Beyond the Weeping Willow

A Story of Survival, Courage & Hope

*

by Robert Hill

Blue Heron Press

First printing December 2023

Beyond the Weeping Willow: A Story of Survival, Courage & Hope

ISBN: 979-8-218-33550-2

Printed in the USA
Design: Sarah McElwain
Cover photo: General Braxton Bragg Home in Mobile, Alabama, ca 1941
Photographer: Highton, Works Progress Administration
Alabama Department of Archives and History.

Dear Reader,

Within these pages, you will dance between the echoes of history and the whimsy of imagination. While you may recognize familiar landmarks of the past, be ever mindful that the tale spun here is woven with threads of fiction and fantasy. The names whispered, the places visited, and the events that unfurl are but the playful musings of the characters who inhabit this world. Any words they utter, or adventures they embark upon are theirs and theirs alone. I merely lent them my pen.

- R.E.H.

Acknowledgments

In the meandering journey of bringing words to life, there are often guiding stars that shine brighter than others. Among those stars, one has been a constant, illuminating my path when it was clouded by doubt and steering me away from impending storms. To Sally McElwain—the best companion a writer could ever wish for on this literary adventure. From the depths of my heart, thank you for everything.

You may not control all the events

that happen to you, but you can decide

not to be reduced by them.

~ Maya Angelou

1

THE NIGHT IN EARLY AUTUMN OF 1943 was as dark as sin in that immense former Alabama plantation house. A gale blew across the lifeless fields and the house, where young Carly huddled beneath the antique bed, hands pressed over his ears against the hellish sounds from the next room. Winnie, Carly's older brother, crouched nearby, staring out the streaked windowpane, watching the bright flashes of lightning as they highlighted sheets of rain skittering across the yard filled with live oaks. The angry words next door exploded like the booming thunderheads outside. Mama wailed while Papa bellowed and cursed, and glass shattered against the walls and unbreakable objects crashed with earsplitting decibels against the walls, door, and windows. The window held fast as an ashtray crashed against it. Water sloshed and splattered against the door when Mama hurled a vase. Books and lamps flew until Carly imagined dynamite was blasting tree stumps from new untilled land.

Carly was a prematurely serious boy who pondered their circumstances, but the constant warring between Mama and Papa already wearied him. As the arguing rose explosively, Carly spoke as Winnie turned from the window. "I know they'll kill each other," he said. "But I'm scared Winnie. They might kill us. Can we go live somewhere else?"

Winnie spoke quietly, "We'll leave this place, find somewhere new. A valley with green grass and cool rivers flowing."

Mama cried, "Voices in my head shout to fight him. He'll murder me if I don't kill him first."

Papa roared back, "Crazy bitch, you break that platter, and you'll wish you hadn't."

Winnie knew the platter Papa meant—a heavy cut-glass beauty from England. Then came an explosion as the platter erupted into a profusion of shards.

Papa wailed, "Jesus, mercy, woman, what've you done to my head? Blood's everywhere, running down my face into my eyes, my nose, and mouth. I can't breathe or see, and I'm unable to walk."

Mama shrieked, "Pray quick to your devil because I'm sending your rotten soul to meet him." More crashes sounded as she struck Papa again and again.

"She's beating the tar out of Papa," marveled Winnie. "I reckon I don't have a dog in this hunt but good for her, I say."

The storm was lost in the war of words and battle. Papa soon yelled, "I quit! You're killing me." He stumbled drunkenly away from the battle, down the hall, his face and clothes bloodied from another clash with Mama. Twice he fell hard onto the wooden floor amidst much groaning, grunting, and cursing before his bedroom door slammed shut. Mama had the madness in her, the family curse. He had the meanness of a rabid dog. Both were broken souls in that dreary place.

The storm suddenly burst loud and blindingly bright as the boys crept outside. Lightning etched the sky, and thunder crashed, but nothing matched the tempest inside that house.

Winnie's jaw set hard, and he said, "You're right, they'll kill each other sure as rain falls. We've got to leave this cursed place, I'll figure a way, just you watch and see. Then we can find a better life. You'll see."

Carly's faith in his brother was complete. Winnie was steadfast and brave.

Winnie, Winston, was a lanky boy, all legs and elbows, with flaxen hair, eyes blue as the sky, and a smattering of freckles across his sun-browned cheeks. He had the prominent Turner nose that marked Carly too, as it did all the Turner men, though Winnie called it their curse. The boy had a thoughtful mind, always searching out some dog-eared book to pore over. Old beyond his years, he kept to himself but excelled in his schooling.

Little Carly, Carleton, a sprout compared to Winnie, was a whip-smart boy with blond hair and laughing eyes. Tall for his young age, he had lost his baby fat. He trailed after Winnie, peppering him with questions that never seemed to cease. Carly favored his brother in looks, minus the freckles, his skin yet unlined by the elements. Despite their sorry home situation, optimism bubbled up in the boy.

*

The next morning, the boys ate their meager breakfast. No steam rose from the biscuits piled on the oilcloth. Baked the previous afternoon, Winnie scraped on jam or jelly, listening to the endless questions from Carly that marked each morning. Shafts of sunlight through dusty windows shone on the grim scene, making interesting patterns on the marble floors and the old oilcloth table covering. Carly and Winnie were weary from the events of the past evening. Carly watched a shaft of light bend as it went through his waterglass. He picked up an almost empty pack of Camel cigarettes that Papa had left and made an interesting observation.

"I can make this camel turn around to head in the other direction," Carly said.

Winnie looked in his direction, then ignored him until Carly placed the camel behind his waterglass. The camel faced the opposite direction. Winnie was amused and laughed. Mama, limping badly, shambled in wearing only a filthy robe, open in front with no undergarments, and hanging loosely on one shoulder, a sight that wasn't uncommon. Carly and Winnie turned away from the embarrassing sight but too late. A demon seized Mama and she flew at them, cursing, scratching, and striking. "So, you think so low of me you refuse to look at me." She slapped each of the boys, hard across their faces, for the final effect.

Afterward, Papa slunk in, limping on a gimp leg that Mama injured in their latest fight, his head wrapped in a piece of blood-soaked pillowcase, only partially covering where Mama split his scalp with the platter.

Carly was anxious when he saw Papa's blood-soaked bandage and clothes, "Does Papa need to see a doctor?"

Winnie was adamant, "No. If he dies, that'll be good. Leave him be."

"Not one word," Papa's hate-filled look warned. But Winnie softly asked Papa if he wanted salt or pepper, and Papa lashed out in rage, knocking Winnie off his chair. His head made a loud thud as it struck the wall. He landed dazed and bleeding on his back. His head was leaning akwardly against the wall. Carly quickly helped him to his feet, and they hurried to Winnie's room to ponder escape.

Papa knew Winnie would inherit the farm someday since his own Papa had disinherited him. The prospects looked grim. Carly worried that Winnie might not live that long.

"We'll make it," Winnie said. "Just hold on."

Carly nestled close, believing they just might. He was comforted by his brother's words. Winnie always took care of him and shielded him from the worst of their parents' poisonous wrath.

When the bus came, Winnie left for school while Carly stayed back. Their uncle Matt came by later, collected Carly as he did daily and took him fishing by the creek. Red-winged blackbirds circled low over the water as they sat on the bank. Carly smiled for what felt like the first time in forever.

*

Mama was a wisp of a woman, with sad-eyes as blue as a Robin's egg, and with yellowish blond hair. She was tall like her own mama. Her mama had battled demons in her mind till she met her end, hanging by her own hand, when Mama was only eight. Now Mama flew into frequent rages without rhyme or reason. When she wasn't like a wild animal, she was withdrawn and unhappy. The doctors said she was schizophrenic with severe depression, but they didn't have any cures for it, and no medication could help what plagued her.

Mama got worse as she got older, talking nonsense no one could follow, and seeing things others couldn't. She'd be smiling one minute then fly off in a tear the next. Her temper was a sudden summer storm, fierce and unpredictable. The meanness in her wasn't her nature, but the sickness twisted her mind until she didn't know herself or anyone.

Papa had darkness in him, buried deep as the deepest sea. As a boy, he first felt its cold hand squeeze his heart when he saw a father and son walking, laughing together. In that moment, he saw what he lacked. Over time the darkness grew, until it became his companion through life. He drowned it in liquor's embrace.

The immense house creaked as it cooled from the heat of the day to the coolness of dusk. On the back stoop, Papa stared off at the withered fields, as he did every evening, seeking solace from the Mason jar. Grandpa Turner had never shown love to Papa. He had chosen to have no contact with his son. The lines on his face told of a lifetime of sorrows. Papa took to the bottle when Mama got sick soon after they were married. He spent his days in a stupor, finding oblivion in white lightning from old man Cunningham's liquor still down by the river. Papa's own papa had disinherited him, and he was jealous of Winnie because he'd inherit the farm, being the first-born grandson and all. Papa had always been a gloomy person, even when he was a boy. He never got a loving hand from his own folks, so he didn't know how to give it to his own boys, either.

Inside, the boys played checkers, waiting, hoping, praying for the day they could break free of this cursed place. Winnie said he aimed to take Carly away from there, maybe find a new life out west. He had read about the Salinas Valley, where the grass grew high, and the days stretched long.

In the deep bond of brothers, Carly wholly trusted Winnie, whose strength and courage never wavered. Carly would follow his brother anywhere, even the dark side of the moon. Winnie was the only light he had in that desolate life.

2

LIVE OAKS MEADOW was the large farm where the manor house sat, twelve miles out of Marston, Alabama, once a sleepy country town. The Civil War had destroyed much of the city, and Reconstruction brought economic ruin, but it regained a sound agricultural economic footing afterwards. It had grown into a bustling city after The Great War with a noted university, hospital, and top-notch schools.

The endless arms of the plantation reached the river in the west. Back in its heyday, Live Oaks Landing had served as the plantation's port on the river. Bounteous fields produced untold bales of cotton and tons of grain, loaded onto barges and shipped to market by the hands that slaved there. The landing received shipments—fertilizer, tools, clothing, sugar, salt, spices, seed and ice—everything needed to run the farm and supply the county folk who traded there. A ferry ran from the Landing across the river. It was stopped in 1934 after cars and trucks were uncountable, and a bridge was built to span the river. Live Oaks Landing was destroyed by Federal Troops during the Civil War. The farmhands continued to live in the houses provided by the farm, and some had bought their houses from the farm. The community, now with many homeowners, became unofficially known as The Landing.

Although Federal troops destroyed Live Oaks Landing, they left the home at Live Oaks Meadow intact, which was used as a hospital and a headquarters for Confederate officers. Federal forces advanced on the farm, the Confederate troops abandoned the headquarters, saving the farm from being razed.

The manor house was built in the early 1840s by Great, Great Grandfather Turner after he arrived from England as a young man. The immense house was built grand, with a marble floored kitchen that could feed an army, an adjacent nook with table and chairs dating to the inauguration of the house, a fine parlor for greeting guests, a library, picturesque fireplaces, and a magnificent curving stairway leading to bedrooms and an office.

Beyond the entryway, the living room with its magnificent massive fireplace posed a stunning, imposing surprise when entering it. Comfortable and attractive, it was beautifully arranged. A chair, not systematically placed, was sitting directly in front of the fireplace, a seat claimed by Papa.

*

Winnie recalled Mama and Papa before Tillie's death. Tillie was Winnie's younger sister. They laughed and played with his sister and him, which was fun. But things changed during Tillie's gradual and prolonged illness and eventual death. She developed Bright's disease of the kidneys, and, for over a year, slowly died. According to Winnie, the extreme desperation and anxiety caused by her sickness had precipitated Mama's mental illness. That became Winnie's supposition over the years, but he never confirmed it. After Tillie's death, Mama and Papa became cold to Winnie, and more self-destructive in their behavior.

Mama discovered she was pregnant again. Mama's sadness improved when she found that she would have another baby. She spoke about how happy she would be when she delivered another little girl like Tillie. With her delivery approaching, she was obsessed with the prospect of another daughter and was sure it would be a girl. She no longer yelled or screamed.

The time came for the birth, and the midwife, Artentious Jackson, and her helper, Dottie Mae Swain, came to the house to deliver the baby. Winnie, ordered out of the house for the delivery, waited a safe distance from the house in an area he called his camp, eager for a new brother or sister. When he heard a baby crying, it was as if he had the winged feet of Mercury. But when he breathlessly arrived, there was no baby. Winnie was surprised and confused when the workers told him he was mistaken because there hadn't been a baby's cry. Winnie thought maybe the baby had been born dead, but he knew he heard a baby's cry, and he asked everyone in the house, but no one told him anything. Over and over, he asked what had happened to the baby, but no one answered his questions. No one would speak about it or explain what had occurred at the delivery and he learned nothing about the shrouded event.

It was as if it had never happened. Mama cried nonstop for months and became more withdrawn, resuming her seclusion in her bedroom. Winnie eventually stopped asking about the strange event but never stopped thinking about it. Papa blamed Mama for whatever had happened at the delivery. Mama knew why, but she would never talk about it.

*

Young Carly came into this world in that house on a brisk autumn day in 1940, delivered by the midwife, Artentious Jackson. His brother Winnie remembered it well, how their Mama hadn't wanted another boy. Carly wasn't welcomed by Mama or Papa. Mama could never forgive him for not being born a girl. Despite that abusive treatment, Carly kept a happy personality, attributable to Winnie's love and devotion to him and the love and caring of his Uncle Matt, Mama's brother.

Drunk as usual, Papa had entered Mama's bedroom and raped her under the cloak of darkness. The courts didn't recognize rape of a wife by her husband as a crime. She was pregnant, and she again obsessed for a baby daughter, even though it was the result of rape. She was sober during the pregnancy, again, an auspicious time for her, and her anger outbursts were few. But at the delivery, Carly was born. This was a distressing disappointment for Mama, causing her to relapse into the black abyss of her mental challenges and alcoholism. Her aberrant mental state resulted in her two-fold hatred of Carly: he was not a girl, and he was the result of Mama being raped.

Papa was a viciously mean drunk who knocked them around when he was drinking. He paid the boys no mind, leaving their care to Winnie. Winnie was older, nearly a man it seemed to little Carly, who followed his big brother everywhere. They'd fish down by the creek when home life got bad. Winnie was the light Carly hardly had in that dark place.

Several years later Papa raped Mama again. She believed hatred rather than lust was the reason for the rape, and she knew it was to show her he had that power over her. She was pregnant again, and because it was rape again, a loveless delivery brought Josie, the little sister of Carly and Winnie, into the world.

*

Carly and Winnie knew that if Papa kept the moonshine coming to Mama from Jedidiah Cunningham, there would be a slight decrease in her abuse of them. It caused more drowsiness and napping and kept her more confined to her room than when Papa didn't make his trip to Jedidiah's. He and Winnie accepted any degree of respite, no matter the size or circumstance. But her angry outbursts toward the kids were vicious, scary, and damaging.

Winnie learned to live a life of silence and obedience when Papa came home with the moonshine. He told Carly he was applying this principle to his existence at home, and he taught Carly to follow his example. He was learning to cope with life at home, offer no resistance, because resistance created pain. The physical pain of referring to Papa's drinks with the misnomer of 'moonshine' forbade the use of that term. Winnie had long ago assumed the role of Carly's protector, ushering him out of the paths of parental wrath, and teaching and warning him at all junctures of their lives.

On a day when Carly especially felt Mama's wrath, he looked into her eyes and said, "Mama, why don't you love me?"

She responded by slapping him hard across his face, knocking him to the floor, and she continued to pummel him while he lay defenseless, bloodying his mouth good. But Carly didn't cry out. Winnie had taught him not to let them see you hurting. Winnie grabbed

Carly, pulled him out of Mama's reach, and delivered him to the safety of his room.

After supper each evening, before Winnie began his homework, the boys relaxed at the large table in the breakfast room and talked and laughed. One evening, as they sat enjoying each other's company, Mama surprised them by walking into the kitchen. An evening visit was unusual, didn't happen on ordinary occasions and didn't ever bode well. She was her usual undressed self, her eyes were red and swollen from crying and heavy drinking, and she singled Carly out and made eye contact. He didn't blink or look away, which infuriated her. In an uncontrolled drunken outburst of rage, Mama grabbed Carly by his shoulders and shook him violently, so brutally he bit his tongue and lip, and blood sprayed from his mouth into the air, onto his chin, and down his neck.

She shrieked and slurred, "I wanted a girl! You were supposed to be a girl! I won't ever forgive you, and I won't ever love you!"

Mama slapped him hard across his face, light flashes streaked through his vision, and he almost fell to the floor but regained his balance. Carly neither shed tears nor cried out because he wouldn't give her that satisfaction. That was Tillie's birthday.

Their relationship with Mama and Papa had deteriorated to the point of abrogation, and there was no room for further decrease. As the boys matured, they knew there would be no hope for a positive change in future interconnections with Mama and Papa, and they knew significant changes would be necessary if they were to survive. Winnie was the sole reason Carly was alive, or at least, free of broken bones, and he was thankful for his big brother and protector.

Winnie promised they'd leave someday, take off and make a new life. Carly dreamed of the day they'd strike out together. Until then, he'd keep laughing, no matter how bad it got.

3

1943

. . . .

A DAY IN OCTOBER BEGAN like most other early autumn days; the sun was bright, lovely, scarcely moving fluffy clouds floating aimlessly, and a typical autumn briskness had crept in overnight, making for a sensational day. Mama remained in her bedroom.

Still a thoughtful lad who dreamed of a bigger world, Winnie prepared jelly and jam on stale biscuits for breakfast and got ready for school, Papa grumbled about whatever, but no one cared. Carly watched in silence. Winnie had said he thought Mama would soon have a baby, but no one had told the boys about a new baby. None of her routines changed, and she continued to incubate in her bedroom. Winnie said her belly had gotten large during the last months. They'd watched the bellies of cows and horses get big while carrying their babies, thus his conclusion that a baby was coming.

Winnie was eager for a baby sibling, and both boys were hoping for a miraculous change in Mama's disposition. Mama was still furious that Carly was born a boy, not a girl. Perhaps she had changed, but Winnie experienced a sense of foreboding if their sibling was another boy.

"Carly, we should pray for a healthy sister," he said. "But it might be too late for God to intervene."

That afternoon, Winnie arrived home from school to find that his hunch was confirmed. A baby's birth was imminent, and Carly toddled out to meet him at his bus stop. Winnie knelt with his back to Carly.

"Want a piggyback ride?"

Carly climbed aboard, and they walked back to the house. Winnie told him a baby was coming, and Mama would be center stage.

Artentious Jackson, the Black midwife who had delivered Winnie, Tillie, and Carly, was in attendance, having arrived in her familiar horse-drawn buggy. Her horse grazed the knee-high hay grass at the yard's edge. Carly dismounted from Winnie's back, trotted over and patted the horse's neck as he fed, and the stallion whickered in acknowledgment. White ladies from around the community had parked a half-dozen cars in the yard to attend the birth.

"They're not here to help, only to satisfy their curiosity," Winnie said dryly, displaying his blossoming cynicism.

"But they brought pies," Carly grinned.

Carly had watched cows give birth to their calves, and he had seen a mare give birth to her foal. He understood pregnancy in four-legged animals and assumed two-legged animals weren't much different. But that day's event stirred more excitement on the farm than when the farm animals gave birth.

Artentious had a prominent growth on her nose's upper bridge between her eyebrows. The strange appearance of the overhanging protrusion hid what it might be. Was it a unicorn's horn? Carly, in his innocence, had once asked if she was part unicorn. Artentious was always friendly and talkative, but the significant unicorn horn-like thing between her eyebrows caused such a distraction that Winnie couldn't converse politely. Carly was too young, so they didn't expect him to try. They sat and stared while others talked.

Artentious boiled water when she arrived. During the butchering season, Carly had seen farmhands plunge hogs into barrels of hot water to scrape off the hair, preparing it for butchering. Carly scanned the surroundings and asked Winnie, "Where are the hogs?"

Winnie laughed. "I think boiling water is normal to prepare for a baby's birth, but I'm not sure why. Women are closed-mouthed about the goings-on of baby deliveries."

"Take that child, and you two get out of here," Artentious shouted to Winnie.

Winnie and Carly wanted to avoid the entire house, so they grabbed some freshly baked biscuits and a couple of wieners and hurried to their camp, a safe place Winnie had set up a hundred yards from home. An unused grain crib sat on the campsite, and Winnie occupied it to store food and camping supplies, and they used it to escape harsh weather and their nasty home life. Winnie always let Carly tag along to the camp.

Mama's loud cries of pain informed the boys of the happenings at the house. But when Mama initially screamed, it alarmed Carly. "Is Mama fighting with Papa?"

"No, I reckon pain is part of having a baby."

Unlike cows and horses, Mama's pain created screams and caterwauling. The fuss she was kicking up was loud and seemed to carry for miles, and the cacophonous howling and barking of dogs answered Mama's cries.

Carly laughed hard when Winnie told him the screams and howls reminded him of last spring's uproar when a panther visited. "The difference is the panther was trying to get pregnant, and Mama is trying not to be."

They laughed again when Winnie kept talking. "Do you think Artentious has been giving Mama moonshine from her Mason jar?"

They thought Mama was going for an acting award from all the commotion and nervous disturbance she was causing. They giggled some more.

Suddenly, out of nowhere, Artentious surprised them by appearing at their camp, halting Winnie and Carly amid their laughing and giggling. They snapped to attention when she gave them a scowl that would stop the old grandfather clock. She updated them on the birth's progress.

"Wait for just a little longer, boys. Soon you'll have a new brother or sister. Your Mama's doing fine, and everything's normal."

Winnie looked surprised that someone would bother to include them in an update. Artentious turned, and both boys hugged her with closed eyes to avoid embarrassing her or themselves by staring at the protrusion between her eyebrows.

Alone again, Winnie solemnly said they shouldn't laugh anymore because it would be disrespectful. He said they should remain quiet in their thoughts for a while. Carly couldn't understand why. After a bit, he recalled Winnie's story about the panther trying to get pregnant, and they were giggling again.

Winnie told Carly about his plans for the two to leave the farm to live somewhere safe. He said his plans weren't complete yet, but they would need to gather many supplies and lots of food from around the house and farm. There was an Amish-type buggy that was never used that they could "borrow" to haul their stores, and they could grab one horse to pull the buggy. They would slip away under cover of darkness to a secret place where no one could find them, never to return to their dismal life in Hell.

Carly didn't understand everything Winnie said, so he told Winnie, "I want to go when our baby's born."

"We can't go yet because we have a lot of preparation before we can leave. But remember, we can't say a word about this to anyone. We can't go if we do, and they'll beat us. Do you understand?" Winnie said.

"Yes. I won't say a word, ever."

"We need to swear never to talk about this to anyone but us. Let's pinky swear."

Carly knew it was necessary because pinky swearing was even more serious than swearing on a Bible, and Winnie had told him his pinky finger would be cut off if he broke the promise.

Carly and Winnie did their pinkie swear, locking their two pinky fingers, signifying their unbreakable promise had been made.

Just when the atmosphere had grown dense with anticipation, the distinctive cry of a newborn pierced the silence. The loud jubilations of the attending ladies that followed made it official.

Winnie stood. "Sounds like Artentious just delivered another Turner baby! Welcome to the world, Little Turner."

He knelt. "Climb aboard."

Amid the golden glow of a setting sun and the spectacle of colorful fall leaves, Carly climbed onto Winnie's back and looked around, anticipation sparkling in his eyes. They were embarking on a mission, with the impending dusk setting a picturesque backdrop. The air was nippy, and it was a beautiful, brisk autumn afternoon. He looked at Winnie's face and saw a picture of sheer happiness. Thinking it would be a fun ride back to see the baby, the ride began. They barreled toward the house, with Carly hanging on for dear life, but he felt safe. Each gallop and dash evoked a sense of urgency, a yearning to meet the newest member of their clan. Though low-hanging tree branches were slapping Carly's face, their spirit was undeterred. It was the allure of family, the magnetic pull of new life that spurred them on. Winnie tried to sidestep a small ditch, but stumbled, fell, rolled, and got up; Carly fell off his back and skinned his knees, but nothing was as important as seeing the new baby. They continued their race homeward, a race against an unperceived opponent, and they intended to prevail, but it felt like time was standing still. They couldn't get to the house fast enough. Finally arriving, Winnie rushed, breathless, inside to see the newborn baby and Mama with Carly close behind.

But their journey faced an unexpected detour. A lady intercepted them just inside the entryway, and instead of being ushered into a room filled with soft cries of a newborn, they were directed to the kitchen nook for supper. They ate beef stew and cornbread, a meager consolation for their thwarted efforts.

Winnie and Carly lay in their beds, but sleep was elusive. The quiet night was punctuated by a distant owl's hooting and faint wails of the hungry infant. They listened restlessly almost all night for untoward sounds that might inform them something was wrong. Both boys arose early but wouldn't see Mama and the baby until mid-afternoon. They learned, come morning, of their new sister, Josephine.

Their first glimpse of Josephine was a moment frozen in time. Her cherubic face, her soft, cooing sounds, and the way her tiny fingers wrapped around Carly's was a grip that felt like a promise.

Papa had arranged for someone to help Mama while she recovered. Dottie Mae Swain lived only four or five miles away and sometimes worked in their house. Mama held a distinct dislike, even hatred, for Dottie Mae, which might have been why Papa hired her. That may understate it a bit. Mama hated Dottie Mae's guts. According to Winnie, Mama had liked her until she helped Artentious when there was a delivery with no baby.

Eva Lou came with her mother, Dottie Mae. Carly thought Eva Lou was the most beautiful girl in all the world and she was his best friend. She had captured Carly's young heart while they walked or played together and hugged him when they met every morning and when she left for home in the afternoon. She and Carly were born the same year; he had loved her from his earliest memories. Now Dottie Mae and Eva Lou would live in Carly's house to help while Mama recuperated from Josephine's birth.

Winnie and Carly saw Josephine lying on her back in her crib, without a blanket around her, cold and screaming with hunger. Both knew there would be no change from the unending domestic physical and psychological abuse. They saw Mama, inattentive, lying on her side, looking at the wall away from Josephine, offering neither love nor comfort, showing less concern than they had seen when she cared for a small bird with a broken wing. Dottie Mae fed Little Josie from a warm bottle, and soon she slept.

Winnie and Carly agreed Josie, lying in her crib, was prettier than they could have imagined with her perfect little face. A tiny squirming bundle, she was sleeping soundly. She cried when she was awake because she always wanted to eat. Her little hands and feet were so pretty, so perfect.

Mama's disposition didn't change. Winnie had long ago ceased to hope for redeemable value in Mama, so he was hanging close to Dottie Mae and Eva Lou as they attended Little Josie, trying to learn about newborn baby care, and Carly stayed close. Even at an early age, Eva helped her mom care for Josie. They watched Eva when she carefully removed Josie from her crib, with intention, so that she could feed her. Eva adeptly kept Josie's blanket tucked around her. She held the baby's bottle with milk in her hand and sprinkled some of the milk on the inside of her forearm to test the temperature. Eva cradled Josie in one arm and held the bottle to feed her.

It amazed Carly that Eva knew how to do these things. Winnie contemplated that the natural care-giving instincts of girls were born with them, woven into the fabric of their souls, and the ability became available to them when they needed it, even before adulthood; for instance, at that early age, Eva was helping her mom care for Josie. Winnie ended his argument by pointing out that for males, every bit of knowledge was hard-won, every morsel of understanding must be earned through observation and need.

Beneath the wonder and the lessons was a simmering worry. Winnie's apprehension continued; he talked with Carly about his concerns, and, over time, his agitation became worries. The specter of their parents' unstable tendencies loomed large. Both parents were mean drunks, both were handicapped by severe mental challenges, and neither could even care for themselves now, especially the added responsibility of a newborn baby. The paramount question remained: In a home filled with tumult and uncertainty, what would become of little Josie once Dottie Mae returned to her home to live?

4

1943
. . . .

IN THE HEART OF THE IMMENSE Live Oaks Meadow Farm stood a figure as timeless as the land itself: Matti Palosaari, Mama's brother. Known fondly as "Uncle Matt" in Mama's softer moments and rare nostalgic tales, his presence was an unspoken promise of stability in Carly and Winnie's turbulent household and often chaotic world. His hands, weathered from years of labor and wisdom, wove stories of resilience and ingenuity, and the wisdom lines on his face testified to a profound understanding of the world. Uncle Matt had been on the farm long before Carly and Winnie were born. His mechanical ability was innate, and he was a true jack-of-all-trades.

On those brisk mornings, after Winnie had left to catch his bus to school but before Mama and Papa had brushed off the night of alcoholic stupor, Uncle Matt would silently swing by, much to the relief of the domestic helpers, to rescue young Carly, leaving behind the morning chill for a day of education, adventure, and excitement, and ensuring he was safe from the tumultuous environment at home.

The weight of World War rationing darkened many childhood dreams. Carly dreamed of a wagon, but metal wasn't available for children's toys. War rationing had not dimmed Uncle Matt's spirit.

"I've got a project," Uncle Matt told young Carly, "And I need help."

Uncle Matt's eyes sparkled with mischief and wisdom, and Carly remembered pestering him, trying to glean the details. He'd come to know that gleam in Uncle Matt's eyes—meant adventure, learning, and bonding.

With deft fingers and a craftsman's soul, he encouraged Carly to help him at every stage and brought into reality a brilliant red wagon for Carly, a beacon of hope amidst the grayness of war.

Carly's tiny footsteps were always windmilling, each step trying to mirror the rhythmic strides of his mentor. Though these steps were on the soil, they were etched on Carly's heart. The years brought wisdom as Uncle Matt instilled in Carly the essence of life, skills of the farm, and an intense love of sitting at the feet of a true raconteur recounting tales from a life gone by.

The sweltering heat and hum of the blacksmith's forge, and the ringing of red-hot metal being hammered on the anvil into useful tools and thingamajigs was a lullaby to Carly. Uncle Matt's sayings became a treasure trove of lessons of life. "Strike while the iron is hot," Uncle Matt would say, his words resonating deeper truths.

In a teasing way, he would tell them when he dropped "a pearl of wisdom" and he always followed with valuable information. When he received notice of his IRS audit, he was insecure and didn't fare well with the audit. His pearl was, "You know you are in trouble when only dogs can hear you fart."

The lessons continued as they danced through the nurturing art and science of gardening, the secretive art and science of making wine and potent moonshine, and the craft of basket weaving.

Weekends were special. Uncle Matt would gather them after school or when he got off work, and they would head for the river, camping under the wide-open sky, beneath a vast expanse of twinkling stars. The evenings rang with singing and harmonica tunes that echoed with the soulful Delta Blues. Bedtime required a scary story that sounded too true. Their days were filled with fishing, precision carving, and archery. It wasn't only about fun; survival was an important part of his teaching. He required they learn to recognize the four kinds of indigenous poisonous snakes, rattlesnake, water moccasin, copperhead, and coral. Emergency treatment for bites was high on his to-teach list. If they were careless enough to receive a snake bite, a lesson about treating snake bites followed. He warned them about the medical thinking that recommended that they cut the fang marks with a knife and suck out the venom, but he said, "Don't do it. It will become infected, and you might as well rub cow shit in the wound." That graphic warning stood the test of time.

Wrapped in the warmth of their campfire, Uncle Matt proved to be an unequaled raconteur, regaling them with tales from a world and time that once was. Stories of a young soldier named Matti, a world torn and scarred by the Great War, and whispers of a heritage from far-off Finland. There were tales of World War I, adventures in Italy after the war, and playful jabs about their Finnish heritage. Uncle Matt's narratives weren't just tales from the past; they were windows into worlds Carly and Winnie had never seen. The boys would jest, teasing Uncle Matt about some of his wilder stories, but beneath the laughter lay a deep reverence. Deep down, they cherished every word.

Shadows often lurked beneath their sunlit memories. Winnie and Carly would often quietly discuss their plans to leave the farm. They were desperate to leave, to escape the oppressive atmosphere of their home to fulfil their dreams of someday arriving at a safe sanctuary. But how could they tell Uncle Matt? The man who had been their mentor, protector, and confidant. Should they entrust their plans to Uncle Matt? Would it endanger them if they let him into their world? Their hearts grappled with loyalty, trust, and the fear of the unknown consequences if Uncle Matt tried to stop them.

"I don't want to leave without telling him," Carly confessed one evening, his voice hushed. "He is our best friend and our only family."

But Winnie, the pragmatist, countered, "It's too risky. He's our lifeline, granted, but if he should think we were wrong to leave, we can't risk the wrath it might bring down on us."

For the boys, Uncle Matt wasn't just an uncle. He was the father they wished for, the mentor they needed, and the advocate they wanted to stand with them. The day they'd finally part from the farm would be bittersweet. And though paths might diverge, Carly held onto a hope—a hope to sit with Uncle Matt once more, sipping homemade wine and bridging the chasm of time, getting lost in the tales of yesteryears. Their departure stayed a silent promise, as days turned to nights and nights to days.

5

1946
·······

EVA LOU WAS A SIGHT TO BEHOLD—a beautiful girl, slim, as tall as Carly, and taller than the kids the workers brought around to keep them company. She had radiant tan skin without a blemish, sparkling blue eyes, like jewels of light that reflected her changing moods, and Carly was constantly trying to guess what secrets they hid. Her light brunette hair was always trimmed short. Eva loved the outdoors, and even though she was adventurous, showing no fear of snakes, lizards, turtles, possums, or raccoons, she had a peculiar aversion to armadillos. Carly was always mesmerized by her demeanor, her spirit, and her laughter. To him, she was as beautiful as a porcelain doll.

Carly, on the other hand, had his distinct features: brilliant blue eyes just like Eva's and a penchant for wearing overalls, a staple among the boys his age. Sweaters? No way. He'd rather embrace the cold. He wasn't one to care about his appearance; scuffed shoes and tattered clothes were just part of his everyday getup. Such superficialities were unimportant to him.

The opening day of school loomed ahead, and Carly and Eva Lou were expecting their first day. While playing outside, a shadow crossed their carefree existence. Carly asked Eva if she would sit beside him on their bus, and she became quiet, appeared sad, just sat diddling in the sand with her toes.

Carly placed his hand on her soft cheek. "What's wrong? Did I say something wrong?"

Eva said, "We ain't gonna ride the same bus."

"What do you mean?" asked Carly.

"We ain't going to the same school together."

"How come?" Carly wanted to know but was becoming upset.

"Carly, sweet Carly, you never noticed that I'm Black and you're white, have you?"

Now Carly was upset. "No, but I've noticed your tan skin. What difference does that make? Is our skin color why we can't go to the same school? It don't make no difference. Your tan skin is pretty."

Eva edged closer to him and spoke in a lowered voice.

"Mama said white folks won't let Black and white children go to school together."

"Why? That don't make no sense. We play and eat together. We've lived together in this house."

"When I asked Mama the same thing, she said that's the way it's always been. I don't know what that means, except we can't go to the same school."

"We ought to go to school together. We're alike, and we've been together all our lives. You're my best and onliest friend." Carly felt like he might have his first tantrum. He had seen kids have them, and their mamas beat them. He reckoned he'd try not to have one. A terrible pain was in his chest, and his breathing was hard. The world was spinning like when they played whirling dervish. Was he losing his mind, going crazy? Was he going to die?

Carly could hear Eva Lou saying, "Carly, just be calm." But she sounded far away, drowned out by a loud noise inside his head. He tried to be calm but didn't know how because he didn't know what it meant. Eva went inside and came back with a paper bag.

"Here, breathe in this bag. I've seen people get upset and blow into a bag, and it helps."

It helped, but not quickly. Carly's spinning world slowed down a little but just in case, he hung on to the bag. After that, they didn't find anything fun to do. They sat, moped, and played in the sand with their toes.

"We ought to go to the same school." Carly wouldn't let it go.

Their bond was palpable and beautiful, but the world's prejudices, it seemed, were determined to wedge them apart. Their different paths became clear the following day. While waiting for his bus, Eva's bus rolled by; she smiled big and waved, and Carly waved back. His bus was going in the opposite direction of Eva's. He saw differences in their buses. Eva's bus was old and looked like a wreck, but his bus seemed shiny and new. How come? A profound realization weighed on Carly's young mind—society's skewed beliefs had bled into every aspect of his young life. Carly reckoned bigger world problems had caught up with Eva and him. He couldn't get a hold of them with his mind. Maybe the differences in the school buses were just a part of the bigger problems that he didn't understand. Carly wanted to talk to Eva about her school, but dreaded what she might say. What if her school was a wreck, like her bus?

Carly would never talk to Mama and Papa about anything because he knew they'd hit him. When he got to school, he asked his teacher, Mrs. James. "Why can't me and my best friend, Eva, go to the same school?"

She yelled at him. "Is Eva Black?"

"No, ma'am, she's tan."

"Stop your sassing." She sent him to the principal's office. Carly wanted to ask somebody why she sent him to the principal's office and what would happen when he got there, but he had no one to ask. He later learned that the principal, Mr. James, was his teacher's husband.

"What's the problem?" Mr. James asked.

"I don't know," Carly said, but then told him what happened, about asking Mrs. James why he and Eva Lou can't go to the same school, and that she got mad.

Mr. James' face turned as red as a ripe tomato. He yelled, "Is Eva Black?"

"No, sir, she's tan."

"Don't sass me, you little bastard."

Carly thought, here was that word again. What does sass mean?

What had he done to make everybody mad at him? He still didn't know why he and Eva couldn't attend school together.

Mr. James yelled at Carly to put his hands on the desk and bend over. He bashed Carly's ass six hard strikes with his wooden paddle. Carly didn't know what was happening, but he would be damned if he cried. Besides, Mama and Papa did worse just about every day. Mr. James told Carly he needed to discuss this problem with his parents. Yeah, Carly thought, fat chance.

After his first day at school, Carly knew more than when he left home that morning, but the world was more confusing. His question remained unanswered. "Why can't we go to the same school?"

*

A few days later, the school moved Carly to the second grade. No one had told him anything, so he didn't know why. He reckoned he must be smart but thought he might be a problem like at home. Mrs. James didn't like him, which might have been why they moved him. He didn't like her either, so he was happy with the move. They tried teaching him to read with books about Dick, Jane, and Spot, but he told them he wouldn't read them because he they were for dumb people who couldn't read, and he could already read.

All he had learned in school was that the World War had ended, and millions of soldiers had returned to the USA. He wouldn't have known that if he hadn't been a ravenous reader. His reading was already years ahead of the middle school books, and his arithmetic was ahead of Winnie's school grade, but not ahead of Winnie. The school had put him in a deathly dull class. He sat there trying to concentrate, but the teacher's voice soon reminded him of the buzzing of a bee caught behind a screen wire, and he stopped paying attention.

Winnie rode his bicycle and delivered *Grit* newspapers every Saturday to people who would buy them. The banner read *Grit, America's Greatest Family Newspaper*. Boys distributed *Grit* to small towns and rural areas all over America. It cost only a dime for a twenty-page newspaper that included local, national, and world news, a serial novel, and comics. Carly wondered why Winnie sold the *Grit* newspapers when they weren't a family. But Carly liked to read the paper each week, and that's where he learned the news of the war's end.

Carly's school day began with someone from his class reading Bible verses, followed by the Pledge of Allegiance to the flag. Most days, they all said the Lord's Prayer after the Bible verses, and grace before their lunch meal. Since Carly didn't have money for lunch, he remained in the classroom but joined in saying grace in case God was watching.

Carly had spent significant time thinking about religion. Since all of his friends were forced to go to church each Sunday, he heard them talking about it each Monday. He had heard people say God answered their prayers, but he thought they lied. God had never answered his prayers. Besides, he couldn't understand who they prayed to. Was God supposed to answer the prayers, if so, how could He answer them? God was absent on Sundays, which was supposed to be his day. He thought maybe God took the day off like humans. Carly never saw God during the week either and didn't understand when God worked. He saw people working, but not God. So why pray to an invisible God who never worked? Carly thought this whole religious thing might be phony. But not knowing enough to be confident about this yet, Carly kept reading, thinking, and working on it. Carly reckoned he better be careful when he started distrusting God because the Bible said God smote his enemies. He didn't know anything about smote and didn't want to find out the hard way.

Winnie and Carly had said a simple prayer for a healthy new sister rather than a brother. It was a girl, and she was born healthy, but Carly thought she might have been anyway. Despite his prayers, Carly's parents were still nasty, angry, and mean alcoholics. He reckoned some things were too severe for God to change, and those things might come from the Devil. It wouldn't hurt to keep trying with the prayers. It would require more study for him to understand the difference between God and the Devil. He thought God didn't even see the difference. Did God only answer prayers for grown people who could put dollars on the plate in church? Carly had no dollars, so that could be the big hang-up.

✳

A couple of months into the school year, the school advanced Carly to the third grade. His new teacher, Mrs. Brownlie, gave him an incredible amount of free time for reading. She discovered that he could read years ahead of his grade level, and she told him his assigned school level hindered him from realizing his real potential, which he didn't understand, but he liked the benefits. She gave him reading assignments that were years ahead of his classmates, and the material interested and energized him. Since he stayed in the classroom to read during lunch, Mrs. Brownlie nourished his intellect by teaching him high school English grammar, composition, and diction and coaching his speech. She majored in English in college and studied English literature which she taught Carly. Mrs. Brownlie spent hours teaching Carly literature and loaned him her college texts and novels.

He found Dickens's *Oliver Twist* fascinating, followed by *Great Expectations*. He agreed, Dickens was a genius. She introduced Carly to Shakespeare with *Julius Caesar,* an unexpected jewel written by another genius.

6

. . . .

THE SUN ROSE OVER ANOTHER school year, and Josie, just a petite five-year-old, surprisingly found herself in the first grade; probably a clerical error, but fortuitously, she was more than prepared. Mrs. Brownlie learned of this and arranged for Josie to join her teaching sessions alongside Carly. He'd already been a beacon for Josie, teaching her to read, and she continued to learn so rapidly that Carly believed she had a knack for teaching herself. Mrs. Brownlie saw her potential and taught her at a level just below Carly, and Josie's progress at absorbing knowledge astounded her. She half-jokingly mused that she might pass him up on her educational quest. To ensure her continued tutelage of Carly and Josie, Mrs. Brownlie didn't promote him from the third grade, which suited him. The school promoted Josie to the third grade before the end of the school year. Mrs. Brownlie said she planned to keep her there. The numbers, the grades—they didn't matter to them. They reveled in the joy of learning.

In Carly's life, where happiness was a rare treasure, the rich collection of books left behind by his late Grandfather, Bernard Turner, became a sanctuary. Carly once described the collection as more a museum than a library, but Mrs. Brownlie, ever the wise sage, reminded him, "The classics remain timeless, Carly. Immerse yourself in them." He read them nonstop as fast as possible.

Carly, always pushing boundaries, unearthed school textbooks from a closet in his classroom. With Mrs. Brownlie's guidance, he learned algebra, geometry, chemistry, and a profound passion for physics. He dreamt of delving into Isaac Newton's *Principia Mathematica*.

Having exhausted all the resources at the small school library, including a thorough read of The Encyclopedia Britannica through 'H,' Carly asked Mrs. Brownlie how to get books from Marston's Carnegie Library, and she promised to investigate.

Winnie, always supportive, assured Carly, "Mrs. Brownlie was the best person to ask for help. I'm sure she'll help you."

And she didn't disappoint. Soon, books started flowing from Marston's library, including three books about being medical students and becoming doctors, which Carly consumed with fervor.

Over the years, despite the push from the administration, Mrs. Brownlie resisted promoting Carly and Josie to a higher grade, keeping them under her careful eye and tutelage. Consequently, they were privy to college-level composition, English Literature, and American Literature. She welcomed her friend from City University to teach advanced math and physics to them.

The school administration eventually prevailed. After exhaustive testing, Carly was moved to the eighth grade, and Josie was moved to the fifth grade. Mrs. Brownlie asked Carly to see her after school, she had an important item to speak to him about. He arrived at her desk early, and she had not yet arrived. He noticed two papers lying on her desk, one with his name, and Josie's name on the other. They were the results of the intelligence quotient tests they had completed. He edged closer, his was on top, his score was 183. He slid his over a bit to see Josie's score, 185. He returned the papers to an untouched appearance and walked over to gaze out the window to wait until Mrs. Brownlie arrived. He didn't know the significance of their scores, and he wasn't curious enough to research their significance. Those numbers did not impress him.

She told him the school placed him in the eighth grade, and Josie would advance to the fifth grade starting the next school year. He was melancholic all summer, thinking he would have to leave

Mrs. Brownlie. When the school year began in the fall, Carly was euphoric when it turned out that Mrs. Brownlie was his eighth-grade teacher, and she continued teaching Josie and him without interruption. Carly knew they must be the luckiest people alive.

Winnie had graduated from high school and was now a sophomore at City University. He lived at home and commuted.

As he grew older, Carly realized he and Josie were lucky to have Mrs. Brownlie as their mentor and advocate. He became more aware of her tremendous effort to ensure that he and Josie would be beneficiaries of such priceless, astonishing educational opportunities. They felt indebted to her for always looking out for them. Their education opened doors that would have otherwise remained closed. He surmised she saw in them a glimmer of light worthy of her time and energy to nurture and encourage that spark to glow to its fullest potential. They never slacked off or gave anything less than their total intellectual energy to Mrs. Brownlie's untiring efforts.

*

Uncle Matt's surprise for Carly and Josie was a delightful black-and white puppy, the markings of a Border Collie. Winnie was less interested, saying he didn't want the added responsibility of a dog. The pup's history was bittersweet—Uncle Matt found an entire litter of identical puppies in a cardboard container on a railroad track. Someone had placed them on the railroad tracks hoping a train would kill them. Uncle Matt rescued the pups after seeing them as he drove over the crossing. They appeared to be six or eight weeks old. The joy was palpable when they met the puppy, and the puppy returned their love, washing their faces with kisses, bouncing from one lap to the next, and beating them with her perpetually wagging tail. The three were together for a few minutes, and they quickly agreed on her name, Jenna. They took her to a veterinarian at Mallory's Mercantile and had her spayed. She barely blinked an eye with recovery.

Carly and Jenna shared a secret. There was a rule that dogs were forbidden in the house, so Carly placed Jenna beneath his bedroom window each evening and opened the window and brought her inside to sleep with him. Soon she went to the window and waited for him. When Jenna was old enough, she jumped through the open window in the evenings and left through the window each morning, creating memories that cemented their bond forever. Jenna became an integral part of the lives of Carly and Josie, teaching them about love, resilience, and the beauty of simpler things.

7

SEVERAL YEARS HAD PASSED since Winnie and Carly began planning to abscond with Josie and leave the farm and their dreadful lives behind. They had often talked of leaving. But it wasn't whimsical daydreaming. Preparing a plan was much easier than activating it, especially when it demanded a complete life change for everyone. Life on the farm had been tough since their births, but it had turned tougher and potentially deadly. Carly and Winnie would have left home in a heartbeat without shedding a tear or a drop of sweat because they had lost their emotional investment in the farm and its people almost at birth. Uncle Matt was the notable exception. The thought of leaving him caused considerable sadness. But removing Josie from home, from the only stability she had ever known, and moving her to a permanent camp-out was even more challenging to defend.

Carly and Winnie finished breakfast and, filled with their usual chatter and laughter, walked to their rooms to get ready for their day. The familiar sound of boots came from behind. Papa. That was the third time in a week he had arranged sudden confrontations, yelling at them, insulting them, and striking them. That bullshit was not good when it began, but it had now become a distressing ritual. Papa's vicious taunting reminded Carly of an aphorism often quoted by workers on the farm, enough is enough and too much is a dog's bait! This bullshit was a damned dog's bait. Papa zeroed in on Winnie, who tried walking around him, but Papa swung his fist and struck a hard blow to Winnie's chin.

A burning rage overcame Winnie, and he went berserk, screaming at Papa, "I have had enough of your bullshit." He retaliated by swinging wildly, surprising Papa and causing him to recoil in defense. Winnie connected a solid blow to Papa's face, knocking him off his feet. Winnie tried to leave the scene, to walk away. While Papa was still on the floor, he swung his legs, sweeping Winnie's legs from beneath him. Winnie hit the floor hard, and Papa was astride him instantly, beating Winnie senseless and unresponsive with his fists. Carly hurried into the nearest bedroom and brought out a heavy, solid oak bedside table. Using both hands, he swung it with all his strength, hoping for a death blow when it soundly struck Papa's head. Papa slumped onto Winnie, who was stirring. With all his power, Carly held the weaponized table high above his head and again delivered a solid battering blow to the side of Papa's head, causing him to tumble off Winnie. Papa didn't move or twitch. Winnie tried to sit up, and Carly helped him to his feet.

Bloodied and panting, Winnie met Carly's gaze. "We can't stay here," Carly whispered. Winnie nodded, and not giving a damn whether Papa was dead or alive, they scrambled out the back of the house, seeking safer quarters. Both boys ran to the main barn, climbed to the hayloft, and hid amidst a wall of baled hay. Winnie displayed bruises and skinned areas on his face, and an early shiner was developing around his left eye. They remained hidden, speaking softly, fearing he would come looking for them. Soon they heard a siren at the front of the house. Both returned to the porch. Trying to remain camouflaged and out of sight, they saw the most beautiful sight imaginable; two medics loading Papa's unresponsive body into an ambulance. They thought a more beautiful scene would have been a hearse.

Entering the house, they found an agitated group of domestic workers. Josie had walked into the hallway to investigate the unusual noises coming from the ruckus between Papa and the boys, and she saw their desperate act but remained silent. There were loud voices coming from Mary Ann and Carl, the domestic workers, and Mama couldn't control her cries and screams.

When she saw Josie, all hell broke loose. Mama screamed, demanding, "Who attacked Papa." Josie said she knew nothing. Mama slapped her twice. "You are a damned liar," Mama was screaming.

Winnie had recovered enough that he and Carly rushed to Josie's defense and, surprising Mama, they grabbed her arms and shoved her into a nearby chair. Winnie said, "We knocked hell out of Papa after he attacked us. We had no choice."

Only inches from Mama's face, Carly screamed, "If you ever lay a hand on Josie again, even to touch her, I will do worse for you than I did for Papa, and a hearse will come for your body. You had best damned well believe that because we've had enough of your shit." Mama looked stunned and remained silent and motionless.

Later, Carly asked Winnie, "Why should Mama care so much about what happened to Papa since they fight more than Joe Louis ever did?"

"I think she wants the thrill of delivering the coup de grâce to Papa, and she takes a dim view of losing," Winnie said.

Their home situation had deteriorated, degenerating into more desperate circumstances by several orders of magnitude. Their weariness of living in such a terrible environment had reached the breaking point. Papa was angry at everyone and had become much more belligerent and threatening to both boys but more so toward Winnie. If the boys spoke to him, Papa would curse and strike them; if they didn't talk to him, he would curse and bash them. His clothing was filthy, tattered, and threadbare, and he wore the same clothes for weeks. His unbathed body issued the foulest of odors. His teeth were rotten, and shaving was a rarity. Would a doctor prescribe medications to help Papa? Carly considered that a rhetorical question without even the remotest possibility in Hell.

Mama was an alcoholic, her mental challenges caused hurtful behavior, and they had grown weary of enduring her angry outbursts and physical assaults, but they didn't believe her to be a grave or lethal threat like Papa. They didn't know of any resources that might be available for her and didn't know how to search for potential help.

The house was no longer safe for the three kids. They had not yet set a departure date but knew they must leave soon. The recent violent turmoil had finally forced their hand to push ahead with their plans to go.

Winnie and Carly listed everything they thought might be necessary to survive for at least six months, allowing them time to find a campsite and make it livable and permanent. They were preparing as thoroughly as their knowledge allowed for their imminent departure. They wouldn't dare tell anyone of their plans to leave the farm, not even Josie. Carly and Winnie would share their plans with her only hours before they were to leave. But she must go with them, or they wouldn't leave. Mama and Papa continued to heap unrelenting physical and verbal abuse on the three. Still, Winnie and Carly considered the abuse they suffered differently than Josie's because they could fend for themselves, but not Josie, and they wouldn't let it continue.

Papa continued to present a grave, lethal danger to the three. They considered him a deadly threat, and they tried to avoid him at every turn because he was a viciously mean, devious, dangerous, drunken SOB. He was an unpredictable, cruel, embittered alcoholic who drank daily and whose every move meant unmitigated malice and hostility.

*

Winnie and Carly sat on the large table outside the back of the house, the golden hues of the dusk painting their faces. The memories of little Clifton Gable, a fragile soul from their school, weighed heavily between them. Clifton wasn't like the other kids. His skin, pallid and stretched tight over his frail bones, seemed almost transparent. He appeared sickly, underfed, too thin, and he came to school with tattered, filthy clothes, no socks. His shoes, worn out long before, bearing more holes than leather, whispered of hard times and abject poverty.

All the kids made fun of him. Carly remarked that the kids had made up a senseless but hurtful ditty schoolyard chant that they sang in his presence, "Clifton Gable skinned his nabel on the table." Clifton would display a wan smile and shuffle away, as if trying to convince the world—or perhaps himself—that he was unfazed.

Carly's voice quivered, "I saw him once without his shirt in the locker room. He had huge welts and bruises on his arms, legs, face, and neck. His father beat him with the buckle end of his belt, which cut his skin in many places, and no one had covered the cuts with bandages, and they were still bleeding." Carly 's eyes said more than his spoken words ever could.

Winnie nodded, the weight of Carly's words pressing on him. "He once told me that every morning he made the tiring trip to school, not for education, but because it was safer than staying home. Clifton believed his father would soon kill him. He said he was so tired, hungry, and weak, he no longer had the strength to avoid his dad's beatings, and he hoped his death would be soon."

Winnie spoke with a sheriff's deputy about Clifton, pleading for his help, but it was late in the day, toward the end of his shift, and he showed more interest in leaving when his shift ended.

Carly felt guilty that Clifton had no clothes, so he gave him clothes that he and Winnie had outgrown, presenting him with pants, shirts, socks, lots of socks, two pairs of shoes, and a coat. Clifton had worn his shoes through, now full of holes, showing his bare feet and toes. The mornings were frosty, and Carly hoped socks would help warm his feet. The sheer wonder in Clifton's eyes and his smile were unforgettable. "I just wanted him to know someone cared, even if just a bit," Carly whispered.

Soon, Clifton stopped showing up for school. Clifton's absence from school was the kind that slowly grows from a whisper of concern to a roar of alarm. Three weeks passed. No word. No sight of him. Then came the undeniable, gut-wrenching smell and the neighbors detected a stench of carrion coming from the Gable house. The sheriff was contacted, and the unimaginable was found. Clifton, his life stolen from him at the heart of his youth, lay dead in his home, the victim of his drunken father, who admitted he had stomped him to death—whose defense was nothing more than the intoxication of his mind and senses. It shocked the now guilt-ridden students.

"How can a father kill his son, even if he is drunk?" asked Carly, disturbed and reflective.

Winnie, more reflective than most, sat in deep thought and heavy silence.

As news of the tragedy spread, shock, horror, and pity enveloped Marston. Considerable public outcry spread throughout the surrounding counties. The Marston Herald covered the story extensively about Clifton, but the front-page story dealt with the new, intriguing defense attorney hired to defend Mr. Gable. But, as with most tragedies, the clamor waned as the days passed.

The trial began and the courtroom was abuzz with excitement. Observers were outwardly taken aback, upset by the composition of the jury. Of the final twelve jurors, one had a second-grade education; another had reached the sixth-grade level. Another had finished a ninth-grade level, but none had received a high school diploma. Two known alcoholics served on the jury. The defendant's lawyer had seated a slam-dunk jury for his client with little opposition from the prosecuting attorney. It was clear to even the least clever that the scales of justice were heavily tilting in favor of the defendant.

As the trial played out, the prosecuting attorney's exceedingly lax, some said lazy, presentation of the facts to the jury, he came across as if he knew the defendant was guilty and nothing more needed to be said. His argument did not occupy the jurors for the full morning of the first day. His demeanor contrasted sharply with the defendant's vibrant arguments.

The defense lawyer's mastery over rhetoric meant his arguments went, true as an arrow, to the jurors' hearts. In his closing, he argued that whiskey had impaired Gable's judgment, and they should not find him guilty of murder. "Besides," he teased, "there but for the Grace of God go many of us." That brought laughter from the jurors.

The verdict was swift and shocking; not guilty. As the courtroom's murmurs faded, Winnie and Carly found themselves grappling with a sense of loss as great, or greater, than Cliftons death. The denial of justice for little Clifton meant the loss of belief in a system that was supposed to bring justice to the innocent.

Winnie had described Clifton's plight to the deputy and begged him for help, which did not come. After Clifton's death, Winnie asked him why he didn't help Clifton, and he whirled around and walked away without answering. His avoidance stoked the fire of anger, disappointment, and even hatred.

Later in life, Carly often morosely replayed the sad story of Clifton Gable in his mind, trying to parse why such a spectacular failure of the judicial system had occurred and why there wasn't an outcry from society. How did the legal minds escape discussing the challenges the present jury system presented to the judicial system? The most learned jurists, the community, the very fabric of justice— everyone had forsaken Clifton. The intricate dance, supposedly complicated but splendid between law and society was flawed, and Clifton paid the ultimate price.

✳

Winnie and Carly had shifted into high gear to gather the food, materials, equipment, and hardware they would need to survive for at least six months when their endeavor to leave the farm came to fruition. They had purloined a sack each of dried black-eyed peas, pinto beans, and lima beans. They planned to take a smoked ham and pork belly from the smokehouse. The farm butchers had smoked and salt-cured the ham and pork belly, and with wintry weather coming soon, both should be fine for a month or more. Dozens of jars of canned vegetables, fruit, and meat had been confiscated and stored in the unused grain crib, where they secreted their newly gained possessions.

While Winnie was in the smokehouse selecting the meat, the butcher in charge went into the main room to check on something, not knowing anyone was inside.

Winnie saw him enter and eased to the back of the windowless, dimly lit room smelling of smoked meat, he hoped to blend with the hanging animal carcasses, knowing if the man discovered him, it would require explanations. He was not as smooth with deceptive explanations as Carly. As if completing a cursory inventory, the man walked around the room, surveying the entire collection of meats. Winnie kept easing around a large hog carcass near the far back corner, trying to keep the pork between him and the butcher. After an eternity, the butcher walked out of the smokehouse, and Winnie breathed easier until he heard the unmistakable sound of the door latch falling into place. But he knew there was a leather thong attached to the door latch and threaded through a drilled hole to the inside, to gain an exit in situations such as he was in. He found a cloth sack to hold the meat he selected and added two sides of pork ribs as compensation for being locked inside. He made his way through the haze, only to find the leather thong was not through the hole. His immediate reaction was, "Damn, that poses a problem!" There was no access to the door latch from inside the smokehouse. Carly knew he was coming to steal the meat, so Winnie would have to wait. He sat on the floor while waiting, quietly sitting and thinking, and remembered they would need to pack an oilstone and files for sharpening knives and gardening tools.

Carly eventually came looking for him, and they decided it was best not to carry a big sack of meat around the farm on their shoulders in the daytime, and they would grab their bag of meat after dark.

They successfully stole the meat after darkness had settled.

The boys robbed, purloined, appropriated, snatched, borrowed, and stole canned food, garden tools, horse feed, matches, kitchen items, seasonings and lard, tarp, rope, soap, and the list became almost endless. The boys continued to amass more items. Carly collected a box of books from the study that he had yet to read, and he found a stash of Harlequin Romance novels that he included with a package of books for Josie. He had never heard of a *Harlequin Romance,* but he thought maybe it was something a young girl would like to read.

Carly and Winnie stored everything in large burlap bags for easier handling and more compact packing. They stashed the filled bags of material in the grain crib in their camp. Their mode of transportation would be a one-horse, four-wheeled Amish-type buggy, and they planned to pack items onto the cart after school each day until they had gathered all the items on their list. There were a couple of horses, and they had to choose one. Carly's dog, Jenna, a loyal pal and a significant part of his life, would accompany them with a standing invitation.

After supper, under the cloak of darkness, they moved the buggy and parked it beneath the shed attached to their campsite grain crib. The four-wheel Amish buggy was at least thirty years old, but hardly used, and squeaks were heard coming from two wheel hubs. They repacked all the wheel hubs with much needed axle grease before loading it. Packing the buggy like a sardine tin, they ensured room for Josie, their most precious cargo. The horse's gear was hanging, ready to go on the chosen animal in a flash.

The boys had saved 78 dollars to see them through when they reached their destination and set-up their camp. They planned to sell the horse and buggy to raise money for survival. Complete, total secrecy was their plan, and they were not to discuss it with Josie until their escape. They knew they would pay with broken bones or even their lives if a slip of the tongue alerted someone to their plan.

Winnie had discussed the selection of three potential sites suitable for a campsite, and they planned to choose one after examining each location. The sites were beneath large bridges that would shelter them from the weather, near running streams, and all were far from the farm, an essential detail.

*

"We have ninety-five percent of the items on our list, and I think we should leave tonight or tomorrow night at the latest." Winnie was ill at ease and anxious.

Carly disagreed. "We can't come home for items we don't have. Why the sudden hurry? We need our list to be 100% complete before we leave."

"Papa has become angrier than I have ever seen. I don't understand why, but it seemed to become pronounced with my eighteenth birthday. I have a gut feeling something terrible will happen if we stay longer."

His tone surprised Carly. "What do you think will happen?"

The question upset Winnie, causing him to shift and look away while he talked. His voice choked. "He stays angry enough to kill me, and I think he might."

But Carly didn't think they should go until they finished appropriating all the supplies and provisions on their list that they might need, and he told Winnie his fear of death was hyperbole. After talking and arguing for another half-hour, Winnie agreed they would stay until they completed the list.

Another week passed, and they finished gathering all the items on their list. Everything was ready, and after school, Winnie and Carly decided they would leave that night near midnight. They sealed their decision with a handshake and a hug, but both were apprehensive. If an obstacle delayed them, or someone discovered their plans, they would be in for a bone-breaking beating, or worse.

Winnie and Carly ate a nervous supper and went to their rooms, ostensibly to study. Josie always wanted to hang out with Carly and drifted to his room.

"Get your coat, gloves, and hat and bring them to my room," Carly spoke softly. "We're going for a ride later tonight."

"Will we ride in the car? Will Winnie go?"

"We are going for a buggy ride, and Winnie will go with us."

"Oh, good! I love to ride in the buggy. Where'll we go?"

He placed his finger over his lips, hissed and lowered his voice to just above a whisper. "Winnie and I are leaving the farm forever tonight. We will find a safe place to live more normal lives, and we hope you'll come with us, but we can't force you. If you decide not to leave, we won't either. Will you come with us?"

With a momentary look of surprise, she looked at Carly and without hesitation she whispered, "Every inch of the way, I'm with you. I'm scared to live here. Wherever you go, I'll go with you."

With a surprising move, she leaped toward Carly, wrapped her arms around him, and held him in a long, tight hug. When Carly explained the importance of their insistence on absolute secrecy, she answered in a serious tone, "I know, mum's the word."

Amid the pain and chaos, the bond between Carly, Winnie, and Josie grew stronger. The home that once stood for comfort now stood as a prison, reminding them of their Papa's unchecked rage and Mama's downward spiral into alcoholism and dangerous mental challenges. The weight of their past and the hope of a better future loomed large. They were each other's beacon of hope, and together, they would navigate the path to a new beginning.

8

·······

PAPA WAS SITTING in his chair in the dimly lit living room with no lamplight, drinking moonshine from his Mason jar in a brown paper bag, yelling and cursing. As usual, no one paid him any regard because he had become a blood-sucking predator who preyed on them, and they had hoped he would become less so if they shunned him. The room glowed by the fireplace's open fire, lighting the area around the hearth but giving off a dim light beyond and sending shadows like rhythmic dancing ghosts onto the walls and ceiling. The smell of the burning firewood pleasantly permeated the air, but in Carly's mind, Papa's extremely drunken state mitigated the pleasant aroma. He was slurring every screamed word, but there was a difference this time. He was lacing his yelling, screaming, and cursing with more venomous anger than ever.

"Winston, God dammit, get your damned ass in here!"

Winnie remained quiet, absorbed in his studies, but he thought Papa's screams weren't new. Winnie had heard them many times before, and there was never an urgency to go to Papa because he still considered him nothing more than an asshole.

Papa yelled a second time, much louder and with furious anger. Carly knew this episode might not end well when Papa shrieked at the top of his lungs, "Winston, get your ass in here, you damned little bastard!"

Winnie didn't answer. Josie realized, too, this encounter differed from other times. Though 10, she jumped onto Carly's lap like a toddler, hugged him, and placed her face against his. Her breath was a deep, rapid pant. She squeezed her eyes shut, and Carly felt her thin body trembling, but she didn't cry. Carly hugged her, held her tight, and under his breath, told her he would keep her safe.

Carly had grown over five inches the past year, pushing five feet ten inches and weighing nearly 160 pounds. He was taller and more muscular than Winnie. Still, at thirteen years, Carly knew he didn't have the cutthroat viciousness, the overwhelming meanness in his system as Papa, so he doubted whether he stood a chance with him in a fair fight. Besides, Papa didn't know the ethical meaning of the word "fair."

Josie and Carly listened as Winnie left his bedroom. They heard his footsteps on the hardwood floor in the hallway, heading toward the living room. He had made this walk an untold number of times, and there was never a need to rush to Papa.

Then they heard Winnie say, "Papa, what can I get for you?"

Papa slurred when he half yelled, "Fucking thief! You're stealing my farm!"

They heard a loud thud and a sharp crack, like a breaking stick, followed by an ominous sound as if a firewood log had dropped onto the hardwood floor. Except it was not firewood. It was Winnie crashing to the floor. Winnie never uttered a sound. Papa had struck Winnie with an object, breaking bones in his face, skull, or neck. The cracking was a dreadful, ominous sound. Carly had heard this sound when livestock sustained broken bones. Josie and Carly were near the panic stage, but neither made a sound, barely daring to breathe.

Slurring, Papa screamed at Winnie, "Still want to steal my farm, you sorry-ass bastard? Get up!"

Loud, slurred cursing followed.

Josie and Carly were nearing hysteria, but neither dared to make a sound. They were helpless against their drunken, raging, fiery mad Papa, and they were afraid that if he discovered them, he would murder them. Then, it sounded like Papa got up from his chair and, cursing, with a loud grunt, kicked Winnie, and Carly could hear bones crack, accompanied by Papa's loud cursing. The sounds petrified him, and he was beyond horror-stricken. But there was an even more ominous sign; Winnie remained quiet.

Desperate, Carly first recited the Lord's Prayer, then beseechingly offered a spontaneous prayer. The most horrifying, dreadful, spine-chilling sounds began, sounding like Papa was stomping Winnie while he lay helpless on the floor! Each time Papa crushed him, he cursed Winnie, and they heard the hideous, sickening sounds of bones cracking and snapping! Carly vomited, projectile. Then Josie pressed her face against his neck and shut her eyes tight. Neither dared to make a sound while breathing nor twitch a muscle.

Carly's primary concern was keeping Josie safe. Papa was murderously insane enough to kill him at once, and then he would make quick work of Josie. Papa was snorting, cursing, gasping for breath, and wheezing as he extinguished the life from Winnie's body. The horrendous noises continued for what seemed an eternity. Carly thought Papa had to tire. There was a sickening sloshing sound like Papa was walking in mud. Papa had executed Winnie, and he had a madman's curse in his mind to exterminate all evidence that Winnie existed to prevent Winnie from stealing his farm!

When Papa grew too exhausted to continue his accursed, wicked execution and was too fatigued to stand, they heard him fall back onto his chair, wheezing, coughing, and gasping for breath. Within a few brief minutes, he was snoring as if he had done nothing more than a mere dance around the room. Listening to Papa's snoring, Carly hoped he was far enough gone to allow him to go to Winnie. He cautioned Josie to remain seated and stay as quiet as possible, assuring her he would return to her at once. Carly stood and, on tiptoes, eased past Papa's chair, ensuring there was no immediate threat, and knelt beside Winnie's lifeless body.

The smell and feel of hot, sticky blood were unmistakable to Carly. He had encountered it while helping butcher animals. He was close to passing out. The room was dim and seemed spinning, lit only by the dying fire of the open fireplace. He was on the verge of screaming as the reality of what had happened became clear. Winnie was a bloody mess. His face, now swollen and bloody, wasn't recognizable, and a massive amount of blood covered the floor, the wall,

Papa's chair, and even the ceiling. Winnie's blood covered Papa from his head to his feet, and blood flowed across the floor into the fireplace, extinguishing the flame.

Kneeling by Winnie, Carly slowly reached for Winnie to feel his pulse, knowing but dreading what he would find. Papa suddenly stirred and sat forward, looking around like he would attack. Carly stood, and, with all the force and courage he could muster, he planted a full, robust, solid kick squarely into the front of his head and face, and he welcomed the sound of breaking bones. Blood sprayed from Papa's face, and his breathing became a gurgling sound. Carly remained standing but unmoving, petrified, not even daring to breathe. His heart was racing, held between beats by unprecedented fear and anger.

Papa fell back into his chair and remained motionless, with irregular breathing but no snoring. It was clear Papa would not move, and Carly breathed again. Kneeling beside Winnie, he tried to stifle his uncontrolled sobs. Tears blurred his vision and flowed down his cheeks. Winnie had no pulse. Winnie was not alive! He was dead! Paralyzed, Carly continued to kneel, and he tilted his head upward as if to speak with God, his arms and hands outstretched, searching and begging for help that was not there. Horrible anguish beyond what Carly could ever have imagined filled every crevice and cavern of his mind, brain, body, and soul. The scene overwhelmed him with feelings of helplessness, hopelessness, fear, and alone. Winnie's body lying before him was now indelible in his mind, and nothing could undo it. Winnie's unmitigated slaughter had deeply implanted uncontrolled anger in his soul. Carly hoped he had killed Papa, but he was still breathing.

Carly's primal hatred for Papa was categorical, and he wanted revenge. Looking upward, Carly could only whisper. "Where were you, God? Don't you give a damn?" If there was a God, Carly guessed God thought the question was rhetorical.

He called out to Uncle Matt, "Uncle Matt, I need you! I need you by my side to give me the strength necessary to deal directly with this horrendous, bloody execution of Winnie. Uncle Matt, should I murder Papa? He murdered my brother!" Uncle Matt wasn't around to answer, but the moment gave Carly the strength to save Josie and the clarity of mind not to murder Papa.

Carly briefly said goodbye to his big brother, confidant, best friend, and protector. He recalled their conversations about Clifton Gable. But trying to parse the similarities between Winnie's and Clifton's death was brutal. Too much information was crowding his mind. He couldn't process it in that fleeting moment. He must grab Josie and leave for safety at once. If they reached a haven, maybe someday he would have the time and calmness to clear his mind of this unspeakable, catastrophic bloody slaughter.

Carly considered Mama a non-entity in this equation, and he initially gave no thought to letting her know what had happened. He knew she had passed out from drinking rot-gut moonshine whiskey. Carly wondered what the scene would be like when Mama and Papa stirred the next day. He decided it would be best to try at least to alert her to what she would find the following day. He went directly to her room and entered without knocking. But she had passed out from alcohol and was not arousable. Despite yelling her name, screaming, and strenuous physical shaking, he couldn't suffi-ciently rouse her to have her understand what had just happened. An unlikely thought flashed through his brain; maybe Mama and Papa would commit suicide. That thought annoyed him; there was no time for dreaming. He turned to return to Josie but stumbled on an object lying on the floor. He picked it up and examined it. It was a stick of firewood with hair embedded in the bark. It was the club that Papa had used to kill Winnie. He dropped it as if it were ablaze.

He turned to run to Josie, but she stood in the living room, star-ing at the bloody scene. She had seen too much for her age, but so had he.

Carly gathered Josie, their coats, and hats and made a determined dash for the campground and their means of escape! He bridled the gentlest and best-looking horse of the bunch, a beautiful, large, dark mare named Mary. They hitched her to the loaded buggy in record time, and as an afterthought, he grabbed the saddle and threw it atop the burlap storage bags.

Josie eagerly climbed aboard the buggy. "I hate this damn place and all the people in it. I want to leave and never come back."

Carly rushed to make sure Josie was comfortable in the seat next to him, covered her with a blanket, placed her hat on her head, and left at a fast gallop, headed to God knows where, hoping never to look back. Carly's dog, Jenna, was in the lead, like a dashing dark shadow, leading Mary. The full moon gave enough light for him to see her running as if she knew where she was going, and she knew their leaving was permanent.

Josie said nothing about leaving Winnie behind; she had not shed a tear. She would talk when she was ready. Carly didn't know if Josie realized Winnie was dead, but she had seen more than enough while watching the scene to realize it was true. He was dealing with an impossible rage, and so was Josie, but she didn't show it. He was slowly gaining the insight that Josie grieved privately. Papa, the damned drunken son-of-a-bitch, had just murdered their brother, and Mama was too damned drunk and mentally challenged to realize what had happened and that she was now alone. And God was MIA.

But this was no time for grief or self-pity. Carly had to focus all his energy on their escape, on finding a safe refuge for himself and little Josie. Josie, 10, and Carly, 13, were alone, isolated, and this realization settled on him as if the weight of the moon and planets had descended on his shoulders. He knew he must now base his decisions on reason, not anger. Glancing down at her as she huddled against him, he vowed to himself that he would let no harm come to her. The foremost thought in Carly's mind was that she was his sole responsibility now, and he would care for her as Winnie had cared for him.

With this renewed sense of purpose, Carly flicked the reins again. The loaded buggy bounced along even faster, putting more distance between them and the horrors they left behind. The future was uncertain, but together they would face it with resilience and hope.

9

1953

THE BUGGY JOLTED ALONG the washboard-rutted dirt road, its aged wooden wheels creaking with each rotation. Young Carly hunched over the reins, urging the beautiful mare to greater speed. His sister, Josie, huddled beside him on the bench, her small frame trembling against the chill of the autumn night. Although covered with her coat and a light blanket, Carly had forgotten to bring a heavier wrap for her in his haste to flee that house of horrors.

Behind them, the farmhouse had receded into the darkness, looking almost peaceful in the silvery moonlight. But Carly knew better. He had borne witness to the unspeakable violence within those walls and had seen his brother beaten to death by their rabid, drunken father. Never again would he and Josie have to endure that man's vicious, drunken temper and heavy fists. They were free! Yet freedom came at so great a cost. Were they free? As long as Papa was alive and walking free, would they ever be free?

Carly swallowed hard, fighting back the tears that stung his eyes. Dear Winnie, always so quick to protect him from their parents' wrath, now gone forever. The image of his battered body lying lifeless in that pool of blood was forever seared into Carly's mind.

Their progress was slow. Carly felt each jolt and bump, traveling the back dirt roads to avoid recognition by someone who could report them to the sheriff. The loaded buggy was easier to handle than imagined, but the dirt roads did nothing for comfort. Josie fell asleep in post-adrenalin exhaustion minutes after they began riding. The night air was crisp and calming to breathe. Even in the palpable tension of their escape, Carly was aware of the brilliant harvest moon shining a bright yellow orange, no clouds obscuring its beauty, and millions of stars sprinkling the night sky like diamonds on velvet, each trying to outdo its neighbor with competitive interstellar beauty.

The calmness was shattered as vehicle lights approached from ahead. As they drew nearer, and as the vehicle passed, Carly saw it was a pickup truck. But not just any—it bore the unmistakable flashing red light of a patrol truck. He needed to get off the road. The pickup slowed, stopped, turned around, and trailed close behind their buggy for a short distance. Carly's heart raced, each beat echoing louder in his ears. His chest hurt, and he gasped for breath. He covered Josie and sat forward on his seat, hiding her from sight, and praying she wouldn't stir. He gripped the reins against his lap to hide and try to steady his shaking hands.

There were ditches on either side of the dirt road, but he guided Mary to a stop. A cold sweat bathed him, and the brisk night air covered him with goosebumps. He hoped the darkness would hide the dribbles of sweat running from his forehead to his face. If the officer returned them to the farm, Carly knew Papa would kill them both. But the events surrounding Winnie's bloody death were now becoming surreal in his mind and dim in his memory, and he was finding it difficult to believe what happened was real. The state patrol officer came beside Carly, shining his flashlight over the horse, buggy, and cargo.

The officer approached and asked the obvious question, "Where are you going at this hour?"

Without blinking, Carly forced himself to look into the deputy's eyes and crafted a story. "Papa, Mama, my brother Winnie, and I are going camping for a few days, and Papa wanted to make sure this gear load was okay for the horse and buggy. I think it's an okay load. It's such a peaceful night I lost track of time." He held onto hope that it would be enough.

The officer warned him it would be safer if he carried a light, and he gave Carly a spare flashlight. "Leave it at the police desk when you come to town."

Carly thanked him. The officer walked by Mary, the horse, looking at her size and beauty, patted her on her withers, and she returned an appreciative whicker.

As he turned toward Carly, he smiled and said, "Stay safe and enjoy your camping trip."

"Thank you, Sir. May I ask your name?"

"Petty, Officer Petty. Oh, let me see your identification just to make it official."

A lightning strike couldn't have hit Carly harder. He was short of breath again, trying not to gasp as he felt a panic attack rearing its ugly head, just waiting for the proper missed heartbeat to land with full force, and he didn't have a paper bag. His hand tremor had become uncontrollable, and sweat was streaming down his face. The officer could have brushed him aside with a feather. Struggling to speak, he managed only to mumble.

"Uh, officer...."

Just as things seemed to take a turn for the worse, a reckless car came over the little hill in front of them, speeding toward them like a bat out of hell, and got dangerously close to the buggy and Officer Petty's truck, causing the officer to dodge. He slipped on the gravel and ended up flat on his ass, and was he ever pissed!

"That SOB. You go ahead, son."

He jumped into his truck, turned it around, and with the red light flashing and the siren screaming, he sped away. And with that, their escape continued. But not for long. Another vehicle approached from behind. This vehicle was closer than the first and may have spotted them already. Carly's heart raced, fearful that it was Officer Petty again. He tapped Mary with the rein, clicked his tongue, and she responded with a fast gallop. Carly was desperate to get off the roadway because the fast gallop on the washboard dirt road was jarring his teeth and insides, and Josie's. A full moon allowed almost maximum night visibility in the cloudless sky, giving the moving landscape imaginary scenes of beautiful, ghostly, dancing fairies. The moonlight limned the leaves of the trees and bushes in a fairy-tale, ethereal, silver highlight.

Jenna found an almost invisible turnoff, more imaginary than real, and Mary followed her onto an overgrown, long-ago-used field road. Carly guided Mary behind a hedgerow, stopped, and waited for the vehicle to pass. Both animals took a needed breather It slowed and stopped, backed up, and the engine stopped. The car door opened, then slammed shut, and Carly could hear the crunching of someone's shoes on the clay-gravel road. Who was it? Had the state patrol officer returned? He had trouble handling the reins because his hands wouldn't stop trembling. He thought the damnable night would never end. In a cold sweat bath in the light breeze again, his teeth chattered, and goosebumps covered his entire body.

He heard more dirt-gravel crunching shoe sounds; the car door opened and slammed again, the engine started, and the car drove away. After long minutes, his breathing calmed, and they resumed their getaway, following a vague, unused path from long ago that had lain idle for years, away from the main road. Jenna led, and Mary followed without hesitation, wandering through fallow farmland. Although Jenna was trotting to an unknown destination, Carly was now at ease, allowing her to lead, which was out of character for him. Jenna was taller and heavier than the usual Border Collie but had the black and white markings typical of a Border Collie, although she was larger than typical Border Collies. She had inherited both the superior intelligence and the instinct to herd her four-legged brethren and people that Border Collies have. The other mix in her breed was unknown, but he suspected Pit Bull. She had become fiercely loyal and allowed no one to step between her and Carly, even if the purpose was friendly.

A dark farmhouse silhouette was faintly visible in the darkness; no lights showed, no dogs barked, and Carly thought the house was vacant. Jenna and Mary stopped in front of the house. Years of neglect of the yard had left it overgrown. They had not yet reached any destinations that Winnie had named, but they, including Mary and Jenna, needed rest. He rummaged through a burlap bag to find another flashlight.

The house was shadowy but promising, silently holding on to its stories, waiting patiently for someone to listen. A cursory check-out of the house and close surroundings found it vacant. A thick growth of bramble, sassafras, hickory, black gum, and wild plum bushes surrounded the house, and there wasn't a visible path leading to the front porch.

Josie continued to sleep, but Mary smelled water and walked ahead. Carly stopped her, unhitched the buggy, and propped the gear against a tree trunk. Mary and Carly walked a short distance, following Jenna to a creek with clear, running water. Carly stomped down the overgrowth on the faint path and cleared a rough, temporary trail to the porch. The floor appeared solid with no dry rot. The prior occupants had left the front door unlocked. Giant spider webs in the doorway proved no one had entered the house in recent months or years. But inside, Carly was surprised that someone had abandoned a furnished home. Dusty furniture told tales of once-happy moments, of laughter, of warmth.

An oil lamp was on the mantlepiece, another was on a long table beneath one window. Another lamp with a frilly shade sat on the kitchen nook table. Someone had left in a hurry, planning to return, but had not. Now, everything stood still, silent witnesses to a new chapter in the lives of Carly and Josie. There was no evidence electricity ever being installed. Carly was sure electricity had been available for many years. Could the house have been vacant that long? The interior was in excellent repair.

The beds invited his tired body to sleep, but they were too dusty to sleep on. Josie was now wide awake and eager to see their new surroundings. She walked through each room with childlike wonder, excited about staying the night at the house. Josie still said nothing about the unimaginable horror scene they had fled earlier. It had become dimmer in Carly's mind, like a broken dream, and he hoped she would not want to discuss it soon.

Carly checked one of the oil lamps, cleaned off the dust, including the lamp's chimney, and found it filled with kerosene, with one match, the lamp was bright.

Carly went outside to care for Mary, fed her several ears of corn and hobbled her in a patch of good grazing. He and Josie retired to the not-so-soft pallet he had thrown together, and Jenna slept by their side. Josie's breathing slowed into the rhythm of deep sleep, but sleep didn't come for Carly. The events of the night, a mishmash of fear, relief and disbelief, played in a loop in his mind. The quiet house seemed to lean in, listening, providing shelter and silence for Carly's thoughts. Too much mental noise flooded his brain, although he wasn't sure why.

10

·······

CARLY JERKED AWAKE FROM a restless nap at the sound of the front door shutting. His first instinct was an intruder, but Josie had returned, announcing she had to pee. She'd ventured outside in the pre-dawn darkness without waking him. As Carly tried to grapple with the wave of relief and fatigue, the distant crowing of roosters filled the quiet. Were they feral, roosting in the nearby trees?

He walked onto the back porch, paused, and let the refreshing brisk morning air fill his lungs. Dawn was turning the eastern sky to a lovely red and blue hue. A few big fluffy clouds hung motionless in the bright sky, and a light breeze completed the beautiful October morning. The porch was a testament to days gone by with two tables with weathered wood loveseats and chairs, set upon a floor of sturdy cedar boards that had taken on graceful, weathered gray hue.

He and Josie wandered into the backyard, and Josie shot him a cautionary glance, reminding him they should be hyper-alert. He nodded quizzically, not understanding why, but he didn't voice his confusion. They saw no nearby houses, and a large barn was on an overgrown path behind the house. The surrounding nature hinted at years of solitude; towering pecan trees, gigantic, majestic live oaks, water oaks, and large magnolias stood as if guarding an age-old secret. Amidst this, a weathered muscadine vine snaked upward among the sprawling limbs of a water oak. The extensive vines and undergrowth surrounding the trees stood as evidence of long abandonment. Carly and Josie took Mary to water and left her hobbled and grazing in the front yard.

The pair, accompanied by Jenna, searched for drinkable water.

An old covered well at the back of the house had a bucket, rope, and windlass, but the rope crumbled into dust in his fingers, showing its weathered age. The water level was less than ten feet from the well top, and he had brought a rope that could reach that depth ten times over and installed it on the windlass. There were no gutters and downspouts from the roof, the well had the promise of being spring fed and potable.

Their exploration farther along, walking upstream from Mary's watering point, led them to a large stream feeding the creek. As they followed the stream, they discovered a fountainhead up the slope from the house's back. The view was breathtaking. The spring was as beautiful as a page from a fantasy storybook. A picturesque Weeping Willow stood guard over the spring, its beautiful slumbering limbs protecting the clear water and whisking a large limestone rock at the upper edge of the spring. Close by stood a majestic Magnolia tree. It seemed they'd stumbled into a secret sanctuary.

But as they basked in the tranquil beauty, A strange wave of dizziness accompanied by mild nausea overcame Carly. He sat down in the grass. The world around him was a blur. Confused, his connection to Josie and his own identity seemed to vanish. He grappled with this unsettling amnesia for what seemed like hours before clarity returned. Shaken but determined, he fetched water from the spring, the site now holding a deeper significance. He had unanswered questions, but the pastoral setting was so soothing, his mind was relieved of burdensome anxiety and depression. He regained his self-identity, and Josie's name and her relationship with him returned. There was not a dramatic difference in the house's level and the level of the spring up on the ridge, but it was enough to give one the sensation that they were looking down on the house. The descriptive terminology of "up the slope to the spring" was born, something they would often say to each other. They headed to the barn along a trail overgrown with weeds, briars, and bushes. Attached to the barn was a feedlot or corral with wood rails that were in good repair. The barn showed little evidence of wear and tear. They climbed to the hayloft and found baled and loose hay filling over half of it. They stirred up chickens using the loft and stalls to build nests and lay their eggs. Hundreds of pigeons used the hay loft to roost, breed, and hatch their young. They flew in and out, reminding Carly of outsized bees with a colossal hive.

They discovered a horse's skeleton in one stall, bolstering Carly's supposition that someone had made a hasty departure. A clean stall on the barn's end near the house would be perfect for Mary at night. There was enough grass in the feedlot that she could graze for weeks if they were to stay that long.

An outhouse stood about two hundred feet from the house's mudroom door. Carly fetched a large kitchen knife from a burlap bag on the buggy and used it as a temporary yard tool to cut the vegetation around the outhouse. Jenna gave welcome assurance there were no snakes or rats holed up, and Carly ensured no Black Widow spiders lurked beneath the toilet seat.

As they settled in, the pair began to adapt to their newfound sanctuary, aware of the challenges and mysteries it held. But how long could they stay?

11

AMIDST THE REMNANTS of a long-ago abandonment, Carly found a bookcase built into a living room wall that held dusty books, some which might interest Josie. An adaptive learner, she advanced far beyond her peers under the tutelage of Mrs. Brownlie. He found a fascinating book about karate and read it while taking a break before tackling the kitchen.

The tidy but antiquated kitchen held relics from another era. An old, dented percolator coffee pot sat atop the wood-burning stove with its top ajar, flanked by two flat irons, one with a broken handle. Hints of faint aromas of past meals lingered though the house had been empty for who knows how long. He cleaned thick dust from the counters. The prior occupants had stored dishes and flatware in the kitchen cupboards and drawers. A sturdy table and four match-ing chairs sat in an adjacent breakfast nook.

The brisk fall air chilled the house. Carly brought wood and kin-dling from outside and started fires in the stove and fireplace. As the rooms warmed, Jenna collapsed into a deep sleep near the fireplace, and Josie slept on the pallet, wrapped in her blanket alongside Jenna, her head on a pillow from a bed and her arm over Jenna's neck.

Three furnished bedrooms were dusty, making washing bed linens and curtains necessary. Dust-covered floors, windows, and furniture would need extensive cleaning. The beds were tidy from however many years ago, suggesting a neat housekeeper, adding to the deepening mystery. A large, empty room with only an ironing board leaning against one wall separated two bedrooms, and a hall-way connected to a third bedroom, all furnished.

A sizable storage room was in the house's backside. At least a hundred Mason canning jars were on the shelves, some with canned food, but most were empty. A bustling utility room had washtubs and a scrub board; outside the utility room, a cast-iron wash pot stood ready in the yard, and heavy wire clotheslines were still standing on metal posts. All these hinted of a family life abruptly abandoned. But why?

Carly lowered the smoked salt-cured pork belly, ribs, and ham into the well, just above the water, protecting the meat from marauding critters and taking advantage of the cooling effect. He filled the stove reservoir with water and stoked and fed the stove fire to have warm water for Josie's bath.

*

Carly had made a disturbing discovery. He and Winnie had saved 78 dollars to see them through and cover initial living expenses until they could sell their horse. The money was not in the buggy but remained in Winnie's pocket. They had a quarter, a dime, and three pennies, 38 cents. With Carly's fractured memory, there were so many unclear things in his mind. He couldn't remember why they must sell their horse, and asking Josie was too embarrassing. Maybe Winnie was planning to join them. He would get everything cleared up when he next saw him.

Carly's pocketknife was a treasured gift from Uncle Matt and was the only thing he owned outright. Beyond that, he had borrowed, purloined, or stolen all their belongings, but he couldn't remember why. Besides his pocketknife, his most treasured belongings were his pencils, paper, notebooks, books from the farm, borrowed books from Mrs. Brownlie, and books from the school closet. He could not understand why they left the farm. He assumed job prospects for a boy of thirteen were not bright, but he would have to do something because Josie depended on him. But why? The constant demands of surviving on the abandoned property kept him busy. He was sleeping well, and Josie relaxed, but they stayed alert. So many things were a mystery. He wasn't sure why, but he didn't dwell on his memory lapse.

Food was a pressing concern, and Carly knew it was his responsibility to supply it. They had canned and dried foods, but fresh vegetables were essential. With no money, his options were few, and after discussing the situation with Josie, he decided he had to steal from neighbors' gardens, but not close-by neighbors. The word 'steal' sounded too harsh, so he chose the euphemism, borrow. Under the veil of dusk, for his novice trial, he would go to a well-kept garden about three miles away. With neither fence nor gate to interfere, there should be less likelihood of complications.

With a small backpack, he left the house as the sun was setting, appearing only as a smoldering cinder but beautiful colors of red, orange, and yellow etched the scattered clouds in the western sky. He arrived in the garden's vicinity a bit early, so he sat in the shade of a hedgerow and admired the sunset's remaining red and golden colors. Frogs were croaking and ribbiting, and crickets were chirping, but nothing else encroached on the pervasive silence. After darkness had settled, he edged into the garden. His heart raced, and his breathing was as rapid as if he had run a mile. He began harvesting vegetables into a tow sack pulled from his little pack, filling it with turnips, greens, onions, collard greens, kale, carrots, and garlic.

As he was leaving the garden, a car turned onto the narrow driveway leading past the garden to the nearby house. The lights were about to bathe him when he slammed his body flat against the earth in the middle between two rows of vegetables. He remained motionless, waiting for the car to pass and continue to the house. But it stopped beside the garden. A man climbed out of the vehicle, left the engine running and the lights on while he gathered something from the garden. Had the man seen Carly, and was he coming to assault him?

Carly was sweating, not knowing whether to jump up and run like hell or remain flat on the ground and risk having the man stomp the crap out of him. He tried to stifle his breathing but was unsuccessful. In the reduced ambient night light, the man looked older, in his 60s or 70s, and hummed a catchy little tune. Carly breathed a sigh of relief when he decided the tune was a good sign the man had not spotted him, unless he was just a happy murderer. He would remain still unless the guy assaulted him while he hummed his little ditty. The man went to the onion row, still humming his tune, pulled up several onions, returned to his car, and continued to the house. Carly got the hell out of the garden with his bag of goodies and ran toward home. He noticed his breathing was quieter after running three miles than when lying in the middle between the vegetable rows.

Carly spent an evening each week plucking turnips and greens, rutabagas, collard greens, kale, tomatoes, and anything that looked nourishing from the gardens a few miles away. Three neighbors had sweet potato hills in their gardens and unknowingly shared their tubers. Choosing those gardens with more affluent houses a distance from his home, meant he would never enter the close-by neighborhood gardens. Ashamed of being a burglar, he knew it was not his neighbor's responsibility to remedy his misfortunes. The road to Hell is paved with good intentions was a well-known expression, but he vowed to see them compensated someday. But it was strange that he couldn't remember why they were experiencing the misfortunes. He felt embarrassed to ask Josie to help him remember; otherwise, he was okay.

*

Josie went for a long morning walk with no purpose or destination in mind other than she needed to get away from the house and Carly for some free time. The morning was beautiful, in the mid-70s, scattered cumulous clouds floating, and nothing needing her to hurry home to tend. The sun peeked above the eastern horizon painting the sky blue and red with a wide brush. The birds were singing as if they were a chorus. Squirrels were busily gathering and stowing acorns and nuts for the coming winter. Since she had not yet developed an exact sense of estimating distances, she left that to Carly. But because her feet and legs were getting tired, she figured she had walked several miles when she came to a mailbox packed with mail and newspapers. Was someone away, sick, or dead? A narrow driveway led into the woods, apparently to an unseen house. Curiosity was an inborn trait of Josie's, and she plucked a letter from the packed mailbox to see whose name was on the envelope and dislodged a yellowed newspaper that fell to the ground. The letter was addressed to Ross Hutchinson, which meant nothing to Josie, but she would pass the information along to Carly. After stuffing the envelope back into the mailbox, she picked the newspaper off the ground. The yellowing of the newspaper showed it was old, and the date on the paper concurred. It was a copy of *The Marston Herald,* and when she glanced at the headline article, she was momentarily stunned to see her name and Carly's. The article described the sheriff announcing the presumed deaths of Carlton and Josephine Turner. The sheriff described the horrendous murder of Winston, but he and his deputies had been unable to find the bodies of Carlton and Josephine Turner, the brother and sister of Winston. According to the sheriff, there was irrefutable evidence that Carlton and Josephine Turner had also perished, and he declared them dead. She folded the newspaper beneath her arm and turned to head home.

Josie knew this was an important piece of information because now that she and Carly were presumed dead, no one would officially be looking for them. However, the heinous specter of Papa was always looming. She and Carly must discuss this finding and decide what effect, if any, it would have on their daily lives. That question began a cascade of related thoughts that were still in their formative stages because Josie had noticed that Carly had been unusually happy, carefree, displaying no evidence of depression since they arrived at their new location This was unusual. Also, he hadn't mentioned Winnie since arriving, and didn't seem to fear the consequences that being discovered might bring Papa. She had repeatedly warned him to be careful, remain secretive, and not to draw attention to them. He acted as if the warnings weren't registering. She wasn't alarmed, but the change had been abrupt, appearing when they arrived at their new location, perhaps a result of the relaxed atmosphere of their new home in its beautiful pastoral setting. But taking all this into account, maybe she should wait to discuss the newspaper article with Carly. She wanted to know that he was okay.

Their journey had only just begun, and while the future held many uncertainties, Carly and Josie clung to hope and each other.

12

As November dawned, the palette of nature changed. Leaves turned yellow, red, and golden hues, but beautiful persistent evergreens stood firm against the encroaching winter, providing a backdrop of unyielding green. Stately live oaks were semi-deciduous and didn't shed their leaves in the fall. As the days passed, Thanksgiving neared, and the siblings, fueled by a nostalgia spawned from voracious reading of books, Carly and Josie decided to attempt Uncle Matt's cherished hasenpfeffer recipe. Though they lacked the authentic ingredients of Uncle Matt's design, Carly's resourcefulness and Josie's memories came together to improvise a version close to their heart. Carly and loyal Jenna went out in the early morning hours before dawn. Jenna had gotten their Thanksgiving rabbit when the sun began to paint the eastern sky with beautiful red and blue hues.

Josie had set a beautiful table, placing a colorful tablecloth that earlier occupants had packed in the pantry. She added autumn leaves for a touch of the season, brightening the room with earthy red, yellow, brown, and green colors. Both were involved with the meal preparation. Accompanying the hasenpfeffer were collard greens, turnips and greens, baked sweet potatoes, and a pan of cornbread.

They sat at the table, and Josie asked to say grace.

"Dear Lord, thank you for the food you have given us. We are especially thankful that you led us here safely to be together. Please lead and bless us as we make our way through life. Amen." Josie continued, "That's all I know; I've thought about this for days and practiced it too. I think I got it right, though."

Carly said, his voice tinged with emotion, "That was much better than I could have said. I'm thankful we're together." Josie's heartfelt grace reminded Carly how their journey, with all its challenges, had strengthened their bond.

The entire hasenpfeffer meal was delicious and was something they could be proud and thankful for, each bite reminding them of memories of Uncle Matt.

Jenna devoured her share and also seemed thankful.

*

Autumn passed quickly, always short in the Deep South, and winter subtly ushered in with no fanfare or arctic storm. They would soon celebrate their first Christmas enjoying their new liberty in their new home. It wasn't just their first Christmas in their newfound home, it was their first true celebration of the holiday. They still did not know how long they could continue squatting, but they hadn't heard from the owners or anyone. The prolonged absence of the owners was puzzling. But they would continue living daily, prepared to leave at a moment's notice. Carly didn't know why they were squatting, but he seemed happy not knowing. Why they would not spend the holiday on the farm was confusing to Carly, but he was happy not being there, and he wouldn't ask Josie.

Their formal education remained paramount in Carly's mind, but Josie said returning to school now wasn't safe. They wanted to remain in contact with their teacher, Mrs. Brownlie. The college English textbooks and English novels Mrs. Brownlie had loaned them remained boxed from the move. Re-reading his books a third time, Carly also practiced composition and learned advanced algebra from textbooks he had found in a closet at his school. The Romantic authors' novels and poems were incredible. Memories of Mrs. Brownlie continued to drive him. He was desperate for more reading material and dreamed of attending college someday, although he had no funds.

A few days before Christmas, Carly asked Josie, "Want to join me on a trek to find the perfect Christmas tree?"

"I'd love it. Where do we go?"

"Let's bundle up like Nanook of the North, hitch Mary to the buggy, and head to places unknown. If we're lucky, we'll find a small cedar tree that will be pretty."

They were excited because neither had ever selected a Christmas tree. They never had a Christmas tree on the farm. Nor had they ever celebrated Christmas. They traveled north, following an overgrown field road, not knowing where it led. Carly assumed it would be on land belonging to the house's owners, but he was unsure. Riding in the buggy in the brisk morning was enjoyable, and they cherished the new feeling of freedom. Everything, the trees, sun, even the dead snags, looked more beautiful than they could remember. Soon, they stopped beside a tree that looked promising. It was the right size for their living room, about five feet tall, and its shape was beautiful. They had stumbled across the one—the perfect Christmas tree that embodied the spirit of the season. They placed it on the buggy and headed home.

Carly trimmed the tree's base, nailed two boards across it for a stand, and placed it in the living room, looking as regal as one they had seen in pictures of Buckingham Palace. Carly had borrowed several ears of popcorn from a neighbor's garden. They shucked, shelled, and popped it, then strung it as a garland to decorate the tree. There were no lights or store-bought decorations, but they didn't mind. They admired the beautiful tree from every angle, strolling back and forth, sauntering around it. The addictive redolence of the cedar filled the house, and they sat, with two oil lamps burning, adoring the beauty and breathing deeply to enjoy the aromatic essence of the cedar fragrance.

They had no money to buy gifts, but their joy at Christmas was filled with intangible treasures—an enraptured experience, albeit unfamiliar, a priori, and they didn't want it to end. For the first time, they felt safe, were happy, and shared an unbreakable bond.

13

·······

WHEN WINTER'S GRIP BEGAN to loosen, almost overnight, signs of spring were everywhere. The days were getting warmer and longer, beautiful wildflowers had blossomed in abundance, and birds were out in great numbers, singing their little hearts out, trying to attract a mate to start a family.

They managed to survive the winter, living on borrowed vegetables from local gardens; dried peas, dried beans, canned vegetables, and smoked bacon and ham they had brought from the farm. There was a plentiful supply of chickens and eggs, and Jenna was a proven expert at catching rabbits and squirrels. Carly had mastered his cooking technique on a spit over hot coals and a low flame.

One morning, Carly saw a majestic black bear on the edge of the woods behind the house. With its identifying ursine gait, it meandered out of the woods into the edge of an open field. Unhurried, it dug for roots and grubs, unearthing natures buried treasures. It tore into a rotten log for larvae and insects. It either smelled or heard him and stood on its hind legs looking in his direction, but it was doubtful it saw him. He had read that a bear's distant vision was not great, but their sense of smell was phenomenal, as much as seven or eight times greater than a bloodhound. He, or she, then sat on its prominent haunches and scratched its ears, appearing thin, just out of hibernation. He knew he must be careful when letting Jenna outside, ensuring he was with her until warmer weather made food for the bears more plentiful.

Jenna was on the trail of something up on the ridge. She was an excellent dog for small game, having brought home two rabbits in the prior two weeks. He had prepared the rabbits, the first to bake in the oven and the second to fry on the stovetop. They had lard, salt, and pepper, making the rabbits quite tasty, and he shared both with Jenna. Scarfing them down, she agreed; they were flavorful.

Jenna was tussling over something, shaking it vigorously, and Carly headed to investigate. She tried to trot toward him, but something was wrong. She had difficulty managing her unstable walk. Unsteady on her feet, she came to him. He checked around her head and neck and saw multiple puncture wounds on the left side of her neck and chest, consistent with several snakebites. The area was swelling rapidly and bruising already. He sifted through her coat but found no more wounds. Searching farther along the ridge, he found a rattlesnake with multiple puncture wounds, dead from Jenna's teeth. He turned to return to Jenna when he heard the chilling rattle of another rattlesnake. Unable to immediately figure out the location of the rattling, instinctively, he began scanning the immediate area for the source. A lightning-like movement caught the corner of his eye, and something struck his lower right leg, just above his high-top shoe, followed at once by intense burning pain. Then, another burst of severe searing pain occurred at a higher point on the same leg. And a final "thump" on the side of his shoe confirmed Carly had found the companion to Jenna's rattlesnake. It was huge, around four or five feet long, and he looked at it slither into the brush. He stooped, pulled his pant leg above the shoe top, and saw four puncture wounds typical of snake fang puncture marks from two bites. Two punctures, almost invisible, were on the side of his shoe. Like Jenna, the tissue around the bite marks was already turning blue and swelling. Jenna had taken on one snake, but its companion had exacted its revenge on Carly. He went back to Jenna who was having more trouble walking, and as she fell, he scooped her up in his arms and headed for the house.

Jenna was drooling heavily, and her neck already showed considerable swelling. He carried her into the house, Josie met them, and they took Jenna to the utility room. Carly asked her to look after

Jenna's neck and chest wounds, but he didn't mention she had snake bites. He had to remove his shoe because his foot was already swollen to an enormous size. His instinct was to elevate his foot, but he sat, his leg lowered to rest his foot on the floor trying to slow the venom's upward spread. According to Uncle Matt, the current thinking of snakebite treatment involved cutting the fang marks and sucking out the poison, but he warned against that procedure. Carly was reluctant to commit to anything that drastic unless a doctor ordered it. He had also recommended a sizable chew of Red Man chewing tobacco, making a paste, and applying it to the bite. That wasn't happening, either.

The venom surged, clouding his senses. Dizziness had overcome him, his leg was throbbing with an agonizing pain, and he was on the verge of vomiting.

Josie washed Jenna's neck and chest wounds with soapy water and brought a basin to clean Carly's bites.

He told her, "I need to go outside for a moment."

Unsteady as he walked, once outside, he vomited everything he had eaten the past week, plus the currency token he swallowed when he was three and dropped to his knees. His head, face, and chest were wet from copious sweating. His heart was pounding, and his head pounded in sync with his heartbeat. His nausea continued. He was retching with dry heaves but had nothing left to come up, no longer a critical threat to vomit. Returning to Josie's care, he knew he must lie down. The floor was the closest horizontal surface, so he lay on it.

She washed the wound and his sweaty face and asked, "How big was it?"

"It looked well over four feet." He held his hands wide apart to show the length, which grew bigger as he thought about it and showed its size.

It puzzled Carly how Josie knew those were snake fang punctures. She was scary clever, and intuitive.

The pain remained intense, but the swelling leveled off after about seven or eight hours. His nausea continued until the next day, he had no more vomiting though it had killed his appetite. His right foot and leg looked at least three times their usual size, and extensive black and blue bruising extended from his toes to his pelvis.

He was in bed, applying tincture of time, planning to catch up with reading. Starting with Sheridan's *The School for Scandal*, a hilarious book he needed to lift his spirits, he planned to follow with Charles Dickens' *David Copperfield*, interspersed with the English romantic writers' poems. Goldsmith's *She Stoops to Conquer* was one of Mrs. Brownlie's favorite comic masterpieces and would follow the book of poetry.

Jenna was recuperating slowly from her snakebite, but she was ahead of Carly. She had neither energy nor appetite and didn't eat her dinner of leftover rabbit. Her neck was enormous, but she was drinking water.

He and Jenna were out of commission, and days turned into nights as Carly recovered from his ordeal, giving him time to think about where they were and what their plans were. The first was much simpler than the latter. He assumed they were marking time, but he wondered why. He looked at himself in the mirror, and the dim light gave him the pallor of a corpse. As he looked at his face, he concluded his physical concessions to his Mama were his blue eyes and blond hair. His only resemblance to his Papa was his Turner's nose, which sat on his face like an English curse, too large to be Roman. These observations could apply to Josie's features as well. He would avoid further interface with mirrors while recuperating, for peace of mind.

He had questions about the house and the surrounding farmland where they lived. Foremost, he didn't know why they had moved there. Second, why did the prior occupants abandon a well-built farmhouse, farmland, a good barn, and excellent water? There were no answers to this nagging mystery. The neighbors should have helpful information, but that would not happen soon because Josie said he should not answer questions and they should keep a low profile for their safety. He couldn't understand what she meant. He was afraid to discuss his memory problems with her because it would only upset her, and he didn't know how to get help. Although he was getting some information about their neighbors, he and Josie wouldn't soon reciprocate.

Josie insisted they try to enter or leave only after dark to prevent the front entrance from looking used. He was clueless as to why they were being so secretive. He and Josie had kept busy and didn't wander far off the place. The food problem was a concern for him since he had been out of commission. He had gathered greens, yams, beets, cabbage, and salt meat from night-time forays into gardens and root cellars around the area before the snakebite. Onions and an adequate supply of potatoes were available.

Jenna was healing but was still lethargic and had little interest in going out alone. But after another week, she went outside and returned with a rabbit. Carly hoisted himself off the sofa to dress it for cooking, but Josie had already done this. He gave cooking instructions to Josie, but she didn't need his input. She added potatoes and onions, and when finished, Josie feasted as if it were a meal for royalty, but the diminished appetites of Jenna and Carly meant they could manage only to sample it.

Carly began to find solace in the rhythms of the world, the beauty of spring, the chirping of birds, and the promise of a new day brought hope. The trials of winter and the perils they'd faced were now memories, reminders of the unpredictability of nature, the fragility of life, their resilience, and strengthened the bond they shared.

14

. . . .

THE SCARS ON CARLY AND JENNA had faded over the three weeks since they tangled with the rattlesnakes and lost but still inferred to the traumatic ordeal they'd endured. Their recovery had taken longer than expected, but both were sufficiently recovered to carry out their everyday activities. Jenna's boundless energy had returned, and Carly was back to near-normalcy. After they gathered eggs from the barn loft, Carly cooked breakfast, bringing a big smile to Josie's face. "You've been missed," she teased. Beneath her playful words was an undertone of concern. He had been careless, and his recklessness resulted in snakebites, but he couldn't afford to be that bold again. It was a stark reminder of the fragility of their situation.

As night descended, Carly prepared for his covert operations—garden raids that ensured they didn't go hungry. The adrenaline rush, the thrill of the unknown, was addicting. But with every trespass, the weight of guilt grew heavier on him. He spread his vegetable heist around the countryside to support diversity and inclusivity. He was asking different people to help, though they neither knew that he was asking nor that they were helping. Although he felt guilty of what he was doing, he and Josie would starve if not for the gardens of neighbors.

He picked up his tow-sack and headed to gather food for the coming days to complement their rabbit, squirrel, and chicken diet. No armadillos. He planned to visit two gardens he had never dropped into before. The scenario of sneaking and stealing created an adrenaline rush. The night was clear and adequate night visualization came from a beautiful gibbous moon bathing the earth in its silver glow. Infinite stars, space dust, and gas of the Milky Way filled the velvety sky. The first foray on his evening circuit rewarded him with peas, lettuce, green onions, turnip greens, and collard greens, gathering enough to last at least a week. He took his leave before discovery. The success of his first stop relieved him of anxiety, and, confidence brimming, he felt no fear as he headed to his second and final assignment for the evening.

A six-foot-high chicken wire fence surrounded the garden, designed to keep out deer and rabbits, and the owner had placed a gate with a chain but no lock. Carly removed the chain, making more noise that produced a pang of anxiety, but he forged ahead because the house was a fair distance from the garden, and he felt safe with no adrenaline rush coursing through his veins. After he gathered a good supply of veggies in his tow-sack, a voice echoed through the stillness, loud enough to leave little doubt that anyone in a half-mile radius would hear it.

"Who the hell's in my garden? Answer me, or Imo start shooting!"

Panic took over, and with no intention of hanging around for the introduction the man intended, Carly, the hunter-turned-hunted, grabbed his tow-sack of veggies and beat cheeks toward the gate. A gunshot blast rang out, and shotgun pellets smashed into the weeds ten feet behind him. He shifted into overdrive. The gate was thirty feet before him when a second shot exploded, and pellets blasted down weeds five feet before him. Screeching to a stop, he made a sharp right turn, away from the blasting shotgun, and headed for the chicken wire fence. He hit the wire fence, dropped to the ground, clutched the bottom of the wire, ripped it upwards, and rolled underneath it as another shot rang out. The scattershot struck where he had rolled under the fence. He was running like hell, still holding onto his sack of veggies. Not knowing the lay of the ground ahead, he knew he must trust luck. He stumbled through a hedgerow into an unexpected deep ravine, tripped, and tumbled ass over teakettle to the bottom. Still holding onto his sack of veggies, he crawled away from the shotgun with all the speed he could summon on all fours, interspersed with belly crawls.

Suddenly, the world seemed filled with threats. Carly feared crawling into a bed of rattlesnakes or copperheads, and the thought of a repeat snakebite made his flesh crawl. An innocuous rustle was suddenly another predator. But it was a rabbit scared from sleeping in his bed. Another shotgun blast brought him back at once to the present, and pellets tore into the vegetation above him. He continued a vigorous crawl into thick undergrowth surrounding a large thicket of sassafras and wild plum bushes. He slid on his belly deep inside the patch of weeds and bushes with branches and briars, grabbing and clawing at his shirt, pants, face, ears, and eyes, going as far as possible and laying still, trying to suppress his noisy, anxious breathing.

A bright light searched through the garden and thoroughly combed the ravine banks. Carly could hear the shooter's footsteps and high adrenaline-stimulated breathing not twenty feet away. He thought his panicked breathing was as loud as his pursuer's. The light splayed toward his sassafras and low bush cover, and it rested less than five feet from his head, but after lingering for an eternity—only a minute or two—the shooter turned off his light and returned to his house. Hearing the door slam shut, Carly sprang upright at once, running like an ostrich protecting its young. This time, he was running toward home, about four miles away; but he tired more quickly because of his recent rattlesnake entanglement.

After returning home, he sat to catch his breath, placed the veggies in the pantry, and contemplated the events of the evening. He had a close call, and he must change his modus operandi.

*

Searching for berries to complement their pancakes and omelets, Carly and Jenna discovered a large patch of plump huckleberries. Areas of fresh animal digs were in and around the patch, but Carly, thinking they were from squirrels, hardly noticed. In short order, he picked a half pail of berries and sat in the shade with Jenna. There hadn't been a day as perfect as this in a long time. As Jenna sniffed around the base of every tree within five hundred feet, a fox squirrel chattered his disapproval. Jenna's hackles were standing, but Carly was enjoying the huckleberries. A yellow-bellied sapsucker was riveting horizontal holes in the bark of a medium-sized sweet gum tree, letting the sap drain to capture insects. As he looked up, Carly spotted one of their heron friends flying to the west.

He was munching on huckleberries and talking with Jenna when a rustling sound in the trees up the slope behind them caught his attention. As he glanced around to see what was making the noise, a dump of emergency adrenaline flooded him, and it was now fight or flight. Less than three hundred feet away, a black bear was coming fast toward them, upset that they were feasting in his pantry. They had intruded on his digs among the huckleberries. Carly grabbed his pail of huckleberries and alerted Jenna that they must run, and they both made their way in a hurry toward a safer place. The bear was faster than they were, and it was closing fast. They ran with no specific location in mind but getting away from the bear's clutches was Carly's top priority. He was running across a small clearing toward a hedgerow that shielded a deep ravine. Not his first choice for refuge, but there was nothing else nearby. It was a race to see if they could make it ahead of the bear, huffing and puffing behind them, getting louder as they ran. Carly was sure he could feel the hot breath on his back. They reached the hedgerow and broke through, but Jenna wasn't with him. He glanced back to find her, tripped at the rim of the ravine, and tumbled head over heels to the bottom. He thought he was already dead, and total body pain suggested he was in Hell, but the darndest ferocious animal noise he could have ever imagined brought him back to Earth. With the most fearsome knock-down-drag-out growling that Carly had ever heard, Jenna sounded like she was facing off with the bear. Carly scrambled back onto his feet, clawed and crawled on all fours back to the rim of the ravine, where he found the bear cowering from Jenna, who wasn't about to give another inch. Not yet mature, the bear slowly slunk into the woods. The adrenaline-fueled excitement of Carly and Jenna had reached its apogee, and, filled with fear and excitement, they needed soothing to calm them.

Carly had read stories of bears reacting in fear and fleeing when dogs chased them. Incomprehensible as it sounded, it had happened, perhaps because the bear had not reached his fully grown status. Carly knelt beside Jenna, held her tight against his chest, and tears ran down his cheeks while she bathed him with her kisses. He buried his face in the thick coat of her neck. Something released inside him, tension, anxiety, anger, fear. Everything came out in a cyclone of sobbing. That was the only way he could express unconditional love for his best, most loyal friend.

Back on his feet, aching all over more than anywhere else, it aggravated Carly big time that he spilled their huckleberries. But he had a bumper crop of beggar lice and cockleburs clinging to his pant legs and socks, which would occupy much of his time removing them.

*

Soon, Jenna caught another rabbit, which Josie boiled. Carly found a generous supply of mushrooms at the barn and included them in the pot. Since Josie wasn't a mushroom connoisseur, she preferred her rabbit sans mushrooms. Jenna devoured her dinner. Carly wanted to complete a book he was reading, so he would eat dinner later. Jenna liked the rabbit and mushrooms.

Soon after eating her meal in the early evening, Jenna became restless, pacing and uttering a low growl with her hackles raised. Neither Carly nor Jenna noticed anything amiss when they checked the front and rear doors, and they walked around the house and found nothing suspicious. Following their baths, Josie fell asleep. Carly ate his late dinner and stayed up reading. The meal of rabbit and mushrooms was five-star. A short time later, he felt tired, dizzy, and sluggish. Sleep fell upon him as he dropped into bed with a foggy mind. During the night, quite a commotion occurred in the kitchen; Jenna was barking fiercely, and growling, rousing Carly. Still almost asleep, he headed to see what was up, and Carly stopped in his tracks! Jenna, in an uproar, was barking at two wraiths. A man with no visible facial features wore a long-sleeved yellow and black plaid shirt untucked in his baggy pants and high-top shoes, holding the hand of a teen boy dressed in pants and a long-sleeved blue shirt.

Despite not believing in ghosts, spirits, apparitions, or anything paranormal, Carly had no success convincing himself that the scene was a nightmare. Bright colors of cobalt blue, crimson, green, and yellow were abundant. Curved doors and walls created a diverse and intriguing feel to the rooms.

A crone wearing a dull-colored, bulky, ankle-length dress typical of the late nineteenth century appeared through the door to join the two men. Her entrance was through an unopened solid wood door. She raised one knee about waist high and raised her right fist. She wore high-top brogans and a bun in her hair and carried a black gum twig in her edentulous mouth, typical of many older women who used this method to dip snuff. Carly looked down, and beside him, Josie was watching this spectacle.

Jenna was beside herself. Could Carly have been delirious? Amid the chaos and out of his mental element, he didn't know how to handle it. The apparitional trio vanished through the solid wood door as he was gawking and panicking. He stood, sweating and hyperventilating, for several more minutes. Josie revived his sense of reality when she took his hand and led him back to his bed. His reaction was to lie awake for hours, trying to process what had happened. Josie probably fell asleep within a minute. The haziness in his mind made him feel like he was looking into a foggy mirror.

As dawn broke, Jenna sat at his side, but she wasn't hungry, which wasn't typical of her because she was always ready for food. Josie woke later, and Carly prepared breakfast. Josie looked puzzled when he asked if she wanted to talk about last night.

"Do you mean when you were up?" Josie asked.

"Weren't you up also?"

"Yes, to get you back to bed. I guess you were having a night-mare."

"I presume you didn't see any visitors. Was Jenna barking?"

"No visitors," she shook her head. "And Jenna was sleeping."

After this conversation, Carly was in a state of mental turmoil. Was he losing his mind?

Doubt clouded Carly's thoughts. He revisited the previous day's activities to regain his bearings, searching for anything unusual. When he arose in the morning, he made breakfast, eggs, and grits, and a glorious morning met him when he went outside. There was bright sunshine, a mild temperature and humidity, and a gentle breeze. The next task of the morning was brushing Mary in the barn. As he walked to the barn, an armadillo scurried along the path, heading into its den. That was the first live armadillo he had ever seen, having only seen roadkill before. He enjoyed brushing Mary as much as she enjoyed having it done. When finished, he returned to their house and drew water from the well. He wasn't hungry, so he skipped lunch, as was his usual practice. He then sat and read for a couple of hours. Late in the afternoon, he returned to the barn to feed Mary.

While she ate, he leaned on her feed trough, talked to her and brushed her neck and withers. He had discovered a crop of mushrooms growing in the barn stall that held the horse skeleton, and he gathered some to cook with the rabbit for his and Jenna's supper, but Josie didn't like mushrooms. Josie and Jenna ate supper. Jenna had detected something outside that upset her, but she and Carly investigated and found nothing. He finished Hemingway's *A Farewell to Arms*, bathed, read some more, ate his late dinner, and retired. He found nothing unusual for the day. Was he going nuts? Was he already crazy?

15

THE SUN PEEKED OVER the Eastern horizon, casting long shadows across the yard as Carly, feeling like a man who'd wrestled with his demons overnight, began another day. The old shop was beckoning, promising a distraction from the turmoil within. As he rummaged through its multitude of contents, an antique stoneware crock with a heavy solid wood cabbage tamper, reminiscent of bygone days of fermenting sauerkraut, caught his eye. He hefted the tamper, about three feet long and weighing ten or fifteen pounds, and its weight alone had him imagining its potential as a defensive weapon. Times had changed, and these items would never make sauerkraut again, but they would add character as kitchen decorations.

Soon after they had moved in, he noticed nestled at the back of the shop, neatly stacked lumber seemingly out of place in the chaotic space, and it continued to gnaw at his curiosity. Had they stacked the lumber to hide an object or objects? His distrustful or paranoid nature might have been working overtime, but soon, when he had regained enough energy to attack it, he would rearrange the lumber to satisfy his curiosity.

Under a separate pile of junk, Carly found a new fishnet still in its original packaging. Despite not knowing how to set it up, he would put it in the creek, hoping to lure a fish to their table. They could move it downstream, even to the river, if they catch nothing nearby.

With no prior experience, Carly waded into the creek to set the fishnet. Josie joined in, and they horsed around in the water for fun. If they caught a fish, he planned to fry it for a fresh meal but wouldn't heat the lard until he had the fish in hand.

The late afternoon sun shimmered on the water's surface as Carly and Josie checked the fishnet. Their excitement was palpable, and Josie said it was like unwrapping a gift package. He pulled the end of the net and felt a tug. As Josie squealed with delight, a good-sized young catfish was ensnared in the net's embrace and fought for release. They would eat well at suppertime.

Carly and Josie's conversation turned to a trip to the river later that week. Memories flooded back. Seeing Arthur Cunningham from school would be a treat for him. Arthur was the son of Jedidiah, the infamous moonshiner, who led Carly on a secret trip to the still deep in the woods.

They had become friends, and Carly had made forays into Arthur's world, who took him deep into the woods to see Jedidiah's liquor still. Despite its simplicity, or because of it, the moonshine still impressed Carly. When he was home, he drew every aspect of the still from memory. Carly could still draw every detail.

Josie cautioned Carly, it was too soon for social calls. They could go to the river for a fun day of swimming and fishing.

Besides rabbits and chickens, Carly felt pressure to produce food for the summer, fall, and winter.

"Why don't we plant a large garden?" Carly asked.

With enthusiasm and eagerness to learn something new, Josie concurred with his suggestion. "When do we start?"

The selected spot of ground was rich loam soil that appeared to have been cultivated years ago, which, using a pickaxe and a mattock, Carly hoped would be easier to till by hand, but it didn't mitigate the heat and humidity. The sun was scorching, the humidity was oppressive, and they were sweating. As he toiled, Carly engaged in idle conversation with Josie, asking, "Why do people say sweating like a hog? Hogs don't sweat because they don't have sweat glands. They wallow in mud to keep cool."

Josie replied, "Should I pour a bucket of water to make a mudhole for you to wallow?" Carly answered with a humorous frown.

They were pacing themselves and taking frequent water breaks.

He hadn't yet thought how to find a source of seeds and plants, but it was high on his to-do list.

In the early morning of the following day, he and Josie rode to find someone selling garden plants in the surrounding countryside. After discussing their approach, they decided to play the destitute, dirt-poor card, which was spot-on, requiring no acting talent, hoping it would win some leniency. A handwritten cardboard sign on a side road read, GARDEN PLANTS FOR SALE. After exchanging anxious glances, they slowed Mary to a walk. Josie suggested they not use their real names, and Carly agreed but thought it was a game.

"How does Callaghan sound?" he asked.

It sounded like a traditional Scots-Irish name to both. The narrow, winding dirt road was lined on each side with shallow ditches and thick growths of wild plum and sassafras bushes, and blackberry briars with many years of growth. They slowed when they saw an older gentleman in overalls, holding a hoe, and wearing a wide-brimmed straw hat, standing in front of a quaint old farmhouse. A woman with a sun bonnet rocked while shelling peas in the morning shade of the large porch that ran to three sides of the house. The unpainted, weathered house was a pleasing sight, suggesting that it had been the object of tender love and care for generations. Two friendly, rambunctious dogs greeted them, jumped around, licked them, and thumped them with their tails. The gentleman introduced himself as Ray Jackson and explained that he was born and raised in these parts. "Don't worry 'bout them dogs; they'll just beat you up with their wagging tails."

"Good morning, Sir. I'm Carly Callaghan, and this is my sister Josie. We saw your sign down the road announcing that you were selling plants. Would you consider letting Josie and me work a spell for you, and we would take plants for payment?"

"So, you starting a garden, just the two ah you?"

"Yes, sir."

"But you don't have no money?"

"Sir, we've got 38 cents," said Carly, both hands in the pockets of his tattered pants, and as he looked at the ground, he kicked the dry, dusty dirt with the toe of his worn-out shoe.

"Where d'ya live? Where yo folks?"

"Sir, we're living in an abandoned house. Mama's sick, and we don't know where Papa is. We're hoping to plant a garden for food this fall and winter. We struggled this past winter, and we don't want to go through that again," Carly answered somberly.

The old farmer was quiet and looked away, hoping they didn't see tears as they welled in his eyes, but Carly noticed.

Farmer Jackson choked a bit as he said, "I ain't gone be selling you no plants this spring, but there is plenty more in the ground. You dig all you need and, come gathering time, bring me a mess of vegetables. That's all I'll charge you. And here's a packet of mystery seeds that'll be a secret till they bear. Plant three or four seeds in hills about six feet apart."

They thanked him. The mystery seeds would bring a bounty or be a lesson in agricultural surprises. "We'll bring vegetables from our first harvest."

He patted each of them on the back.

"Stay healthy, young lady, young man. Y'all will go fer."

They pulled many tomato, lettuce, onion, and cabbage plants, and several they couldn't name. They would surprise them when they grow. This gift of plants thrilled them as if it were Christmas.

Carly was out of bed before dawn, eager to plant their garden, and Josie was up before him, cheerful and keen to learn something new. They would make use of gardening lessons that Uncle Matt had taught. Despite the clouds masking the sun, they couldn't escape the scorching heat and brutal humidity. Large dark cumulus clouds were building in the southwestern sky, promising an afternoon thunderstorm.

Carly made rows with the hoe and dug small holes for the plants, and Josie dropped the plants where he scored. They planted the packet of 'mystery seeds' in seven hills, about six feet apart, and he poured a can of water around each plant, and the seeds as Josie looked on.

"Why did you pour water around the plants?"

"To make sure it rains." He chuckled, recalling the words of Uncle Matt.

After a dinner break, they finished planting, stowed their garden tools, and went inside as a sharp lightning bolt and a loud clap of thunder came with rain. A good soaking rain fell during the thunderstorm that lasted nearly an hour.

Josie chuckled when she said, "It's good you watered all the plants."

A lightning bolt ended the thunderstorm with a deafening thunderclap, and an explosion that rattled the doors and windows, typical of a close-by earth strike. When he opened the back door, Carly saw the smoking, broken ruins of a large, wild black cherry tree split in two on the far edge of their yard. The lightning exploded the tree as if someone had placed a dynamite charge inside, and the fresh smell of the lightning strike permeated the air. The lightning bolt dug up the earth around the tree's base, where the high voltage blast followed the tree's roots into the ground.

Carly's memories transported him back to early childhood. He and Winnie had experienced a similar thunderstorm, except it was an evening storm. Mama and Papa fought in the next room, and Winnie and Carly were unaware of the proximity of the lightning strikes, and although Winnie tried to comfort him, Carly feared their parents might murder them.

A wan smile crept across his lips as he returned to the present. He and Josie were safer now. The rain had soaked the ground to give the plants a good start.

The pleasant sound of raindrops on the roof and the pleasant, earthy scent of the rain as it fell on the dry earth comforted him as he read.

As the evening settled, Carly and Josie discussed the intense need to generate income. Because of his frequent visits to the winter gardens and root cellars of rural neighbors several miles away, they survived the winter, but sometimes it was a struggle. It wasn't uncommon for his neighbors to come within a hair's breadth of catching him.

Carly had borrowed enough corn in the fall to last Mary through the following summer. He and Josie supplemented their meals with chickens and rabbits, but now, they must think beyond that. Carly never wanted to borrow food again. The term "borrow" was a euphemism for stealing.

As he sat alone, contemplating his life as a garden thief of the night, he tried to think of a source of income from the farm. He mulled over every aspect of the farm and his mind settled on the barn. Chickens were multiplying like crazy, and he and Josie could sell them.

He leaped into the middle of the room, ran to Josie's bedroom, knocked, and called.

"Josie, I need to talk with you."

Josie sounded sleepy.

"Come in."

He opened her door and entered. "What would you say to the idea of selling chickens to earn some money?"

Now wide awake, she sat upright.

"I've been thinking of that. We could process the chickens before we sell them, and we could charge more. But in reading about fowl, I came across another jewel we ought to consider, pigeons. We could sell the young pigeons, called squabs, to local fancy restaurants. They could offer squabs on their menus. We get them before they start growing feathers. I read that in many fine restaurants, the diners are connoisseurs of gourmet squabs. They're a delicacy, and I'll bet the fancy restaurant at the Hanford Hotel would buy them. And we have a hefty supply."

Carly stood in deep thought, not moving. "That's a good idea. We're getting good at roasting chicken on a spit over hot coals, and maybe we could take orders and prepare them, cooked, for a price. We should sit to pencil all the business aspects."

Their conversations had grown in sophistication. They were growing in years and intellect, and their trust and bonding were limitless as they planned together for a safe and secure future.

16

....

CARLY'S DETAILED DRAWINGS of Jedidiah Cunningham's moonshine still were in a book in his private box, with all his papers and books. He'd made the drawings following a clandestine tour by his friend Arthur. Retrieving the plans, the paper crinkled under Carly's hands as he unfolded the aged drawings. He studied them and made a list of materials needed to construct a complete liquor still. Carly knew these were desperate times, demanding desperate measures, and he knew he was on the edge of a moral chasm. He consulted Josie and asked what she thought about his idea of making and selling moonshine. With only a moment's hesitation, she looked at him and replied, "We must survive. But I want it clear—this is for survival, nothing more. We will plan to do it only short term."

As Carly delved into preparations, consulting the storage room with crowded shelves of Mason jars in pint and quart sizes. Josie's voice haunted the back of his mind. It was a gamble, dealing with the likes of Jedidiah Cunningham. Trust was a luxury they could ill afford, but choices were in short supply. "We will deal wholesale with Cunningham if we can," Carly mumbled, partly to Josie and partly to the silence enveloping their house. "Retail would attract too many eyes."

He hated the idea of the retail sale of moonshine, so he planned to talk with Jedidiah Cunningham about selling it wholesale to him.

Josie said, "It sounds okay, but what will you do if Jedidiah refuses? Would you trust Jedidiah not to report you to the sheriff if you sold retail?"

Carly said, "If he refuses to buy it wholesale, I'll have to sell it retail, even though it's a detestable idea. I don't know whether Jedidiah is trustworthy or whether he would view me as a competitor. That's a worrisome question. Am I willing to go to war with Jedidiah if he views me as a competitor? We'll stand our ground, like we always do, Josie"

Carly already knew that their financial situation would decide the answer. But he must have a predetermined endpoint for as many scenarios as possible.

The shop supplied the materials to construct the liquor still, except copper tubing. Carly needed copper tubing from the thumper keg to form a spiral coil inside the condenser. He pondered this problem for a few days until he remembered an old refrigerator in the toolshed, now used for junk storage. It was a kerosene refrigerator from the 1920s or 1930s, like those used across rural America before electricity was widely available. He recalled the bit of trivia that Albert Einstein invented and patented the kerosene refrigerator. They were popular during the depression and the dust bowl.

Tenacity drove his path as Carly plunged into disassembling the refrigerator—a relic from another era, recovering more copper tubing than he needed. Carly had several packets of yeast that Winnie had packed, hoping to make bread. They should work. He gathered the materials, loaded them on the buggy, and hitched Mary. He and Josie hauled metal, copper tubing, and Mason jars to the farthest northern point of the property, to a site alongside the creek that ran through that location, the same stream that meandered past their house.

They unloaded the equipment and assembled the still, and Josie watched, a silent sentinel, as Carly meticulously followed his precise drawings to assemble the still. Jedidiah's liquor still appeared over-simplified, and Carly found he was putting in a large amount of skill and an enormous amount of challenging labor to keep it simple. But with each bead of sweat that dropped from Carly's brow, a unity of purpose strengthened between the siblings, a quiet acknowledgement that each kernel of corn added to the concoction was another step toward safeguarding their future. At the end of the second day, they added cracked corn, water, and yeast and began the waiting period for fermentation.

✳

In the dim glow of early morning, Carly stooped to select a young rooster, its flailing stopped when his practiced hands immobilized him by crossing its wings on its back.

They were up getting ready for their Sunday meal, and Carly had de-feathered and de-haired the chicken. There weren't actual chicken hairs, but filaments left when removing the feathers. A brief open flame to the bird's skin signed the filaments. He gathered mushrooms from the barn and added them to the frying skillet, except Josie's piece, which Carly cooked separately. The chicken was excellent, brown, and crisp, and its tantalizing aroma was ambrosial. Lettuce, tomatoes, green onions, and radishes were from the garden. Josie was becoming a superb cook.

The aroma of crisping chicken wafted through their home as the chicken cooked. Carly admired Josie's ladylike mannerisms. She was growing up, outgrowing the stash of clothes they had brought. She was tall and slender with beautiful, straight blonde hair cascading like silk; her skin was perfection, and her bright blue eyes, like Carly's own, mirrored his unspoken fears and unwavering resolve. Regret ebbed at the edge of his thoughts—had he robbed her of a mother's warmth by his choices?

His remorse was always short-lived. But she needed a female in her life. Mamas were important to girls. Yet in Josie's eyes he saw no reproach but an echoing assurance.

The delicious aroma filled the house as the chicken was cooking. When the meal was served, it was a delight. Of course, Jenna received her share. The three were happy to be together, but Carly and Josie were uneasy about their new venture.

17

. . . .

CARLY FELT A HEAVY WEARINESS blanket him shortly after their evening meal. His vision blurred as a lull beckoned him into a dreamless abyss. However, Jenna's agitation cut through the fog of his drowsiness. Her low growls, her raised hackles, and her rigid body stance clearly indicated she was alarmed, making Carly uneasy. He stumbled to his feet, crawled out of bed, took her outside, and walked her around the house but found nothing. The source of her agitation remained elusive.

Slipping into unconsciousness once more, Carly was soon jolted awake by Jenna's frantic barking in the kitchen. Staggering out of bed to investigate, a vivid spectacle reminiscent of a past vision seized his attention. A sense of déjà vu was quick to overwhelm Carly. It was a beautiful scene, with beautiful colors flashing on the walls and door. A loud sound produced brilliant crimson, yellow, and cobalt blue. Ephemeral phantoms—a faceless man was holding a boy's hand about fifteen to eighteen. These apparitional wraiths were unchanged in their dress from their earlier audition, including the old crone. She came through the door again, a snuff twig in her mouth, wearing period attire, an 1890s dress.

Was this a nightmare this time? He thought two identical night terrors ought to be impossible. As before, he watched the apparitional trio disappear through the closed door. He knew Josie had seen it because she was standing beside him. They retreated hand in hand, back to the sanctuary of their bedrooms.

Come noon, Josie had been up for hours and glanced up from her book as Carly galumphed in, followed by a tired-looking Jenna.

Carly sat, afraid to broach the subject of the previous evening, so Josie opened the conversation. "What I saw was identical to the time before."

Because he knew he was loco and had lost his mind, he remained silent for a long time, at least a couple of hours. He was trying to make sense of this nonsense in his misfiring brain. In his mind, nonsensical elements finally amalgamated into a facsimile of rationality. Carly stood bolt upright!

"That's it! Loco! It's loco, as in locoweed, except we don't have locoweed here. Mushrooms preceded the two episodes, and I have read that psilocybin mushrooms have a substance called psilocybin. Psilocybin can cause hallucinations. A long history of their use in ancient religious ceremonies has resulted in weird hallucinations among worshipers, often leading to religious martyrdom and suicides. Because she shared my meals, Jenna behaved like before."

Carly began to ponder other ramifications of the mushrooms. He had read they were called magic mushrooms. Could magic mushrooms be the reason for the sudden abandonment of the farm? In that case, was more than one family involved? What is the history of the farm? Who could provide him with this information? Could they risk visiting Mr. Truman Mallory at his general mercantile store? They had been inside his store and had seen him waiting on customers. He seemed to know everyone and was friendly to everyone. But they didn't have any money and didn't buy anything, even avoided talking to Mr. Mallory. Carly thought he might have a better knowledge of the local history than anyone else.

"Josie, would you like to take a buggy ride today?"

"I would love it. Where are we going?"

"I think I would like to visit Mr. Mallory at his mercantile store. I'm sure he could tell us the history of this farm."

They grabbed their hats, went to the barn, hitched Mary and were soon on their way, hoping to learn a bit of local history. As they rode, Carly tried cudgeling the few facts they had, but there were no facts, only suppositions.

To get ideas for their questions, they rode past the store first. He saw overgrown weeds and bushes along the eastern side of the store, creating quite an eyesore. They slowed Mary to a walk and noticed tons of scrap metal lying around, making it impossible to mow the area. There were old automobile engines, at least one scrap car, old and rusted machinery, and a million unidentifiable metal pieces.

At once, Carly envisioned their future! But several pieces of the puzzle must fall into place. He asked Josie if she was interested in continuing into town, and the look on her face suggested a question, but she said, "Sure I would." Mr. Mallory's mercantile store was about six miles from where they lived, and about four miles west of Marston.

When they got to Marston, Carly stopped near a phone booth, opened the Yellow Pages and found two scrap metal dealers outside the city limits. Memorizing the names and addresses, he drove on.

The first dealer told them he was too busy to deal with street urchins.

"Go play in the sand."

Their second hopeful dealer, Jim Olson of Olson Scrap Metal, treated them with kindness and considerable interest. As Carly introduced them, he asked if Mr. Olson wanted to buy scrap metal.

"Sure do. Do you have some to sell?"

"Depends. What are the prices of metals?"

Jim Olson handed Carly an updated scrap metal price list. According to him, the market was hot, the Korean war was on, and the United States Steel Corporation had labor problems. In his head, Carly calculated the prices and swallowed hard.

As soon as they had settled all their logistical questions, Carly felt terrible that he couldn't buy Josie a cold drink, but he hadn't thought to bring their 38 cents. One of the puzzle pieces had fallen into place, but he had another thought. "Josie, would you like to visit the Hanford Hotel while we're in town?"

"Yes, I'm chewing at the bits to prepare unfledged squabs." Josie chuckled at her display of growing knowledge of squabs.

18

....

GROWING UP ON THE FARM, Carly and Josie had heard references to the Hanford Hotel but had never visited it and never thought they would have a reason to go inside it. They had heard about a snobbish restaurant but didn't know its name. Carly's fingers tensed around the reins as the behemoth Grand Hanford Hotel rose before him, a far cry from the farm life he and Josie were accustomed to. Stepping inside, the opulence struck them—more material wealth than they could have imagined surrounded them. They instinctively knew the hotel catered to a squab-devouring clientele. Beyond colossal doors, two majestic chandeliers above the open gathering area captured their attention. They walked further into the lobby, absorbed by the beauty of the vast granite floors, the likes of which they had never seen. And the immense solid wood reception desk captivated their eyes. When they walked to the counter, grand hanging stairways on either side of the lobby mesmerized Carly. It took coaxing by the person waiting to serve them to get them moving again.

A woman, her attire speaking of a world Carly had never mingled with, approached with a welcoming smile. "How may I assist you?"

Carly was still sightseeing throughout the elegant lobby, he was caught off-guard, and he hadn't planned his question, and his voice hitched. "Ah, the restaurant? So, you have one here?"

Carly watched Josie slowly lower her head, shaking it in disbelief at her brother's stammering inquiry. Help came from a kind gentleman whose demeanor dripped with kindness. "Yes indeed. Evangeline's offers a remarkable array of Acadian-Cajun Cuisine."

Carly regained his composure. "Please lead us to Evangeline's."

Carly, steadying himself, his eyes now meeting the man's. He held a meeting with the manager of Evangeline's and secured a deal for their squabs and chickens. Carly and Josie, children by social standards, had ventured into a world of adults and come out with opportunities in their palms. The two dauntless and determined kids had impressed Evangeline's manager, Hollister "Red" Adair, and he maneuvered contacts with other restaurateurs.

*

In another world, Carly and Josie entered Mallory's Mercantile, looked around, and decided to use their pseudonym, Callaghan, when they met Mr. Mallory. They embraced at the entrance to his office to bolster their courage and went inside. Mr. Mallory greeted them and asked if he could be of help.

His voice solidified from their earlier conquest, Carly said, "Good day, Mr. Mallory. My name is Carly Callaghan, and this is my sister Josie. Would you have a moment to discuss a business proposition with us?"

"Well, by golly, hello, Mr. and Miss Callaghan. Have a seat. What kind of business deal are we talking about?" Mr. Mallory scrutinized them with a friendly smile and a clear, questioning gaze.

Carly spoke of scrap metal, plant overgrowth, and an exchange that would benefit both parties. He proposed removing the large agglomeration of scrap metal, and he and Josie would remove all of the unsightly plant overgrowth, leaving it pristine. They would only ask to keep the scrap metal. "We ask you give us until Labor Day to finish the contract.

"Well, that seems reasonable, but what if you don't perform? There are some heavy pieces of metal out there, several car motors."

"If we can't fulfill our contract, you will still have the scrap metal, weeds, and bushes. It's a no-lose situation for you. We all stand to benefit if you agree to the deal."

"By golly, you propose a fine deal, and I'll give it a try."

"You won't be sorry, sir."

"Many people have been interested in that scrap metal, but by golly, you are the first to offer me something of value for the metal. All the others wanted to 'do me a favor.' Business deals should profit both parties, and I appreciate your perspective."

They shook hands to seal the deal.

Now that the deal was closed, Carly relaxed, and sounded less stilted. "Mr. Mallory, you must be familiar with everyone and everything in these parts. Could you tell us about an abandoned farm on Old Johnson Road? We've seen it as we go by and wonder what the story is?"

In the subsequent conversation about an abandoned farm, Mr. Mallory unleashed a tale that hung heavily in the room, it's tragic undertones echoing across the now dimming space.

"Interesting that you should ask. It has a cluttered history. Thirty-some-odd years ago, a man and his wife bought the farmland, 640 acres, a complete section of land. A carpenter by trade, he built the house, a fine place too, and still is, I reckon. They were successful at farming. But after three or four years, they disappeared. No one heard from them again. One day a dog came dragging up a large bone, and the medical examiner determined it was a human thigh bone, probably female. A hunt was on to find its owner, and after searching unsuccessfully for about six months, someone suggested looking around the farmhouse. Days passed, and the sheriff's deputies found two skeletons, one adult female missing a thigh bone and an adult male."

Josie and Carly glanced at each other, and Mr. Mallory continued.

"They were victims of a murder-suicide, gunshot wounds to the head. The state medical examiner showed the skeletal remains of Mr. Jackey Ellingson and Frances Ellingson, the husband-wife owners of the farm. They had no heirs, and the county took possession of the property for failure to pay back taxes."

"Is there more?" Carly asked.

"The property was going to auction, and another couple wanted to rent it for a period to see if it was worth the value of the taxes. They moved in, but after about six months, the neighbors found the couple's skeletal remains behind the house, murder-suicide victims.

Soon, another family, a man, his wife, and a young boy, if my memory serves, moved in to rent with the possibility of buying. After five or six months, they became a no-show, neighbors summoned the sheriff's deputies to the house because odors aroused suspicions, and the sheriff found bodies of the husband, wife, and child out back of the house, each shot in the head, victims of a double murder-suicide."

Carly turned to look at Josie, who appeared pale and mesmerized. He took her hand.

"Since this last incident, no one, neither the sheriff nor his deputies, not even the tax assessor, will get off the main road to go to the house. Twice they tried to sell the property at auction, but not a solitary bid. I doubt anyone has set foot in the place. The home and farm are for sale for back taxes, but I heard they stopped assessing taxes years ago because no one would buy the property. Most people around these parts say the multiple deaths have cursed the property. That, by golly, makes it a white elephant."

Carly and Josie, riveted by the horror and mystery of the tale, were oblivious to the ticking grandfather's clock behind them. "They sat spellbound as he related this unbelievable chronicle of the place they called home. When Carly heard him say, 640 acres, a complete section of land, he stopped listening and ignored the part about a cluttered history.

The old grandfather's clock chimed three times, and they realized they had stayed longer than was polite. Carly apologized for taking up so much of his valuable time and said they needed to go home to feed their animals. They shook hands. After thanking him for the scrap metal deal and the old Ellingson site's information, Carly asked him for one more piece of information.

"Does Mrs. Brownlie, a schoolteacher, live around here?"

"Of course, she lives less than a half-mile down that road just across the highway. It's a big yellow house on the left, you can't miss it."

Mary headed home without guidance, and they were much happier than they had been in months. They were finding solutions to many of their survival challenges. The heat wasn't oppressive as they traveled, and the trip was pleasant.

A sudden onset of terrible anguish, severe anxiety, and profound depression overtook Carly as they rode. A panic attack engulfed him as he remembered, for the first time in months, memories of the bloody murder of Winnie and the events surrounding that unspeakable tragedy came crashing over him like turbulent waves. He could now understand why they were running away, why they had to avoid the sheriff, why they had to remain vigilant, and why Winnie would not be returning with their seventy-eight dollars. Carly felt his world spinning out of control, and he jumped from the buggy as it continued to roll. He felt nauseous and couldn't breathe. Panicked, he ran three or four steps, stopped suddenly, leaned forward, and vomited. Having survived, although Winnie had died, Carly was overwhelmed and filled with unrelenting guilt. He sat on the side of the road. Josie was at his side.

"What's happening, Carly?"

The events surrounding Winnie's murder and that evening were returning to Carlie's memory for the first time in months. His anxiety, depression, and worry had been absent during that period. She let him talk, and he related everything he could remember.

"My most profound regret is that I didn't act on Winnie's desire to leave at least a week before Papa murdered him. I haven't thought of Winnie's murder in the past months. Sometimes I thought he was still alive and might visit us. Winnie said he believed Papa would kill him. That will forever haunt me, and I think he would be alive if I had not convinced him otherwise. I feel overwhelming guilt for having survived and he didn't. Why didn't I die instead of Winnie? He was a good person, more deserving to live than I."

Was he suffering from amnesia in the past months and now his memory was returning? Carly wondered if a specific form of amnesia occurs after severe psychological trauma. It seemed to him that only portions of his memory were affected, those dealing with Winnie's murder and the events of that evening.

Regaining his lost memories would involve passing an unknown quantum of time, and he didn't know if he could ever recover completely. He would need to learn more about the subject because he knew nothing about its diagnosis or prognosis.

Josie looked at him with sadness but understanding what he said because she was experiencing the same emotions. Carly now saw she kept her feelings to herself better than him. He realized both were suffering, but he was complaining the loudest.

"Josie, I'm so sorry. My self-centered behavior became obvious when I realized you missed Winnie as much as I did."

She leaned toward him, and they hugged for long minutes, a long reverence for Winnie and a quiet period while each tried to unravel their confused, twisted emotions and minds, trying to grasp rationality from thin air.

Josie, ever the silent sufferer, became his anchor, as they grappled with their intertwined past and uncertain future.

"Forgive me, Josie." Carly's voice broke through his shuddering sobs. Josie's arms wrapped around him. A comforting cocoon amidst their storms.

"Carly, there is nothing to forgive. Both of us are suffering, but I guess I'm different from you. I try not to show it, but I can't sleep; I'm having nightmares. Sometimes I'm so scared that I have to sit and pray until I can lie in bed and sleep again. Because you and Winnie were so close, your pain is much more than mine. I think if we could share our feelings, it might be better. I'll share mine with you, and we can discuss our feelings. It would make me feel better."

Carly was ashamed that his little sister had more insight into their grieving process than he did, and she had to inform him before he realized she was so deeply saddened. Looking into her sad, sorrowful eyes again, he was feeling her tremendous pain, and he gave her another hug and kissed her cheek.

There was a brief period of silence, followed by an extended conversation. The two understood each other much better.

Carly smiled. "I'll try not to whine as much."

Josie laughed. "I'll believe it when I see it."

"Ouch."

*

Back in the safety of their home, amidst the duties that grounded them, Carly and Josie found respite, a moment of peace amidst the complexities of their circumstances. Carly used a currycomb from the tool shed to comb Mary down while she grazed in the corral yard. He went inside, and dinner filled the air with an aromatic distraction. Josie was eager to talk, and they reflected on the day's happenings.

"What do you think about our day before your epiphany?" asked Josie.

"Everything went much better than I expected when we started this morning. It would be hard to get a better deal than we got with Evangeline's. We will now negotiate good deals when we meet with the two restaurants for spit-cooked chicken tomorrow. The word will get around, and we might get enough orders from individuals not associated with restaurants to keep us busy. I think Mr. Mallory's Mercantile could be a customer."

"What about the scrap metal deal with Mr. Mallory?" Josie already knew his answer, but it would feel good to hear it.

"It's a really good deal with Mr. Mallory. We're diving into a sea of toil with squabs, chickens, and scrap metal, but we can do it. Not only will we immerse ourselves into more work than we have ever known, but we'll evolve with it and carve out a living from the squabs and chickens. We may stash away the metal profits. We know how to pinch pennies."

"But what about the information about this farm?" Josie was saving what she thought best for last.

"The data Mr. Mallory gave us about the history of this house and land is more important than our scrap metal deal, chickens, and squabs. The magic mushrooms' were unknown to the people who lived here. Over a long period, the mushrooms must have made them desperate and frightened beyond their tolerance, resulting in murder-suicides. Without a way to discover what was happening to them, the mushrooms could drive people to such tragic acts. I wasn't to that point, but I can see how it could happen.

"Besides finding out everything about this house and the land, we should also find the total bill for the back taxes. When we have that information, we can make plans. Everything went well, but the return of my memory didn't serve to cap the events except in an unforgettable way. What do you think? Anything you disagree with?"

Josie's young yet expanding intellect was something Carly had learned to value, despite them being runaways with their respective fears and anxieties. She had taught him to trust her judgment, and he couldn't imagine anything separating them, but he and Josie were runaways. However, Carly still expected a car to drive up any day with Papa or a sheriff's deputy, which would mean separation because he could never go home. Because Carly feared what might happen to Josie, as well as what might happen to himself, it was a constant source of anxiety and worry. But their mutual trust was often a buffer against Carly's near-tangible nagging fear of being discovered by authority or family, especially when a vehicle lingered a moment too long on Old Jackson Road, making his heart race.

Josie agreed with all his points. "The deals, the contacts...they'll help us, Carly." Carly glanced at her, finding strength in her youthful yet mature eyes. "Yes, they will. And we'll navigate the other things too, Josie—together." If a vehicle slowed on Old Jackson Road, it would make Carly's heart race. Carly was ready to run if someone showed them too much attention at Mallory's Mercantile or in town.

Carly suggested they stay alert and speak up if there were suspicions of an untoward situation. His willingness to ask her for advice pleased her, and she said she was glad he recognized she was growing up.

Carly continued to think aloud.

"When we feel safe enough, we must consider going back to school. That's on my mind daily, but we aren't there yet. Someday,

I'll get enough courage to visit Mrs. Brownlie. Besides saying hello, I need to return some books. It would be nice to share our secret with her. If someone were aware of our plight, it might reduce our worries, but I don't know whether we can trust her. What do you think?"

"I think you should follow your heart, but first work on gaining courage, then actions will follow."

Besides planning their trip to the courthouse, they needed to decide when they would begin working at Mallory's Mercantile, hauling away the scrap metal.

Carly informed Josie that he had to make an unfortunate announcement. Josie was alert and concerned.

"About what?"

"I regret to tell you of the death and burial of my plans to become a renowned moonshiner."

"Oh, that's so sad." An impressive joy flashed through Josie's eyes.

"But I will continue my ways as a night burglar of cribs, gardens, and root cellars."

"How could we fail?" She laughed.

He suggested they disassemble the liquor still at the back forty of their property. They hitched Mary and headed over at a lazy pace. As they drew closer to the site, a cacophony of hammering, crashing, and furious noises were heard over several male voices in the liquor still's area. They stopped Mary a safe distance from the still, exited the buggy and crept closer, staying behind concealing bushes. The strong malodor of whiskey hung in the air. They held their breath, their heartbeats syncing in silent fear.

They first saw Sheriff Luke Dunham's Jeep parked on an unimproved path beyond the liquor still, past their property line. The sheriff was sitting on a tree stump with his back to them, fanning himself with his brown Stetson hat. He weighed 250 to 275 pounds, and his butt was hanging over the sides of the tree stump. Temperatures in the high 90s and the oppressive humidity had him sweating, with large wet sweat patterns under both armpits, on the back of his shirt, and below his belt line. In front of him, his deputies were destroying Carly and Josie's liquor still and smashing their Mason jars into millions of pieces. Sheriff Dunham glanced around as more rivulets of sweat poured from his face and ran down his neck, almost as if he knew someone was watching him. He saw Carly and Josie and called them over, motioning with his hand,

"Hey, y'all, come over, heah. What chall doing heah?"

Frozen as if in a photograph, they fought the urge to run like hell. With golf ball-sized eyes, they were trying on the cherubic faces of innocence, and a squeaky voice escaped Carly's lips as he said, "We're just walking, sir, enjoying nature since school is out."

They kept their bug-eyed look and held their jaws at half-mast, thinking they looked innocent, disregarding the fact that they probably looked stupid. Josie spoke, "Gollleee," drawing it out to multiple syllables, as only Southerners can, but Carly had a tough time hiding his jitteriness. In response to the situation, his memory recalled Uncle Matt's words, "You know you're in trouble if only dogs can hear you fart." Making moonshine was punishable by a year and a day in prison, and selling it stacked on more time behind bars. A year and a day ran through Carly's mind as he thought, Oh hell!

"Sir, what is that thing they're busting up?" Carly asked timidly words while his heart was racing madly.

When Sheriff Dunham looked at them, he saw two innocent children. Concealing their knowledge and public appearance of innocence, a contrast of emotions alien to them, and tension was palpable.

"Kids, this here is a moonshine still for making whiskey, or moonshine, it's called. And the moonshiners use those fruit jars to peddle the moonshine to the buyers. A group of evil, non-Christian crooks come in here, prolly under cover of the dark of night, and built this sinful thing here. We come in here using the same trail. The moonshine was ready to run off today, and somebody reported it, and we was lucky we found it when we did. Otherwise, this whiskey would've been in the community by tomorrow. But I'll say one thing, whoever built this whiskey still knowed what he was a doing, cause I've never seen one built so good as this one. But he's still out there, prolly gone build anothern, and that scares me. If you kids heah anything 'bout this, call me now, you heah?"

The sheriff gave them a business card. With pride, Carly silently accepted the compliment on his extraordinary ability to construct liquor stills and took it to heart.

"Of course. Oh yes. I can't believe even non-Christians would be so evil as to build this thing and do this. This thing is so illegal. If we hear anything, we'll call you at once."

Josie nodded in complete agreement, and they turned to leave.

"You kids enjoy yore nature hike now, ya heah?"

"Thank you, sir," and Carly led the way, looking like they were out for a stroll. However, they wanted to run screaming back to the buggy because relief was tangible. After climbing aboard, they snuck back home, unhitched Mary, went inside, took deep breaths, stayed silent for a short time, and then cackled with laughter, relieved to have escaped the moonshine business before it crashed.

*

They got up early, hitched Mary, and headed into town. They entered the courthouse to find the office responsible for tax foreclosure properties. As they walked down the marble-floored main hallway, Carly assumed the tax assessor would be the correct office. They had smelled a strong urine odor when they were at least a couple of blocks away, and it was much more robust inside the building.

A large map of properties, including those on Old Johnson Road, hung on the wall of the tax assessor's office. The name Ellingson was still on their property. Five large filing cabinets stored all the information about properties in the county. According to the property description in the tax foreclosure file, the sale for back taxes was $862.00! That information was nothing short of astonishing. Carly copied the data. Was there a mistake? A woman with a friendly smile who looked in her 60s got up from behind her desk to help them. The name on her tag read Betty Arnett, Tax Assessor's Office. "May I help you?" she asked with a genuine, ready smile.

"Yes, ma'am." Carly went to the question. "If the tax foreclosure file states a sum of the sale, is that the amount to be paid to own the property?"

"That's correct. Is there a property you are questioning?"

"One more question. Do we have to be twenty-one to buy property?"

"Not at present."

"What about this property?"

She looked at the paper that held the complete description of the property. Betty Arnett gave a brief chuckle and pulled the file from a close-by cabinet.

"Do you know the history of that farm?"

"Yes, ma'am."

"Doesn't it bother you?"

"No, ma'am. But I want to get this straight. If we pay $862, will we own the property?"

She checked the cover page of the file. "That's right."

As soon as they left the courthouse, they were walking on air, the happiest two people on earth. Since they were not in a hurry to get home, Mary walked, so they could enjoy the peace of the countryside.

Carly said nothing to Josie, but a distant, unknown observer lingered in his car about a hundred yards behind them, not trying to catch up or pass. It stayed well behind them until they reached their driveway, and as they pulled up to their house, it drove past their driveway, continuing down Old Johnson Road. The driver inspected them and their property, but he was too far away for them to identify.

19

1954
. . . .

A MAJESTIC CURTAIN ON THE eastern horizon slowly lifted, allowing the sun to cast a glowing, radiant sheen of awakening hues—bold reds and tranquil blues—to paint the beautiful cirrus clouds and the heavens of immeasurably deep blue. When punctual Mr. Mallory arrived, Josie and Carly were already outside the mercantile store loading scrap metal onto their buggy, having arrived early before dawn; he smiled, waved, and yelled good morning. Josie waved back to him while Carly, squinting from the sun, offered a nod. In the shade of a sprawling live oak beside the store, Mary grazed hay grass like she hadn't eaten for days. An old, weathered fence post with a short strand of barbed wire, attached to nothing and hanging by a loose staple, stood away from the store, and a brown thrasher sat atop it, singing its heart out with beautiful anthems to springtime. Carly enjoyed listening to the brown thrashers and mockingbirds, but in his opinion, the brown thrasher performed a more extensive repertoire of spring melodies.

Amid the heat that already greeted the day, the discordant whining from insects was initially distracting, but Carly and Josie were soon busy, and the sounds were not intrusive. Carly was pacing himself, trying to keep the punishing heat and humidity manageable. The sun had become less impeded by the thinning clouds, and it honored eagerness with sunburn and the threat of sunstroke. Bothersome gnats and sweat bees swarmed around his sweaty face and neck. He loaded smaller pieces of metal first, soon had a full load, and they headed to the scrap metal yard with their first haul. Because the cargo was heavy, he let Mary choose her speed because the added weight made her less spirited than usual.

They got closer to town, Carly noted the car that had followed them to their house days earlier was following them again, hanging back, not trying to catch up or pass. It followed them to the scrap metal yard and drove past, but the driver looked away as it passed, and, again they couldn't identify the lone driver.

In the scrap metal yard, labyrinthine paths wove amongst vast piles of wrecked automobiles and untold pieces of metal, they went to the scales. The weight master stamped their weight ticket, and the yard workers unloaded the metal. The scrapyard agreement was plain. Carly got a weight ticket with each load of metal, and he presented their weight tickets each Friday morning, and their check was ready by the afternoon.

An unexpected fortune awaited them. Their first check was ready when they made their last delivery in the afternoon. The total was astounding, and they stood in disbelief. They had never had so much money. All but dancing in the street, Carly almost shouted when he said, "Josie, we can buy Fort Knox!"

They walked to the bank to open an account. However, the tangible taste of newfound prosperity soured in the ornate halls of The First National Bank. The bank staff treated them like criminals. As they passed the checks from one to another, the tellers sneered, frowned, and made snide remarks over their eyeglasses. They wanted to leave, and Carly asked the woman to return their check, but she refused, saying she had to investigate.

"There's something fishy going on here. This check is too large for two kids," the leviathan woman remarked.

Josie reached over and snatched the check from her hand. Charging from behind her cage, the enormous woman grabbed Josie by both shoulders, slammed her into a chair, and grabbed back their check, looking angry enough to slap her. But Josie's vibrant spirit, temporarily dulled by the sting of injustice, but ignited in defensive fury, with all her might and a hard shoe, walloped the woman's right shin with a well-aimed hard kick, giving a loud smack. Screeching, the woman fell to the floor, screaming, rolling, and caterwauling, holding her right shin as if it were leaving her body.

Her shrill screams were discomforting, for sure, and the other women were panicking, screaming for the toad woman to return the check. Still, she refused their check, although the other women continued to scream for her to do so.

"I'm calling the police to get our check back and to have this beast arrested for hurting my little sister!" Carly said, almost yelling.

A man with an in-charge bearing approached the fray. "What's going on?" he asked. His authoritative voice cut through the chaos, forcing a semblance of order upon the turbulent scene. Carly explained in photographic detail how he and Josie came to the bank to open two accounts, checking and savings, with their hard-earned money, but that woman had robbed them and hurt his little sister, and Josie was only trying to protect herself. Three ladies in the office had calmed enough to answer and agreed with his description. The bank officer plucked their check from the big woman's hand and returned it to them, along with apologies.

Josie insisted on an apology from the leviathan toad-woman. Helping herself off the floor was quite another show. No one offered to help, and she limped over and offered a meager apology. While laughter tickled his chest at the chaotic scene unraveling before him, Carly's protective instincts cast a shadow of bitter anger across his face, but he thought it would be worth paying admission to watch this sideshow event.

"Go to hell," Carly said on their way out.

As they walked away, their check in hand, they heard the bank officer speak, "Marge, this is the final straw. You have been warned over and over. I'm firing you!" He continued, "Clean out your desk. I want you out of here in ten minutes. Lois, help her, then escort her off the premises."

They walked about two blocks uptown looking for another bank, and they arrived at another one. At Jackson State Bank, they found solace in the sincere smiles and courteous service offered. When they entered, a smiling lady near the entrance asked if she could help them, and they were treated like valued clients. After opening two accounts, checking and savings, they made their deposit and kept ten dollars cash.

As they strolled, window shopping, they peeked into a drugstore window with a soda fountain sign, Baker's Pharmacy and Soda Fountain. Curious, but not having the faintest idea what lay before them, they went inside.

The soda guy was too cheerful when he said with a wide open mouth smile, "Hi, my name's James Henry. What can I get you today?"

Since their knowledge was nil, they sought his advice. Each ordered a milkshake for the first time ever, Carly ordered vanilla, and Josie ordered chocolate. They found brief respite in the enormous, delicious milkshakes. Josie was in heaven.

As they relaxed, quiet in their private thoughts, Josie started a conversation.

"Carly, have you noticed how much you have grown since we left home? I'll bet you've grown at least a foot or more. You can hear corn and bamboo growing because they grow so fast, but if we listened, we could hear you growing."

They laughed at her humorous analogy, but she spoke the truth. Carly's clothes had become too small within months of landing at their home. He was now wearing Winnie's clothes, which were too small for his growing frame. He would need new clothes by Labor Day.

As they continued walking, they looked in store windows until they came across La Belle's, which sold clothes for young ladies. They admired the gorgeous dresses and shoes, but it was after five o'clock, and the store had closed. Josie turned and looked at Carly, raising both eyebrows.

"We'll come back tomorrow when they open and buy some clothes for you." Her enthusiastic smile melted his heart.

Josie was excited, up early, having slept lightly. La Belle's would open at 9 AM, so they had time to kill. Carly intended to take a load of scrap metal when they went into town. He cooked eggs and grits, and they sat, ate, and talked.

After delivering the metal, getting their weight ticket, and parking Mary, they went to the clothing store for another novel experience. Neither had ever been in a clothing store, nor had they been shopping. A pleasant lady whose name tag read Mrs. Ruby Thaxton, Sales Consultant, sensed they were insecure in a strange, new situation. Carly introduced them and addressed Mrs. Thaxton by her name. She greeted them with a bright smile, but before offering to help, she complimented Josie on her beautiful hair and smile. And she told Carly he was a handsome young man, and since she made them feel comfortable at once and offered advice, Carly thought she must have children, and he felt it had been redundant for Josie to tell her they had never shopped. She beckoned them to follow, "Come with me."

She led them to the young lady's clothing section, Josie beside her, and as they strolled through a maze of vibrant, youthful garments, they eased into a friendly conversation. Carly and Josie felt happily normal for a moment amid bright colors and soft fabrics. It was a quiet, understated moment. With a lovely blue dress swirling about her, Josie emerged from the dressing room like a fledgling butterfly, her wings yet to realize the boundlessness of the sky.

Mrs. Thaxton, with gentle hands and a mother's knowledge, assisted her in choosing those often overlooked items—practical undergarments, versatile shoes, and socks. She told Josie, "No fold-over tops this year; that was last year."

An ensemble was born, complete with delicate ribbons, a petite, elegant purse, and a nice comb and brush set. Josie seemed to flutter, not walk, her spirit lifting with each light step, her soul singing a melody of ephemeral happiness as they exited the store.

As they walked, their steps were unhurried, seemingly unburdened. They edged toward Baker's, the drugstore with the soda fountain. James Henry, the ever-eager soda jerk with a disarming innocence about him, was at their table. "What can I get you?"

They looked at each other, and shrugged, then Josie, whimsically, said, "We're thirsty."

"How 'bout root beer floats?"

The giant floats were delicious, but they couldn't finish them. They shuffled out, and Carly patted Mary to let her know they appreciated her patience; she thanked them with a whicker. They were in no hurry, so Mary took a slow walk. It had been a good day, and they sang as they rode home. But there was the perpetual, not-so-subtle, lurking shadow from the past. The shadow of anxiety and worry that ever clung to their periphery, a silent adversary shrouded in memories of violence, fear, and blood.

Ghosts of Carly's recollections—sounds of violence and sights of gore—clawed at him, a perpetual struggle against the macabre that whispered insanity in his ears. Panic lanced through him in moments when those grotesque images were too visceral, too real. Josie, a mirror to his torment, found solace in the echoes of prayerful meditation.

There were periods of worry and anxiety, sometimes concurrent and sometimes interspersed with an intense hatred for his parents, Mama for sure, and Papa for damned sure. Neither he nor Josie could find resources in or about Marston to help them deal with these issues. They didn't discuss their psychological problems with anyone because they didn't trust anybody with that information.

✳

He and Josie gathered vegetables and tomatoes, filling a large basket, and visited their old farmer friend, Ray Jackson, who gave them their garden plants and mystery seeds. Carly considered that trip a necessary fulfillment of their agreement. They met Mr. Jackson as they entered the welcoming atmosphere of his farm.

"You're the Callaghan's."

Mr. Jackson was delighted with their visit and hoped they would return for more plants next spring. "Thank you for the vegetables. Be shore you come back in the spring fer more plants."

They thanked him for trusting them and agreed to return in the spring.

At the store, Carly told Josie they should take a brief break to cool off. They went inside and bought two cold drinks. Josie had an Orange Crush, a delicious, orange-flavored soda, and Carly had a Grapico, a smaller drink than Josie's, but he liked the sweet grape flavor.

The radio was playing in the background, and Mr. Mallory was paying close attention to the news. A significant development had occurred in Phenix City, a town in southeastern Alabama across the Chattahoochee River from Columbus, Georgia. Someone had murdered Albert Patterson who was elected State Attorney General in the last election, but not yet sworn into office. Phenix City, known for its open gambling casinos, was his hometown, and, while campaigning, he had promised to clean it up. According to the Alabama State Police, the Phenix City Police Department and Russell County Sheriff's Department were corrupt and complicit in the murder of Mr. Patterson. As a result, Governor Gordon Persons declared martial law in Phenix City and Russell County, and the police and the sheriff no longer had any authority.

The news was disturbing for both, and Carly looked at Josie. "Are you interested in seeing a picture show tonight?"

She was ecstatic. "Wow! We've never been to a picture show. I've thought about it, but I knew we had no money. That'll be the best treat ever!"

They went into town and found the theater. A spoiler for their outing came when they passed a separate, unpainted door about a quarter-block away from the main entrance to the theater. A small sign showed it was an entrance to the theater, but a large sign, COLORED, was displayed above the door and offered the only access for Blacks. They trudged into the Ritz theater through the Black entrance and watched a western picture show, "Stagecoach," starring John Wayne and Claire Trevor. It was about a group of strangers traveling through hostile and uncivilized Apache Indian country on a stagecoach. The scenery was spectacular, but neither had the experience to assess the acting. One scene near the end was downright heart-stopping! John Wayne dispatched three lawless thugs with his trusty Winchester rifle while throwing himself to the ground! The momentousness of the bigger-than-life actors captured their imaginations from the beginning and kept them glued to the screen until the end.

They talked about that experience for days, and Josie and Carly knew they would remember that outing as one of their happiest and most memorable experiences. But the sign—COLORED—hung there, a stark reminder of the reality marred by division and prejudice, tethering their joy to the harsh strings of reality.

It was dark as they walked from the theater, a half-moon abetting the copious light of millions of stars. Carly could see car lights following their buggy on their way home, again, not trying to catch up or pass. It followed them to the Mercantile Store and continued straight when they turned onto Old Johnson Road to head home. Carly wasn't worried yet, just curious about who was so interested in them. He wasn't concerned that it might be Papa because he would show no restraint. He would pounce for the kill at once. But it was a reminder that even in moments bathed in starlight, dangers could hide in the shadows, unseen yet ever present.

*

In the following days, Carly and Josie found rhythm and routine, navigating their burgeoning poultry and squab business. As they worked, they polished their routines because their customers were clamoring for more, and they were getting busier.

They needed refrigeration, but commercial refrigeration was too expensive for them to consider. Carly employed the idea of an ice box used at the Live Oaks Farm before refrigeration was available, especially before and during the Civil War when the barges delivered ice to the Live Oaks Landing. He designed and constructed an ice box, a large rectangular box about 5 feet long, 5 feet deep, and 4 feet high. It was double-walled, with an eight-inch space on all sides and bottom and a single lid with an eight-inch double-walled thickness. He lined its interior with sheet metal, sealed it watertight, and filled the empty spaces with sawdust, long known for its insulating qualities. Weather strips on the underside of the lid ensured the interior would be airtight.

Carly bought two 50-pound blocks of ice at the ice plant in Marston and placed them in the icebox. He built a smaller, portable ice box to fit on the buggy for delivering the products to their customers.

Their newfound resilience was growing stronger, and their trust and dependence was as boundless as their love for each other. They were silently continuing to strengthen their infrangible bond.

20

CARLY'S HANDS WERE STREAKED with grime and calluses, and the stench of metallic sweat clung to his sun-beaten hands. Each day blended with the next, their sameness interrupted only by the increasingly oppressive sun heralding the morphing of spring into summer. Scrap metal, an important element of his and Josie's everyday labor, had become a shared crucible that strengthened their partnership under Mr. Mallory's omnipresent gaze. On a particularly overcast day, Mr. Mallory ventured outside where they toiled, his presence more business than social. He bore news of an impending weather crisis.

"I've some information on an impending weather challenge for you. Since you don't have a radio, you're probably unaware of the weather reports. A massive tropical depression had sprouted off the Cabo Verde islands, near the African coast, north of the equator. It had evolved into a tropical storm; now, it's a full-blown hurricane. The meteorologists can't pin down its path just yet, but it's headed westward, full of fury. It may seek a path northwesterly into the Atlantic, but I'd recommend that you take precautions if it veers toward the Caribbean Sea. We won't know its landfall point until it draws closer, but I'd advise you to start preparations now and hope they prove unnecessary."

Carly responded, "We appreciate the heads-up. We'll come in after you close up shop."

Mr. Mallory smiled and returned indoors, leaving a wake of apprehension lingering in Josie and Carly. Their eyes locked, both registering equal parts fear and determination. Carly, always resolute, swallowed hard. "We'll come up with a plan, Josie," he whispered, trying to muster more confidence into those words than he felt about their hurricane preparations. Carly admitted his lack of knowledge but hoped that Mr. Mallory would offer guidance.

Carly and Josie continued to hall their scrap metal until the yard closied. Mallory's Mercantile remained open, but its customer traffic was sparse. They headed inside, passing the time reading the local *Marston Herald* and *The Mobile Press-Register. The Marston Herald* boasted its weekly front-page spectacle, a picture of a snake slayer holding his giant prey, while local sports dominated the news. Meanwhile, the Mobile paper offered a balanced mix of local, state, and national happenings. There was a mention of The Caribbean story, but less detail than Mr. Mallory's cursory warning.

They entered his office once Mr. Mallory switched the sign to CLOSED and dimmed the lights. After the pleasantries waned, they delved into the grim prospects before them. Mr. Mallory shared a Red Cross booklet detailing hurricane preparedness, covering everything from the off-season to post-hurricane actions. He emphasized the need to board up windows and amass a two-week food supply. Carly absorbed the information intently, realizing the enormity of the task ahead. His hours would stretch from the crack of dawn to post twilight as he and Josie raced against a Labor Day deadline for their scrap metal contract and fulfilled chicken and squab orders.

"May I borrow this booklet?" Carly asked Mr. Mallory.

"Of course, that copy is yours. I've got a drawer full of them for friends and customers," Mr. Mallory said. "But let's hope this storm turns out to be much ado about nothing."

Carly, mindful of the danger, thought about how they might barricade themselves against a fierce storm. When Josie's fingers brushed over the hurricane preparedness booklet, her eyes flickered with a flash of resolve, "We'll get through this, Carly."

Josie and Carly sat at their breakfast table, crafting a tentative schedule to complete their preparedness project, meet their scrap metal deadline, and process chicken orders. They decided to shop for their food and supplies at Mallory's Mercantile between trips to the scrap metal yard. Together, they measured each window's dimensions and calculated the required plywood sheets—seven sheets with precise cutting.

The moment had arrived to transport the car engines, an endeavor demanding more strength than they could muster. Carly finally found a solution, uncovering a block and tackle in the shop, still nestled in its original crate, unused since Uncle Matt's days. He rigged it up with a chain for added strength, ensuring it could handle the car engines. It promised a 6:1 lifting advantage, anchored to a sturdy live oak tree outside the store. Carly expertly hoisted the first engine, lowered it onto the buggy with Josie guiding Mary, and repeated the process for the second.

Their second engine transport, however, took a precarious turn when the resonant rev of a pickup truck and its belligerent driver harassed them, leaving both their hearts pounding in their chests. He forced them off the road. A confrontation with the intoxicated driver ensued. Carly, always the protector, amidst the chaos, his thoughts were tethered to Josie, ensuring her safety and comfort. Carly led with a swift knee strike to the man's crotch, leaving the man writhing on the road, clutching his crotch, moaning and talking in a falsetto southern drawl. Carly pocketed the man's keys and wallet before continuing to the scrap yard, avoiding further incidents.

The car that had followed them previously, again tailed them to the police station, but the driver quickly departed upon their arrival. They reported the road encounter with the driver of the pick-up truck and handed over his keys and wallet to the amused Police Sergeant, feeling a sense of relief. After completing one more engine haul that day, they finally gave Mary a well-deserved break.

After their lunch break, they bought plywood from Mallory's Mercantile and measured and cut the pieces for their window covers. With their calculations spot on, no material went to waste. There was determination in their movements, but also an underlying tremor of fear, hidden beneath the stoic veneer of rural grit. For them, this was another great unknown.

Over the next two days, they transported more engines to the scrap yard. On the third day, they tackled the final three, saving the challenging engine from the old car carcass for last. Carly hoisted it, but the unwieldy attachments made it precarious. As it swung and rotated out of control, Carly jumped onto the buggy to steady it, but a slipped chain caused it to crash onto the buggy floor. Carly's leg was caught beneath it, and, at once, he knew it was broken. Josie swiftly came to his aid, her empathetic countenance teetering between panic and pain, and she could have been easily mistaken for the injured victim. She spoke softly to Carly, gently touching his face and pushing his hair away. Tears ran down her cheeks. Together, they managed to free his leg. Carly fashioned a makeshift splint from a piece of wood and, gritting his teeth with excruciating pain, used a rope to secure the splint, before instructing Josie to first deliver the engine to the yard and then take him to the hospital.

Dr. John Whitney, a general surgeon, offered his services at the hospital. X-rays revealed fractures of both bones in Carly's lower leg, and Dr. Whitney recommended a closed reduction, meaning he would not do surgery, but he would set the broken bones in their anatomic position. "It will hurt like hell briefly, but I can control the pain, or I can administer general anesthesia."

Carly opted for pain with medication over anesthesia, a choice he would quickly question as an error in judgement because he endured excruciating pain during the procedure, uncontrolled with medication. Once stable, he was discharged with a cast from his mid-thigh to his toes, and Josie drove them to get crutches and pain medication.

Carly's mobility was limited, but he was determined not to let it slow him down. He embarked on hurricane preparations, securing their property and gathering supplies. Josie helped him tirelessly, a true partner in their endeavors.

Carly's research at the library revealed the devastating impact of the 1926 Miami Hurricane, especially the flooding. He began to see their nearby creek in a new, potentially dangerous light. With this new information, they were more determined than ever to prepare for the approaching storm.

With a few days of rest, Carly had learned to walk with his leg cast and crutches but was growing restless. After supper, lights from a vehicle appeared in their driveway, sending their hearts into hyper speed. They were at once in defensive mode, fearing it was Papa or the sheriff. The vehicle parked near their front porch, and they heard a man's heavy footsteps on the gravel driveway. They breathed hard but remained quiet. They listened to the sounds of the footsteps as he ascended their front steps, walked with determination across their porch and knocked on their door.

Still fearful, Carly hesitantly called out, "Who's there?"

A man's voice answered, "Carly, It's Truman Mallory. I need to speak with you two."

Carly sighed with relief and quickly answered the door and invited him in. Before he sat, Mr. Mallory said, "I have a little gift for you, but I'll need your help to bring it inside. I realize you don't have electricity, but you will enjoy this, and it can be quite useful."

Josie joined them, and the three went to the car to retrieve their gift. When Mr. Mallory opened the car trunk, Carly and Josie were astounded to see a gorgeous radio sitting alongside a new battery still in its packaging.

Mr. Mallory said, "This is a high-end radio I used before electricity came to these parts. It comes with a new battery, the ground post and ground wire, the antenna, and the connecting cables." He walked Carly through the steps necessary to bring the radio to life and assured Carly he would have no problems hooking it up.

"You will find this valuable in the next few days, receiving weather reports as the hurricane wanders the open seas."

Carly and Josie were almost speechless. Carly shook his hand and gave him their sincere thanks. Josie stood before him and said, "Thank you, Mr. Mallory, from the bottom of my heart." Mr. Mallory offered his hand, but Josie asked, "Would you mind if I were to hug you?"

Mr. Mallory bent forward and, while she hugged him, he wrapped his arms around the little girl. He gave them a tip for an excellent station at 89.7 on the FM dial. "It's the station on the City University campus in Marston. You will enjoy the sophistication of their programs and the classical music."

Carly started installing their new radio as quickly as a gimp leg, a long leg cast, and crutches would allow. But Josie was his secret weapon. She held the light, fetched everything he needed, and waited for beautiful music. After about half an hour, clear, beautiful music filled their living room. The FM station 89.7 played a beautiful piece by Brahms, *Wiegenlied,* better known as *Lullaby* or *Cradle Song.*

There was a radio program that discussed politics and current events in depth. It appeared the panels were omnifarious. The debate focused on the Jim Crow laws, their unconstitutional abandonment of the Fourteenth Amendment, and how they victimized and dehumanized a large population segment. A heated discussion ensued between a young Baptist minister from Morehouse College in Atlanta, now studying for his Ph.D. at Boston University, Martin Luther King Jr, and an uneducated firebrand snapping turtle, Imperial Grand Wizard Terry Baker of the Ku Klux Klan. King's mind was sharp with his unemotional, thoughtful responses, and Baker, not so much!

When the news came on the radio, there was an update on the hurricane's progress. It was moving westward past the Lesser Antilles in the Caribbean Sea. Instead of heading north into the Atlantic, it was heading toward the Greater Antilles, south of Puerto Rico.

Despite Carly's encumbered mobility, hindered by a sturdy, long leg cast and the persistent companionship of crutches, they pressed on, determined to complete their scrap metal job. Demolishing the old car carcass into manageable pieces proved a formidable challenge but reducing it to a moderately large pile of metal and hauling the metal took several days. They had one more essential task: cut the weeds, bushes, and briars around the store.

Josie carried out most of that task using a scythe, a sling blade, and an axe from the tool shed. The twisting movements required with those tasks caused too much pain in Carly's leg. They finished their work agreement with Mr. Mallory on Thursday afternoon before Labor Day weekend, and Labor Day was their agreed-upon completion date. Mr. Mallory's General Mercantile yard was pristine.

As they finished, Mr. Mallory came outside the store, smiling when he shook their hands. Impressed, he said he had watched them all summer and had never seen two people work so hard. And he could not believe Carly had returned so soon after his accident.

"Why did you do it?" he asked them.

"We had no choice, Mr. Mallory. Autumn will soon be here followed by winter, and jobs aren't available for kids our age. And I returned after my accident because we agreed to finish by Labor Day, and keeping our agreement was foremost on our minds."

They returned to town in the late morning because Carly wanted to go to the library to study the history of the Miami Hurricane of 1926, specifically about flooding in the Bay area. He found volumes addressing in detail the effects of the hurricane. Flooding had been extensive in the eastern Mobile Bay area, causing more damage than wind. The eastern shore farmland was especially hard hit by flood waters, not from a surge but a prolonged torrential downpour, dumping more than sixteen inches of rain in twelve hours. Having the creek less than a hundred yards from their home was usually considered an asset but could be a source of significant flooding. Another detail he must worry about.

After collecting their final check from Olson's, they headed to the county courthouse to determine their property's tax bill and buy it. They parked Mary beneath a large cedar tree. Horses or mules still pulled dozens of wagons, carriages, and buggies, and the city supplied water, grazing, and hitching posts, especially near the courthouse. They walked into the tax assessor's office, Betty Arnett greeted them with a sweet smile, remembering them from their earlier visit, and asked if they were still interested in the Ellingson property.

"Yes, we want to buy it today. Is it still $862.00?

"Yes, it is."

"How long until they issue the deed?"

"It usually takes ten days to issue the deed, and this property will take less than a week since there hasn't been an owner for over twenty-five years."

Carly said, "Is it possible to know when Ellingson built the house? She looked at the record and answered, "1928."

Betty gave the sweetest smile when Carly said, "We'll go to Jackson State Bank and return with the check as quickly as possible."

Despite a long line at Jackson State Bank, they returned to the tax assessor's office an hour later with a cashier's check for $862.00. But when they presented the check to her, she refused to accept it, saying, "Someone just bought that property."

Their hearts sank with profound surprise and disappointment, and both were close to tears. Carly was sure he would vomit amid an impending panic attack.

He said, "May we ask who bought it?"

"When you were at the bank, a man bought the property and left instructions to mail the deed to the property's address."

They were in a state of total quandary and bewilderment. He and Josie stood aside to talk. Josie told Carly not to despair. "We might lease it from the new owner."

She walked back to the lady.

"Will you please give us the name and address of the property's new owner?"

"I'm sorry. We will mail the deed to the property's address, and you must check with the person when the deed arrives."

Josie and Carly looked at each other. They must leave the property in the next few days. Carly hoped he wasn't as ashen as Josie, but she said he looked like a corpse. His head was spinning, and glints of light in the corners of his eyes signaled sensory overload.

They asked if they could sit, and when she looked at them, she said,

"Come behind the counter, sit in these chairs. What just happened?"

Josie and Carly looked at each other and sat, holding hands, disoriented.

"We desperately wanted that property and worked hard to earn money to buy it. It's our lives. Would you please give us the name of the person whose name will be on the deed? Perhaps they would consider leasing it to us." Josie pleaded.

She smiled again, and her smile now pissed Carly off because she was enjoying this game of charades. They thanked Mrs. Arnett, turned, trudged slowly away to return, discouraged and forlorn, to Mary and the buggy to go home. Depression had descended like a heavy, dark blanket, constricting his breathing and compressing the light and life from his body. Was there anything to live for? He felt defeated, hopeless.

But he must not allow Josie to see him like that. Josie made his life worth living; he must always make that known to her.

The evening news gave an update on the hurricane's progress. It was in the eastern Gulf of Mexico, having brushed Hispaniola, but battered Jamaica with sustained winds of 140 mph; it was on a path to hit western Cuba.

Carly and Josie worked together to install the window covers. Josie held the covers while Carly secured them. They finished close to noon when his arm was ready to surrender.

They found lumber that would suffice to cover the lesser-used rear door. They would cover the front door and the remaining back door that led to the outhouse as the storm raced closer.

Their shattered dream of owning Ellingson farm felt like an added tempest, though one of emotional upheaval. Josie's face had crumbled at the news, and Carly, heartbroken yet still unbroken, reached across the abyss of their disappointment to gently touch her arm. "We'll find another way, Josie. Our dreams are bigger than a piece of ground."

21

1954
....

AS THE CYCLONE'S WRATH bore down on Havana, Cuba, leaving a trail of devastation and destruction, and uncounted deaths, it pressed its relentless journey into the warm embrace of the Gulf of Mexico. With deliberate, curvilinear intent, it advanced at about ten miles per hour, leaving forecasters to predict its probable landfall anywhere from New Orleans to Pensacola. Yet the precise path remained elusive, and the cyclone's winds, already at a menacing 130 miles per hour, promised to intensify as it traversed the Gulf's heated waters.

Carly asked Josie to join him as they checked Mary's quarters in the barn. Together they fortified Mary's quarters within the sturdy barn. Each nail driven into the wooden barrier felt like a desperate prayer in the face of impending chaos. Carly said they must sit tight because evacuating was not an option; their house, though sturdy and well-built, held their only refuge. Still, as he spoke, he couldn't help sprinkling many "ifs" into the equation, each one a grain of hope mingled with uncertainty.

Mozart's *Eine Kleine Nachtmusik* and Dvorák's *New World Symphony* played softly but did little to shield their hearts from the mounting dread. Sensing something different was happening, Jenna was restless, not her usual relaxed self, and she wasn't letting Carly walk away from her.

In the midst of rain's rhythmic descent, Carly prepared breakfast, and they sat in somber silence, eating omelets and grits. There was a low, dark cloud cover. The impeded light cast an eerie pre-dawn pallor over their world, and the chickens were still perched on their roost. The forecasters had predicted thunderstorms for the afternoon. They settled down to read, but their anxiousness was too weighty; they couldn't concentrate.

Carly learned that in the Miami Hurricane of 1926, flooding had caused more damage than wind. They had a creek running nearby that was usually an asset but could become a curse in a deluge. How would an extensive flood affect their house and the farm? The spring was "up the slope," a few feet higher than the house's base. That could make a difference when considering drinking water, making it less likely to become inundated and contaminated. But drawing water from the well and filling every container was imperative.

Recollections from the tax assessor's office visit, he had learned Ellingson built the house in 1928, less than two years after the Miami Hurricane of 1926. He seemed like a thorough man and perhaps considered that storm's extensive flooding and high winds when he constructed the house. Only time would reveal the house's true mettle.

As dusk draped its shroud, when the pigeons and chickens had gone to roost, Carly hopped out on his crutches to the barn and lowered the massive, hinged wood door to cover the opening of the hayloft, sheltering the chickens and pigeons from the wind and rain.

The progress of the hurricane given on the evening radio report was alarming. The curvilinear path of the storm was to the north. The storm trackers predicted it to hit land at or near Bayou La Batre, a mere 30 miles south of Mobile, at approximately 3 a.m. and continue north toward Mobile. The sustained wind speed was 138 miles per hour, a relentless march forward at ten mph. Extreme atmospheric electrical activity created severe static on the radio, and he had difficulty hearing the full report. Still, he had understood enough to know they were in for a long, sleepless night.

The storm bore the warmth of the Gulf, turning the house into a stifling oven. Carly's thoughts had become fixated on tornadoes known to spawn at the right front quadrant of the whirling mass of winds. If the hurricane continued its predicted path, the bay's eastern shore would bear the brunt. Most tornadoes associated with hurricanes were mild and short-lived, but some had proven to be lethal titans, a perilous uncertainty that gnawed at Carly's composure.

Carly started a fire in the stove to accept coffee's solace, adding to the oppressive heat. He knew he'd fare better through the night with coffee. But what was the purpose of staying awake? It was a macabre jest suggesting slumber might provide a peculiar sanctuary. Yet, he yearned to witness the impending spectacle, wanted to see the action.

Late evening beckoned the whispered plan to blow out the oil lamps and use only candles and a hushed pact to blow out all candles when the hurricane was closer. The world outside was cloaked in darkness, an inky abyss masking nature's fury. In their resolute wait, they pondered the unknowable like two souls staring into the abyss.

As he sipped his coffee in the relative solitude of the breakfast nook, his repetitive depressive thoughts about their loss of the purchase of their farm weren't fading. They must start loading the damned buggy as soon as the hurricane passes. But where would they go? That scene made him lightheaded, so he pivoted his mind to another subject and involuntarily returned to a painfully familiar one.

"I read that powerful hurricanes push a devastating storm surge, often as destructive, if not more so, as the storm. Are we far enough from the water to be safe from a surge?" Josie wondered.

"I hope so. Time will answer your question. This is a powerful storm, and predicting its destructiveness would be guesswork. I have read that the deeper the water, the larger the surge. The surge may be high at landfall, but the bay is shallow. We should be, and I think we are safe..." trailing off, he saw a new look on Josie's face. "Josie, you're afraid, aren't you?" he said with empathy.

"Yes. This storm is scary because it's an unknown; maybe the next ten hurricanes will make me tougher," she smiled. "I'm still sad and upset because we lost our farm. I don't look forward to the days after the hurricane. We'll be busy moving. Where will we go?" Carly answered with a hug and a wan smile.

"I'm also upset because we lost it. It was our lives. It gave us the only true security we had known. But we will live. Our lives will go on," he said.

Reality, unyielding and unsparing, seized them once more. Something had hijacked time, passing at an infinitesimally slow pace, like cold molasses. Both were sweating, and the weight of their anxious anticipation bore down. The humidity hung heavy, their collective anxiety also wringing water from their pores. They switched to candles, which were much dimmer than oil lamps. Josie smiled when Carly suggested they strike a match to see if the candles were burning. They had flashlights but would use them sparingly to save the batteries. Carly remembered they hadn't eaten since breakfast, but neither had an appetite. He thought hurricanes might be suitable to include in a weight loss regimen.

Carly tried to listen to a weather report, but the static was too great to recognize even a voice. The impact of the rain on the house's east side and the roof was becoming more forceful and louder. Over the next five hours, the increasing sounds of rain and wind reached a point where their conversation was almost impossible. The winds traveled counterclockwise and were still pounding the eastern side of the house. When would the winds lighten up? He was concerned for Josie's mental well-being because this was more stressful over a longer time than they had ever experienced. Carly knew they had not yet entered the front eye wall. The front and back eye walls were the most devastating components of a hurricane. The wind direction at the back eye wall would be from the west, at a fierce wind speed.

In a few minutes, the house vibrated violently. They were in the front eye wall. The noise level from the ferocious wind increased to a horrendous level. The rain was a torrential deluge, and the noise on the roof was indescribable. Will the house survive? Will they survive? The violent turbulence could last an hour or more, depending on the distance through the eye wall. The darkness was absolute, and Josie stood next to him. He held her close and shined the flashlight to ensure she was okay. She was afraid. He was also worried, but, for Josie's sake, he was trying not to show it.

The temperature had reached a miserably uncomfortable level, and sweat had soaked their clothes. Their home had become a crucible of torment. They had been trying desperately not to panic for the last hour, but their resolve was weakening. How much longer could they hold out? They were mentally exhausted. Even in their most dismal moments, they could never have imagined anything this dreadful. They clung to one another, their bond a lifeline in a tempestuous sea.

Then a respite. The extreme noise and turbulence decreased within moments when they were on their last nerve. They were through the front eye wall and now in the restful eye of the storm. Both were grateful for the interval of respite, however brief it might be.

Carly looked at Josie and said, "Maybe God is watching."

"There may be hope for you yet," Josie said, smiling, her faith rekindled.

Heavy rainfall continued unimpeded. The eye size was smaller for intense storms, and this hurricane had proven extremely strong. If the eye diameter was about twenty miles, and the cyclone was moving forward at ten mph, their respite should last as much as two hours. They weren't sure how long the lull would last. Carly explained to Josie why their period of relaxation would end, but she already knew. It was probably daylight outside, but the cloud cover prevented the light from sifting through.

"I hope Mary is okay," Carly was worried. If the barn survives, he felt confident that she, their pigeons, and chickens would be okay. Had the intense rainfall caused flooding? The creek would undoubtedly be out of its banks. He wanted to look outside but couldn't until the storm quit. Sitting in quiet, nervous exhaustion, Carly wondered how the house had survived the onslaught through the front eye wall. He walked through the house and found all the window covers intact and no free water in any room.

After two hours of the lull in the eye, within moments, they were suddenly amid deafening wind, now battering the west side of the house, creating a noise described by survivors of earlier storms as sounding like freight trains. The unbelievable downpour of torrential rain was pounding the roof again. It was dèjá vu, but he wasn't as anxious as the first go, and it wasn't pitch-black dark as before. The house was vibrating again, rattling, shaking, and groaning, but it wasn't giving in to the storm. Josie stood close, and as Carly put his arm around her, she didn't seem as overtly anxious as before, but sweat continued to soak her clothes and his. The temperature remained intolerably hot, much too high for comfort.

The continuous vibration, creaking, rattling, shivering, and groaning associated with the unrelenting deafening noise again grated on their nerves. They weren't due for relief for at least another hour into the back eye wall. Another hour passed, and within a few minutes, there was a cessation of the noises and turbulence of the vicious winds. They were out of the back eyewall, and it was as if the storm had passed, but the noises from the less terrifying but dangerous wind speed and torrential rain would continue for another four or five hours.

In his mental exhaustion, complicated by prolonged sleeplessness and unending deafening sound, Carly hallucinated, imagined he was at the helm of a ship, guiding it through the storm, much like a half-remembered dream while not fully awake. After the back eye wall had passed, and during the last part of their journey through the storm, he was in and out of this state of mind, having to exert mental effort to bring himself to reality. While at the helm, his primary goal was to see Josie through the storm and get her safely to port. Seeing Josie safely home was a duty or responsibility, not a burden, and he knew he must remain awake to finish the journey.

The storm persisted for another five and a half hours after the back eye wall passed. The savage wind had diminished, although the gusts remained dangerous, and although thunder and lightning were persisting, they barely perceived them, and the rain continued though not as intense. Carly and Josie collapsed in their beds and slept for over fifteen hours. When they finally tumbled out of their beds, Carly prepared an excellent breakfast of bacon, eggs, and grits to assuage the return of their ravenous hunger. They were starving.

Desperately needing to see the after-effects of the hurricane, they knocked away enough of the front door cover to exit onto the porch. They had the surprise of their life. Water was as far as they could see in all directions, and it appeared to be moving with the creek's downstream current. Wind-blown tree limbs floated everywhere, but no downed trees were in their yards. They were flummoxed, not yet up to understanding how to navigate through or around those hurricane after-effects.

Carly needed to get to the barn to check on Mary. The hayloft window needed opening to give the pigeons and chickens access to food and water.

He removed the covers of the two back doors and almost waded into the water to check for water damage to the underside of the house, but Josie yelled at him to stay inside, "Sit and quit being a pain in the butt, or you will ruin your cast, and it won't help your leg either." Feeling appropriately chastened, Carly sat and moped.

Josie looked beneath the house and reported to Carly, "There's a line of mud on the pillars underneath the house, marking the highest water level, and it's at least two feet below the floor joists. No water damage is present."

Ellingson had scored huge in Carly's eyes for having built the house higher than the flood in 1926. But his joy was short-lived when he remembered they would move as soon as the water receded.

He surveyed the yards from their doorways. All the live oaks in the yards were still standing, but small and medium-sized limbs were on the ground, the larger significant limbs were intact. The pecan trees lost limbs, but they stayed upright.

Josie grabbed a pair of rain boots, rolled up her pant legs, and decided to brave the journey to the barn herself. The water came up to her mid-calves in places, but she managed to make her way over, carefully avoiding any potential hazards lurking beneath the water's surface.

Although it wasn't easy to see the difference, the barn site was higher than where the house sat, and its flooding was minimal. The barn appeared untouched by the storm, the roof and sides remained intact. Mary was standing in six inches of water, agitated but otherwise unharmed, and Josie knew she must be moved. Entering the hayloft, she opened the wood cover over the large window among a flurry of activity as hundreds of pigeons scrambled outside for food and water, and the chickens clambered for water. She shelled some of Mary's corn to feed them.

Mary was still skittish when Josie haltered her and led her out of the stall. Josie grabbed her brush, and they waded to the house, and both went inside the storage room. Mary offered no resistance to follow, and Josie dried and brushed her until she was calm. She placed a large tarp on the floor, hobbled her, and fed her more than usual, which she consumed quickly to show her thanks. Josie returned to the barn and spread corn and horse feed in the loft for the chickens and the returning pigeons.

They didn't know how long the flood waters would last, but Carly and Josie had enough food to last weeks, and their ice would hold for weeks. They both sat down, letting the weight of the last days sink in.

The storm had tested their limits and home, but not their bond. Through it all, they had emerged unbroken, stronger than ever. The future might be uncertain, especially with the loss of their farm, but they were sure of one thing: together, they could weather any storm.

But their imminent move was the looming 800-pound gorilla that neither wanted to mention because the wound was too acute and painful.

22

1954
·······

THE RELENTLESS PASSAGE OF TIME seemed to have ground to a halt, leaving Carly and Josie adrift in uncertainty. The air hung heavy with the wet remnants of the hurricane and the melancholic aura enveloping Carly and Josie. Their shattered dream of buying the farm seemed to hang, suspended in devastated lands amidst their erstwhile buoyant hopes. The aftermath of the hurricane had cast a somber pall over their days, compounded by the loss of their dream of buying the farm where they lived. And the weight of their existence hung heavily upon them. They knew they had to shake off this melancholy and act, so they reluctantly returned to packing their trusty buggy.

Carly couldn't muster the motivation to begin the arduous task, but he knew they couldn't afford to continue to wallow in despair. He moved the buggy to the front of the house into plain sight, a silent prod to get them moving, albeit through the grit of despair. As he contemplated their seemingly endless state of despondency, Carly couldn't help but empathize with the ghosts of his parents. Did they endure this daily, soul-sucking depression? He understood now how the desperate pursuit of solace could drive a person to seek refuge in the bottle as Mama and Papa had done.

In a moment of providential distraction, Carly was staring out of the living room window, surveying the landscape marked by standing water and the indelible scars of the hurricane. He noticed the mail carrier making his way to their mailbox. To procrastinate further and delay the onerous task before them, Carly seized his crutches. He dragged his injured leg towards the front door, planning to trudge through the ubiquitous drying mud that seemed to cling to every surface.

"Misery might appreciate some company, Josie. Walk with me to the mailbox?" His eyes pleaded more than his words. Although Josie didn't relish the idea, her acquiescence was more resignation than agreement. Yet the semblance of an activity, no matter how mundane, was a subtle balm to their morose spirits. Together, they embarked on a desultory journey down the muddied road towards the mailbox. The absence of their usual sense of purpose made their conversation unusually idle.

Just as Betty Arnett had foretold, they found a large first-class letter waiting for them, nestled alongside some less significant pieces of mail. Carly suspected that the bulky envelope contained the deed to the farm, intended for the new owner and tenant. He handed the unopened envelope to Josie and turned, resigned to face the grim task of packing.

Making their way back home, Josie opened the envelope. But then, Josie's voice rang out, carrying a hint of curiosity and questioning. "Carly," she said. His mind was elsewhere, and he didn't respond. He continued his sluggish journey homeward.

"Carly!" she called out with urgency and excitement. He slowed and finally stopped, half-turning to face her with his attention only partially engaged.

"It's the deed and title to the farm," she exclaimed, her voice filled with astonishment.

"I know. That's why I passed it to you. I don't care anymore. We need to move on." Uninterested, he turned to continue hobbling toward the house.

"But Carly," Josie continued, "They have our names on them, Carlton Turner and Josephine Turner. The deed and title are ours."

"Josie! How in heavens...." His voice trailed off, suspended in disbelief. Carly was now engaged but flabbergasted. He tried to unravel this rapidly baffling mystery, but it was like trying to assemble a jigsaw puzzle with pieces missing and others mixed in. "What on Earth, Josie? How is that possible? Let me see that."

Their world had been thrown into a whirlwind of confusion. How could their names possibly be on those legal documents? Carly grappled with the idea of a courthouse error or the exceedingly unlikely scenario of someone buying the property for them. He chuckled when Josie suggested that standing in the middle of a muddy road wasn't conducive to solving this enigma. With the deed and title bearing their names, they couldn't solve the puzzle, it deepened the mystery. Carly's mind raced, his thoughts entangled in a web of possibilities versus probabilities.

After hours of fruitless debate and no closer to solving the puzzle, they harnessed Mary to the buggy and headed straight to the courthouse for answers. Betty Arnett in the tax assessor's office confirmed there was no mistake, and the names on the documents were indeed correct. However, she had been sworn to secrecy and couldn't reveal the identity of their benefactor.

"You'll find out soon, and it will pleasantly surprise you both," Betty assured them. "Meanwhile, congratulations, and enjoy your new farm." Filled with unbridled excitement and gratitude, they were eager to discover the person they owed an immeasurable debt to. But who was this mysterious benefactor, and why had they done this? Carly declared that when he found them, he would first unleash a torrent of sincere gratitude and then give them a stern piece of his mind for putting them through such emotional turmoil. With the deed and title now in their possession, they knew they had secured their place on the farm they had worked so hard for. Josie walked silently to and fro, holding the deed and title to the property over her heart as she stared vacantly at the cloudless, heraldic azure sky.

They celebrated this unexpected turn of fortune by visiting the local drugstore with the soda fountain. Upon arrival, they took a recommendation from James Henry, the soda jerk, and each ordered a banana split, though James Henry timidly suggested they share one due to its immense size.

Waiting for their delicious treat, Josie spoke from the heart. "Carly, I want to tell you something. I love you for bringing me along on this journey. I know it hasn't been easy, providing me with a home, food, and being a brother, a mother, and a father to me. But if you hadn't taken me with you after what happened to Winnie, I don't think I'd be alive today. It's been an incredible experience, and I wouldn't trade it for anything. Thank you. I love you."

Carly was deeply moved by her words and took a moment to respond, quietly. "There was never a question of whether to bring you along. Your safety was why we started planning our escape to freedom. Winnie and I loved you, and that love never wavered. We wouldn't have embarked on this journey if you hadn't chosen to come with us. Always remember that. Maybe our luck is finally changing."

Josie probed further, asking if Carly believed it was all just luck. He admitted that he had asked himself that question countless times, but it remained unanswered. He was determined to keep seeking an answer, even though it eluded him.

As they sat together, enjoying the sweet respite from their troubles, Carly couldn't help but reflect on how far they had come. Their journey had been filled with good and bad fortune, and as he pondered their current situation, he couldn't deny the role that luck, or perhaps divine intervention, had played. However, the silence of God in the face of Winnie's death still loomed large in his mind, and until that question was resolved, he couldn't fully embrace the notion of divine intervention.

Their jumbo banana split arrived, and they indulged in its sweet extravagance, though they couldn't finish it. As they relaxed and conversed, Josie commented on Carly's continued growth.

"Are you going to grow to be seven feet tall? You're like dough rising before baking," she teased.

Carly responded in mock horror, and they both laughed heartily. Josie's laughter was infectious, and she laughed with her entire being. Carly realized he needed new clothes, as his current attire was tattered and threadbare, starkly contrasting his rapidly growing physique.

Josie quickly pointed out his need for a wardrobe update, but Carly feigned indifference, attached to his old clothes as they had once belonged to Winnie. They were his last physical connection to his brother, and he wasn't ready to part with them just yet.

He turned the question, "But look at you," said Carly. "I think you are approaching five and a half feet. And you don't have an ounce of fat."

Josie then turned the spotlight on herself, jokingly mentioning that she should measure and weigh herself when she didn't have a banana split weighing her down. Their banter continued as they enjoyed their newfound sense of security, courtesy of the deed and title that now proclaimed them property owners.

"If we'd been smart, we should have read the names on the large envelope from the courthouse, our names. That would have been a helpful clue," Josie said.

Carlie looked stunned, in deep thought. Then he slapped his forehead in comprehension. They laughed together. The weight of uncertainty had lifted.

After working so hard all summer, Mary deserved a treat so they would stop at Mallory's Mercantile. Carly remembered they originally intended to sell Mary for survival money, but they had survived the winter with 38 cents, and they couldn't sell her now. She and Jenna were essential members of their small but growing family.

They stopped at Mr. Mallory's store and bought some grain for Mary.

A few months ago, he noticed he was taller than Mr. Mallory. Measuring at least five feet ten inches and pushing 160 pounds, he was a brawny, powerful young man with broad shoulders, a slim waist, and narrow hips. He had blonde hair, blue eyes, and robust facial features. He appeared years older than his age of 14. His clothes were tight-fitting, too small for comfort, and, as Josie had said, the pants resembled pedal pushers. Headlong into full-blown puberty since leaving home, his voice was now a rotund baritone, and his muscle development was astonishing. His penis and testicles had grown large, along with pubic and chest hair. Winnie never spoke with him about such matters. He had been Carly's primary reference for everything during his formative years.

They shared the good news of buying their new home with Mr. Mallory and thanked him for the informative discussion about the property. Was Mr. Mallory their secret benefactor? But Mr. Mallory stood speechless, out of character for him, and despite suspecting that he was the one who bought their property for them, seeing him with such genuine surprise removed him from consideration.

Carly knew they would never have to worry about returning to the farm, but he couldn't ignore the looming threat Papa still posed should he find them. The cloud of anxiety had hung over them for so long. What would their lives be like if that cloud dissipated? Would the residual stress and worry diminish with time? He doubted he would live long enough to realize that dream.

23

1954
·······

CARLY'S EYES PIERCED THE HORIZON where the hurricane flood water had receded. His usually steadfast voice wavered with a soft, lingering emotion as he turned to Josie and asked, "Do you think she'll remember us?" Josie, gently clutching the hem of her pink dress, responded, her voice barely a whisper, "She has to. Mrs. Brownlie always said we were unforgettable." Memories of Mrs. Brownlie's kindness fluttered through their memories like cherished pages of a beloved book. Their beloved tutor had instilled in them not just a love for reading but a flame of hope that refused to be extinguished.

Carly ran his hand through his hair, remnants of grief embedded in his eyes, yet a spark of adventurous spirit lingered. He and Josie gathered the well-read books and embarked on a journey toward their past, stepping into Mr. Mallory's Mercantile with hearts as turbulent as the recent cyclone. They asked him for help selecting a gift for Mrs. Brownlie. He sounded like he knew her well when he said she collected porcelain dolls. He had a new shipment she had never seen. Their choice, delicate and vibrant, caught Josie's eyes. Wearing a sunflower-yellow dress—it seemed to whisper memories of brighter days and promised futures. Mr. Mallory said she would love it because yellow was her favorite color. It came with a certificate of authenticity from Asia.

They planned to visit unannounced. Would she still remember them? They could talk about their life since she last saw them if she showed any interest.

Josie looked like a living doll in her new pink dress and new shoes. Carly still wore Winnie's clothes, although they were too small.

As they approached the picturesque yellow farmhouse of Mrs. Brownlie, their hearts were entwined with anticipation and fear. The porch extended to three sides of the house, and white wood furniture adorned a space near the door, an invitation to a friendly home. The plants and the extensive green lawn around the house were gorgeous and perfectly complimented the scene. Both were uncomfortable with this visit and still wondered if it was a good idea, but they shuffled toward the door. Carly was about to knock when the door opened, and Mrs. Brownlie stood with her extended arms. And there, in the embrace of a woman who defied forgetting them, they found solace. Mrs. Brownlie, her voice drenched with emotion, declared, "Carlton and Josephine Turner, welcome home!"

"Ma'am, how'd you know it was us?"

"I've been waiting for you. Everyone thought you were dead. A report from the sheriff's office concluded that you both died. The newspaper quickly picked up the announcement with headlines, and everyone stopped looking for you. I knew you were alive, though."

"How did you know?"

"A voice told me in a dream, letting me know you were okay, and I would see you again one day. Since that dream, I've waited patiently, knowing you were fine. The two of you have grown stronger and more mature, but I would have known you with your blond hair and beautiful blue eyes." Her smile was as graceful as ever.

They presented their gift to Mrs. Brownlie. Surprised, she examined every aspect of the little doll. She thanked them and led them into a room brimming with a stunning collection of porcelain dolls crafted in Asia and Europe, dressed in every imaginable costume. They seemed to nod approvingly at their heartfelt reunion. "I'm an avid collector of porcelain dolls, have been for years, and I'll treasure your gift."

They exchanged stories encased in a bubble where the past met the present. Josie and Carly answered Mrs. Brownlie's questions as they talked, but out of deference to their privacy, she asked nothing about their life before their escape. Maybe she thought it would be enough to learn more later. After discussing their work history from spring through the summer, they told her about the house and farm-land they had just bought and now owned outright.

She sat speechless, blinking to clear her welling tears. She expressed amazement that the two had achieved so much, so young.

Mrs. Brownlie recalled when Carly started school and got into trouble when he wondered why he couldn't go to school with his little friend.

Carly nodded. "She was my dearest friend and still is, I hope. I miss her so much. We couldn't go to school together, and I haven't seen her since we started school. I have never received an answer to my question, 'Why can't we go to the same school?' She lived relatively close to our farm, and I assume she still does. I would love to see her. Her name is Eva Lou, a lovely name for a beautiful person."

After several hours of talking, Mrs. Brownlie insisted they stay for supper.

Before they sat at the table, Carly brought in the long-overdue books. Mrs. Brownlie told them about her husband, who worked as a professor on a project known as the Great Books of the Western World. They were to publish the most important literary, scientific, and artistic works in the Western world in a single set that anyone could buy, like an encyclopedia.

For his work on the project, the university awarded her husband a set of Great Books. They arrived, but her husband had become ill and could never enjoy them before his death. They were still in the original shipping crate. Mrs. Brownlie wanted Carly to have them. After he'd studied them, he should give them to Josie. Mrs. Brownlie then turned and pointed to a couple of boxes.

"Josie, I have more boxes of books for you. I hope they will be okay at your achievement level."

Carly asked Mrs. Brownlie if Josie could show her something.

"Of course."

He selected a book, opened it to a random page, and gave it to Josie to read. Mrs. Brownlie objected, thinking it might be too hard to read. Josie then handed the book to Mrs. Brownlie and recalled everything on the page. Again, Mrs. Brownlie was almost speechless.

"She has a photographic memory, a rare genetic gift. Do you have it, Carly?"

"Yes, ma'am, I do."

Mrs. Brownlie asked them to sit. She had more to say. "I'd like to propose an education for both of you." They could respond after they have thought it over. According to Mrs. Brownlie, the public schools in the town would not provide them with any advantages in their educational pursuits. Recalling his earlier experience, Carly agreed.

Their conversation meandered toward an educational proposal that promised a beacon of hope yet was shadowed by the societal struggles of integration and acceptance. She proposed taking them as private students in a program with City University. They would receive official credit, and with proper guidance, they could reap untold educational benefits. The program would prepare them for the world's best universities. Mrs. Brownlie had dreamed of a situation like this throughout her teaching career. Now she knew it was possible because of her earlier experience tutoring them. Carly and Josie listened, a mix of aspiration and apprehension flickering through their youthful eyes. Mrs. Brownlie unveiled an opportunity masked in triumphs and challenges. "This isn't just an education, dear children. It's a revolution."

The opportunity was like something out of a fairy tale, Josie and Carly told Mrs. Brownlie. "Mrs. Brownlie, we would do this in a heartbeat, but we don't have the money for such a program. So, we must decline your offer," said Carly.

"Not so fast, young man." Mrs. Brownlie explained she had thought this through and had thoroughly developed the program. "I have a grant for the project, and the funding foundation is eager to start. The foundation funding the program mandates three participants, but full disclosure, at least one person, must be of color. I designed this program to integrate the all-white City University. The program will carry out that with the least societal disruption and antagonism. The program will accept young individuals like you two because you project a less threatening image to society than young adults. But you would likely meet the Ku Klux Klan and its sycophants daily throughout the school year. Understanding what you could encounter is essential."

Josie and Carly looked at each other with eyes wide open in excitement.

"Your education will be unparalleled and set a historical precedent to last beyond your lifetime. The funding will cover your expenses and pay you a stipend because the school year is twelve months, so you can't work summer jobs. The Grant will also cover post-doctoral expenses."

Carly said, "Mrs. Brownlie, we're young. Some would say we're kids, although we don't think of ourselves as such. But will we be able to handle the work at the college level you are describing?"

"Carly, you and Josie handled college-level studies when I tutored you. We'll evaluate you initially and document your progress as you go along. We'll begin teaching at the level you test at the beginning. Each course is at a level you can handle, but the program will challenge you at all levels. City University will administer this program, but I'll be in charge. I have already lined up the professors eager for the opportunity to participate. The Grant will pay the university and the professors for taking part in the program. If you accept, I'll search for the third student."

Carly shifted in his seat. "A project of this undertaking would require an overwhelming time commitment from you, perhaps creating difficulty for you."

"No, I would never consider teaching a hardship. It's a calling that I'm answering."

Eyes locked, Carly and Josie found a united resolve. "Of course, we'll do it."

And that was that.

Carly whispered, "If the world expects us to be washed away, let's teach them how to sail."

His descriptions made her laugh. He added he wanted to sit in college-level courses and wanted the same for Josie.

Carly wanted to know the university's position on implementing the program.

"Dr. Hennessey, president of the university, supports the program and its dual purpose, but the dean of students, not at all. When I told Dr. Hennessey of the grant's requirements, his face lit up, and he said, 'Good. I've been seeking an opportunity to integrate the university, to have it enter the twentieth century.' The president is happy the school is integrating. He knew it was coming one day soon, and he agrees perhaps this program will be the least socially antagonistic way for it to happen."

After saying goodnight, Carly and Josie climbed aboard their buggy with their boxes of new books, Carly clicked his tongue, and Mary headed home. A beautiful harvest moon and a clear night made for a perfect slow ride. Mary wasn't in a hurry, and neither were they. There was a lovely briskness in the air. They couldn't wait to start, almost floating on clouds and happy beyond words.

The morning sun greeted them and soon omelets were sizzling softly in the background, but he and Josie were uncharacteristically quiet. Considering the previous night, Josie asked if he had any further thoughts. He smiled and spoke reluctantly and slowly, "Nothing could make me believe last night could even be a reality. What have we done to deserve this? Should I believe in fairies and unicorns?"

"I can think of nothing we've done. Maybe it's good luck. Perhaps it's our turn," Josie said.

Carly replied barely above a whisper, "I hope so, damn I do. But my God-given skepticism makes me question the true intent of the program. She made a one-sided presentation of many pluses for us with an artful persuasion that the program would racially integrate the university. Will the university's attention to our education decrease to a sideshow with less emphasis and importance while the integration process becomes center stage? I don't know how to get a guarantee our education will not slide. But I'll keep mulling over this question until I'm satisfied with my answer."

After daydreaming in the afterglow of their evening with Mrs. Brownlie, they shelved their new books. Carly placed his books on the shelves and stood admiring them. The collection was fifty-four volumes of beautifully bound books from Homer to Freud, and each title had a different color according to its genre. It was the most beautiful, precious gift he could have received.

Carly asked, "Why do you suppose Mrs. Brownlie gave us such a gift?"

Josie shrugged like the answer was obvious.

Although initially overjoyed, his survivor's guilt soon bore down and devastated Carly with a piercing depression. Why wasn't Winnie celebrating this gift instead of him? Josie noticed the change, walked over to Carly and put her arms around him.

"Don't do this, Carly. I know it's about Winnie. Please don't. If you do, I will go along with you; Carly, it's too painful. Why can't you let it go? Winnie is watching, and he's happy for us. We don't know why he died, but we must try to accept that there was a reason for it. Carly, nothing can change it. Our lives will continue, but we must let it go."

"I know what you are saying, Josie, but I must feel it, and I don't. I'm trying."

"Okay," said Josie and began shelving her two boxes of books, selecting one to start, *The Red Badge of Courage* by Stephen Crane. Carlie picked two volumes: Isaac Newton's *Philosophiae Naturalis Principia Mathematica* and Thucydides' *History of the Peloponnesian War.* He hoped a night of intense concentration would help clear his mind.

In the comfort of their abode that evening, amidst the tranquility of newfound books and under the watchful eye of the gentle moon, Carly and Josie whispered promises of courage, education, and change to the night.

As they delved into the tales of bravery and historical sagas, physics and mathematics, the siblings silently vowed to march forward into a future they would carve, not just for themselves, but for those forgotten by the world.

24

·······

SEVERAL WEEKS AFTER LABOR DAY, they grabbed tools from the tool shed and shop and the battle against the entwining menace of scrub bushes, briars, and vines surrounding the house began with grim determination. Carly reminded Josie to watch for copperheads and rattlesnakes.," Remember, Josie, copperheads, rattlesnakes..." his voice, a gravelly murmur, threaded through the lush, unkempt overgrowth. Josie's response was a silent nod, her attention already partly sunk into the wild environment, partly into her task, and ever so slightly alert to the venomous threats Carly had whispered about.

Their work rhythmically progressed faster than they had dared to hope, and they cleared the porch and one side of the house by dinnertime. They discovered old flower beds around the front porch, their potential masked by years of neglect and needed topsoil and new plants to revitalize them. Soon Carly heard the ominous, fearful rattling of a rattlesnake, sending chills down his spine as an adrenaline dump infused through his body. As he fearfully searched for the vicious reptile, his eyes darted towards Josie. She calmly, with a precision that seemed to mock the danger, decapitated the rattlesnake with her gardening tool and was standing, holding the writhing reptile vertically by its tail, minus its head. Her eyes, steady and unfazed, met Carly's. He stared silently, gave her a thumbs up and slowly returned to the task at hand.

When dusk fell to the darker part of twilight, they had cleared the house's entire periphery, and the day ended.

When morning came, Carly and Josie, their muscles protesting, moved their tools to the driveway at the junction with Old Johnson

Road to contend with the rampant brush and bramble along their long driveway. Carly estimated work on that project would last several days.

Carly intermittently stole glances towards the horizon, and the rumble of an approaching tractor vibrated through the still morning air. He stood by Old Johnson Road, postured with a tempered readiness, and moments later the tractor with a bush hog attached came into sight. The driver was a man in his sixties wearing overalls and a large straw hat with a green plastic piece sewn into the front brim to protect his eyes from the sun but allowed upward visibility. Carly flagged him to stop.

The man stopped his tractor, removed his straw hat and a large bandana from his pocket, and mopped his sweating brow, his eyes squinting in the sun.

"Morning. What kin I do fer ya?"

Carly introduced himself and Josie, using their real name, Turner. Despite still feeling insecure, it felt good to use his real surname. He said, "I would like to hire you to make a couple of passes with your bush hog along both sides of this path, up to the house and back. I will pay you."

"Do you live here?"

"Yes, sir."

The farmer, shading his eyes as he surveyed the house and land, asked, "Do you own this place now?"

"Yes, sir, we bought it and are trying to do some cleanup. Quite a job with a sling blade, ax, and mattock."

"I'll make a couple of passes, look at it, and if it looks decent, I'll quote you a price. If it don't look okay, you won't owe me nothing."

"It's a deal. What's your name, sir?"

"My name is Birchfield. I'm yer next-door neighbor 'bout two miles down the road."

He made two passes along either side of the path, plus passes around the house, then returned.

"It don't look good, so I reckon I won't charge nothing. Consider it a housewarming gift. Where yer folks?"

"Inside. Thanks so very much, Mr. Birchfield. What you have done for us means a great deal, and we won't forget."

"Wait, now, not so fast. Yer just kids, awfully young to be hiring me to do work around here. I want to meet yer folks."

Carly said, "Well, Mr. Birchfield, it's just Mama, and she's sick. The doctor thinks she could have the consumption, so we have to keep her isolated until he knows, but he thinks Mama might die. Papa took off when Mama got sick; we don't know where he is. We can go inside and see if she's awake."

By the time Carly stopped talking, Mr. Birchfield had backed off about six steps. He said he'd wondered about the curse on that place, "Don't it worry you none? I'm uncomfortable being here right now, and I think I'll be running along now."

He climbed aboard his tractor before Carly could answer, started the engine, and in his hurry to leave, tried to put it in gear without depressing the clutch, causing a terrific grinding of the transmission gears. When he successfully got it in gear, he lost no time hightailing it down Old Jackson Road.

Mr. Birchfield's rapid departure, mingled with the tales of curses and Carly's hastily woven story of consumption, left an echo of trepidation lingering in the stillness.

The sun was sighing into twilight, and Carly and Josie sat on their front porch, enjoying the grassy beauty of the newly mowed area. They watched the setting sun as it turned the sky reddish orange before dipping beneath the western horizon. As evening caressed the land, Carly and Josie moved inside, lit the oil lamps, picked up their books, and settled in for the evening. But an uneasy dance by Jenna, her growls a low rumble of warning in the otherwise peaceful evening, disrupted the serenity.

They put their books aside, listened, and heard slow but heavy footsteps heading along the side of their house toward the back. Then, the steps were on the back porch, and the man bumped into a table or chair, prompting a string of cursing. Heavy footsteps were approaching the back door. As the doorknob turned slowly, Carly held his breath, his heart racing. They heard the heavy footsteps of the man who had entered their house, and they were coming closer. Although they kept quiet, there was no escape for Carly or Josie.

An enormous, obese man over six feet tall appeared from the back hallway. He looked 20–25 years old, wearing an old US Army jacket with Sergeant's stripes over a sweaty, dingy tee-shirt and filthy pants, and brandishing a gigantic revolver. His massive gut stretched the shirt beyond its limits, exposing his hairy abdomen. There was a name above the right breast pocket of the jacket that read "Stewart." The smell of alcohol, cigarettes, and grease, combined with the odor of his unwashed body, generated a stink that was disgusting and sickening. He radiated the temper of a vicious, angry man. Josie stood closest to him, and he surprised her by grabbing her, holding his arm around her shoulders and chest, and pointing the gun against the side of her head. Stewart demanded money, and Carly held both hands, palms up, and emphasized, "We have no money."

Stewart was still holding the gun barrel against Josie's head. "Give me the damn money, or I'll kill the bitch!" Carly's eyes flickered, not with fear, but with a calculated assessment.

Carly edged closer to the behemoth. Josie was talking to him, stalling, asking his name and what kind of trouble he was having. Becoming increasingly angry, he shoved her aside, kicked her butt, and called her a "little bitch." She fell, crying and screaming, pretending to be hurt. Stewart's eyes were momentarily diverted to Josie as she got up slowly, faking pain and having difficulty walking, and Carly, taller than Stewart by six inches, moved closer to him. Less than a yard from the terrifying intruder, Carly gave Josie a perfunctory nod, which she reciprocated.

Stewart was furious, "Quit stalling and give me the damn money!"

Seeing no response from Carly, he raised the revolver point blank in Josie's face, pulled back the hammer, and his finger was pulling the trigger.

In a not-so-subtle nod, Carly gestured to Josie, who at once fell to the floor, pretending to have a seizure. Simultaneously, using the proximal joints of his fingers, Carly flexed his right hand into a sharp wedge and, quick as a rattlesnake, shot his hand forward, putting all his strength behind the potentially fatal strike, aiming for Stewart's Adam's apple, landing a vicious blow resulting in crunching noises in his throat and an intense look of surprise on Stewart's face. Suddenly, Stewart fired the revolver with a startling, explosive blast, and the bullet tore into the hardwood floor with a loud splat less than four inches from Josie's head. Josie, even while playing her part in their survival script, felt an unbidden shudder when the revolver discharged explosively so near, and her heart throbbed like a drum in her ears.

25

1954
·······

GROWLING FEROCIOUSLY, JENNA was airborne at once, landed on Stewart's chest, and knocked him to the floor. His head struck the floor with a loud thud, and the revolver spiraled across the floor. Jenna was going for the intruder's face and throat; blood was flying in the air and across the floor. Josie leaped up, shot across the floor and retrieved the revolver. Stewart screamed with pain and profound fright, begging Carly and Josie to call off the dog. Carly could see he was no longer a threat, he called to Jenna, and she stood by his side still giving long, ominous growls. Stewart lay relatively motionless, groaning with pain, showing no ambition to sit or stand. A large puddle of blood was becoming larger on the floor around his head and neck.

Carly was concerned that Stewart might die from blood loss. The copious gush of blood continued. Carly grabbed a couple of towels to apply pressure, hoping to staunch the blood flow. After long minutes, he helped Stewart sit, then, with urging, he stood rather shakily. Carly was stunned when he saw the man's face and neck. Jenna had torn multiple large gashes across his face and neck. An incision cut across his left eye, cutting the upper lid lengthwise and the lower edge drooped with a large opening, and the eye looked permanently open. Carly was concerned that the cut may have destroyed his eyeball. A large laceration extended across the right side of his head and almost ripped off his right ear. His wounds were a stark testament to the violence of survival.

He told Stewart he would get the buggy, take him to the hospital, and asked if he was okay with that. Stewart nodded vigorously and mumbled something that Carly didn't understand. Carly noticed Stewart was breathing with difficulty, likely from his throat punch.

Carly asked Josie to apply constant pressure to the wounds while he brought the buggy to the front. Soon, he rolled up to the front steps, and they both applied pressure while Stewart struggled to the buggy. Carly asked Josie to go with him to the hospital. Afraid to remain home alone after that scary encounter, Josie readily agreed. Jenna went along to keep them safe because it was her duty.

When they arrived at the hospital, Carly and Josie helped Stewart to the admission desk, Jenna insisted on going along, where a nurse at once whisked him away.

At home, as the door closed, enveloping them in their familiar living room, Carly and Josie, shaken yet solid, faced each other.

"Was your seizure real?" Carly asked.

"It was getting very close to real. But I would not be alive if you had delayed another second."

Carly agreed and asked where she had placed Stewart's revolver.

"In the kitchen counter drawer nearest the hallway."

"That's the perfect place for it, handy for the next time," he said with a grin.

Their conversation, punctuated by half-chuckles of relief and residual fear, simmered with the unspoken acknowledgment of their collective ordeal and the uncertainty that lay ahead.

26

1954

. . . .

IN THE AUTUMN OF 1954, when the humidity had retreated mercifully and the temperature held its gentle sway, Carly was immersed in choreography of tasks around the farm. Amidst the rustling leaves that carpeted the yard, he diligently raked them into piles while also plucking the last of the watermelons from their vines and gathering the remaining tomatoes in their garden.

The watermelons were the fruit of an enigmatic packet of "mystery" seeds given to them by their farmer friend, Ray Jackson, and had flourished into impressive giants. Their vivid, two-toned green stripes concealed the sweet, bright red hue of the watery flesh. As he worked, Carly pondered plans for a garden the upcoming year, considering the prospect of planting pumpkins for a burst of color and potatoes to yield starchy delights.

However, this tranquil scene was soon disrupted by the sudden arrival of a flashy red convertible, veering off Old Jackson Road and making its way up their driveway. Carly's Pavlovian anxiety sent a surge of raw adrenaline coursing through his veins, his heart racing as the vehicle came to a stop before their porch. Could it be Papa? His apprehension ebbed somewhat as he saw a stranger climb from the car, dressed casually in an untucked batik shirt. But Carly's momentary relief was swiftly replaced by incredulity and disgust as he watched the man brazenly explore his nose and consume his findings. The man was a "snotter," as Carly promptly deemed him.

The stranger spotted Carly in the garden, descended the porch steps, and approached him with a briefcase clutched in his left hand, while he held important-looking papers in the other hand.

"John Slaughter," the man introduced himself, though he made no offer of a handshake.

Carly was relieved that he didn't have to touch the man's snot-covered hand.

"I'm looking for Carlton Turner," Slaughter declared.

Carly, momentarily taken aback, decided there was no reason to hide behind a pseudonym now. "I'm Carlton Turner," he replied, revealing his true identity. This marked their first encounter, but Carly recognized the name from a sign outside a law office in town. Slaughter extended a document toward Carly with his right hand, and Carly accepted it cautiously, avoiding the snot-picking fingerprints.

Carly examined the document for about half a minute before glaring at Slaughter, who seemed unusually self-assured. "This document is riddled with three glaring errors, which I won't address here," Carly declared, his voice steady and confident. "I'll save those discussions for my countersuit. Your lawsuit is baseless and fraudulent. I have no doubt you'll eventually withdraw it, and when you do, my countersuit will continue, and you will suffer substantial losses."

A pregnant silence followed as Carly fixed his stare on Slaughter, who no longer appeared smug and wouldn't make eye-contact.

"You're going to lose everything you own, and you'll find yourself behind bars because this complaint of yours is nothing but a sham. Your mistake, Mr. Slaughter, was assuming that I am young and gullible."

Slaughter swallowed hard, his expression shifting from confidence to unease.

"You have been sorely mistaken," Carly continued.

Carly finished his gardening and retreated inside to relax. Josie inquired about the visitor, and Carly showed her the paper, explaining the fraudulent scheme Slaughter was trying to perpetrate.

"His name is John Slaughter, a shady lawyer from town who served me with a complaint," Carly began, revealing the identity of their uninvited guest. He continued to outline the claims made in the complaint and pointed out its glaring errors. It claims we signed an illegal contract with the county to buy our house and section of land. It also says we didn't do a complete search for the original owner's legal relatives and now a legal relative has shown up who will claim to own the property, a Samuel Riddell, no address," Carly continued. "He made three mistakes in the complaint, first, the incorrect address of the property and second, the legal description of the property is wrong. We'll go to the courthouse tomorrow to find the incorrectly described property. Third, he had the names of the original owners wrong. The correct names were Jackey Ellingson and Frances Ellingson. The complaint lists them as Francis and Jackie Ellison. Slaughter claimed he had the original deed with the lawful owner's signature, Samuel Riddell, with no present address, but we will find him if he exists. He must show us that document, and we'll prove it's fake."

Josie looked concerned but found reassurance in Carly's demeanor. Carly discussed their limited options due to their financial constraints when Josie suggested hiring a lawyer. However, Carly rejected the idea, believing that Slaughter would likely represent himself in court, and that he could handle their legal defense while Josie acted as co-counsel.

Josie agreed to join him in this endeavor.

Later that day, Carly suggested sharing some of their bountiful watermelons with their farmer friend, Ray Jackson. They made their way to Ray's farm, where Carly presented him with the green treasures, resulting in a warm and genuine smile from their farmer friend.

"Yew two is welcome anytime. Come spring, y'all come back fer more plants now, you heah?"

As they returned home, Carly contemplated the significance of the complaint that Slaughter had served on them and the actions they needed to take. It was clear that their lives were becoming intricately entwined with a web of deceit, and they were determined to expose the truth.

The next day, Carly and Josie went to the Court House to gather information. Betty Arnett, the tax assessor's office employee, confirmed their suspicions about Slaughter and Riddell's inquiries into their property.

Carly showed her the legal description of the property that lawyer Slaughter had erroneously put on the complaint he served Carly and asked her to help him find the property on the map. She pointed to it without hesitation.

"Why are you able to show us that address so easily?"

"John Slaughter was here asking for information about this property and yours.

That information didn't surprise him. "So, both properties were sold for back taxes?"

She said, "On the same day."

The glaring mistakes in the complaint that Slaughter served on him prompted his next question.

"When Slaughter came in, did he seem distracted?"

"A young woman from another law office got hot and heavy with him. I considered throwing ice-cold water on them, but they left together."

"I guess you are familiar with everybody in the county. Who is Samuel Riddell?"

"Slaughter's mother's Christian name is Riddell. Samuel Riddell is John Slaughter's first cousin, living in the southern part of the county. Please don't deal with them because they're dangerous men. Both are well off, but many people are poorer because of it."

"Is this the correct office to check on deeds?"

"No, you need the County Recorder's Office, down the hall, on the left."

They continued their investigation, seeking information about property deeds in the County Recorder's Office. In this part of the courthouse, they met the stark manifestations of racism and segregation for the first time, a surreal scene they did not recognize enveloped them. It was their first time seeing the public restrooms, male and female labeled WHITE, and between the restrooms stood a water fountain labeled WHITE. Across the wide marble-floored corridor were male and female restrooms marked COLORED, and between the restrooms stood a water fountain labeled COLORED. No one cleaned the bathrooms marked COLORED often enough, which resulted in a strong, unpleasant urine odor that wafted for blocks.

Despite reading about segregation, Jim Crow, and racism, they barely touched the surface of the subject in school and had limited personal familiarity with such issues. There were no Black students, teachers, or janitors at their school. Race relations weren't taught in their world. All the schoolteachers must have received similar instructions about race. Most of their meager knowledge had come from their peers in school, giving them a one-sided racist view of a part of civilization. Having lived a reclusive and sheltered life since leaving home, they had not worried about the societal ills of Jim Crow and segregation. Carly remembered his first day in school. He met segregation's demonic emotions when he had to attend a school different from his best friend, Eva Lou. He discovered the disturbance caused by questioning the system when he asked why they had to attend separate schools. The principal administered stern punishment with his wooden paddle.

The name on the door's frosted glass window read: Mary Louise Rogers. A well-dressed lady of diminutive stature with wire-rimmed glasses, graying hair and a pleasing ready smile, helped as they explained the essence of their problem, and their need for information. Mary Louise stood silently looking at them, sizing them up, then put her index finger to her lips, denoting secrecy, turned and retrieved sheets of unfiled information from the back of a drawer of a filing cabinet. As she handed him the sheets, she made him promise never to tell anyone where he got them.

They were seated in the hall down from the County Recorder's Office, and happened, by chance, to see Mary Louise leave. When they checked it out, she had placed her "Gone to Lunch" sign on the door, which remained unlocked. While Josie guarded the door, he quickly collected the data about defrauded property holders. Just as he suspected, Carly discovered that Mary Louise had an unofficial file in the back of a drawer, not intended for public consumption. The sheets held a trove of information, including names, court dates, copies of deeds, dates of property sales, and documents of checks, much more than he had hoped for.

"There are names and information here that will make big news," Carly whispered, and remembered everything verbatim, then returned the sheets to Mrs. Rogers file cabinet, knowing this information would be explosive when he released it to the newspapers.

After leaving the courthouse, Josie and Carly went to the library to get cards to check out books. Carly thought the librarian came across as a stern disciplinarian. Josie suggested she wears hobnail boots to be so obnoxious. Would she show them more respect if they gave an SS salute? The librarian ran the library like her personal fiefdom. She would only allow them to register for library cards if their parents were with them. Carly tried to show her the recorded deed to their property, showing their names, addresses, and ages but she rejected the deed as a fake and refused to look at it, and she declined to register them. She walked away, unwilling to listen to their pleas. Carly changed his opinion of her. She wasn't a disciplinarian, just a mean bitch.

They left the library, climbed aboard their buggy, and gave Mary the reins. She had the unforgettable directions imprinted in her brain by now. As they neared Mr. Mallory's store, Carly remembered Mrs. Brownlie was getting books from the city library for him before Hell emptied its devils on them, and they stayed. She might not remember, but he could propose it again.

"Why don't we stop by Mr. Mallory's store and say hello? Maybe he isn't too busy."

Josie agreed with a nod and a smile.

They parked Mary in a good grazing patch in the live oak shade and walked inside. Mr. Mallory put aside a copy of the New York

Times when he saw them, greeted them, and invited them to sit.

Carly said, "I often see you reading. Did you go to college around here?"

Mr. Mallory said he received a BS degree from Duke and a master's from Columbia University. That information surprised Carly. He knew he sounded educated but hadn't suspected Mr. Mallory had such an educational background.

"What were your areas of interest?"

"At Duke, I studied math and physics with a smattering of philosophy. Later, while at Columbia, I switched to English literature. I authored my thesis on Milton's work and haven't regretted it for a minute. Oxford University had accepted me to study Milton, but, by golly, I met a woman and fell in love. My love for her was much stronger than my love for Milton, so I now own a general mercantile store. My wife died of breast cancer eleven years ago. She was the love of my life, and I didn't want to remarry. Now, what's your story?"

They were momentarily frozen. Carly had left them wide open for unexpected questions. Although reticent, Josie and Carly shared details of their earlier life, except for Winnie's murder. Neither of them wanted to discuss that tragedy with anyone. They skimmed over most of Papa's information, but Carly said he had created tremendous contentiousness and presented an obvious ongoing danger to them. Mama's story was brief. Mr. Mallory listened, offering no criticism, only gracious comfort, welcoming them into the community.

"This is a loving and forgiving community you can call home, and you'll never be sorry for doing so."

Carly looked at Josie before he continued. He decided it would be okay to ask for one more thing that involved Josie and him.

"Mr. Mallory, we've given you our information, and we ask you to please hold it in strictest confidence because we consider Papa a continuing grave threat to both of us if he learned about our location. I must confess to you, our actual surname is Turner," said Carly.

Mr. Mallory smiled and said, "I know."

Carly and Josie discussed their difficulty with the librarian at the Marston Library. They needed library cards to check out books, and Carly needed access to the books in the Law Room, but he needed a card to get them. Upon hearing Carly's motivation to enter the law room, Mr. Mallory became curious.

"Why do you need access to the Law Room?" Mr. Mallory wondered.

Carly recalled everything in precise, photographic detail that had occurred with Slaughter and Riddell. Taking notes, Mr. Mallory asked pertinent questions, which they answered.

"Where did you first meet Slaughter?" Mr. Mallory asked.

"In our garden, when he served me with the complaint."

"Where did you meet Samuel Riddell?"

"We haven't," said Carly.

Mr. Mallory closed the office door, turned back to them, and lowered his voice in a cautionary tone.

"By golly damn, you two are dealing with dangerous individuals in Slaughter and Riddell, and I want to warn you to play your cards close to the vest. Be careful who you speak to about this matter. You should know that those two thugs work for Judge David Hardie. A judge who is a powerful and crooked man with tentacles reaching statewide. Before playing your cards, you must ensure you have a royal flush. Get them dead to rights, and, even then, expect to be blindsided."

Carly sat. "Do you speak from experience?"

"Let's say I received an education, but by golly damn, they paid for it. Someday I may fill you in with the details."

"Are they dangerous in the sense of physical harm?"

"Yes, but I'm sure the thugs expect a walk in the park with you. Be careful. I'll be watching you two. Anytime you want my opinion on something, run it by me. I'm always available, never too busy, and in your corner."

After a long, contemplative moment, Carly spoke, quoting Carl Sandburg. "Do you have a criminal lawyer in this burg? We think so, but we haven't been able to prove it on him,"

Mr. Mallory smiled at him. "Carl Sandburg, *The People, Yes.*"

They referred to Carl Sandburg's last book poem, published at the height of the Great Depression, dealing with the perseverance of American society and customs.

"I can take care of the library cards right now. I'm the chair of the board of trustees of the Marston Library."

He pulled an official-looking folder from his desk and filled out two Marston Library cards.

"I'm speaking off the record now. We get complaints almost daily about the librarian, and no one wants to fire her because she has been there since they unloaded the last load of bricks to build the place, but we all want her to retire."

He smiled, they shook his hand and thanked him like he'd given them a birthday gift. "We know your time is valuable so if we come by to talk, remind us you are busy. We have no such time constraints. Thank you so much."

Carly thought Mr. Mallory had become a staunch friend. But had they said too much? Less talkative in the future might be a good rule.

27

1954
• • • • • • •

LEAVING HOME ON A DAY veiled in clouds and brushed by brisk winds, they rode to the library. Inside, they braced themselves for a confrontation with the librarian who had the bearing of a stormtrooper. Josie approached the card catalog while Carly went into the Law Room. After memorizing the Dewey decimal numbers, Josie moved to the stacks. Carly gathered the books he needed for reference and sat quietly taking notes in his spiral binders. Josie soon joined him with a stack of books. It wasn't long before they were joined by the book Nazi of the highest order.

"What are you doing in the Law Room?" she demanded.

They replied, in unison, "Reading."

"You are not adults; the library only allows adults here."

"Why?" Carly asked.

"This room is for adults only." She was getting pissy already.

"Where does it say, adults only?" Carly asked.

"It is an implied rule. How dare you question my authority."

"The board must approve that rule, and they wouldn't approve it." Carly reasoned.

"How do you know that?" the librarian queried.

"Because it would be a stupid rule," Josie interjected.

"I'm calling the police!"

"That'll be a big mistake," warned Carly.

"Why would it be a mistake?"

"Because it'll make you look like a fool," Carly boldly declared.

She stormed out, her flaming red face only a shade lighter than her hair. About twenty minutes later, she returned with two police officers.

An officer named DeLoach asked Carly, "What's the problem?"

Carly addressed the Officer. "I don't have a problem, Officer DeLoach. The librarian apparently does."

"They're unsupervised here, in an adults-only room, without a library card," the librarian now had taken a superior tone.

"First, there is no adult's only rule, no written policy," Carly said. "She only wants that rule. Second, I'm supervising my sister, Josie, who is trying to read while not disturbing anyone. I'm her legal guardian. Third, we have library cards. We hoped to research our projects and wanted to be in a quiet place to study."

"Why didn't you show your cards to the lady?"

"She never asked to see them. Besides, she is no lady. Here are our cards."

He examined their cards and chuckled at Carly's 'she is no lady' wisecrack.

The stormtrooper librarian, unwilling to yield, said, "Let me see those cards," reached over and snatched the cards from his hand. He ordered her to stand aside, or he would arrest her, and he grabbed the cards from her hands. The officers and the book Nazi saw that Carly and Josie had gotten their cards from Mr. Mallory, the chairperson of the library's Board of Trustees, and now the librarian was ill because she appeared like a fool. Carly smiled, remembering he had tried to warn her.

"It's good to see you kids so intent on getting an education," said Officer DeLoach, handing back their cards. He read the riot act to the librarian outside the door, but not out of earshot. After the officers left, she left them alone to study in the Law Room. When left alone, Carly copied verbatim the purloined information from Mary Louise's office for future reference.

*

Their impending visit to Mr. Mallory's store to discuss final matters was looming, and they were nervous and eager. Carly realized the far-reaching consequences the release of this information would have on many people's lives, but the crooks brought this to themselves. He was thinking how close he and Josie had come to being victimized and the nine families who lost everything to that pack of thieves.

The sun had not yet made its dawn entry, but it had painted with a wide brush the eastern sky with lovely but transient reddish-blue hues. Mr. Mallory arrived at his Mercantile Store when Carly and Josie rolled up. They asked him for a few minutes to run something by him and get his advice. He happily invited them inside. Carly got on with his discussion right away. He gave a photographically detailed outline of their discoveries, including the article he lifted from Mary Elizabeth's filing cabinet. He ended with a brief summary of the entire case they had made.

There were nine earlier cases involving the swindling of property owners who bought properties by paying overdue taxes. Two are going to trial.

Judge Hardie handled all nine cases and would be the judge in the two upcoming cases, one of which was theirs.

Slaughter was the Plaintiff's attorney, and his cousin Riddell was the 'discovered heir' in all nine cases and will be in the next two.

The law firm of Benson, Miller, and Chown were involved from the outset.

State Attorney General Elbert Boutwell and the Chief Justice of the State Supreme Court received checks from selling all nine properties.

As Carly and Josie deliberated the conclusion of their investigation with Mr. Mallory, they found themselves grappling with a pivotal question: who should they contact to navigate the legalities that lay ahead? The local law enforcement was a non-starter because of the Judge's influence over them. Since there were highly placed state officials, contacting the Attorney General's office was equally fruitless.

Mr. Mallory thought briefly and offered a solution: contact the FBI. He offered to make the call, but Carly, resolute in seeing the project through to its conclusion, said no, he had started the project and would complete the task.

Carly placed the call and talked with Special Agent Salter, who harbored a bit of skepticism until Carly's photographic memory impressed him. They talked for an hour. Special Agent Salter assured Carly the FBI would take the case forward.

With determination and a sense of purpose, Carly released to *The Marston Herald* and the Mobile newspaper a comprehensive summary of the information he purloined from Mary Louise's filing cabinet in the County Recorder's Office. It outlined all the perpetrators of the crimes: Judge David Hardie, John Slaughter, the firm of Benson, Miller, and Chown, Samuel Riddell, Attorney General Boutwell, and the State Supreme Court Chief Justice. The information was front-page headline news. When Carly saw the newspaper article, he knew several lawyers would be busy until the victims had received proper compensation.

Once the cleanup started, the stage was set for a swift operation. However, the wheels of justice, though set in motion, possessed an unyielding propensity to grind with exquisite precision. After the dust had settled from the arrest of Judge Hardie and his cohorts, Josie longed for a day of respite.

28

On a sunny morning following a hearty breakfast, Carly, Josie, Mary, and Jenna rolled out without a care in the world to see the river. The cotton fields stretched out, their white bolls ready for picking. The cornfields' diffuse golden-brown ocher hues were in beautiful contrast to the brilliant, cloudless blue sky. The brisk air and the harvest aroma accentuated the beauty of autumn. Carly recalled F. Scott Fitzgerald's quote, "Life starts all over again when it gets crisp in the fall."

Their excitement was palpable. Carly had not visited the river valley since long before leaving the farm, and Josie had never seen the river. A picturesque stretch of the river came into view, accompanied by its unmistakable aroma. Rivers, like the salty sea air at the beach, had captivating, distinct scents that were addictive. They had chosen a route that would lead them to Buck's Landing, allowing access to the river.

A thicket of blackberry briars, wild plums, and sassafras bushes with reddish-golden leaves flanked a narrow, rough path framed by ditches and hedgerows, leading to Buck's Landing, a clearing on the riverbank that was about three-quarters of the length of a football field. Centuries of human invasion had ensured the river landing lacked trees and bushes. Otherwise, a dense forest and thick underbrush edged the riverbank, shadowing slippery, dark mud banks. Nearing the clearing's upriver boundary, a large catalpa tree grew near the river's edge, close enough to the water to feed the fish with falling catalpa worms. They weren't actual worms but were the caterpillars of the beautiful Catalpa Sphinx Moth. The caterpillars ate only the foliage of catalpa trees.

A large sycamore sweeper was less than a hundred yards farther upriver from the clearing. A windstorm had blown it over years ago, but the tree was still alive, leaning horizontally just above the water, its branches extending above its trunk and branches below into the water, resembling a natural sieve. The moving stream's surface was swift and scattered submerged rocks broke its surface.

A junk pickup truck rolled up just as Josie and Carly got comfortable doing nothing. Will Cunningham, Jedidiah's brother and uncle of Carly's best friend from school, Arthur Cunningham, was driving. Carly knew Will was there to ensure they weren't from the sheriff's department.

The sight of Carly startled Will. "Carly Turner? Everyone thinks you're dead! I almost didn't recognize you. You've grown into a man."

Carly laughed and reassured Will that he wasn't dead, and he wanted to ask Will to please say nothing about him being there, but he realized he was weary of playing that game. Still, he was fearful of Papa finding them, and he shifted the conversation to a different topic. He asked about Jedidiah, Arthur, and their family. Jedidiah had died, and Will and Arthur continued to run the moonshine business, which was brisk. He predicted it would be over two years before Arthur could help because the sheriff had arrested him for moonshining and other charges. The judge sentenced him to three years in Kilby prison outside of Montgomery. Arthur's job would wait for him until he returned. Also, he was confident the moonshine business would remain brisk if the churchgoers continued to vote for the state to remain "dry."

Moseying along the riverbank, approaching the sycamore sweeper, they exchanged small talk as they were getting re-acquainted. Carly noticed an oddly shaped dark object among the branches reaching into the water beneath the sweeper. It wasn't unusual for things to get caught while floating downriver, and he mentioned it to spark conversation. Until they were close enough to see it no one paid much attention to it, but as they got closer, Will waded into the water, almost chest deep, and tried dislodging the object. But it was impossible. He needed help. Carly didn't want to wade into the cold water, but Will asked him to help. It required all the strength the two could summon to disentangle the massive object. Will complained that the mud coating made the thing as slick as owl manure on a banana peel, and he couldn't get a handhold.

At that point they made the shocking discovery that the object was a human body of enormous size. Carly helped Will wrestle it ashore, requiring all their combined strength. A thick layer of river mud covered every inch of the body, head to toe, a slippery factor that figured in the difficulty of getting it to the riverbank. Will estimated it had been in the river for weeks, if not months. They used buckets from Will's truck to wash the mud from the body with river water as best they could.

Turtles and fish had eaten away the soft tissues of the face, throat, scalp, and neck, leaving only the bare skull. Physical facial features would not be available to help identify the body. The soft tissues of the hands were also absent, but the bones were large and appeared to be those of a male.

Josie and Carly stood motionless, silent, stunned as they watched Will wash the body with river water and saw it at the exact same moment. Josie's expression showed that she shared Carly's dumbfounded realization. The corpse wore an Army jacket with Sergeant's stripes and the name "Stewart" above the right breast pocket!

Stewart's presence was a stupefying surprise, and Carly uttered an expletive louder than he intended. "I'll be damned!"

Josie whispered back, "You read my mind."

While watching Will wash the mud from the body, Carly thought it best not to mention their brief but scary encounter with Stewart. Josie looked at Carly, who shook his head, and she nodded in agreement. Mum's the word.

"Will, we are supposed to meet someone at noon; if you don't mind, we'll go now, and we can call the sheriff's office. I suppose they would be the authorities to notify," Carly said.

Carly called the sheriff's office from Mr. Mallory's store. He and Josie discussed the serially recurring body of Stewart, and both wondered if that story was finally behind them. They were bewildered how he had managed to wind up in the river. Did he drown or was he killed and dumped in the river? They probably would never know.

Jenna and Mary were glad to be home. In the western sky, scattered clouds were a beautiful red and orange when the sun was low on the horizon. Josie, Jenna, and Carly were in their favorite spot to relax, sitting on the giant limestone rock by the spring fountainhead. Attempting to forget the saga of Stewart, they talked, had a few grins, and forced themselves to relax. The redolent Arabian jasmine wafted through the air, and as light breezes stirred the Weeping Willow leaves, the setting sun cast dancing shadows across their faces.

✳

The Marston Herald published an interesting article approximately two weeks after Carly and Will retrieved Stewart's body from the river. The article stated a mud-covered male body had been found in the river, removed from the water, and turned over to the sheriff. The body was male, had not been identified but wore an old Army jacket with Sergeant's stripes and the name Stewart sewn on. An autopsy found that he had not drowned. He died from a gunshot to the chest, which penetrated his heart. The sheriff was asking for help in identifying the body.

29

·······

CARLY HAD NEVER CELEBRATED BIRTHDAYS, neither his own nor Josie's. Their parents were too self-absorbed, perpetually drunk, and sick to pay attention to such occasions. But as October approached, Josie reminded Carly that she had a birthday coming up, and since he didn't even know his own birth date, she suggested he pick a date for himself. He wondered how he could register his birth to receive a birth certificate. He knew he could always ask Mrs. Brownlie.

"Why is my non-birthday on your mind?" asked Carly.

Josie, in her growing empathy, explained, "I think you need a birthday gift. You've been wearing Winnie's clothes for so long and have outgrown them. Your shoes don't look like shoes anymore, and your threadbare pants will soon reach your knees like pedal pushers. You look like a ragamuffin. Let's go into town and get you some clothes that fit."

"You should think about what you want for your birthday and not worry about my absent birthday," he said.

A gratifying aspect of Josie's development was her growth as an empath. Their mother had been a terrible role model for Josie and him. Women were more highly evolved than men and had a higher essence of being, and he wondered how this could be. In their pursuit to improve men, they appeared to be on an eternal quest. Even Josie couldn't help it. Was it genetic? God bless women, he thought.

"Carly, why do you say that? You do a lot for me, but these are not gifts. We do these things because we're family. How else will we survive? Now, how about some new clothes?"

"God, Josie, you're growing up too fast. You drive a hard bargain!"

She didn't miss a beat when she said, "We're free all day today and tomorrow. Which do you choose?"

He breathed a deep sigh of resignation, but her sincerity touched him, and he said, "Let's go this morning, and we can also go to the courthouse to see if someone filed for our birth certificates."

As Carly scrambled to leave, he was thinking about their imminent educational events. After working on their reading assignments, they awaited their next meeting with Mrs. Brownlie. His thoughts were pleasant for a change.

Josie and Carly found a watering trough and a hitching rail for Mary near their shopping destination. Josie stayed in the buggy while Carly walked to the bank to withdraw cash to cover his shopping. Welfare checks arrived the day before, and men were waiting in long lines for the bank to cash them. Carly took a position in line to wait his turn. Four men were ahead of him. The other three lines were longer, so he was okay. The lines were slow to move, but Carly made his cash withdrawal.

He walked with Josie, window-shopping at the men's clothing stores. They saw some nice men's clothes in Cromwell's. Carly was self-conscious about his appearance because his pants were over six inches too short, and his shirt was at least two sizes too small. He had no belt and desperately needed a haircut; his hair reached almost to his shoulders. He looked like Josie had described him, a cast-out ragamuffin from the streets, white trash. Despite looking at them when they entered, no one offered to help. Being well dressed, Josie didn't share his self-conscious feelings and walked over to the nearest clerk and asked for help.

"What do you want?" the sales clerk asked in a nasty tone as she leaned on the cash register with her elbow propped up and her hand under her chin. Her name tag read Nellie Holmes, Sales.

"To buy some clothes if we aren't disturbing your sleep."

Josie refused to suffer sass from anyone.

"You go somewhere else. We don't need your kind in here."

"And what do you mean by our kind?"

"White trash."

"So, you recognize us as your equals. Let's go, Carly. We'll find a decent place that will take our money. We don't need her crap."

Another men's store a few blocks up the street looked promising, Bradford's Men's Club. They saw a demo of their bright clothing line as they peered through the window. A young man named Dan Rothman, Sales Associate, greeted them as they entered. Probably twenty years old, he engaged them in intelligent conversation as he led them to men's clothing. He studied math and chemistry at the university but had included enough pre-med courses if his dreams remained mixed.

First, he measured Carly's height, who stood 5 feet 11 inches.

There were scales on the floor near the wall, and Carly asked Dan to weigh him.

"Of course."

Carly stepped on the scales.

"165," Dan announced.

With Dan's advice, Carly chose pants and shirts, dress, casual, and work. Then came the "accouterments befitting a gentleman of your age." When Dan made that pronouncement, Josie chuckled. Dan helped Carly choose belts, one black and one brown, and an everyday work belt, underwear, socks, two pairs of shoes, a pair for everyday and a dress pair, and a wallet. Carly had neither owned a wallet nor such beautiful clothes. He had been using a rope for a belt for over a year and had used the rope to tie his splint in place when he broke his leg.

Carrying bags of clothing, Carly was merry as they approached their buggy, but Josie appeared subdued. Carly let her be, knowing everyone has down days, but since this safari was her idea, it was unusual. As they passed Cromwell's, Carly looked in the window and saw Nellie, the rude salesperson, still leaning on the cash register. They entered the store, and as he walked past Nellie, a polite older gentleman asked if he could help. Carly stood with his shopping bags. "We'd like to speak with the owner or manager, whoever is available."

"I'm Richard Cromwell, the owner; how may I help?"

"We came to your store earlier to buy clothes, and your salesperson treated us rather rudely. She told us to leave because you don't want 'our kind' here, explaining that 'our kind' was white trash. She made a rude mistake."

He and Josie held up the bags of clothes.

"Who treated you like that?"

"Nellie Holmes, she is leaning against the cash register."

The owner was quite apologetic and asked that they please return in the future. Carly secured their shopping bags in the buggy, preparing to go in search of birth certificates. Josie asked if it would be okay if she remained in the buggy while he checked on the birth certificates.

Carly said, "Of course, it'll be boring, I'm sure."

Carly hoped to cut his visit to the courthouse short, but several people were waiting when he arrived. After an hour, he finally reached the window and asked for his and Josie's birth certificates, and files showed that they each had a recorded birth certificate.

He wondered aloud, "Who the hell was ever sober enough to file for our birth certificates?"

The clerk had him fill out the short form for each of them. He paid two dollars, and she said the certificates should arrive in one week. With so many unknowns in his life, he found it reassuring to have proof that he'd been born.

Carly returned to the buggy to find Josie sleeping. She was leaning smartly to one side, and when he straightened her a bit, he felt her face flaming hot with fever.

"Would you like something cold from the soda fountain?"

Josie said, "No, I want to go home."

He pulled her coat around her neck and face, clicked his tongue to Mary, and they headed home. Josie wasn't responsive when they arrived home. On the verge of panic, he picked her up and moved her into her bedroom. After covering Josie with a sheet, Carly put a gown on her. Even though he covered her with the sheet, the incident embarrassed him. Josie remained unresponsive, which was unusual since she was a light sleeper. Their house had nothing that could combat fever except water. Carly applied cool water to her face and neck with a wet cloth, letting it evaporate. An earlier tenant had left a bottle of rubbing alcohol in a cabinet, so he mixed it with the water, hoping it would enhance the cooling effect. He didn't have a thermometer, but he assumed her body temperature was too high if she felt hot to his touch. That scene continued for another two hours. Josie's face was still hot, she remained unresponsive, and Carly was increasingly anxious, but he wasn't sure how to get medical help at this late hour.

The hospital must have an emergency room, but he felt going out in the chilled night air wouldn't be the best decision. A doctor was unlikely to make a house call, especially at that late hour. He would address these problems later, but now he must deal with the current pressing issue. He thought Mrs. Brownlie is home. I'll ask for her help.

He didn't want to leave Josie alone, so he carried her outside to the waiting buggy. When they arrived, he saw the light in Mrs. Brownlie's study. Carly hurried to the door, and he heard her coming.

"Carly, are you okay?"

"I beg your pardon, ma'am. I'm desperate for your help. Josie is in our buggy, and she has a high fever. She doesn't answer when I call to her; I can't rouse her."

Mrs. Brownlie rushed outside in her bathrobe before he could finish speaking and headed to the buggy much faster than he thought possible.

He shined the flashlight beam on Josie so Mrs. Brownlie could see.

"Carlton, can you get Josephine inside at once while I call a doctor?"

"Yes, ma'am. Where do you want her when we get inside?"

"Place her on the living room sofa. Un-bundle her so she can lose body heat."

Carly placed Josie on the sofa. Mrs. Brownlie was talking to a doctor. As she put down the phone, not on the hook, she brought a thermometer and a watch and instructed him to record her temperature, pulse, and respiratory rate. He recorded her pulse, 128 beats per minute; respiratory rate, 40 and shallow; temperature, 104.4°. He gave the paper to Mrs. Brownlie, who repeated it to the doctor.

She whirled. "We must get her to the hospital. I'll drive to the front door. Bring her to the car and put her in the backseat!"

Carly carried Josie to the backseat of the car, crawled in the back, and held her hand while sitting on the floor. They made the trip to the hospital in record time, uncertain about what lay ahead.

30

The hospital, devoid of an emergency room, admitted Josie in haste. The nurses placed Josie on a gurney and rolled her into room 106, conveniently located near the nurse's station. They were setting up an oxygen tent on the bed in a flurry of activity. The doctor had already arrived; he introduced himself, Dr. Martin Fischer. The nurse recorded Josie's vitals while Doctor Fischer examined Josie, listening with his stethoscope and thumping with his fingers and hand.

"She has severe pneumonia. We need to get a chest radiograph as soon as possible," Dr. Fischer said.

Besides ordering blood and sputum cultures, he instructed the nurses regarding intravenous fluids and antibiotics. Josie was on the gurney awaiting transfer to the oxygen tent bed and suddenly had a grand mal seizure. Nurses held her jerking body to prevent her from falling from the gurney. A nurse grabbed her jaw to keep her from biting her tongue, and another inserted a wedge-shaped rubber object into her mouth, serving the same purpose. A nurse identified a syringe with phenobarbital as she handed it to Dr. Fischer, who injected it intravenously. The first signs of decreased seizure activity came within minutes, but as the phenobarbital concentration increased in her blood, the seizure activity decreased further and soon stopped, but Josie didn't respond to the painful procedures, and Dr. Fischer looked worried as he spoke with the Charge Nurse, who left the room and quickly returned with equipment wrapped in a white outer cloth.

Doctor Fischer talked with Mrs. Brownlie, who suggested he include Carly in his discussion. He addressed both, "Her high fever, seizure activity, and non-responsiveness to painful stimuli raise the question of central nervous system pathology, such as meningitis or encephalitis. But pneumonia and high fever can cause similar signs and symptoms without brain pathology. We have no other clues. I need to do a lumbar puncture, often called a spinal tap, take a spinal fluid specimen, and have it analyzed. If the results are normal, I can relax. Do either of you have questions?"

"Is that a dangerous procedure, Doctor? Is there a danger of damaging the spinal cord?" Carly thought inconsolable worry was one of Mrs. Brownlie's cherished hallmarks.

"No, I will insert the needle lower in the spine, well below the tip of the spinal cord. This procedure is safe, and it will give essential information. There is nothing more you can do. You should go home and get some rest. The results will be back before the morning rounds.

Carly and Mrs. Brownlie went to the Admission Desk, and he informed her that Callaghan was the pseudonym he and Josie had been using.

"I need your advice. Using it made us feel safer and more secure, but we are safer now that we own our home and farm. Would it be okay to register her with the Turner name?"

"Carly, if it relieves stress and anxiety, use it. I think you will resume using Turner soon. I have already told Mr. Mallory of your identity, and he said he had solved the little deception already, but he would go along with it if you needed it to keep you safe."

He registered Josie under her name, Josephine Turner.

Mrs. Brownlie gave him a long embrace inside the hospital's entryway, and he found it comforting, but he suspected it was also for her as he held her hand.

"I'm sorry I put you in such a predicament at this hour. I could call only you, and I was desperate, so you got the short straw. After Josie's well, I'll put fail-safe plans in place. I always learn from my screw-ups like this."

"Carlton Turner, you and Josie are dear to me, and I'll be there for you. Do you understand?"

"Yes, ma'am, and you don't know what that means to me."

She embraced him again, and they walked to the car together. The unknown vehicle was lurking behind them again. When they arrived at her house, the tailing vehicle stopped and parked on the side of the road, apparently waiting. When Carly and Mary started home, the car turned around and sped away. He thought it was suspicious, but probably a coincidence. But he did not believe in coincidences.

When he arrived home, he stopped to check his mailbox and found the latest edition of *The Mobile Press-Register*. Carly had subscribed to the newspaper, taking advantage of their drastic cut-rate three-month offer, and he enjoyed the paper from the front-page headline to the last page of want ads.

The prolonged adrenaline surge kept Carly awake, and he fed Mary and Jenna. Now more at ease but still anxious, he remembered he hadn't eaten. Sitting at the table and nibbling leftovers from last evening, Carly wasn't hungry enough to fix more food. A beautiful, relaxing piano concerto by Brahms was playing on the City University radio station.

A front-page article in the newspaper followed a recent thread in the news about the murder of a Black teen boy in Money, Mississippi. The 14-year-old boy from Chicago, Illinois, Emmett "Bobo" Till, visited relatives in Money, a small town in Mississippi. Someone kidnapped Till, shot him in the head, and tied a cotton gin fan to his neck with barbed wire. Days later, the sheriff's deputies pulled Emmett Till's body from the Tallahatchie River. A white woman, Carolyn Bryant, claimed Emmett wolf-whistled at her, leading to his murder. The article said the sheriff had arrested two white men for Emmett Till's murder: Roy Bryant, Carolyn Bryant's husband, and John Milam, Roy's brother. That news made Carly feel sick, almost ready to vomit. He knew the likelihood of a conviction in Mississippi was nil. When would this damnable Neanderthal bullshit stop?

✳

Mrs. Brownlie and Mr. Mallory joined Carly standing near the nurse's station. Dr. Fischer had arrived much earlier and was assimilating new data from the lab studies done during the night. Carly looked better dressed than ever in his new clothes, but his grimace betrayed his deep worry. He was silent while the adults talked, mostly about nothing. Besides discussing the weather and cotton crops, they also discussed the stalled Korean truce talks. Their obligatory conversation ended when Dr. Fischer came over to them.

He said, "Results of the studies show no evidence of meningitis. The chest x-ray reveals bilateral lobar pneumonia. Josie had persistent chills and fever throughout the night. She's not sweating and is still not awake, not talking, but I hope to see an improvement in her mental status soon."

It didn't relieve Carly.

"Thank you, doctor. Last night you said her pneumonia was likely a common type. Could it result from a less common type of bacteria or even a virus? Do you think you'll have to add another antibiotic?"

"Excellent question. The present antibiotic, penicillin, should be the drug of choice. If it proves otherwise, I shall regroup and make whatever changes are necessary. If there are no other questions, I'll give a progress report this evening."

31

AS HE TURNED TO GO into a patient's room, Dr. Fischer stopped beside Mrs. Brownlie and asked, "Is the young man who asked the erudite question Josie's brother?"

"Yes, he's Carlton Turner, an orphan, raising Josephine, his sister, alone," she said. "He and Josephine are so young, but they recently bought a home on 640 acres of farmland. He believes he's not exceptional, though he is a genius and is studying *The Great Books of the Western World.* But Josephine, a remarkable girl, is also a genius. They're inseparable; he'd die for her if the situation demanded. Both have endured hardships beyond imagination, yet their achievements have been remarkable. Perhaps, when you have a moment to spare, you could spend some time with him?" she continued, "It would be worthwhile for Carlton. He's at an age where guidance and role models matter. The medical profession would do well with someone of their potential."

He smiled and nodded, then headed into the patient's room. Mr. Mallory stood near the nurses' station and Carly moved closer to him.

"Mr. Mallory, thank you for coming. I'm grateful for your support. I feel there's a rainbow of hope now. I trust Dr. Fischer; my sister should receive excellent care."

"By golly, you're wise to have that opinion, my boy. Marston is fortunate to have a doctor of his caliber. After graduating from Yale Medical School, he interned at The University of Pennsylvania School of Medicine and came to the Deep South to practice medicine. Talk with him if you get a chance. You should share interesting conversations. When I heard Josie was here, Carly, I wanted to come. Your sister is a fine young lady. We are all pulling for her and you. Everyone appreciates the positive mark you're making on our little burg. You both left a positive impression with Mr. Olson at the scrap metal yard, the two cops at the Marston Library, and the librarian."

He laughed.

"Your sister is making her mark, and it's good. Mrs. Brownlie is the staunchest supporter for you both."

*

Josie was still unresponsive after 48 hours post-hospitalization, and her fever was abnormally high. Dr. Fischer said her pneumonia was caused by atypical enterococcus bacteria not sensitive to penicillin, necessitating an uncommon antibiotic, chloromycetin. It wasn't in wide demand and was unavailable locally or even in Atlanta. Still, the hospital pharmacy had ordered it from the manufacturer Parke-Davis pharmaceutical company in Detroit. However, the wait for it to arrive was over seventy-two hours.

Dr. Fischer said, "Her immune system and the antibiotic will need time to fight the bacterial infection."

It was a long, intense twenty-four hours of insomnia and anxiety for Carly. Dr. Fischer again met with them near the nurse's station to give Josie's progress report.

"There is no improvement in Josie's overall status: instead, her condition has declined. She continues to run a fever, is still unresponsive, and requires medication to control seizure activity. I'm sorry, but I must tell you, I have placed her on critical status. We are at the mercy of the swiftness of the modes of transportation between Detroit and Marston. Parke-Davis is aware of our critical situation, but I am fearful the package handlers are neither involved nor committed to speed along the way. I will repeat the spinal tap to assess the critical issue of central nervous system involvement."

With heavy hearts, Mr. Mallory, Mrs. Brownlie, and Carly looked at each other.

"We completed a face-mask modification for administering oxygen instead of the oxygen tent, which should increase blood oxygenation to the brain, helping her mental function. Any questions?"

They slowly shook their heads in reply.

Mr. Mallory and Mrs. Brownlie gathered with Carly outside the hospital entry following the progress report. The sun was bright, causing them to squint but it was sharing the sky with towering cumulus clouds. Since Josie's illness, Carly had been alone and isolated, so he was eager to talk with anyone, even if it was about the weather. As his depression became more pronounced, Mrs. Brownlie poured comforting thoughts upon him, but they had no lasting impact. Besides being his sister and soulmate, Josie was synergistic with his heart and soul.

*

Mrs. Brownlie worried about the potential impact of anxiety and depression on Carlton's health and decided he needed relief. She remembered his mentioning his "best friend, Eva Lou" when he got in trouble asking why they couldn't go to school together. Although Mrs. Brownlie thought that was the correct given name, Eva Lou's surname escaped her if he even gave it. Perhaps she would drive out that way to see if she could find her to have her visit him, which might help with his depression.

She drove among the thinly scattered houses in the community and selected two that she thought could be Eva Lou's house. Approaching the first, she could hear children playing inside. She knocked, and an attractive young lady, about thirteen or fourteen, with a captivating smile and beautiful tan complexion, welcomed her. Her beautiful blue eyes and sweet ethnic dialect made her stand out. Mrs. Brownlie introduced herself and asked if the young lady was, by chance, Eva Lou. It caught the girl off-guard and surprised her when she called her name, but Eva Lou smiled.

"Yes, ma'am, I am. How can I help you?"

"Eva, I'm in contact with your dear friend, Carly Turner, who wants and needs to see you. Do you remember Carly?"

Eva Lou was taken aback and leaned against the door frame for support. She appeared dizzy and faint, and her breathing was rapid. She was finding it difficult to process information, fumbling with words as she invited Mrs. Brownlie inside and asked her to sit.

"Yes, ma'am, I remember Carly. He was the best friend I ever had, and still is, I hope. People in these parts thought they were dead..." Her voice trailed. "With that awful murder and stuff at his house, folks thought he and his little sister, Josie, were dead. The sheriff even made it official when he announced they both were dead, but they found no bodies. Nobody searched for them after that announcement. But I knew they were alive, and everything would be all right one of these days."

"You were right, Eva. Carly and his sister, Josie, are alive, but he longs to see you. Josie is gravely ill. Carly is not handling it well and is severely depressed. He's having a challenging time. Will you please consider coming with me to visit him?"

Eva's excitement was now palpable. In one graceful motion, Eva stood upright, almost leaping off the sofa. "Let me get some of my things together. Should I plan to stay for a couple of days? I'll need to tell my Mama, so she won't worry."

"Of course. You're such a dear girl to do this. If you would like, you may stay with me."

"Ma'am, I've prayed that this day would come. I never lost hope, though it's been a long time. Help me, sweet Jesus! The wait is now over. Carly, sweet Carly, I have missed him so much. Every day I think of him."

Eva Lou collected her belongings, and within minutes she was ready to leave, but she went to the kitchen to tell her Mama she was leaving. "Mama, my friend from before we started school, Carly Turner, is having a tough go of it and has asked to see me. Josie is in the hospital in a bad way. I'll go over to see him with Mrs. Brownlie, his teacher. I will stay a couple of days, hoping he can find some peace."

Dottie Mae screamed, and loud talking followed for a prolonged period. "Eva Lou, don't you go over there and shack-up with that boy.

Don't you do it. If you have sex with him and you get pregnant, don't you never come back here. Ever since you got outta high school you been wanting to go out and have sex. Well, I'm done with you. Don't come back here no more."

Dottie Mae came into the living room and tried hard to convince Mrs. Brownlie all was okay. But she understood enough of their one-sided conversation to know Dottie May's reaction was far from supportive of Eva Lou's decision to visit Carly.

"Lord have mercy, Mrs. Brownlie. I have always believed those two would show up again, and I thank my Jesus they have. So, you want Eva to visit them for a few days?"

"Yes, Mrs. Swain, she can stay with me, and I'll keep her safe." She knew she must use whatever persuasion was necessary to get the deed done.

"It's okay if it's not too much trouble for you. Eva Lou seems happiest since before those two had to start in separate schools."

"Thanks, Mrs. Swain. Josephine is critically ill, and Carlton is so depressed. He, too, will soon be in the hospital if this doesn't work to cheer him up."

Eva Lou walked out of the kitchen with her head held high, picked up her bag, showed Mrs. Brownlie her radiant smile, and spoke sweetly, "I'm ready to see Carly, Mrs. Brownlie."

While driving to Carly's house, Mrs. Brownlie filled Eva Lou in on Carly's life, including Josie's grave illness. Eva didn't show any anxiety over her conversation with her Mama. Instead, she was eager and unflustered, her anticipation building as they approached Carly's house. Mrs. Brownlie said to Eva Lou, "It's best not to mention Winston's death unless Carly is the first to bring it up since he's not ready for that discussion." Mrs. Brownlie turned onto Carly's well-trimmed driveway, creeping toward his house. She hadn't visited his house but had often driven past. Eva's face was close to the windshield, her hands on the dashboard, and her feet bounced on the floorboard at the front edge of her seat. Like a young girl, she was in such a state of excitement that she could barely contain herself. Before the car stopped moving, she took an exuberant step out of the car, followed by a sprint to Carly's front door. After knocking, she pranced eagerly. While waiting for their meeting outside her vehicle, Mrs. Brownlie stood, holding Eva Lou's bag.

When Carly opened the door and saw Eva Lou, he stood speechless and immobile in the doorway. Eva Lou squealed and raced into his arms, and they collided in a clumsy, uneasy embrace for long minutes, appearing beyond happy. Her heart warmed by the reunion Mrs. Brownlie handed the bag to Eva Lou. Her mission was done.

Eva Lou said, "Mrs. Brownlie, can I hug you?"

The happiest she had been for countless days, Mrs. Brownlie embraced Eva, said she would see her at the hospital the following day, excused herself, and drove away.

32

EVA WAS ALMOST AS TALL AS CARLY, her posture radiating poise and grace. Her smile was almost magical, and Carly recalled her eyes, gleaming like blue sapphire. She appeared before him, a vision of unparalleled beauty.

Their conversation flowed effortlessly, hours melting away like the morning mist. They took a late lunch break, and Carly, eager to hear about Eva's experiences, was engrossed in her stories. As they sat, Eva held his hands, and his mind harkened back to their pre-school days when Eva would hold his hands, and he cherished the warmth of her touch.

After their leisurely lunch, they took a short hike up the slope and sat on the limestone rock by the Weeping Willow. The lovely aroma of the Magnolia blossoms wafted so gently on the breeze. Eva placed her head on his shoulder, and Carly held her tight, and their words flowed freely. Neither wished for the day to end.

Their next stop was the barn, where they tended to Mary, and Eva's curiosity led them to the hayloft, where the chickens nested, laid their eggs, and roosted. Carly talked about surviving the big hurricane and asked how she fared during the storm. "It was the worst thing I've ever experienced, and I hope never to be in another one," Eva said.

As the day progressed, their laughter filled the air, leaving them exhausted. Eva lay on the sofa with her head in Carly's lap, humming a familiar catchy tune, and he asked about the song.

She said, "The Black Blues singer Huddie 'Lead Belly' Ledbetter wrote "Good Night Irene" when he was in Angola prison in Louisiana."

"Sing it," Carly said, "I remember how you used to sing to me before we started school. You have a beautiful voice."

Her voice was beautiful, reminiscent of a professional Delta Blues singer.

When she finished, Carly said, "Eva, that was great, your voice is as lovely as I recall. How did you learn so much about the Blues?"

"Mama loves listening to Blues artists on the radio. I reckon I asked millions of questions about Blues, and I remembered all the answers. Soon, my friends considered me an expert on all kinds of Blues. I love listening to Blues, male and female, especially Black Blues artists. I enjoy Howling Wolf, W. C. Handy, and Charlie Patton, but my favorite is Son House of Mississippi. He is a great artist but doesn't seem to catch on, so he isn't so famous, but I'll bet he will be. Son House taught Muddy Waters, and I like him too. And I like Mamie Smith because she opened the Blues for women with her "Crazy Blues.'"

"Wow, Eva, your knowledge of the Blues is impressive." Carly was amazed.

As they prepared for bed, Carly suggested the bedroom where she could sleep. In a tight embrace, she placed her arms around him and pulled him close. Fearing that this magic moment would dissipate like a will-o'-the-wisp, he held her slim and beautifully proportioned body without moving or speaking. He was aware of her graceful curves that had developed over time.

"Carly, Sweet Carly, Goodnight. Sleep tight. See you tomorrow."

"Good night, Eva. Sleep well. See you in the morning."

The sweet embrace left him speechless. Eva was sure to be sound asleep, but Carly remained wide awake! He exited the back door and went up the slope to the spring. The millions of sparkling diamonds in the velvet sky and the beautiful quarter moon, partially obscured by clouds, registered in his mind as extra special. He sat by the spring, listening to the lapping water. Then he heard footsteps, initially giving him a start. But the steps were light.

He called out in a subdued voice, "Eva Lou!"

Eva answered softly, "I was hoping you were here. I want to sit with you until I'm sleepy. Is that okay?"

"Of course. Come, sit beside me."

They sat together, holding each other close, their heads on each other's shoulders. Eva admitted, "I probably shouldn't tell you this, but I went to your bedroom looking for you, and I'm almost disappointed you weren't there." She chuckled.

Carly looked up.

She said, "Carly, can you believe we're 14, still teenagers? Do you think it was luck that put us together again? Why do you suppose we are brought together while we're still teenagers, and not when we're adults? I'm not complaining, just wondering." They sat and talked until the wee hours as if time were fleeting. Eventually, Eva said she was getting sleepy, and they walked back to the house, hugged, and went to their bedrooms.

With the break of dawn, they were up early. After breakfast, Carly asked if Eva wanted to go with him to the hospital. He explained the visits had not involved seeing Josie, only getting progress reports from Dr. Fischer.

Her smile was lovely as she said, "I'd love to go."

Carly smiled, embraced her, and soon they were underway.

Mr. Mallory was already at the hospital when they arrived. Mrs. Brownlie joined them and looked stunning in a cobalt blue dress. She talked to Carly and embraced Eva Lou. Mr. Mallory was talking with someone in a small waiting room. When Dr. Fischer joined them, Carly introduced Eva Lou as his dear friend who came to visit Josie.

Dr. Fischer began his report by reviewing Josie's vital signs, which were unimproved after the improved method of delivering oxygen. Her mental acuity had not improved, she was still unconscious, and her fever remained unchanged. That report brought worried looks all around.

"I'll give the next report in 24 hours. Are there questions?"

Carly asked, "Does she continue to have seizures?"

"Yes, she continues on phenobarbital, an anticonvulsant."

Carly intended to ask about visiting hours at the nurse's station, and Eva Lou was at his side. Before he could ask his question, a formidable white woman behind the desk, not a nurse, bellowed for Eva Lou to get out. The woman didn't ask Eva to leave. She screamed, demanding her to get out as if there were a fire.

"Why?" Carly demanded.

"Hospital rules do not allow her kind here." Still bellowing.

"Why?" Carly pressed.

"Because she's different."

"Why?"

"She's Black, that's why," continuing to bellow.

"But you are morbidly obese, which makes you different. Yet you're still here."

She was astonished, but then she became angry that anyone would question her authority, especially about the race issue. She was in charge, and no one should question it.

"Get Dr. Fischer on the line." Mrs. Brownlie had become entirely heated by the discussion.

"Why?" the bellowing woman demanded.

Mrs. Brownlie was angrier than Carly had ever seen.

"I want to speak with him now."

The woman vehemently refused. Carly had an overwhelming buildup of anger that was out of character. He banged his fist on the desktop, the sound echoing through the hallways, his face flushed red, and his anger-filled tone wasn't mistaken as a request when he demanded, "Call the Hospital Administrator and call Dr. Fischer NOW!"

Mr. Mallory approached, sensing the urgency, and joined the fray. "I am on the hospital's governing board. Get the administrator here now! And call Dr. Fischer now!"

The nurse was dialing, as was the Leviathan woman. It wasn't long before Dr. Fischer and the administrator appeared almost simultaneously. Mrs. Brownlie, Carly, and Mr. Mallory cornered the two gentlemen, and when Carly spoke first, his voice was shaking with anger.

"We have two problems. Eva is my lifelong friend, and she is visiting a patient, my sister. That woman," Carly pointed, "ordered Eva to leave because, and I quote, 'hospital rules do not allow her kind in here because she is Black,' but there are no rules to that effect. I ask the administrator for clarification."

They looked at the administrator and waited, but he was silent. Mr. Mallory spoke in a loud voice. "Well?"

The administrator appeared ill, pale, and withdrawn. He admitted he had acted without authority when he told the staff to discriminate against people of color from coming on the premises.

"Discriminate?" To say Mr. Mallory was less than pleased would be an understatement.

"Well, sir, we should not encourage coloreds to come here." said the wimpy administrator.

That racist statement sent Mr. Mallory into enraged agitation. "I suggest, no, by golly damn, I demand, you make it known to all personnel that discouraging coloreds from coming to this hospital is a non-policy. This hospital is a tax-supported institution, and Blacks pay taxes too. Understood? The hospital board has made that the official policy."

"Yes, Sir." The administrator was on the verge of fainting, vomiting, or both.

Mr. Mallory continued. "You will not give authority to egos in the future. Is that understood? The head nurse is the charge nurse on this floor, and she may delegate someone to be in charge in her absence, but never the ward secretary. Is that understood?"

The administrator was almost beyond resuscitation. Prominent beads of sweat were streaming down his face. "Yes, sir."

And Mr. Mallory wasn't finished. "Give the ward secretary the rest of the day off without pay. There should be a program to combat racism, and if not, make one."

When Dr. Fischer asked about the second issue, Carly had cooled, and he said, "Resolving that problem made the second issue non-existent. If that were hospital policy, I would have asked you to transfer my sister to Mobile General Hospital."

"I would have transferred her," said Dr. Fischer.

Everyone breathed and joined in a communal sigh of relief.

Mr. Mallory wanted to meet Carly's friend. Carly introduced Eva, and Mr. Mallory gave her a warm, welcoming embrace.

After the tumultuous morning, Carly and Eva returned home. They had a light breakfast, and Eva wanted to see more of the farm. Carly whistled for Jenna, and the three walked past the barn into the woods. Autumn's vibrant colors painted the landscape. Squirrels were out in numbers, chattering warnings that the intruders weren't welcome near their homes. They walked almost an hour to the edge of the giant swamp, where Carly and Jenna often came to watch the waterfowl. A colony of Great Blue Herons nested on the swamp's opposite side. He and Jenna had wandered into their midst occasionally, and when they aroused the herons, their cry could be mistaken for a barking dog. One could quickly identify the Herons in flight as they held their necks in an "S" shape with their feet straight behind them.

They sat on the trunk of a downed tree and watched Jenna sniff every blade of grass and every tree trunk in view. Her keen senses alerted her of the essence of the squirrels at the base of most of the trees. In the distance, probably one hundred yards, a black bear was tearing into a widow-maker snag to get to the insects and grubs. They watched until it left to wander elsewhere.

They ambled back home, rested by the spring and Weeping Willow. They lounged and talked until the last vestige of visible light from the sun flickered beyond the crest. The air was brisk, and Carly asked if they should go inside.

"No, not yet. It's a perfect day, and I'm not ready for it to end."

"You say that after the incident at the hospital?"

"I say it because of what happened at the hospital. You went to battle for me, and no one else has ever done that. I will never forget what you did. It was my perfect day."

After darkness had settled, they moved inside, sat on the couch, and talked about various random subjects. They held each other, not speaking, and Carly said, "Would you sing for me? You have a beautiful voice. That was a beautiful Blues song, "Goodnight Irene" you sang recently."

Eva said she would dedicate a song to him because, over the years, she sang it when overcome with loneliness for him. She put her heart and soul into an old Spiritual, "Sometimes I Feel Like a Motherless Child." As the intensity of the lyrics flowed, tears streamed down her cheeks, and Carly felt Eva's bared soul. When the song ended, Carly's heart ached. He gave in to tears, and then sat silently, thinking how different their subjective lives had been. As they embraced, Eva said her tears were for him because he was a motherless child.

Carly watched Eva's angelic face as she sat silently with a faraway look in her eyes and a hint of a smile, and he wondered what the future held for them.

33

CARLY INFORMED EVA HE was going to the hospital to check on Josie and she asked if she could join him. They left after breakfast, hoping to get to the hospital during visiting hours.

Upon their arrival, they were met by Dr. Fischer at the nurse's station, who, with a somber countenance, gave a brief update on Josie's condition. In concert with his sad, worried countenance, the brevity of his statement was more than a suggestion that Josie's prognosis was grim. It was a declaration. Josie had not improved; she was weakening. He recommended that Carly delay his visit, possibly until the next day, pending the results of the bacteriology culture on her spinal fluid. Carly knew Dr. Fischer was withholding information, but he was too apprehensive to press for the complete report because he feared the truth. What did the microscopic study of the fluid show? He would wait another day. Maybe the new antibiotic would have arrived in the interim.

Carly asked if Eva would mind him checking out a book at the library. She was happy to do so, saying, "May I join you? I've never been inside the library. It should be interesting."

That statement begged his question, "Why haven't you been inside the library?"

Her response was laden with the weight of racial injustice: "I'm black. They refuse to help us, and we can't check out books. I want to learn how to find books with the Dewey Decimal System. Maybe you will teach me someday."

Carly empathized with the racial obstacles Eva faced daily. "Of course, I'll teach you. I'm sorry these racist obstacles confront you at every turn."

When they arrived at the library, Carly was distrustful of the book-Nazi librarian. She had left Josie and him alone since they got cards from Mr. Mallory. But taking Eva into the library might be an entirely different problem. The incident over the library cards was personal. This event was staring in the face of the fixed, morally binding customs and habits of ethnic groups in the Deep South, and the librarian had the full force of the legal and judicial systems backing her. However, to their relief, they weren't met with the hostility they had feared. Greatly relieved, they went about their business at hand.

While Carly selected books, Eva went with him, he took the opportunity to teach the Dewey Decimal System, which she learned quickly. With newfound confidence, Eva picked two books and asked if Carly would check them out. He asked if she would like to get a card, and she was delighted when the card was issued without fuss.

Carly took longer to find his book, and she encouraged him to speed up.

"Why?" he asked.

"I have to pee!" she volunteered.

"Go to the restroom." Carly advised.

"There are no restrooms for Black people, only for whites."

That bit of information shocked Carly. They hurried to the courthouse, where there was a Colored restroom she could use, which was closer than the hospital and much closer than home.

Back at home, by the Weeping Willow, Carly apologized for the restroom situation at the library. He was recognizing the racial problems she had faced every day of her life. Eva dismissed his apology as unnecessary.

"Societal injustice isn't your fault, Carly. There's a restroom for white people, but I'm not ready to fight that battle yet."

"But it's society's fault if it can happen unchallenged."

"Don't worry, Carly. I don't like it, but I've grown accustomed to a lifetime of that treatment."

That statement struck at the core of his being; Carly couldn't accept her resignation: "Eva, please, never grow accustomed to something morally, ethically, and socially wrong! Although there are laws supporting segregationist and racist practices, they do not make the practices right! We must all stand against such unjust laws and practices. Our churches support Jim Crow practices and are often guilty of concocting the laws that enslave our part of the nation. I wonder if it's better in the North."

Their conversation delved into the issue of racial divide in society.

"Carly, sweet Carly, my uncle Rodney has returned from years of living in the north. He said it's called de facto racism in the North, and it's as insidious as legislated racism here in the South. I asked him to explain it to me. He said there were no laws for segregation in the North, but prejudice and racism were everywhere. He said that in the South, we know when somebody will stab us in the back because we have laws telling us when somebody will stab us. But, up North, he was always surprised who was about to stab him because it's sneaky racism. I have no experience with de facto racism, so I'm uneasy about it and looking for answers. But he told me that 31 states in the USA have Jim Crow laws. So, it isn't just the South that's guilty. Northern states are also, but it makes the news in the South, not the North."

After silent thoughtfulness, Carly asked Eva about her dreams and aspirations. "What do you want to do with the rest of your life?"

"I'd like to be a nurse. But I also love literature, so maybe I could be a teacher. But I don't have any money, and education is expensive. So, I haven't seriously pondered either."

"Set your goals high, and we'll work to make them happen. You could be an exceptional nurse or a brilliant teacher. Choose whatever you want, and we will make it happen. Don't just settle for something based on convenience."

Eva and Carly's hands were interlaced as they talked throughout the evening and recalled their childhood. The half-moon was bright, reflecting off the shiny leaves of the nearby magnolia tree, beckoning them to the spring. They sat on the limestone rock and held each other in silence. The incessant lapping of the water on the rocks was almost hypnotic. Carly talked with Eva on random subjects to keep Josie's desperate crisis from drowning him with sorrow. The moonlight filtered through the Weeping Willow branches, revealing snippets of their faces. No hindering clouds threatened. The night was perfect. Finally, as sleep approached, Jenna led them to the house, where they walked to the hallway, embraced, and went to their bedrooms.

Carly was cudgeling an idea that he would like to ask Josie about. But he was not able to discuss it yet.

He contemplated asking Mrs. Brownlie if she would consider offering Eva the same program she planned for Josie and him. He was confident Eva could do the work. She was brilliant. Of course, he knew when they started, the program would be a complex and challenging path for all three. Whether she would have the desire was unknown. On his way home, he would go by Mrs. Brownlie's house to present his idea.

In the morning, they were up with the sun. Carly extended an invitation to Eva, wondering if she would like to join him on a ride to the hospital again to check on Josie.

"If it's okay, I want to stay here today. Several things will keep me busy, and I promise I won't get bored," Eva replied.

"I want to swing by Mrs. Brownlie's on my way home, but I shouldn't be late," Carly said.

Dr. Fischer was at the nurse's station when Carly walked in, ready to give another succinct report. Josie remained unchanged, and her condition remained critical. He said he was expecting the new antibiotic the following day. Carly was severely depressed following the report and, after saying goodbye to Dr. Fischer, headed to the buggy where forever loyal Mary was patiently waiting. As they left town, his thoughts about Dr. Fischer's words were heavy, leaving him in a state of profound despondency. He listlessly gave Mary the reins, wherever she wanted to take him, until he remembered his intention to go by Mrs. Brownlie's. Mary seemed to be a mind reader. She had turned left at Mr. Mallory's store instead of right, and they were in front of Mrs. Brownlie's house within a moment. Before Carly could even knock, she opened the door and welcomed him. He still marveled how she always anticipated his visits, but he'd solve that another day.

Carly sat, ready to discuss the purpose of his visit, when Mrs. Brownlie became serious-minded. "Carly, have you any good news yet?"

Unable to bear breaking down in front of her he reassured her, mentioning the arrival of the new antibiotic the following day.

Her spirits lifted slightly, Mrs. Brownlie pivoted to a new topic. "Carlton, I want to tell you, after spending time with Eva Lou, I have come to realize she has a brilliant mind eagerly yearning for education. She's a remarkable young woman, and I want to provide her with the same program I have in store for you and Josie. I thank my angel for sending Eva Lou to me. I see Eva as the embodiment of the basic tenets of the grant, the integration of a Black student into a predominantly white university. Integration of the university was a primary requirement for funding the program while providing a world-class education for each class of candidates in the program. I'm enthusiastic about this program, but it will create a societal change of tsunami proportions, still less socially antagonistic than attempts have been at other locations. This program means more to me than I'm able to express. It's the culmination of a lifelong dream."

Carly could barely contain his excitement. What had just happened? "Mrs. Brownlie, this means so much to us."

"She'll receive the benefits of an outstanding education, a priceless gift. But first things first. I'll speak with Eva in a couple of days, and then start a rigorous military-style boot camp." She chuckled and continued. "I intend to have all my students properly schooled in English, diction, enunciation, pronunciation, grammar, and eloquent choice of words when speaking and writing. Eva needs this, but it will be open to all, and all should attend for moral support. If you get my drift."

Indeed, he got her drift, loud. Carly silently recalled Eva's words, "Help me, Jesus!"

She asked what Carly needed from her.

"Uh, I was going to; I wanted to check the testing schedule. When do we start the testing?"

"We'll begin when Josie has recovered. But Boot Camp will begin ASAP. So, you and Eva Lou can start quickly, and Josie can start when she is well enough to withstand the stress. I'll come out to your place the day after tomorrow to explain everything to Eva Lou to make sure she understands what the program expects of her and agrees."

"We'll wait to hear from you. I'll share the fantastic news with Eva, including the news of the Boot Camp. I'm sure she will be as delighted as Josie and I."

Josie's illness continued to burden Carly on his way home, but he couldn't wait to share the splendid news with Eva. As Mary pulled to the house, he bailed out of the buggy while it rolled. He hurried inside and found Eva had washed all the bedding, curtains, and clothes for Josie and him. Just outside the utility room, strung assertively across the yard, were two long clotheslines of clean washing, drying by the warmth of the sunlight and a gentle breeze. She greeted him with a smile, and Carly experienced mixed emotions. Eva was energetic and had done all this work for Josie and him. Although delighted, he was exhausted and depressed.

When Eva was at a point to rest, she sat with her hair covered by a piece of cloth from a pillowcase, tied in a perfect tricorne headdress. She was as beautiful as a photograph of a posing model. She asked about Josie, and Carly explained the report continued to be brief, but Josie had shown no improvement. Still, he held on to the glimmer of hope that the new antibiotic due the next day might bring a much-anticipated positive change. Then, he excitedly recounted what Mrs. Brownlie had said, that she wanted to include Eva in the same program he and Josie would receive. Eva's response was unexpected. She was suddenly silent, and her countenance shifted from cheerful and energetic to somber, perhaps even angry and sad.

Carly picked up on the sudden mood change. In his ignorance, he had imagined the new information would thrill her. Acknowledging his misjudgment, he said, "Eva, I've offended you, you're upset, and I'm so sorry. Please tell me what I need to do to make this right."

"No, Carly, there is nothing to forgive or do. This opportunity you talk about sounds incredible. But right now, it overwhelms me. It terrifies me. This program puts me in a world that feels foreign and makes me uncomfortable, but if I want to be with you, I'll need to grow and adapt to your life and your world, which differs from the world I've known all my life. But please be patient. I need time to think about this. and I know it's an opportunity that comes around only once in a lifetime, but it'll be an earth-moving change for me, like an earthquake. Can I even meet the program's expectations? Carly, sweet Carly, I'm so deeply touched by your generosity. I can't thank you enough for this chance for an education. It's unbelievable, but I'm beyond frightened."

"Eva, I realize now I should have discussed this with you. But Mrs. Brownlie just sprang this idea on me minutes before I came home, and I was so excited, I came on like a freight train. I was unaware this would be so scary to you, and I promise never to pull a stunt like that again. Nothing irreversible has happened, and it won't. Take your time as you make your decision. Whatever you decide, you will remain my dearest friend."

Eva continued her work, much subdued, in deep thought until she finished. Then, she sat with Carly, held his hand in both hers, her gentle touch but a whisper, and looked into his eyes as she spoke softly, "Carly, I want to do this, and I'm saying yes, but I need to discuss this with my Uncle Rodney. You understand this is a major decision affecting my life, family, and friends. Nothing like this has ever happened in my family, and I don't want to announce it after the fact. This undertaking isn't a big deal to you, but it'll be like a volcano erupting in my little world and life. Do you understand what I'm trying to say? I don't have the words like you do, but I'm trying."

"Eva, I understand exactly what you're saying, and I can't tell you how pretty your words are to me. I share your fears because I'm terrified about what lies ahead for us. Will this program make our future easier? I don't have the answer to that question. Still, education should improve our lives, amplify our contributions, and offer our children opportunities for a better life even greater than we can imagine. I insist you talk with your Uncle Rodney. I envy you the chance to do so."

Eva leaned over and embraced Carly, holding him close. "I want to go to my uncle's house this afternoon. He's the most educated of all my kin. He's traveled a lot, and he's worldly. Maybe that's good, but he's offered me a lot of advice. He lived up North for a long time, but he says he returned when the tug of his roots became too strong. I can talk with him, and we can come back in time for supper. Or we can go tomorrow. It's up to you."

Carly smiled warmly, "Let's go as soon as you're ready." He embraced her and whispered. "Your words are prettier than I could ever hope to speak."

1954
·······

THEY HEADED TO EVA'S Uncle Rodney's house underneath the vast expanse of towering, fluffy white clouds, locked in a celestial battle with the radiant sun, vying for control of the heavens. Yet the weather forecaster had predicted impending rain. Eva was quiet, in deep contemplative thought, while Mary trotted, guided by her own instincts. Carly, uncertain, asked if he should leave, wait in the buggy, or go with her inside.

She was quiet while thinking and finally responded. "Can you come to pick me up tomorrow before dinner? Is that okay?"

"Okay. Should I come in to say hello to your uncle?"

"No, I'll talk to him privately. He'll be fine."

"Okay. See you tomorrow before noon." Carly kissed her on the cheek, climbed aboard, clicked his tongue, and Mary briskly responded. As he waved goodbye, a fleeting moment of joy washed over Carly, which was swiftly replaced by an overwhelming sense of desolation. Loneliness was beginning to permeate his mind, and soon, it would be overshadowed by a creeping sense of depression. Upon returning home, he led Mary into the feedlot to graze. He put her feed in her trough, and she could eat when she wanted.

Carly sincerely longed for a talk with Winnie, in his moments of solitude and despair. There was an incessant yearning to hear Winnie talk to him, connection that even death couldn't sever. He had questions he wanted desperately to ask. But Winnie's silence remained steadfast. He pondered the mysteries surrounding Mama's pregnancy after Tillie's passing, a puzzling tale with unanswered queries. What did Winnie discover about that delivery? It remained an enigmatic episode. There was no baby, and no one spoke of it. Winnie said Mama had withdrawn into her bedroom, weeping daily for months. Carly couldn't fathom how, but he held onto the hope that someday, the missing pieces of the puzzle might come to light.

Carly walked up the slope to the ridge and sat on the limestone rock. While sitting for hours, he listened to the murmuring of the rippling water. Yet solace eluded him. The sun dipped lower toward the horizon, appearing and disappearing, playing hide and seek with the gathering evening clouds. It turned them to a beautiful reddish orange, suggesting the adage of weather lore, "Red sky at night, sailor's delight. Red sky in morning, sailor's warning." Carly recalled Shakespeare spoke of this in *Venus and Adonis.*

In the barn, Carly talked to Mary, scratched her, and brushed her down. Mary's happiness was palpable, she enjoyed the attention, and a bit of her happiness passed to Carly. He marveled at how Mary could share her magic.

In the tool room, Carly remembered the meticulously stacked lumber, and thought it would be an excellent time to re-stack it, satisfying his curiosity about why someone had taken such care in stacking it.

He carefully re-stacked the lumber into a different but equally neat pile. At the central core of the lumber pile, he uncovered a tarp that covered an unknown object.

Carly carefully removed the tarp and three layers of quilted padding covering the object, revealing an exquisite chest. The chest was approximately five feet tall by four feet wide and three and a half feet deep. He brushed off a thin layer of dust and wiped it down with a cloth. Extensive inlay woodwork adorned the front and sides of the chest. The master carpenter had embellished the chest with many gemstones that appeared genuine. It was a work of art, but Carly was oblivious to the chest's story, its origin or its purpose. He resolved to research its history, discover its master craftsman, and unravel why someone needed to conceal it in that house. The chest boasted five drawers, but a lock was near the right end of the middle drawer with a weirdly shaped aperture. He wondered where he would ever find a key to unlock that drawer.

Nevertheless, he decided to move the chest inside while he researched it. However, when he tried to move it, he was confronted with its immense weight—several hundred pounds. How on earth would he manage to get that thing moved?

Soon the sun was setting, and darkness was settling in, but he was in neither the mood nor temperament for sleep. Overwhelmed with loneliness and melancholy, Carly missed Josie and Eva and their sharp wit and vivacity. He spent a dark, empty night tossing and turning, listening to the whippoorwill's call. Carly found solace in anticipation of the forthcoming morning.

Following breakfast, he harnessed Mary and rode to the hospital, hoping Josie was awake. Dr. Fischer began his report by reviewing Josie's vital signs, which improved after twenty-four hours of receiving a second antibiotic and the improved method of delivering oxygen. "Her mental acuity has improved, but she isn't up for visitors yet. But Carly, you may see her for a few minutes. She began oral fluids for breakfast and will start a soft diet in the morning if it's tolerated. I'll give the next report in 24 hours. Do you have questions?"

Carly asked, "Will you continue phenobarbital as an anticonvulsant when you discharge her?"

"Yes, she will continue on an anticonvulsant until we are sure she isn't prone to epilepsy."

Carly was pleasantly surprised when he saw Josie propped semi-upright on pillows, making an effort to smile. He gave her a long hug, though she had a terrible cough. Carly told her he was heading to the library to gather reading material for her, and Josie's pleading was weak and hoarse, "Oh, please! Bring me something to read."

Carly returned to Josie's room in the hospital with several books that he felt she would enjoy. She appeared more alert and was a bit more talkative, and Carly was much more optimistic about her complete and prompt recovery. He was always too quick to look at the glass half-empty when considering Josie's health.

Carly left the hospital and rode to Eva's Uncle Rodney's house, where the cacophony of barking dogs announced his arrival. He climbed out of the buggy and massaged Mary's neck and withers. Eva attacked him from behind when he turned to head toward the house. She was happy beyond words. Her hugs and kisses were non-stop. Carly thought she must have gotten Uncle Rodney's approval.

"Should I talk to your uncle Rodney?" Carly asked.

"No, he's fine."

Eva hopped in the buggy, Carly followed suit, and they started home.

Eva had brought a couple of filled paper bags, and Carly asked what she was bringing home from her Uncle Rodney's. "Oh, nothing. Just some stuff Uncle Rodney gave me," she said, appearing mysterious. Before leaving the yard, Eva hurried to his side of the buggy seat and turned to face him while lying across his lap.

"Carly, sweet Carly, I missed you something terrible. I had a lonely night, tossing and turning. How is Josie?" Carly noted her slight reversion into her cute ethnic speech.

Carly's heart warmed at the mention of his sister. "She's better, more alert, and will soon be eating soft food."

"I'm so relieved she's better. That's a prayer answered. I want to ask you something?"

"Of course. What do you want to ask?"

"Would it make you nervous and put you off if I told you I love you?"

Startled, he sat up straight.

"Now I've ruined it, haven't I?" Eva looked scared, on the verge of crying.

"No, of course not, Eva! Those words, coming from you..." stuttered Carly, "are the most beautiful words I've ever heard. Josie is the only one who has ever told me that."

"Carly, I love you so much."

"And I love you, Miss Eva Lou." He was feeling a kind of love that rarely strikes, but when it does, it's like lightning, only once in a lifetime. For some, maybe never. It blinds while imbuing one with a sense of boundless mastery of the universe. Now he was head over heels in love. It was okay to be in love, even if they were young. There was a phrase he'd heard since his memory dawned but never knew its meaning: "puppy love." He assumed he shouldn't make this into something serious because it most likely was puppy love. He wasn't aware of a test to make that distinction.

"And, Carly, we will be together forever?"

"We will be together forever."

She continued to shower him with hugs and kisses along the way. Mary was driving. He had long ago relinquished the task of navigation to her. As always, she delivered them safely home.

Before they relaxed at home, Eva carried the filled paper bags into a room apart from their bedrooms. Trying to hide them well as she stashed them, she saw a condom fall from one of the paper bags. Quickly picking it up, she wanted to squirrel it away before Carly saw it, but he asked, "What are you hiding?" At the zenith of embarrassment, she must explain. "Uncle Rodney wouldn't believe we weren't having sex and sent me home with two paper bags filled with rubbers for sex. Lordy Carly, if we used all these, you would be in a wheelchair." They laughed together, and Carly calmly said, "You know, Eva, wheelchairs aren't all that bad. Given your prediction, I wouldn't mind being in one. I think we should consider it." They laughed some more, then sat by the spring, relaxed, and talked.

"I talked to Uncle Rodney, and he was so excited. He asked what this would mean for his favorite niece, and I told him what you had told me before I was a part of the program and that we would do testing. I explained the courses would be with Mrs. Brownlie and the professors at City University. He couldn't believe his little niece could be so lucky, nor can I. This program will be harder than anything I've ever been up against, but I'm willing to give it my all, and with you and Josie helping me, I won't fail; I can't fail, and I refuse to fail. My family and my entire community are counting on me.

So, if I fail, it won't be just me. I will let many people down. Do you understand, Carly?"

"Of course, Eva."

*

Carly returned to the hospital the following day. Eva asked to stay home. He went by the library again, replenishing Josie's book stash.

Josie was sitting in bed at the hospital after brushing her hair and applying makeup, and the nurse had helped change her gown. She complained of pain and tenderness in her right calf and thigh and said she had shown it to Dr. Fischer the previous evening, but he didn't think it was a concern. But it had become more painful overnight. At Carly's urging, Josie agreed to show it to Dr. Fischer again. It was refreshing to see she was no longer neglecting her vanities, a sure sign of progress. They embraced. Then he listened to how everyone mistreated her and how her life was miserable. She was weary of lying in bed, only getting out to walk to the bathroom. The food was terrible, and only Dr. Fischer came around all day to talk.

"Dr. Fischer and I have interesting conversations when he visits. He enjoys general practice but will return to the university for a residency in internal medicine. He wants to save a little money before he returns to academia."

"Sounds as if you two are an item. Did you ask Dr. Fischer for a date yet?"

She grinned, threw a pillow, and called him stupid. He noticed she grimaced from the pain in her leg when she tossed the pillow.

"He wants to talk with you as well. But why should he bother to talk with an idiot?" They laughed.

"Has the doctor been here yet?"

"No, not this morning. Dr. Fischer may be late today; he delivered a baby late or early, depending on your perspective. It was about 3 AM."

"Did the nurse tell you that?"

"No, he stopped by after the delivery. I was still reading, so he stopped to visit and chat."

"This sounds like it's getting serious. Have you told Dr. Fischer how old you are?"

"I told him I'm 21. I'm not sure he believes me, but at least he pretends."

They laughed hard, which ended with Josie having a long, hard coughing session. The nurse came in, gave her medication, and soon the cough had calmed but wasn't gone.

It was refreshing to see Josie laughing and teasing, evidence she was on the mend. Carly had watched as she had been so ill over the past weeks; the image was burdensome and affected his psyche.

Now he could relax, but he asked her where she was learning this stuff.

"From that huge stash of Harlequin Romance trash, you gave me. Where else?"

"What is a Harlequin Romance? I don't even know what they are. Should I burn them?"

"Too late. I've read all those smutty stories. What an education. I suggest, though, don't upset me. The gendarmes would be interested in the smut you peddled to me." She cackled with laughter when Carly slapped his forehead and groaned. It was delightful to see her regaining her frolicsome personality.

*

Dr. Fischer was discharging Josie from the hospital, they left home with time to spare, and they didn't want to be late. When Carly and Eva arrived at the hospital, cars filled the hospital parking lot, and they parked at the far end of the lot on a grassy plot where it met the tarmac. As they were about to climb out of the buggy, an obese, filthy man who looked to be in his 40s approached, dressed in greasy jeans and an unbuttoned long-sleeved plaid shirt in dire need of washing. His exposed hairy belly, which had long ago exceeded critical mass, was now bursting gigantic and spilling over his belt. Unshaven, with oily, red hair and a weathered face, his maker had decided he didn't need a neck and positioned his head on his shoulders. Holding a half-burned cigarette in his yellow-stained fingers, his other hand carried a paper bag with a Mason jar tucked inside, the trademark of a moonshiner's product, too familiar to Carly. Jenna gave a long, low growl, and the hackles stood on her neck, shoulders, and back as she crouched, alerting Carly that trouble was afoot.

When the uninvited visitor was about a yard from the buggy, he barked in a gruff, loud voice, almost yelling, meant to intimidate. "Yew, boy, git yore Black bitch and git yore asses out of this town, yew heah?"

Without a word from Carly, Jenna was in the air as quick as a lightning flash, hitting the man in the chest and knocking him backward and off balance, his head making a loud thud when it struck the tarmac. His jar of moonshine splattered when it hit the hard surface, and its familiar scent filled the air. His yelling and rolling on the tarmac had brought on asthmatic wheezing and a severe bronchial cough. Dazed, he hardly knew what to do.

"Call off yore dawg. He's gonna keel me!" Hack, hack, cough, wheeze.

"Yep, looks like she might," Carly called her off.

The man was slow to climb to his feet and was limping from the scene when Carly spoke.

"Before you leave, you owe the lady an apology, and if I think you may try to run, I'll sic my dog on you again."

The man was slow to answer, appearing to assess his options, and finally said, "I'm sorry."

Carly said, "No, you address her like the lady she is."

"Ma'am, I'm sorry, I was rude. Please fergimme."

"Get patched up if need be." He had no visible wounds.

They waited until the man had left the parking area, and Carly suggested they take a stroll downtown until they were sure there were no further threats, and he could calm down. Eva concurred. They strolled until they came to a peaceful park and sat to pass the time.

"Carly, I know you don't like people saying nice things about you, but this is the second time you've gone to battle for me, and he said mean, hurtful things. I have nothing but love for how you handled that."

"Eva, I had nothing to do with that. It was Jenna's idea, and I was brave enough to stick around when I saw she would win. A couple of minutes longer, and you and Jenna would have been on your own!"

She laughed, striking his shoulder, causing him to feign injury. He hoped the maudlin crap had ended.

They walked back into the hospital and through the lobby. He was aware of unusual stares from people he had seen daily since Josie's admission, but he thought no more about it. No one was at the nurse's desk when they approached it, apparently giving meds. He was confused when they walked to the open door to her room and looked inside. Her bed was empty. A hospital housekeeper scrubbed the room's contents, and she stripped the sheets from the bed. Maybe she was getting a study elsewhere. But nothing else was present in the room. Where had they moved her, and why? He returned to the still vacant Nurse's desk, propped on the desk, and Eva waited beside him.

The Charge Nurse came out of a patient's room and saw him leaning against the desk. She took a few steps toward him, appeared to have forgotten something, and whirled to dart back into the patient's room. She stayed for long minutes. Carly was becoming aggravated, but because Eva was present, he waited patiently. He saw the nurse sticking her head out of the room and slowly edge into the hallway, moving hesitantly toward the desk. The nurse never made eye contact. She fixed her eyes on the tiled floor. She slowly walked behind the desk, perfunctorily fiddling with some paperwork, occasionally glancing toward Carly but kept her back to him, never speaking.

Carly finally asked, "Where did you move my sister, and why?"

The nurse stood erect as if struck by an electric current, staring at the wall away from Carly, not moving. Slowly turning to face him, she walked woefully to stand before him, but try as she might, she couldn't speak. When he saw tears streaming down her cheeks, his brain at once perceived the answers to his questions, and his world ceased to exist. His legs gave way, his vision dimmed and darkened, and he slid alongside the desk to the floor. No words could make Carly's life whole again. He could neither talk nor hear. He sat on the floor with his back propped against the desk, his head bowed with his chin on his chest as people huddled around him, but he wanted to be alone and far away.

Why couldn't they understand? He had nothing to submit, no more to give. The so-called God of love had sucked the very life from his body and soul, and he had nothing further to offer. He sat with a vacant mind. An unbearable, indescribable pain was beyond measure in his soul. He felt a subliminal tugging in his mind, and he thought he needed to do something, to finish something, but he couldn't grasp the detail. After an eternity, he thought someone was calling his name, but he couldn't focus on answering. The voice was inside an echo chamber and kept calling. Eventually, he grasped they were trying to talk with him, and he slowly recognized the voice of Dr. Fischer. But an answer required much more effort than he could summon.

Someone or something was lifting him. Now they were moving him through the air. There was little awareness of anything else, except he wondered if he were dead. He could only hope. Something lowered him to a soft surface. Was it a bed? A female voice was crying in his ear, calling his name, and saying she loved him. A sharp pin stuck in his upper left arm, followed by a burning sensation. Was that a rattlesnake bite? Soon, he was aware of nothing, not even aware that he was alive. When he awoke, it was dark, eerily dark. He didn't know where he was and needed to speak with someone. Within moments of waking up, a lady with a hat like a nurse turned on a dim night light and came to his side, spoke pleasantly to him, and he felt a needle stick followed by the same burning sensation as before in his upper right arm. Soon he was relaxing, and then he lost consciousness again. When he next awoke, it was daylight.

Looking around, it looked like a hospital bed. Confused, a nurse call-button gadget was on the bed handrail, and he pressed it for the nurse.

He was trying to make sense of the strange situation when a nurse came into the room, maybe twenty-five, no older than thirty. She was pleasant but refused to answer his all-important question. "Where am I?"

"Dr. Fischer will be in soon and answer your questions," she said.

Accessing only vague flashes of the incident at the nurse's station made him wonder if it had been a hallucination. Maybe God was testing him or playing tricks on his mind. Where was he now? Carly couldn't remember when he left the hospital or where he had gone. Why was this a hospital bed instead of his bed?

He lay in a half-awake state of confusion, like a half-remembered dream, afraid to allow himself to realize his memories fully, but his efforts to shield himself from his thoughts were futile. In his groggy state, he thought he could control his mind and direct them to pleasant memories, but there were no pleasant memories.

Someone opened the door to enter. Facing the window, away from the door, Carly did not acknowledge the visitor. The person came closer, placed a hand on his shoulder, and a female voice whispered, ever so softly, "Carly." Who was it? Was it a nurse? But he thought he recognized her voice. He slowly rolled onto his back and looked toward the source of the voice. Even with difficulty focusing, he recognized Eva's beautiful blue eyes and angelic face. They embraced, afraid to let each other go, and Carly felt safe in her arms. Both were sobbing silently and uncontrollably.

"Did she die?" Carly finally whispered.

Eva kissed him and whispered, "Yes, Carly, my dear sweet Carly. Josie passed away." Her voice choked.

The scene from the previous day was becoming real, but he had many questions, as did Eva. Carly was in shock and disbelief, and he was finding it difficult to understand that his sister, his soulmate, his best friend, was no longer with him, was dead. Before he and Eva could talk, Dr. Fischer knocked and walked toward his bed.

Dr. Fischer looked tired, his eyes were red and swollen, and he needed sleep. His white coat partially hid his wrinkled shirt that hung untucked in his trousers, and his melancholy countenance expressed marked sadness. He stood without saying a word and appeared to be searching for the proper words. In lieu of words that wouldn't come, he leaned down and hugged Carly. Unable to control his emotions, Carly sobbed. Dr. Fischer held him for long minutes, finally releasing him, and said, "Carly, I'm so sorry this has turned out so badly. She was responding to the new antibiotic and was rapidly returning to herself."

Carly asked, "Dr. Fischer, do you know her cause of death?"

"I have an opinion, but it cannot be final unless we do an autopsy. Josie had developed tenderness in her calf and thigh, which I mistakenly dismissed when she first mentioned it to me. Then, yesterday morning, she said you told her to show it to me again. It had become much more pronounced, typical of thrombophlebitis. I at once ordered heparin, an anticoagulant or blood thinner. Before the nurse could administer the heparin, Josie died suddenly, I believe, from a large Pulmonary Embolus, or blood clot, to the lungs. I believe it was a massive saddle embolus, a large clot at the bifurcation of the main pulmonary artery, blocking blood flow to both lungs. Death was instantaneous."

Carly said, "Is it possible to get an autopsy?"

Dr. Fischer said, "Yes, we can, and I'm glad you asked that question because it could be beneficial for treating future patients. Pulmonary emboli are uncommon in pediatric patients, and deaths in pediatric patients from pulmonary emboli are rare. She was on total bed rest for days, a perfect set-up for blood clots in older patients, but not for young people. If this is a saddle embolus, I will write a paper, perhaps alerting other doctors to the tragic possibility. We will go ahead with the autopsy today. If you feel like going home, I'll discharge you this morning."

"Thank you, Doctor. I prefer to go home."

"I want to caution you; this isn't over for you. Josie was more than a sister to you. She was your soulmate, and, in many respects, she was like your child. Your grief will be lengthy and intense because you deeply loved and cherished your sister. You may experience overwhelming sadness, crying spells, and feelings of emptiness. You will find engaging in regular activities challenging and have trouble sleeping and eating properly. We expect these entities in the normal process of grieving. I want to see you in my office in one week. Meantime, you must sleep seven to nine hours each night."

He shook Carly's hand and turned to speak to Eva. "Eva, you'll endure grief and sorrow and experience the same symptoms as Carly. Call me if you need help during this process, either for you or Carly. Please come with Carly to my office when I see him in one week."

"Thank you, Dr. Fischer. You are so very kind. This tragedy will take the wind from our sails, but we must be strong and forge ahead for Josie's sake. God, I'm going to miss her." She wept.

Dr. Fischer looked at both. "What I have to say next is directed to you both. With grief, depression is a familiar guest, and that invites anger. Be careful and alert to detect these changes. Don't start blaming each other for things that don't go well. You need each other more now than ever. You must depend on each other, help each other, and, above all else, listen to each other. Spend time talking about Josie, don't make her off limits in your talks. Celebrate her life by talking about her and laughing with her."

He hugged Eva and slowly walked from the room.

35

1954

· · · · · · ·

THE AIR REMAINED STILL with the weight of Josie's passing. Carly had found little solace within the four walls of his home, trying to lose himself in thought and the occasional book. The absence of Josie rendered him hollow, a silhouette of a man but no heart. His appetite was scant, eating one or two small meals daily and was beginning to look meager, but he wasn't concerned.

Observing from a distance, Eva finally ventured, "Carly, let's walk up to the spring once the sun is up. I would love your company."

The eastern sky lost its reddish-blue hue after the autumn sun first peeked above the horizon. The briskness of the morning wore off, and Eva and Carly made their short walk toward the spring. Neither was enthusiastic about going up the slope to relax beside the Weeping Willow because the world was oblivious to their grief. The slope seemed sacrosanct, unfitting, and taboo for the two to ascend so soon after Josie's passing. Carly had only one uninterrupted thought on his mind. After a bit of light conversation, Eva wanted to steer the subject to factors affecting their lives. "Carly, I've been thinking about the series of tests we'll soon take. How do you feel about them?"

"I hate sitting on my butt several hours a day, but the tests are not pass-fail, which takes the pressure off, no anxiety of failing." Carly spoke unenthusiastically.

"But I disagree because I will have failed if my scores are low. Do you understand?" Eva's voice held a note of vulnerability. She then unraveled her pent-up nervousness because of her past—the hardships, the racial injustices, the emotional battles.

"I understand what you're saying, but I disagree. First, they won't tell us our scores. They're relevant only to those deciding our level to begin studies. Second, we're in this together, and we'll help each other every day, all the way. Don't worry that you won't measure up. Eva, you're brilliant. Mrs. Brownlie and the professors will teach you to activate that ability, and you'll be off to the races. Tell me what else is bothering you. I don't think it's the testing alone."

"Carly don't take this as an 'oh, woe is me' shit speech because it's a simple truth. I'm Black, and I've only known Black schools. I went to all-Black schools with Black teachers in Alabama all my life, as you know. We didn't have things like white kids did in school. Fifty of us shared five or six textbooks. We didn't have chalk. We had chalkboards, but what good were they? My uncle told me how Jim Crow laws prevented our Black teachers from obtaining proper educations."

Carly nodded, and Eva continued.

"Our friends and classmates were sometimes criminals. A boy stabbed a kid with a big knife in our classroom. We watched him die on the floor in an enormous pool of blood. The deputies arrested three boys for burglary. The sheriff arrested two boys for rape. That doesn't count the rapes that the girls didn't report because they thought it was natural for boys to rape them. Some girls didn't even resist when the boys raped them because they thought it was natural. These are shadows of Jim Crow, the lack of resources, and a history of emotional battles."

Carly was astonished. He looked at Eva's face with a piercing stare but didn't know what to say.

Eva continued, "I've never been in a class with white kids, which may scare me initially. Our teachers never taught us how to speak because no one taught them to talk. My Mama taught me to speak, and she speaks like she has a mouthful of butter. Uncle Rodney made me see the terrible effects of Jim Crow and its poverty. I could keep talking for hours, but you get the gist of what I'm saying, don't you? I'm not just worried. This idea of sitting with all of you in classes scares me shitless! I don't want to fail, and I'll do everything in my

God-given soul not to fail, but if everything is so far over my head that I'm drowning from the time I'm out of the chute, then I may not make it, but I'll die before I fail."

Carly, a world of emotions behind his eyes, pulled her into an embrace. "Eva, I'll help you if you help me. No one guarantees us success just because we're white. But you have qualities I can only dream of because you've had a Mama guiding you. Everything that makes us successful isn't in books. Let me help you, and please, help me. The images we have conjured of the classes scare me. I think it would be initially like drinking water from a firehose. Maybe I won't be a shining star to start, but I'll give it one hell of a try."

Eva clung to Carly. "I sure love you, Carly. You are like Josie; I remember her every time I turn around."

"She was my soul, so it's reasonable that we were alike."

Eva had more questions about things that only boys could answer, but she was too shy and reserved to ask. They turned and walked silently back to the house.

*

Mrs. Brownlie visited Carly and Eva to evaluate their emotional state, her keen observation skills taking in their demeanor. "You're both strong. But let's not rush things. There's time." But both said they were grieving but had too much time to wallow in pity and would prefer to begin the academic program. Pleased with their report, she presented the details for the upcoming weeks.

Mrs. Brownlie talked with Eva alone and said she needed to speak with her Mama about the plans to include her in the Stars of Infinity Program. "I can go alone, or we can go together to visit her. It's your choice. It has been a bit since you were home."

"I'll go with you because I need to get a few things from home. I'm sure she is still mad as a hornet because I disobeyed her. Please don't be offended by anything she says, and I'll try not be embarrassed." Eva said.

Eva found Carly in the yard. "I will go home when Mrs. Brownlie talks with Mama about the program. It won't go well. She will kick me out, disown me, so I will need a place to live. I don't want to wear out my welcome with you, but may I live with you while we complete our program? I will contribute to the costs from our stipend."

Carly was astonished. "She may still be angry, but why would she kick you out? Before you answer that, please understand, you don't need to ask to live here. You are a member of this household, that's an accepted fact. It would break my heart if you didn't live here."

Eva said, "She thinks I came here for sex with you and won't listen to reason. The fight won't be pretty, and I dread another fight, but we may as well finish it. I won't be bullied. She has a closed mind when it involves you and me, and I don't know why."

"Eva, I'm so sorry. What can I say? Maybe things won't go that way, but you should know this is your home. I desperately want and need you by my side."

"And I so profoundly need you with me, and I want us to walk side-by-side through life," Eva said, looking into Carly's eyes.

✳

The sterile smell of Dr. Fischer's office was strangely comforting. They were sitting in Dr. Fischer's office, the weight of their grief between them, having come at the Doctor's behest when he discharged Carly. Eva had suggested she didn't have to visit, but Carly insisted she come along because she was experiencing intense grief and sorrow, the same as he was. Activities to divert their attention had transient benefits because both quickly and repeatedly fell into the same rut. They talked about Josie, cried a lot, talked about other subjects, then cried some more when Josie's name came up, and repeated these or similar cycles ad infinitum. Then they went to bed, tossed and turned every night, and felt drained in the mornings, dreading facing another day.

When the nurse called Carly, he asked, "May Eva come with me?"

The nurse explained that Dr. Fischer prefers to see each separately, then he will talk to both in a closing summation. Carly followed the nurse to the examination room. Dr. Fischer opened the door. The greetings were short, and the Q and A session began. Carly explained he was suffering from depression and had little or no interest in his life. His attention span was ephemeral, nothing beyond a few minutes. No, he didn't exercise, wasn't sleeping well, and wasn't taking the barbiturate to calm or help him sleep. He had taken a tablet the first night after his hospital stay, but it defeated its purpose for at least two days because it left him logy and depressed. He said he would need exercise more demanding than tossing a ball or running, preferably something viciously challenging, to get through this period with an intact psyche. His session lasted about 15 minutes. Then Eva was called to see the doctor. She stayed roughly the same length of time, fifteen minutes. Soon, Carly was called to join Eva in the office.

Dr. Fischer explained that both had similar experiences while dealing with intense grief. Both loved Josie, and unsurprisingly, her passing affected both similarly.

"There are a few points I will suggest or prescribe, if you will. Do either of you know anything about Martial Arts?"

Carly had read a small amount, but he hoped to become involved someday. Eva said much the same. She said she would eventually like to pursue it for personal protection. She added that she needed something physical to calm her anger and prevent her from ripping someone's throat out and eating it while the donor watched and died.

Dr. Fischer jotted a note and laughed in agreement. "If it were possible to start a Martial Arts program now, with the fees paid, would you be interested?"

Eva and Carly looked at each other and nodded. "Yes, we would. I assume the intent would be to get us exercising but why martial arts?" Carly asked.

"Because physical activity can be a balm for the soul. City University has a unique program for males and females starting in one week," Dr. Fischer answered. "I've already made the preliminary steps of registering you, but you must go and complete the paperwork. The Master Instructor is Ronen Hanegdi. I have become close friends with Ronen. He is a remarkable man and is creating an intriguing new program. You two will be his first students. But one caveat, don't question Ronin about his history or his program. To borrow Carly's phrase, it will be viciously challenging, and, Eva, you may get the chance to rip out someone's throat, but you must supply the salt and pepper." The three made eye contact and chuckled.

"Meanwhile, do what you do well—write. Write to express your emotions, create a space to channel your grief into something creative to supply a sense of release and healing. I want to see you both in one month. I may recommend a therapist if I see your grief becoming overwhelming. In the meantime, try to prioritize self-care. Maintain healthy routines, eat balanced meals, try to get enough rest, and I know you will be engaging in physical activity. If either of you quits, we will all go to the University Hospital to remove my foot from your arses, understood?"

They answered in unison, "Understood."

*

After arriving home, they tried to relax on their back porch. They heard a car at the front of the house. Mr. Mallory was at the door, and seeing tears streaming down his cheeks was too sad for Carly and Eva. Carly at once clasped him in a long hug. Both were sobbing. Then he and Eva hugged in a long embrace, both crying.

Inside, Mr. Mallory sat quietly, and initially, neither Carly nor Eva spoke. Mr. Mallory finally broke the silence, offering unending compliments of Josie. He paused, resumed talking quietly, just above a whisper, and said, "The world lost a precious jewel when Josie passed. I have never met a more intelligent, spirited, yet humble young lady than Josie. It hurt me like my own death when I received the news. She is a once-in-a-lifetime friendship."

Carly and Eva remained too choked to reply, but Mr. Mallory understood. He said he wanted to bring Mrs. Brownlie, but she hadn't been home the last few days. They thought that was strange, but perhaps she was visiting friends or relatives.

<h1 style="text-align:center">36</h1>

. . . .

IN THE SWELTERING DOG DAYS of summer, the relentless heat began to recede as the sun moved south, the shadows grew longer, and the waning days of the season ushered in a less oppressive warmth to the night air. Carly asked Eva if she knew anyone to help move that chest inside the house. Eva promptly offered to enlist the services of her Uncle Rodney. "If you can take me over there, I will ask him today," she suggested.

They were on the road in less than half an hour. They were to meet Uncle Rodney, a giant of a man who revealed a friendly demeanor and rather eloquent speech. He readily agreed to arrange for a friend to help in moving the chest. They arrived later that afternoon, and Uncle Rodney's friend, equally robust, joined the effort. With the apparent ease of moving a feather pillow, they wheeled the chest into the back bedroom. As per Eva, Carly brewed a pot of coffee, Uncle Rodney's favorite beverage, and the four settled down for a pleasant chat that stretched well past an hour.

Autumn approached, and a refreshing briskness infused the air, reinvigorating one's soul. Classes at the university would soon begin. Only a few years had passed since Eva attended high school, so she claimed more recent familiarity with their necessary school supplies, which were available at the university bookstore.

They had been attending Mrs. Brownlie's rigorous English boot camp, taught by profs from the university. They may have initially grumbled about the demanding daily grind, but over time, it had transformed from a grind into a polishing process. Eva, radiating cuteness, displayed pride and happiness in her accomplishments for having made such profound changes. "I wish I could have attended this boot camp in high school. At least, I wish I could have received proper instruction in English, but it helped that I had an intense interest in English Literature and read a great deal," she confessed. Carly couldn't have been prouder as he said with a truthful note, "Damn, I think you're smarter than me."

When Carly asked how long Mrs. Brownlie would enroll them in the boot camp, she replied, "As long as it takes."

In addition to their academic pursuits, they had ventured into the opening classes of martial arts. There were eight students, all driven by a singular question, but Carly and Eva remembered Dr. Fischer's clear warning, akin to the sun on a cloudless day. But they wanted to ask Master Instructor Hanegdi one question, what the hell had they gotten into? They attended the sessions many hours every day, starting at 5:00 AM, off at noon for a thirty-minute lunch break, then met with MI Hanegdi for a two hour and a half discussion session. Finally, they would drag-ass home, too exhausted to eat. They had sore muscles that had never been described by human anatomists. According to Eva, she saw a bright light in all this. "At least we won't have to sweep our floors," she said. "My ass is dragging and doing a respectable job." They weren't wallowing in their grief or pity. Carly didn't need the barbiturates for sleep. Both were confident they could soon snatch throats out at will and consume them even without salt.

Master Instructor Hanegdi placed a faintly glowing candle at the end of their martial arts tunnel when he suggested their schedule would change when their classes began. They would have two-hour sessions on Monday and Thursday evenings and three hours every Saturday morning.

*

Josie's desire was to be cremated, and Carly fulfilled her wish. They placed the urn holding her ashes in the ground beneath one of the younger Live Oaks in their yard, selected to have a longer life than the older, giant trees. A beautiful granite headstone marked her grave. Weren't all the trappings surrounding death—lovely funerals with elegant eulogies, flowers, nicely dug graves or entombed in opulent marble mausolea, and imposing engraved gravestones—meant to assuage the guilt of those overseeing the arrangements of the funerals? Josie would be happy with what he and Eva had done, he was sure.

Each evening, Carly stood beside her grave at twilight and talked to her, but the conversation was one-sided, reminiscent of his talks with Winnie. It was cathartic to tell her what he and Eva were doing and how much they missed her. Most sessions ended in tears, but his spirit was bolstered with each conversation with her.

He and Eva visited Dr. Fischer at their scheduled time. They were humorous when both joked with threats to break his bones for getting them into a program with that formidable beast, Master Instructor Hanegdi. But they quickly let him know it was the best medicine he could have prescribed, and the program became more accessible with each session. But they were curious. When could they ask Master Hanegdi questions? Dr. Fischer said, "I found he loves Scotch, and I soak him with it every chance I get, and he becomes quite talkative."

Carly asked, "Do you suppose rot-gut moonshine would be an acceptable substitute?"

Dr. Fischer laughed. Then he was serious when he said, "My close friend and colleague, Dr. Jacob Bovermann, is Chair of the Department of Psychology at City University. I have spoken to him about the intense grief and sorrow you two are experiencing, and he would be happy to see both or one of you professionally if you feel counseling would be helpful. He mentioned that participating in a support group for young people who have lost a loved one could be beneficial. Consider these suggestions and let me know if you need my help."

Dr. Fischer changed to another subject of utmost interest to Carly and Eva. "The autopsy of Josie revealed the cause of her sudden demise—a massive saddle pulmonary embolus presented a situation of no recourse. The source of the clot was the vein in her right thigh. I must tell you, if I had picked up on this and started the anticoagulant the day before her death when she first mentioned it to me, there may have been a chance to prevent her death. I will permanently carry this burden on my heart."

Carly was silent, absorbing the weight of his words, and spoke softly, "Dr. Fischer, please don't try to 'what if' this scene. It won't change it. Nothing can make it otherwise. Eva and I know you did your best. Sometimes the human factor enters the equation, and often the ending is unpredictable, but you know that. I will be forever grateful for the loving care you gave my sister. Don't burden yourself with unnecessary guilt."

37

. . . .

THE PREADMISSION TESTS WERE behind them, tiring but not grueling as Eva had worried, and Carly and Eva breathed easier. Eva had been apprehensive about the testing, but once done, her spirits soared. Mrs. Brownlie looked at the results and saw an interesting correlation between Carly and Eva's IQ exam. Carly's was no surprise at 185, but Eva's was 186. She knew Eva was exceptionally intelligent, but this was an unexpected and immensely gratifying finding, recalling that Josie also had an exceptionally intelligent IQ in the 180s. Crafting an educational challenge for two such prodigiously intelligent students was going to be an interesting endeavor.

The Stars of Infinity Program awaited them at the university campus. When they arrived on the opening day of classes, the large cul-de-sac outside the administration building was in chaos. Men in full Ku Klux Klan regalia, daunting white robes and pointy hoods, and townsfolk in plain attire, their faces twisted with bigotry, were blocking the entrance to the administration building. A cacophony of shouts and jeers came from a group of protesters holding obscene signs protesting a Black girl's admission to the university. Carly doubted the infamous self-proclaimed Imperial Grand Wizard Terry Baker would lower himself to take part in these protests, but his malignant presence was felt because he was calling the plays.

"Let's take another route," Carly whispered, and detoured onto a side street. He found a small unimproved trail that led to a prime grazing area. He hobbled Mary, and they eased inside without protesters.

By lunchtime, after long lectures and note-taking their asses had become numb. But they found the lectures absorbing. Their fellow students, eager to learn about the newcomers, especially Eva, since she was the only Black student, asked where she attended school, and Eva replied, "Ethiopia."

In the students' perverse thinking, it was okay for a Black Ethiopian girl to attend an all-white university, but not the Black American girl who lived only miles away. Eva impressed them when she told them she had studied English to emigrate to America. They weren't sure how long their incredible stories would remain convincing, but they didn't care. They would stick with the stories until the students were tired of asking. The students never spoke of the KKK protests outside of the administration building.

After a year, the protesters remained in front of the admin building daily, and Carly still took the back way to their classrooms. The blockade appeared more symbolic than practical because protesters didn't notice or care about them going around it and continued blocking access to the administration building. The Marston police didn't bother to interfere with the unlawful barricade because many police officers were members of the KKK, and others shared their beliefs.

City University sued in Federal Court for relief from the protesters blocking access to the administration building. The court ruled for the university in a lukewarm decision. It allowed the protesters to remain, but they must allow free passage for the public to enter and exit without hindrance or harm. The number of protesters had decreased over the months, but Carly viewed the Ku Klux Klan in the same context as he would a rattlesnake. If it wasn't striking, it was coiled to strike. He had accepted that the KKK wouldn't buckle under a mere Federal Court order. There were precedents that the Federal Government would do nothing because the South was politically Democrat, and the Democrat-controlled Congress would do nothing to threaten their core base. Carly had told Eva that with the KKK, everything was secret, but nothing was a mystery. It had enjoyed its survival by perpetuating secretive hatemongering and racism.

Exhausted after weeks of grueling tests, late-night labs, drafting papers with little rest, and getting their butts kicked in martial arts, they needed to celebrate, releasing pent-up mental energy. They decided to unwind at the soda fountain; it was Eva's first visit. At home, they changed into comfortable clothes. Jenna jumped into the buggy, they gave her a bone from the butcher, and Jenna, lying contentedly in the buggy gnawing her bone, didn't care that they would enjoy ice cream at the drugstore. Only a family of four was in the shop sitting at a table near the wall close to the door. They chose a table near the large front window that would be private if a crowd should show up.

James Henry, the soda jerk, came to their table with his trademark open-mouthed, ear-to-ear smile. It had been at least a couple of years since Carly last visited the soda fountain, and James Henry had grown taller and more mature, and he was courteous but still simple. They scanned the wall menu, but neither knew what to order. Eva said she liked chocolate, so a chocolate sundae was for her. Carly ordered a malted vanilla milkshake.

They were in a festive mood when an ugly, short, angry man approached their table; he had a lazy eye but didn't wear glasses. His red plaid flannel shirt was untucked in his faded, dirty, threadbare dungarees, and his shoes appeared to have frequented a cow feedlot. It astounded them when he ordered them to leave. Looking at the little, angry, mean-appearing man, Carly thought he would be a lowercase near the zed if he were an alphabet.

"You two, get out of here."

"Why?" Carly asked.

"She's not allowed in here." He pointed to Eva.

"Why?"

"Because she's Black."

"Damn, I hadn't noticed," Carly said.

"You'll get out now!" Baker ordered them in a loud, angry voice.

"Our order hasn't come yet."

"It won't come. I won't serve you."

"Who are you? "

"I'm Terry Baker, the Imperial Grand Wizard of the Ku Klux Klan.

This is my store, and I'll refuse service to anyone I don't like, and I don't like you. I don't serve Blacks or whites who consort with Blacks. Remember my name and remember it good. Fear it. Now, take your Black bitch, and all y'all git the hell out of my place of business."

He had a sinister smile that was more like a feral snarl. Instead of living as a beneficiary of evolution, Baker was a small, desiccated, ossified man who had devolved into an atavistic swamp-dwelling slime creature filled with hate, anger, and a thirst for power. Carly stood face-to-face with Baker but towered over him at 6 feet, 3 inches, and 185 pounds. Baker must have been 5 feet 6 inches with his shoes on and appeared shriveled when viewed in the same frame as Carly. After Baker viciously and obscenely attacked Eva, Carly's temper was uncontrolled, rocketing to the boiling point. He leaned down and picked up a heavy metal chair, lifted it high above his head, and with all his hopped-up adrenalin might, hurled it through the massive plate-glass window at the front of the store, sending tens of thousands of shattered glass shards in all directions. The sound could have been mistaken for an exploding dynamite charge. Carly looked into Baker's beady little eyes, separated by an aquiline nose, and his feral feline face was betraying extreme fear and outright cowardice.

Carly caught a glimpse of James Henry as he high tailed out of sight toward the back of the building. Eva sashayed slowly, confidently, and proudly, towering over Baker, standing at least five inches taller than him. Her face looked down on his, and only inches separated their noses. Baker looked angry enough to slap her but glanced at Carly and backed down.

Eva tore into the Imperial Wizard in an unabashed, apoplectic rage as no one had dared. "My name is Eva Lou Swain. Remember my name and remember it well. I'll be around when you are out of business and in prison. You may be the self-proclaimed Imperial Grand Wizard of the Ku Klux Klan, but I don't give a happy rat's ass about you or your group of shit-head cowards. I see you only as a supercilious, narcissistic son of a bitch leading a pack of servile, gutless sycophants."

Terry Baker stepped back, speechless, stunned, unable to respond, unaccustomed to being spoken to in such a voice by few white men, and no Blacks at all, especially by a Black woman. While back treading away from Eva, he tripped on a heap of broken glass and fell in an ignominious spill flat on his ass.

To emphasize their point, Carly and Eva didn't want to appear in a hurry, so rather than leave through the front door, they strolled arm in arm through the massive opening of the shattered front window, their heads held high, stepping gingerly through the window frame that still held angry shards of glass, their dignified departure making a statement louder than Baker's protesters. They walked with deliberate strides to the end of the block, turned the corner, and, like gazelles escaping a fast-burning firestorm, went tearing down the street to their buggy, where Mary and Jenna were patiently waiting. Mary ran at a fast gallop as they beat cheeks to reach the city limits, an eternity away, then Carly slowed her to a gentle trot.

As they headed home, Carly tried to lighten the mood. "Are you up for chicken with mushrooms?" He meant it to amuse, but Eva had heard about the psychedelic mushrooms and didn't find it humorous.

Once back home, Carly tried to lose himself in a book, but the encounter at the drug store weighed heavily on his mind. His anger toward Baker had been at a primal level, far removed from rational, mature discourse. Nevertheless, he pondered how to combat racism with reason and maturity when it is a product of subthalamic thinking, so how can a reasonable person counter it in a sensible, adult manner? The mental gymnastics for that inner debate left him drained.

Seeking solace, he and Eva walked outside to sit and chat on the back porch, hoping to soothe the adrenaline high. Neither had the energy to ascend the slope to the spring. Conversation flowed haltingly and aimlessly. Eva eventually asked Carly if he had ever had a girlfriend.

"No, I haven't had a girlfriend," Carly said. "Have you had boyfriends?"

"No. I had male friends, no boyfriends," said Eva. "I had to be careful with my male friends, though. The slightest attention paid to a boy could be, and usually was, mistaken as a cue for sex. Some boys raped three girls. I knew the girls were nice to them, but the boys claimed the girls agreed to have sex, and the DA set the boys free. I have wondered if white girls must worry about that as much as Black girls."

Eva turned to him, intrigued. "Carly, may I ask you something? If you don't want to answer, I'll understand. But I'm curious. Have you ever... you know, done it?"

Eva's question caught Carly off guard, and he blushed with embarrassment. "Eva, I can't even imagine what sex is. I've read about it, but it rarely crosses my mind."

He hoped redemptive chores and spiritual exercises would absolve him of such a blatant lie. As a young man going through puberty, thoughts of sex were a constant presence in his mind, but not more often than every five or six seconds. He marveled at his ability to lie about that subject with such piety.

She laughed, "You are lying, Carly Turner."

"Eva, have you ever had sex?"

"I'm alive, aren't I?" She seemed surprised that he should ask such a question since he had met Dottie Mae. "If I ever had sex, my Mama would have known." As she spoke, Eva was cautious, careful, and selective of her words, choosing unusual pauses for her everyday speech. "How she would find out is a mystery to me, but that's how Mama's work. Then, she would have quickly laid me low in my grave with her cast-iron skillet." She laughed.

They snuggled on the sofa. Eva propped on one elbow and was looking down into his face. The sofa had a narrow depth, and they needed to lie close, tightly packed with one's curvatures fitting the other's, much like a jigsaw puzzle, but neither objected.

"When folding and putting away your clothes," Eva was curious, "I found an envelope in a drawer with thirty-eight cents. What was that for?"

Carly told her the history of the thirty-eight cents, the entirety of their wealth when they slipped away in the dead of night and never spent it. That inspirational story left Eva in awe, and her warm smile caused his heart to jackhammer and skip beats as she looked at him, and he felt each dizzying heartbeat in his head, and the celestial giddiness was delightful. Their faces were so close he could feel her warm breath on his face. They talked until sleep overcame Eva. They stood, walked into the hallway, embraced, and went to their bedrooms.

Carly eased outside and eased up the slope to the ice-cold spring, stripped naked, and jumped in. He stifled a scream because the cold water almost caused cardiac arrest. Returning to his bedroom when the desired effects of the cold plunge took effect, drowsiness overtook him, and he slipped beneath the cover.

On the other hand, Eva cautiously went to Carly's bedroom, carefully opened his door, peeked inside, and walked to his bed, but he was sound asleep. She leaned over, kissed him on his cheek, tip-toed out, and quietly returned to her bedroom. She was so proud of him for standing up for her, a gesture no one had ever made on her behalf. Under her breath, she said, "That crazy boy knows no fear." His actions gave her the courage to stand up to Terry Baker, the idiot barbarian.

Carly awoke when he felt someone in his room, but he remained motionless. He was wide awake and taken aback when she kissed him, so startled that he feigned sleeping because he was unsure how to respond. After she left, and he was more awake, he lay contemplating the situation and blundered ignorantly down the hallway to speak with Eva.

He hesitantly opened her door and timidly peeked inside her bedroom. Eva had tossed aside the demure cotton nightgown she'd brought with her. She sat on the edge of the bed ready to slip underneath the covers. Then, she noticed her bedroom door opening slowly and saw part of Carly's head and his timidly peeking eyes. Eva stood, inviting him in with her gaze, waiting for Carly to enter or say something. Carly, seeing Eva without clothes surprised and embarrassed him, and he was speechless and unmoving, frozen. He was about to close the door because he felt he was being sneaky and intrusive. She walked to him, took his hand, led him to the bed, and they sat on its edge. He sat with a passionate desire to look at Eva's body, but not sure if he should, afraid his staring would offend her. So, he catatonically fixed his eyes on the wall in front of him, trying hard not to stare at her beautiful, captivating body.

In an effort to put him at ease, she gracefully moved closer to him, standing in front of him, her presence nearly overwhelming. Carly, unable to resist, succumbed to his desire to admire Eva's body, and he stared like an entranced Odysseus when he listened to the song of the Sirens. In Carly's life, beauty had played no role. He never had beautiful things. If there was beauty, he viewed it at a distance, like watching the flight of the Great Blue Heron or the vast expanse of the blue sky with a solitary lonely cloud slowly drifting. Now Eva embodied a beauty that left Carly awestruck, causing him to wonder if he was in a dream. His gaze roved her beautiful, Elysian face, eyes of blue star sapphire, her slender neck, to her chest, now seeing for the first time the womanly body she'd developed, her curves, breasts, hips, and long shapely legs. Despite trying desperately not to stare, seeing Eva's body was enrapturing, and quietly, he continued to adore every arousing curvature of her exquisitely beautiful body. Her eyes captured his stare, and she smiled as he recovered his voice enough to mutter a few words and stepped toward her, embraced her tightly, and felt he should apologize. "Eva, you are so beautiful. I apologize for coming into your bedroom without knocking." Even in the dim lighting, his face was blushing brightly. This time, her kiss was not on his cheek but on his lips, which he thought must feel dry to her because, at that moment, he realized he was mouth breathing, and they felt parched. They had their first kiss, Carly's first kiss ever.

Eva's radiant smile conveyed her feelings, "Why are you sorry, Carly, my sweet Carly? I'm not." They stood in blissful silence, holding each other, staring into each other's eyes, having neither the experience nor knowledge of what to do next, and not thinking about what tomorrow might bring. They sat on the bed, whispering sweet nothings. But it didn't convince Carly it was safe when Eva lay back atop the covers. He thought things were moving too fast, uncomfortably fast.

"I probably shouldn't say this, but I've dreamed of this night a hundred times since I last saw you, which was when we started school. I knew I would see you again and wanted it to be special," said Eva.

"I'm not sure I made it special for you, but it's a night I'll always remember. You are a beautiful, special girl, and I'm nothing special. So, my memories might differ from yours," Carly said.

"Carly, you are super special to me. I'm so happy, ecstatic even. But I want to set up some ground rules. Though I love you so very much, I won't have sex with you because I'm not ready or mature enough for it. You and I are teenagers, and a pregnancy could disrupt my education. Many girls from my school got pregnant when they were mere children, fifteen and sixteen years old; one was barely fourteen. Now they are so poor, depressed, and lonely; it reminds me of what Uncle Rodney said, "They like the lowly viper. They ain't got a pit to hiss in." I would place suicide high on my 'to-do' list if that happened to me. I want children when I'm mature and knowledgeable enough to be a parent and can afford them."

Carly sat upright.

Eva sat upright and continued. "This program is the best thing that has happened to me, and I won't have sex and risk getting pregnant. I'm sorry if that disappoints you, but please try to understand. For you, sex isn't a risk, but pregnancy is an enormous risk for me and could destroy everything for me. I'm Black, and since I play a crucial role in the mandate of the foundation that funds the grant, my pregnancy could be disastrous for our program, and that involves you. I feel strongly about my position, but Carly, please don't stop loving me because of it. Do you understand?" With a worried expression, she beseechingly looked into Carly's eyes.

Carly spoke to diminish her fears. "Eva, it's okay that you hold that position because I felt a little uneasy that maybe we were moving too fast. I'm as thrilled as you and won't stop loving you. And my promise to you is that I will never push you to have sex," he added, "but you can push me to have sex with you anytime."

They laughed, embraced, kissed, and he stood and turned, but before leaving her bedroom, he asked, "How did your visit with Dottie May go?"

"Just as I expected, not well; she kicked me out, disowned me, and accused me of coming over here to 'shack up' with you. She was a terrible embarrassment to me in front of Mrs. Brownlie. But it's over, and I'm glad. Things had gone from bad to worse in the past couple of years. I hardly knew her anymore. When I recover from the conversation, I'll say more. But Carly, I want to say this. I am so proud of the way you stood up for me tonight, facing that blob of primordial slime, Terry Baker. No one has ever done that for me. I love you for doing that."

"Eva, I really didn't do anything. I had been sitting in that damned chair and its uneven legs got on my last nerve. I just wanted to get rid of it. But what you did, standing toe-to-toe with that bastard, and seeing the shocked look was priceless. That took far more courage than I could ever muster." She playfully hit his shoulder. He kissed her again, eased out the back way and up the slope, and jumped in the ice-cold spring again.

After he returned, Carly sat on his bed, contemplating what had happened between Eva and himself. His thoughts returned to a book he had brought from the farm library, which discussed the Jim Crow laws and their harsh penalties prohibiting miscegenation, dating back to 1901 and were still in the law books. They forbade marriage, cohabitation, and sexual intercourse between white people and people of other races, and the Ku Klux Klan illegally enforced them.

38

1958
· · · · · · ·

TIME SWIRLED, DAYS RUSHED into weeks, weeks into months, until they formed years that whispered by. As Eva and Carly were about to mark their third year's conclusion, they were greeting the three students of the incoming fourth class of the Stars of Infinity Program. Students from the second and third classes also gathered for a cozy chat in an empty classroom. Nervous queries from the newcomers, quite anxious as expected, were met with honest answers.

Yet, outside the classroom, the KKK continued their protests, relentlessly obstructing access to the administration building. Carly recommended that all the class members take the back streets to the classroom buildings to avoid the Klansmen, and he told them about the tiny fallow field trail he had been using for several years.

The opening day of the fourth year came with a drab canvas of gray skies in early September. Towering, cumulonimbus thunderheads hung in the sky, light rain fell, thick with the promise of heavier precipitation. But what awaited them on campus was even grayer—an angry sea of KKK members in full costumes and other hostile demonstrators in front of the administration building carrying obscene signs protesting the admission of Black students to the university. Mrs. Brownlie had enrolled Eva over four years ago. Wouldn't the cretins grow weary of protesting and perhaps get a job?

A gigantic pyre of burning automobile tires and logs, sending plumes of dense black smoke into the sky and encircling the administration building, darkening the already overcast sky and hanging low to the ground to seek the gathering crowd on the tarmac. The thick air held the suffocating smell of bonfire wood and burning rubber, causing breathing difficulties for many. The weather, thick smoke, and protesters combined to craft a dark, depressing day.

The cul-de-sac was choked with the mob's fury. An overturned automobile was in the crowd of shouting and screaming protesters fronting the administration building. Protesters were pounding the car with their fists, stones, and rough clubs, with trapped passengers inside the car. Carly heard their frantic cries and calls for help from inside the car. The vehicle, too close to the fire but not in flames, had a frightful amount of smoke curling skyward from its underside, which was now topside. Riot psychology controlled the prevailing temperament of the crowd, and as they recognized a sense of empowerment, the melee increased in intensity. The crowd packed around the car and grew more furious by the minute. With its screaming siren, an ambulance was trying to muscle its way to the overturned car, making little progress, and it was taking on significant damage from the protesters. The KKK and all the demonstrators enjoyed the full support of the Marston Police Department and knew there would be no police in attendance to keep the peace or protect the victims.

Demonstrators pelted the ambulance with sticks, rocks, and anything not stationary, while others crowded in front of it to block its advance. Although sustaining a broken windshield and an exploded passenger window, after an eternity, the ambulance reached the overturned car. The attendants extracted three individuals amid a shower of sticks and stones. One victim walked with help and two required stretchers. The crowd knocked one ambulance attendant to the tarmac, and he received solid kicks to his body and head before he dashed to the debatable safety inside the ambulance. After they hustled the victims into the ambulance, an attendant slammed the door shut, and it slowly pulled away, trying to avoid more casualties. Its red light was breaking through the dense smoke and rain, and the threading siren continued screaming for the right of way.

Carly and Eva sat in their buggy and watched as the ambulance finally escaped the lawless confines of the cul-de-sac to the main highway, red lights flashing and siren screaming, speeding toward the hospital. Carly and Eva returned their attention to the melee around the overturned car when the vehicle exploded with a deafening blast and a gigantic fireball that reached in all directions, on the ground, and into the dreary, smoke-darkened sky. The percussive explosion blew away the surrounding protesters and blasted out the windows of nearby buildings. People were lying on the pavement with burning clothes. Many people were running away, but some were not moving. Protesters closest to the blast had taken the brunt of the explosion and had somewhat shielded those behind them, but few escaped unharmed. Screams from injured, burning people begging for help filled the air, mingling with the threading sounds of demanding sirens. Though they fared better, those farthest from the explosion received a sub-concussive blow that dazed them, and some were standing, and others left the scene. Although some victims remained standing, many sustained flash burns, and some men and women remained with still-burning clothes. Screams and loud moans continued, but deadly silence hovered over some. Robed Klan members who remained upright shimmied, danced, and tried to rid themselves of flaming bedsheet robes and pointy headgear while those lying on the tarmac burned with their robes. Most of the crowd thinned out at once, and the air filled with more screaming sirens, growing louder as they approached the tragic, burning scene.

The scene shocked and sickened Carly and Eva, but they realized they would be of little help, and their presence would only add to the confusion and hinder the responders, who were proliferating. Carly lifted the reins, and they moved away from the scene as the burgeoning emergency traffic grew more intense.

The newest class of students and second and third-year students met Eva and Carly outside their classroom building. When they reached the door, and before they could enter, the dean of students, Theron Johnson, stood in the doorway and blocked their entry. With a stern countenance, he informed them he had de-registered them and refused to allow them access to the building. The dean turned on his heel and left the scene, refusing to answer their questions or give them any information. They didn't know what had just happened. Why was the dean such an asshole?

Their first impulse was to call Mrs. Brownlie, and Carly asked the polite building janitor, with whom he had become acquainted, to please allow them to use a telephone in the building. He ushered them into the building's office. Carly dialed Mrs. Brownlie's number but got no answer. He relayed this information to the others, whose questioning faces spoke volumes. There wasn't enough information to answer their questions. Carly recommended they go home and assured them he would find answers and provide them with progress reports when he had more data.

Rain was becoming heavier as they rode toward the city center to Irene's, a minor blues joint they could enter without a problem. They had no appetite but ordered something simply to thank the owner for letting them inside on that dreary, tumultuous day. Sirens continued to fill the air, and they were the only customers. Everyone else had left to watch the disaster at the university. They tossed around ideas for their next step. Did Mrs. Brownlie have family members somewhere she might visit? Carly suggested they go home but first drop by Mrs. Brownlie's house, then swing by Mr. Mallory's store on their way home.

Mrs. Brownlie had locked her house tight all around. A doggie entrance in the garage door allowed Carly a view inside, and he saw her car sitting, an unexplained, troubling finding. Eva saw Mrs. Brownlie's tiny kitten inside a window in the living room, appearing hungry and wanting company, suggesting that she wouldn't take a freewill trip far away. The next step would be to visit Mr. Mallory, hoping he might offer insight into the deepening mystery.

They found Mr. Mallory with no customers. When he saw how distressed they were, he asked them into his office. Carly filled him in on the morning's happenings. Mr. Mallory became more visibly upset than they had ever seen. Pale and shaken, he had to sit to prevent falling. He said Mrs. Brownlie had a male guest at her house for several weeks but didn't reveal his identity when she stopped by the store for a few brief visits. She always dropped by three or four times a week, if only to chat.

"She appeared upset," he said, and when I asked if she had a problem, she looked at me as if she would cry, then turned and walked away without answering. She climbed into the car with the strange man, and they drove away."

As Carly paced, he was thinking and muttering. "Where do we go from here?"

Mr. Mallory stood with a worried look. "I don't know yet. When I look at our paltry information, I feel something bad has happened. By golly damn, I shouldn't say that to you, but it's now on the table."

Mr. Mallory looked pale and sad. Carly knew he wasn't looking at all well and insisted he sit again.

"Mr. Mallory, I think I should call a doctor because you don't appear well. Is Dr. Fischer your doctor?"

Mr. Mallory looked sad and pale.

"Yes, Carly. Please call Dr. Fischer. I don't feel well. Bring my car around, and I'm ready to go to the hospital."

Carly asked Eva to call Dr. Fischer's office and tell them he was transporting Mr. Truman Mallory to the hospital and to have the doctor meet them there in about fifteen minutes. Eva asked Mr. Mallory if he had a key to Mrs. Brownlie's house, and she would ride the buggy over and feed her cat, and he gave her a ring of keys.

Carly brought around the car, but he didn't remind Mr. Mallory that he had never driven a vehicle. He asked if Eva would be okay going home alone. "Of course."

Carly drove Mr. Mallory to the hospital without incident and arrived at the same time as Dr. Fischer. The personnel received Mr. Mallory and rolled him at once into room 106, the hospital's standby emergency room nearest the nurse's station. Carly told Mr. Mallory he would be outside, not to go anywhere. They chuckled. Then Mr. Mallory fell back onto the pillow.

Carly sat alone, thinking of all that had happened that day. The educational ramifications of his life and Eva's had taken a rough tumble. They resolved not to let anything deter them from pursuing this unparalleled opportunity for an education. The Supreme Court ruled in Brown v. Board of Education a few months back in May that segregation was unconstitutional. But he knew to effect change and bring integration would take time and much work, and Mrs. Brownlie and the funding foundation had designed the Stars of Infinity Program to speed the process.

His thoughts about what had occurred had become speculation without information. He didn't understand why the university had barred them from classes. And why the dean suddenly appeared as an asshole, although Carly always thought he was an asshole.

Carly assumed someone had not paid the program's tuition, although, without the dean's cooperation, they didn't even have proof of that. Could it come from the governor's office, applying pressure because of civil rights issues? He had no answers for that possibility, either. They needed more information about that mysterious male house guest and his role in this catastrophe.

Carly didn't call the police because they didn't have enough information. What would he say? Mrs. Brownlie is not home. Her car is in the garage, she locked her house, she isn't answering her phone, and her cat is hungry. The low-energy Marston police department wouldn't even bother to take notes. There must be someone or something that would offer a clue to what in Hell had happened. But who or what?

The one fact they owned for sure, the university had delisted Eva and Carly from enrollment, as well as the first, second, and third year students. The reason probably was the non-payment of their tuition, but that was a supposition, not a fact. But it was a fact that Carly and Eva did not have sufficient funds to continue the program. Carly's best friend, Mr. Mallory, lies on a gurney in the next room and may be close to death. Only God had access to his prognosis.

Though answers were scant, only one thing was clear: the future was uncertain. The weight of the day weighed heavily on Carly. Sometimes, he mused, the world's burdens made it tempting to pull the covers over one's head and hide from it all.

39

. . . .

BUSTLING ACTIVITY CONSUMED Room 106 as nurses and technologists shuffled in and out. Each carried something crucial—oxygen tanks, bottles of IV fluids, and hardware that Carly didn't recognize. A technician rolled in an EKG machine, and technologists left the room with multiple tubes of drawn blood and headed to the lab. For two hours, Dr. Fischer didn't reappear from the room. Initially, when the doctor first spoke to Carly, his statements were to calm his anxiety.

"He is resting at present and is not in pain." Carly thought there must be a 'but.'

"But you got him here just in time. Mr. Mallory had a massive acute myocardial infarction, but this wasn't his first. He's stoic and would rather die than allow anyone to evaluate the frequent chest pains that have left him vulnerable. Mr. Mallory has congestive heart failure; if untreated, it's fatal. He might lead a reasonable life with proper treatment and care. Of course, I will give him a blood thinner, and I can control his chest pain. But he is on the critical list, and I will keep him there until I understand the extent of his myocardial damage."

Carly wondered if he could have visitors. Dr. Fischer said, "No, I have sedated Mr. Mallory, and he will remain so until morning." Carly mentioned he had seen Mr. Mallory less than a month earlier, and he didn't look well. Dr. Fischer said, "His chronic cardiovascular disease had slowly manifested itself as a problem over a long period, but I just diagnosed it and initiated treatment."

Carly left the hospital and recalled Mr. Mallory was the first friend he and Josie made when they escaped from home. A genuine friend, Mr. Mallory, had supported them at every turn and welcomed them into what began as a sojourn but became a permanent destination and meaningful relationship. He wished him well.

Carly drove Mr. Mallory's car to their home and discovered Mary and the buggy still parked and Eva waiting for news about Mr. Mallory. Carly filled in Eva with the information concerning Dr. Fischer's assessment of Mr. Mallory, and they were in a somber mood at once. If Mr. Mallory survived, he would probably require a lengthy hospital stay; Dr. Fischer didn't know how long it would take, and he could not meet the demands of the store, perhaps permanently. Carly asked Eva how she felt about running Mr. Mallory's store while he recovered or if someone found a solution to allow them to return to class. Emphasizing, while Mr. Mallory was their best friend, it would give them access to a phone. And they could take payments equal to their stipend from Stars of Infinity.

Eva agreed, saying, "Keeping the store open is a good idea, except for one major problem. Neither of us knows anything about running a retail store." It surprised him. "Well, there is that. But we're resourceful." That brought a brief light moment.

How were they to continue? They sat and chatted for nearly an hour with no ideas. Carly returned to Mrs. Brownlie's house the following morning, searching for a sign, a clue, or a hint of a clue. They desperately needed to solve the mystery. The only thing that seemed odd was in the room where she displayed her porcelain doll collection. All the dolls appeared undisturbed except the porcelain doll Josie and Carly had given her. Someone had tied the doll's arms behind it with a string, and it was lying face down on the shelf. Mrs. Brownlie was compulsive about her dolls, so Carly thought that might mean something, perhaps showing she was being held against her will. However, he wanted to talk to Eva before he made that conclusion.

Carly told Eva about the porcelain doll's strange position and his interpretation that Mrs. Brownlie was in trouble. Eva expressed concern that he was over-interpreting the doll's findings.

"Given Mrs. Brownlie's obsessive attention to detail," Carly said, "it would be out of character for her to leave the doll bound up unless it points to a significant criminal act by someone. That person's identity is unknown, and we can't abandon the search."

They entered the store early in the morning, hours before opening time, and stood dazed, realizing they had never viewed it from that perspective. Carly looked at Eva. "We'll keep meticulous track of every item sold, every item that arrives, and every penny we receive and payout. Beyond that, I don't know what the hell to do. Any ideas?"

Eva agreed the office would be off-limits, except for using the phone, and they would share any epiphanies, hoping one would appear soon. They filled the early hours of their first day by browsing, jotting notes, and memorizing hundreds of items' locations. Carly encouraged the cash register to reveal its secrets. They opened the store at 8 AM with debatable preparation for their first customer.

In no time, Eva allowed Carly to hide in the office. He called the hospital, spoke with Mr. Mallory's nurse, and asked if he could receive visitors. She answered, "Family only." When asked if Mr. Mallory had family members, she said they had none listed. There were legal-looking papers on the desk in the office with the name, address, and phone number of a lawyer, Chester Pilkington, Esq., Marston. Carly called Mr. Pilkington, introduced himself, explained Mr. Mallory's predicament, and inquired whether Mr. Mallory had any relatives. Mr. Pilkington was silent for a moment. "Thank you for the call. This news is so sad for me. No, Truman has no known relatives. He's a good man and a friend. I shall visit him as soon as his doctor allows visitors. I shall meet you and the young lady soon."

Despite the strange statement that he would meet Carly and Eva soon, Carly thanked him. He called the hospital again, and Carly explained that Mr. Mallory had no known relatives and that he and Eva were close to being his only relatives. He called Dr. Fischer's office to pass that information to his nurse and asked them to let him know when Mr. Mallory became stable enough to have visitors.

40

CARLY CALLED THERON JOHNSON, the university's stern-faced and angry dean of students, and requested more information about the non-functioning Stars of Infinity Program. Despite his curt attitude, the dean explained he suspended the students for non-payment of tuition, and it was Mrs. Brownlie's responsibility to make that payment.

On his second attempt to reach Mrs. Brownlie's number, Carly received a chilling message that the number was no longer in service. Someone had disconnected her phone. His calls to Mrs. Brownlie's pastor said she had no family, otherwise he didn't supply helpful information about her location, nor did the post office. Mrs. Brownlie had left no forwarding address. If he contacted the police, they would ignore him. Dealing with the police and sheriff's deputies would be time-consuming, do nothing, and result in mind-numbing, homicidal frustration.

Who was Mrs. Brownlie's male guest, and what was his role in this mystery? As he contemplated the increasing complexity of their problem, Carly analyzed every bit of information hoping fragments would coalesce into more meaningful evidence. He refused to believe Mrs. Brownlie's involvement in this developing tragedy was her intent. Mr. Mallory had said Mrs. Brownlie's disappearance was a crime, but who stood to benefit? Eva came into the office as Dr. Fischer called. He gave Carly an update on Mr. Mallory's condition, which was unchanged.

Carly shared the depressing news with Eva. He asked her to consider who might benefit most from Mrs. Brownlie's disappearance.

The KKK had protested Eva's admission to the university since they entered, and they intensified their protests before classes began this term. They needed clarification of the relevance of that information. It was clear, however, that no good intentions were behind this act. Mr. Mallory's opinion appeared spot-on.

Carly called the Benjamin Griffin Foundation in Atlanta, hoping to learn more about recent developments. He had expected the dean to inform them about the grant issues, but he had not contacted them. Carly talked with Helen, the grant manager at the foundation, and gave her the few details they had. The Benjamin Griffin Foundation froze the funds from the few facts he provided. Helen told him that the FBI must investigate and resolve the enigma before grant funding would resume.

Carly had grown weary of receiving no information or cooperation from the dean, so he drove to the university to speak with him. But the scene around the administration building was eerily quiet— no protesters or residual trash from the prolonged protests. When Carly asked the dean if the university had notified the protesters of the student's suspension, the dean denied anyone had spoken with them. He said that the protesters had suddenly left the campus on the morning of their suspension, which Carly described as, "Strangely coincidental, and I don't believe in coincidence."

Shrugging, the dean's sardonic smile stressed his wiry lips, resembling those of a gecko. Carly suggested the FBI would find any university employees guilty of collaborating with the KKK in this case and hold them accountable for the dead protesters. "It's called manslaughter."

The dean's appearance suddenly suggested he wasn't well. A hideous rictus grin of disgust replaced the sarcastic smile. Carly updated him on his conversation with the Benjamin Griffin Foundation and assured him that a resolution was coming. The dean's face flushed crimson with anger, revealing pockmarks from pubertal acne, which remained pasty. The dean bunched his gecko lips in the middle of his mouth.

"No resolution is fine with me, and I prefer no solution," the dean said. "I dislike the program and its students because Mrs. Brownlie designed the program to integrate the university. I vehemently oppose integrating City University and any university or college in the state."

Carly stood abruptly and said, "You should know this; I know what has happened. You go to Hell."

The rictus grin flickered, then died on the dean's face as he took on the pallor of a corpse. Carly was afraid the dean would hurl on him before reaching the door. He stormed from the office, forcefully slamming the door behind him, and rattling the windows.

Returning to the store, still fuming with anger, Carly told Eva about the sudden absence of the protesters and his infuriating talk with the lizard-lipped dean. Although it made her angry, it didn't surprise her. "Terry Baker had to be the most likely to benefit from Mrs. Brownlie's absence," he continued, "and given the few facts we have gathered, I think we should concentrate on him because he has imprisoned Mrs. Brownlie."

They searched the phone book for Baker's phone number. To their surprise, they found it listed. Carly called Baker's home on a hunch, and a woman answered. He introduced himself as one of Imperial Grand Wizard Baker's followers and asked if he was home. "Yes, hold on, and I'll fetch him." That's all Carly needed to know. He hung up, picked up the phone directory, and found the Federal Bureau of Investigation number.

A philosophical abyss separated Baker and Carly. But when he kidnapped Mrs. Brownlie, it became personal and filled Carly with fervid hatred, so much so that he wanted to bash in Terry Baker's face. Baker was a psychopath. At that moment, in Carly's opinion, Marston had more ignorance per square mile than anywhere else worldwide if someone were to ask.

Carly called the FBI and spoke with Special Agent Gordon Salter. In the following hour, he provided Salter with detailed photographic memory information. Salter sounded skeptical initially but listened as the conversation progressed. When hearing that Eva's admission to a white college was the spark that set off this crime, Special Agent Salter's temper boiled.

"Their plantation owner, Theodore Salter, enslaved my ancestors in the Black Belt of South Alabama. When the Civil War ended, which freed the enslaved people, they had no surnames, so they usually took the name of the plantation owner. My ancestors took the Salter name, so I'm named Salter. This problem has become personal, and I will see this mess cleaned up. With this information, I'm hopeful we can permanently close the coffin of the KKK."

By the end of their conversation, Special Agent Salter had the address of Terry Baker in Marston. The probability of Mrs. Brownlie being at Baker's Marston address was overwhelming, and he dispatched agents to make arrests. The FBI sent agents to the university to arrest the perpetrators responsible for the inside leak of the grant information to the KKK. That was privileged information, and the justice system must hold them accountable for multiple deaths and critical injuries. Carly gave him the names and university positions of the people he suspected were involved in the conspiracy.

In his second call to the Benjamin Griffin Foundation, Carly informed Helen of everything that had happened. While delighted, she couldn't estimate when the foundation funding might resume. The audit of the program's books and the judicial findings would be relevant. Trials and investigations would take a year or more because the judicial system would grind exceedingly fine. Despite the discouraging news, he thanked her. Carly repeated the information to Eva, and he waited for the call from Special Agent Salter, which would bring news about Mrs. Brownlie. After hours of waiting, the call came.

Special Agent Salter called Carly with good news and news that was not-so-good. When they arrived, FBI agents found Mrs. Brownlie being held captive at the Terry Baker residence. She was malnourished, dehydrated, had broken bones, and emergency personnel rushed her to Mobile General Hospital. Terry Baker and his wife were arrested.

Carly stood, speechless, while he assimilated the information about Mrs. Brownlie's condition. He was happy she was alive but flaming angry that she had become the victim of Terry Baker, that psychotic fool. Why has society allowed him to continue to live?

Later in the day, Carly suggested to Eva that they continue to run the store, and she was all smiles and agreed to continue that arrangement. After preparing the store for opening, Carly called the hospital to check on Mr. Mallory, and the news wasn't good. Dr. Fischer was anxious, according to the nurse. He was about to hang up when he had second thoughts. "I won't ask if he receives visitors, but does he have lucid moments?"

The nurse replied that despite being sedated, he was lucid when awake. Carly and Eva offered their good wishes, and she promised to deliver them.

The nurse called the following day to tell them Mr. Mallory was awake and had asked the two to visit him. Eva placed the store's CLOSED FOR LUNCH sign early, and they locked the door. According to the admission desk lady, Mr. Mallory's room was still 106. He was sitting in bed wearing a broad smile and a regulation hospital gown. Besides Eva, Carly also embraced him. Mr. Mallory asked how their lives were going.

Carly told him about Baker's abduction of Mrs. Brownlie and Mr. Mallory's temper flared. "By golly damn, that son of a bitch. Pardon me, Eva."

Eva stepped close enough to put her hand on his cheek. "I agree, Mr. Mallory; he's a son of a bitch." Eva held his hand. "Mr. Mallory, you mustn't let yourself get upset over this. Terry Baker will spend the rest of his life in prison."

Mr. Mallory gave her a long embrace.

They filled him in on the goings on at the store. Since Dean Johnson had suspended them from school, Carly and Eva had kept Mr. Mallory's store open while they were on holiday. That news dazed him. "You've got to be kidding me."

"No, sir, that's what friends do," Carly said.

Mr. Mallory's eyes welled with tears, and he sat, unable to speak. Carly asked him what bank he was with, saying a sizable amount of cash was on hand. Mr. Mallory said the information was in his office, and Carly said they had agreed the office would be off-limits except for phone calls. In disbelief, Mr. Mallory sat looking at them, shaking his head. "By golly, you two are the last two honest people in the state."

Their conversation continued until the nurse asked them to leave. Carly asked Mr. Mallory if he wanted his newspapers, to which he replied emphatically. "Hell, yes, and pajamas too."

The following day, a nurse called but not about Mr. Mallory. "Y'all sure are popular. Dr. Fischer just admitted Mrs. Brownlie, who transferred from Mobile General Hospital, and she asked that we tell y'all as soon as possible that she's receiving visitors."

*

The Marston Herald had recently repeated stories about the tragedy of the protesters and the exploding automobile on the City University campus, which killed seven people and injured over thirty.

*

Before noon, they closed the store and headed to the hospital. The admissions desk lady told them Mrs. Brownlie was in Room 209. She cried when she saw them, and they held her close for consolation. She needed to talk. "You two are superlative. It's so nice to see you. Where is Josie?"

Carly knew how Mrs. Brownlie loved Josie, and he choked when he began to speak about her death. Eva saw his difficulty and said, "Mrs. Brownlie, Josie didn't survive her illness. She was recuperating quite well and died suddenly on the morning she was to be discharged."

Mrs. Brownlie was shocked, speechless, and surprised, and an overwhelming look of sadness enveloped her, and she began to sob uncontrollably. Carly placed his arms around her shoulders, and Eva held her hand.

After long minutes, she regained a facsimile of composure and began to talk.

"I tied the hands of the porcelain doll you gave me and placed it face down on the shelf, hoping you would see it as a subtle clue that I was a prisoner. It had to be secretive, or Baker would have discovered my ruse. Did you find it?"

"Yes, we found it, and it was significant in leading us to conclude that you were a prisoner of Baker." She bounced from point to point recounting her travail, but they followed okay. She filled them in on all the sordid details of being kidnapped and held prisoner by Terry Baker.

"Terry Baker, pardon me, Imperial Grand Wizard Terry Baker, was making my life a living Hell. Someone told that son of a bitch about the Stars of Infinity Program grant money. The FBI must investigate how he knew about the grant; that information was privileged.

"He often came to my home unannounced to sit, talk, threaten, and contrive for hours. I threatened to call the police, and he laughed and told me to go ahead because he had 'friends' in the police department and the sheriff's department. I didn't believe him, so I called Marston Police Chief Roy Brooks, who laughed at me and said he would always believe Terry Baker over me."

"Baker moved into my house and informed me he was taking control of my finances and the grant. He did not fear being reported to the local law because he felt above the law. Baker said, almost daily, that no jury would ever convict him in the State of Alabama. After gaining control of my ledgers, he learned to control all my bank accounts. That's when Baker got dirty, demanding I remove Eva from the program and never allow her to receive her degree. He aimed to prevent the integration of the university and any white school in the state. Baker then said he took all the grant money for the coming year. Baker said he would choke off the grant money and prevent Black admissions."

She continued. "He knew the program would collapse if I didn't pay the tuition, but I refused to go along with his scheme. He was afraid of the FBI and thought I would contact them, so he kidnapped me and forced me to live in his house. When I refused to go with him to his house, he twisted my arm behind my back so hard I heard the bones break, and the pain was excruciating. He refused to let me see a doctor, and it's healing this way." She pushed up her right sleeve to reveal her deformed wrist and forearm. His wife knew what was happening."

Carly was at a loss for words, so he nodded for her to continue.

"Baker has paid substantial amounts of money to well-placed people in the state and county, and he collected vast amounts of compromising information on people in prominent positions. Baker was not reluctant to use the information for intimidation and blackmail. I purloined Baker's black record book, and now the FBI has it. It reads like a Who's Who of the state. People in our county and state will be in prison before this story ends. Though the tragic event is over, I remain a nervous wreck. I have insomnia, severe anxiety with panic attacks, and a wretched fear of opening my door to anyone. The FBI did not answer one important question, how did Baker know about our grant?"

Carly hugged her. "As for the stool pigeons who gave Baker your grant information, I know who was involved, and I've already passed that information along to the FBI. The dean of students, Theron Johnson and his secretary, Carolyn Crawford, were the culprits. Each will likely be indicted for multiple counts of manslaughter and many lesser charges, and if convicted, they will spend years in prison. I will keep you informed of the developments."

41

NIGHT HAD SETTLED OVER the Turner farm. In the dimly lit living room, Carly was engrossed in his latest writing venture—a thrilling tale about a night burglar, while Eva was lost in the pages of her book. Soft music played in the background. Suddenly, the peace was shattered by the roar of loud engine noises grinding up their driveway at a high speed, and multiple bright car headlights were visible through the generated dust storm.

With an adrenaline rush, Carly jumped from his chair and shouted, "Eva, go to the back bedroom now!" Whatever was happening couldn't be good and might not end well.

He grabbed the Stewart revolver from the kitchen drawer and picked up the household's trusty cabbage tamper as he passed through the kitchen. Amid the swirling dust in the driveway, Carly saw cars parking side by side, their headlights directed toward the front of their house. The men were assembling, lined up in front of the headlights. Carly counted seven cars and nine men wearing full Ku Klux Klan regalia of bed sheets and ridiculous pointy hats, brandishing their baseball bats and chains with disgusting bravado, threatening a household with two teenagers. He looked at the shortest and knew it was Terry Baker. Before the Klansmen had time to start an advance toward his house, Carly drew a deep breath and summoning all his courage, he stepped through the doorway onto the front porch and stood firm, holding the revolver above his head in his right hand, and his cabbage tamper in his outstretched left hand. He wanted all to see it wasn't to be a picnic. Jenna stood beside him, her hackles raised, giving a long, low growl.

Carly yelled, "Stop!"

The robed sons of bitches, viewing his revolver, by damn, stopped and presumably stared. He was scared beyond description, but now he must fight for his life and Eva's. A dump of adrenaline in his bloodstream had created a fight-or-flight situation. The flight would mean certain death, and fight didn't guarantee survival, but he would stand his ground, and sure as hell, he intended to take some KKK bastards with him.

"Why are you coming to my house in the dark of night?" Carly yelled.

The short man spoke. Carly recognized the voice of Terry Baker under his hood. The men with Baker were nervously quiet. Carly had expected them to be a rowdier bunch. Were they rethinking their involvement with their assignment?

"There's a Black bitch living here. Git her and the white bitch out here right now! You heah?" Baker yelled in his not-so-manly high-pitched voice.

Hearing that SOB speak obscene, disparaging remarks of Josie and Eva made Carly's blood boil. He raised his hand with the revolver high above his head for all to see. He fought a near overwhelming urge to shoot the son of a bitch where he stood for denigrating his dead sister.

"No, Terry Baker, you unmitigated asshole. Only one girl is living here, a human, and there is no difference between her and any other human. Now, I'm giving all of you one warning: get your collective asses off my property now or suffer the consequences. And you, Terry Baker, I'll shoot you dead where you stand. You have now pissed me off!"

Carly fired a shot, and the bullet splattered into the ground a matter of inches before Baker's feet, spitting dirt and dust. Carly at once wondered if that shot had been a good idea. A few of the men gave audible gasps and scrambled back, and Baker tumbled backward into a humiliating but familiar position, sitting on his ass.

Carly yelled, "Baker, you are becoming recognizable, sitting on your ass." But Baker wasn't waiting around for the next scene of that story. Terry Baker, their leader, was the first man to run, and the rest, now leaderless, stood stunned for a minute, not knowing what the hell they should do. Baker headed unceremoniously into the woods at breakneck velocity with the first shot, his bedsheet robe flapping ungracefully behind him. His headgear remained in Carly's yard.

"I have five more bullets here," Carly yelled, holding the gun high above his head for emphasis, "and more in my pocket. All you men, listen carefully and understand well, there won't be as many of you going home tonight as when you came here. Take a moment to let that sink in. I will gut-shoot the first five of you who step forward. You decide who you want to sacrifice." Carly spoke loudly so no one could mistake the serious shitstorm that he was about to unleash.

Then, with a loud voice, he emphasized, "Sic-em, Jenna!"

Chaos intensified as Jenna launched off the porch in a flash, growling like the hellhound Carly had heard only once before when she was facing down a black bear. She tore the bedsheet robe off the nearest Klansman with her teeth, causing him to lose his headgear. The disrobed Klansman was Roy Brooks, Chief of the Marston Police Department. Jenna lunged for the next Klansman, whose shrieking Carly heard above the calamitous uproar.

A lone Klansman had mistaken his stupidity for bravery and jumped onto the porch, only to get the full force of the fearsome cabbage tamper planted in his face. Blood, teeth, and spit exploded, and the man was out of action. Two other Klansmen were rushing onto the porch; one made it to the top doorstep and received the solid effort of the business end of the cabbage tamper to the side of his head, above his ear. He toppled headfirst with a face-plant onto the rocks in the flowerbed. Jenna had come onto the porch to check on Carly, launched herself from the porch and landed squarely on the upper back of the next Klansman, taking a massive chunk of flesh from the side of his neck creating a fountain of blood. Madly screaming for help, the man suddenly stopped screaming and fell like a rock.

The Klansmen, expecting a panicked teenage kid who would be easily bullied and killed, had no game plan for an armed encounter, especially when the kid would defeat them outright. With the sudden loss of four members of their Klan, the remaining five rapidly lost all ambition to face a loaded gun and a killer hellhound straight out of Hell. A blast of the gunshot and the growling fury of the hellhound relieved them of their facade of bravery. Seeing Baker flee the scene and the three falling so swiftly, the pack stumbled, tumbled, rolled, and scrambled for their cars. They turned their vehicles around in a veritable dust storm, spewing gravel and dirt, speeding toward the driveway like it was a racetrack. Carly blasted a bullet through the passenger window of another car as it sped by. He fired a shot through the hood of one car, and it stopped rolling in front of the front porch. The driver jumped from the car and stupidly ran into the midst of rioting cars and was struck by one of them. He was slow getting up, but the last car stopped, and the driver yelled, "Get your ass in here." The man dove through the passenger window and the car sped away. In their panicked attempt to escape, the drivers of the cars raced away from their crime scene at high speed and apparently forgot the road ended at the junction of the driveway with Old Johnson Road. A violent windstorm of dust created a condition of zero visibility for all the drivers except the leading car. The impenetrable dust made vision impossible, thicker than smoke or severe fog. Good visibility was of no benefit to the first driver because he went from the driveway straight ahead across Old Johnson Road into the ditch bank. The cars appeared to play follow the leader and crashed, stacked in a line like a train wreck. The piled heap of cars effectively blocked Carly's driveway and Old Johnson Road. The loud noise of the crashes would have registered in mega decibels. Then all was quiet.

Carly ran inside, grabbed a flashlight, told Eva he would go to the crash site because someone might need help. He called Jenna, motioned for her to follow, and they left to check the crashes. Three cars were still sitting in their driveway, but no one was in them. They made their way toward the intersection without the flashlight's aid, moving stealthily, hoping to stay undetected. Clouds covered the moonless sky, and darkness settled with a profound and palpable effect. They arrived at the unbelievable scene of vehicles, crashed and smoking in a crumpled heap, most with their doors open and headlights still bright. Carly saw no one, and the scene was eerily quiet except for the hissing sounds of punctured radiators, which made his hair stand on end.

"I'm Carly Turner. Does anyone need help?" Carly called. Gunshots rang out from the last vehicle in the piled-up scrap heap, bullets zinged overhead, and Carly responded, "Sic-em, Jenna."

She lunged with those hellhound growls like a cannonball through the open door of the nearest car. A male voice screamed. "Call off your dog. I'm all outta bullets, and I surrender. Help me."

Carly called off Jenna's attack. "Throw that gun out onto the road."

A handgun clattered as it hit the dirt road.

"Come out of the car with your hands in the air."

The man's words came interspersed between yelling and blubbering. "I cain't move. The wreck wedged my foot under the seat, and it broke my shin bone. I'm hurting like hail."

Carly retrieved a revolver from the road and switched on his flashlight. Checking the vehicle, he recognized James Henry, the young soda jerk from the ice cream parlor. The crash broke both bones in the boy's lower left leg, creating a 90-degree angle midway between his knee and ankle. His foot was immovable, crushed, and wedged beneath the front seat. Extracting it would cause intolerable pain. A large volume of blood had soaked through the boy's pants, and the sharp, jagged ends of bones were sticking through the cloth of the pant leg. Carly hoped the fracture wouldn't obstruct the blood supply to his foot, but he felt his hopes were in vain.

The boy groaned and screamed with excruciating pain, but he yelled his name clearly to Carly, "I'm James Henry Jones."

"I know, we've met," Carly said. "I need to remove that dress from you."

Carly used his pocketknife to remove the bedsheet robe and cut off the pant leg. He saw the boy had compound fractures of both bones in his lower leg, remembering the medical books he had read. Two saw-toothed bone ends jutted through his mid-lower leg muscle and skin tissues. Attempts to free the boy's foot met with considerable difficulty and brought on pain so severe that James Henry passed out. Carly released the boy's foot by removing his shoe, held his leg steady, and rolled him onto his back before the boy regained consciousness. Trying to straighten his leg was a non-starter, and again because of the intolerable pain the boy passed out. While unconscious, Carly used his belt to attach a dried, dead limb to James Henry's straightened leg, fashioning a facsimile of a splint with ties from James Henry's ripped-up bed sheet robe.

The boy needed medical care, but with the pile of wrecks blocking the driveway, Carly couldn't pass the wrecks with his buggy to call an ambulance. He had no choice but to saddle Mary, ride to Mrs. Brownlie's, and summon an ambulance.

He told the boy his plan. "I'll have to leave you to call an ambulance, but the young lady you wanted to kill earlier tonight will come out to try to stop your bleeding until the ambulance comes. Are you okay with that?"

The boy wept while apologizing. "I'm sorry fer being a asshole. I cain't believe you'd help me after the crap we tried to pull."

Carly smiled at him. "You'd better stop while you're ahead. I haven't thought this through yet."

Carly chuckled, patted the boy's shoulder, turned, and walked away to search for more casualties. Jenna followed him, they found none, and they hurried home to tell Eva what had happened. He asked Eva if she would consider administering first aid until the ambulance arrived, emphasizing that it would be her call if she wanted to care for the boy, but he'd understand if she declined.

She stood at once and began gathering items for the boy, including soap and water.

"It's pretty grim," Carly warned her.

"I've seen grim," Eva said.

Carly returned the Stewart revolver to its proper place in the kitchen drawer nearest the hallway, placed the newest revolver beside it, and replaced the trusty cabbage tamper.

"I had only four shots left, but they didn't call my bluff. Now we have a second revolver. We're working toward an impressive gun collection and at this rate, we'll need to find a larger drawer."

He left toward the barn through the back door to saddle Mary, and Eva left by the front door with her supplies to care for James Henry. When he arrived at Mrs. Brownlie's house, she met him at the door before he could knock. Does she ever sleep? He apologized for disturbing her at that time. She replied that his apology was nonsense. He inquired about her health. She was feeling quite well. He explained the purpose of his visit. He called the ambulance and told them about James Henry. He called the sheriff's office and left a long, photographic memory detailed report with a deputy who became disinterested once the information included mention of the KKK.

Mrs. Brownlie caught Carly's sleeve before he left. He turned toward her with a questioning look. "Carly, I would like for you to take Baker's black book that I stole, look at it and give me your opinion. Is it safe for me to turn it over to the FBI? Will I be in danger if word gets around that I have the book, and I'm going to give it to the authorities? Do you mind doing that for me?"

"Of course not. I will be happy to do so. If I think it's useful evidence, do you want me to deliver it to the proper person? That would remove you from the loop, and you should be safe," Carly said.

"Please, I will be grateful if you do that," she said as she handed the top secret to Carly.

Carly apologized again to Mrs. Brownlie, and he was off.

As dawn broke, Carly's gaze caught the aftermath of the previous night's chaos before he left on his way to Mallory's Mercantile. As he rode out of the yard astride Mary, vision was dim, but he saw a torn KKK robe, several pointy headgears, and a small black object on the ground near where Jenna disrobed the police chief. Carly dismounted to pick it up, it was a wallet. Looking inside, it belonged to Roy Brooks, and he pocketed it. As he looked around, the sun edged above the eastern horizon. In the daylight, visibility was improved, and he discovered three bodies lying near his porch. One body was dead from a massive gash in his neck. Two more were alive but were unconscious from head and facial wounds. Three cars were still in his front yard. The one with a hole in its hood sat closest to the porch. Two others presumably belonged to those who lay in his yard. Neither the sheriff's department nor the ambulance had arrived, and he had called them about 8:30 last evening. Carly knew they were deliberately delaying a visit because they knew the KKK was involved. It would surprise them when they discover that the dead and wounded do not include two girls and a boy.

Carly arrived at the store, sat with Mr. Mallory and the conversation was tense and decisive. He called the ambulance service again to collect the casualties. With his repeat call to the sheriff, he left a warning that he was calling the FBI. After filling Mr. Mallory in on the previous evening's events, Carly asked if he should give a photographically detailed report to *The Marston Herald* or report the accident and let them investigate. Mr. Mallory thought for a moment.

"By golly, Carly, report the accident and ask them to investigate and name the owners by the vehicle license plates, but you can give an anonymous detailed report. But, by golly damn, you and I will pay a visit to the illustrious Marston Chief of Police, Roy Brooks, soon to be ex chief."

"Mr. Mallory, are you sure you are up to this?" Carly asked.

Mr. Mallory said, "Of course I am. This is too damned important to sit on the sideline, and I don't see an army lined up supporting you. So, let's go."

Mr. Mallory and Carly made the trip to The Herald, giving them the detailed anonymous report. He recommended the reporter go to the hospital and ask about James Henry Jones and enquire if any dead or wounded individuals with wounds came in overnight. Carly gave a vivid description of the location of the three decommissioned Klansmen lying just off the porch at his house, and the reporter ran out the door of the Herald with a camera in hand.

Their next stop would be the Police Department to visit police chief Roy Brooks, aka Ku Klux Klan member Roy Brooks. In his office, Brooks looked rugged, with multiple cuts on his face, neck, hands, and both arms. His right arm was in a cast and rested in a sling. His eyes sported black shiners, and his nose looked twice its standard size. But his eyes were more bloodshot than any Carly had ever seen, and he described them to Mr. Mallory as red as a fox's ass in a Pokeberry patch! Roy saw Mr. Mallory and Carly, and his face paled as if he had seen a ghost, making his red eyes more pronounced, almost comical. He sank low into his chair like a kicked hound.

Mr. Mallory took the lead. "Roy, you have a choice, unlike the people you terrorize. You can resign today. Or tomorrow, your name and pictures will be headlines in The Herald and picked up by CBS, NBC, and ABC, as well as newspapers throughout the nation. The choice is yours. Which will it be?"

The police chief tried a threatening ploy. Rising with difficulty from his chair, he leaned on the desk with his one good arm and favored an impaired lower extremity.

"Carly has that black gal living in his house, and that ain't Christian. Now, I'll throw you both in jail," Brooks said.

Carly spoke up. He had gained considerable confidence from the encounter the previous evening, and the resulting decisions he made to take care of James Henry. His recount at the Herald stimulated his confidence even more. "Mr. Brooks, a wise man once said never get in a pissing contest with a man with a full bladder. Our bladders are over-distended! A boy is lying in the hospital with severely broken bones in his leg and almost lost his life from blood loss, and he will probably lose his lower leg and foot, all because of that bullshit you tried to pull at my house last night. Those two girls you tried to kill; one was my sister who died only a short time ago, the other is my dear friend who supplied lifesaving first aid for the boy. She stopped the bleeding until the ambulance arrived. But the pile-up of your wrecked cars blocked our driveway and Old Johnson Road, causing a critical delay in the ambulance's arrival. I rode my horse to the Mercantile to call the ambulance and the sheriff.

Roy Brooks looked down at his good hand on the desktop holding him upright.

"But neither the sheriff nor police had arrived as of this morning because the KKK was involved, and you were given the freedom to complete your rotten, abhorrent terrorism. Meanwhile, you and your brave cohorts had hauled ass, leaving him to die from severe blood loss unless we cared for him. And you have the nerve to lecture us on what is or isn't Christian. Roy, were you missing anything this morning when you dressed, other than your robe and pointy hat?"

After standing in deep, silent thought, it finally sank through Roy Brooks' slowly functioning brain that he wouldn't win this bout. He sank into his chair, he gave a deep sigh, and said barely above a whisper, "Okay, I'll resign."

Carly turned toward the door and spoke over his shoulder. "When it's official, I'll return your wallet. Admitting to being a Klansman as the reason for your resignation might go a long way to restoring your credibility."

Mr. Mallory and Carly took their leave and walked a block to a small café called Coffee 'n' Moore, owned by a pleasant fellow named Wayne Moore. They drank hot coffee and ate donuts, and Carly said, "I've never seen such bloodshot eyes. If Brooks were to sneeze, he would hemorrhage to death through his eyes."

"Who's the wise man?" Mr. Mallory laughed and looked at Carly.

"Me." Carly chuckled; his face tinged with a soft blush.

"The DA should already be on top of this gathering information for a criminal investigation, but this involves the Good Ole Boy's Club, and I would venture a prediction that not much will happen," Mr. Mallory said.

Carly discussed the powerfully damaging information in Baker's book that Mrs. Brownlie had given him. Mr. Mallory was at once extremely serious. "Carly, turn that over to the FBI at once. If someone got word that you might be in possession of damaging information, your life would be in extreme danger."

Carly said, "I'm of the same opinion. I'll contact Special Agent Salter today and arrange to turn it over promptly."

The headline of the next issue of *The Marston Herald* read: KKK POLICE RESIGNS, followed by three pages of detailed reporting and picture after picture of the wrecked vehicles and the owner's names and addresses. At the hospital, they brought in a Klansman, dead with a large gash in his neck that severed his carotid artery. They admitted one to the hospital, unconscious from severe head trauma. They admitted another to the hospital unconscious, with severe fractures of his facial bones and multiple broken and missing teeth. They admitted a third Klansman to the hospital with a gunshot wound to his right shoulder. Another was admitted with injuries consistent with having been hit with an automobile.

One car belonged to the chief, and it would soon head to the scrap metal yard along with the others. The reporter took a picture of a vehicle in Carly's yard with a bullet hole in the hood of a car that would need to be towed because it wouldn't run. Two cars were pictured, and the owners were not named, because the owners were believed deceased. Carly thought, too bad he and Josie weren't in the scrap metal business anymore.

The Marston Herald reporter interviewed James Henry who gave a detailed report of that fateful night, including the Klan's mission to kill Eva and Josie. The long story about the tragedy of the soda jerk, James Henry Jones, included pictures of him. He told how the doctors had tried to save his foot and lower leg, but in the end, they had to amputate his leg about eight inches below his knee. He said he learned later that Josie had died just days before they were to kill her. The story didn't extol the virtues of the Klan or Imperial Grand Wizard Terry Baker. But James Henry recounted the care he received from Eva and Carly as very good. He was apologetic for allowing himself to become brainwashed by Terry Baker and the Ku Klux Klan.

People in the local community and nearby Marston were asking questions and demanding answers and an investigation about why so many automobiles took part in a high-speed crash at the junction of Old Johnson Road with the Turner driveway. *The Marston Herald* was running several stories daily, answering the questions. The public relations for the Ku Klux Klan must have been at an all-time low.

*

Eva and Carly relaxed after the commotion died away. But the calamity had damaged his relationship with the County Sheriff's Department and the Marston Police Department, and it would take years, if not generations, to repair. Both departments carried out cursory in-house investigations for public relations. The Sheriff's Department lost three deputies, the Marston Police Department lost their chief, and two officers, all forced to resign after an investigation named them as members of the KKK. Both law enforcement departments and the KKK gave Carly the dubious distinction of being named the perpetrator. All escaped having charges filed against them. Although the DA issued a letter of vindication for Carly, it did nothing to mend his damaged relationship with the two departments.

*

Public outcry against the KKK was such the DA could not ignore Terry Baker and his extreme and continuing acts that were transgressions against the laws of civilized societies elsewhere. The DA and local police, and the sheriff's department, had chosen in the past to ignore his illegal civil rights violations against the citizens of Marston and the county. After the DA presented the evidence to the Grand Jury, they charged Baker with misdemeanors, a judge found him guilty of the charges, and the judge sentenced him to sixty days in the county jail and fined him two hundred dollars. The same judge suspended the sentence. The pat on the wrist only got Baker pissed off. The local population sighed in frustration but didn't have the knowledge or resources to seek remedies for the KKK plague.

Carly called Special Agent Salter and explained the trove of damaging information in the black notebook that Mrs. Brownlie purloined from Terry Baker. Special Agent Salter was very surprised and sent an agent at once to collect the book that day. He said, "If it holds the information you describe, it might hold the evidence that could put an end to the criminal careers of many people, in government and in private endeavors.

∗

In the early morning, Carly and Eva were rushing to drop her off at the store, and Carly would pick up Mr. Mallory. An insistent knock at the door interrupted them. He went to the door with no expectation of what awaited. When he opened the door, he received a welcome surprise of his life, a miracle bolt from the blue.

Uncle Matt stood in the doorway, wearing a big smile that brought back many precious memories. A lightning strike could not have been more stunning. Unable to grasp words, Carly fell against Uncle Matt's chest in a tight embrace.

Standing tall with streaks of gray in his once black hair, Uncle Matt had a presence about him that was hard to ignore. Those sharp blue eyes still held that same mischievous twinkle, and the years had only added stories to tell.

Carly was examining his uncle. When he could finally speak, he said, "You look...well. The years have been kind to you."

Uncle Matt gave a hearty laugh, "Oh, don't let this old face fool you. The years have taken their toll, but I've managed to dodge the worst of them."

Carly called for Eva, who came at once. She was momentarily frozen at the sight of Uncle Matt.

"This is my Uncle Matt!" Carly said.

"I know. I remember him well. He was extra nice to me and brought me a piece of candy almost every day," Eva said. "Any family of Carly's is family to me. It's a pleasure, sir." She held out her hand to Uncle Matt who used it to pull her to him, and he hugged her. "I know all about Eva Lou and how smart she is. I've heard about the program you are involved with. That takes more courage than I can muster, and I'm proud of you." Tears welled in his eyes. Carly was surprised by the emotion he showed with Eva.

Finally remembering their manners, they invited Uncle Matt to sit in the breakfast nook and Carly offered him coffee. "It's fresh, and there has never been a Finn who didn't like coffee."

Uncle Matt's face was pensive. "So, you remember." He said, mournfully, "Truman Mallory told me of Josie's death. I have about cried my eyes out. I don't know what to say. Everyone says, 'I'm sorry,' but it's never enough. I dearly loved that little girl, so smart it was scary and pretty as a dew-covered rosebud."

"Thank you," whispered Carly. No words were sufficient to express the loss of his beloved Josie. Eva sadly and silently nodded, and she gave a sweet smile.

Uncle Matt watched them closely as they settled into conversation.

He asked, "So, how are you enjoying your house and section of land?"

Surprised, Eva and Carly looked at each other as a sense of understanding slowly swept over them.

Carly spoke first. "Uncle Matt, you old scoundrel. We've been racking our brains to think who our ghost benefactor could be. You are the one who paid the $862.00 to buy our property for us!"

Uncle Matt smiled broadly, happy that his secret had been revealed.

"How did you know about our whereabouts?"

"Do you remember the lady in the tax assessor's office at the county courthouse who helped you when you first inquired about the property?"

"Of course. Her name is Betty Arnett, a gracious lady," Carly said.

"Betty is a good friend. She called when you two first inquired about your property, and she suspected who you were. I watched you closely to ensure you were safe and that nothing untoward happened to you. Your comings and goings were interesting. Truman Mallory told me you had a contract with him, and I followed you. It amazed me when you worked like Trojans all the spring and summer months, hauling scrap metal to Marston with the horse and buggy. I grew weary watching you work so hard, but I was careful not to break your cover because I didn't know what you two were hiding from, but I followed you multiple times, trying not to disrupt anything in your lives but making sure you were safe. When Dr. Fischer hospitalized Josie with pneumonia, I followed you the night you took Josie to your teacher friend, and she took you both to the hospital. After her admission to the hospital, I followed you back to your place. I was distraught and close to breaking your cover when Truman gave me the tragic news that Josie had passed away, so I held back but kept close tabs on you.

Carly and Eva were on the verge of tears as he talked.

Although it wasn't clear why you wouldn't or couldn't come home, as things unfolded, I tried to figure it out, and I did mostly, but not completely. I knew you, Josie, and Eva were intelligent kids, and eventually, we would meet. I wanted to help you, but I didn't want to break your cover, whatever the reason. Betty promised to call me if you came back to buy the property. It thrilled her you were alive, but I didn't know your plans, and I asked her to keep quiet about you."

"We knew someone followed us many times, but we never knew it was you, nor did we even suspect that it could be you. You quite cleverly made sure we could never recognize you. When we left the farm, the hardest part was leaving you without saying goodbye. But circumstances didn't allow that. How did you learn of our plans to buy this house and property?" Carly said,

"When you went to the courthouse to buy the property, Betty called to alert me. She said you were going to Jackson State Bank to get a cashier's check, and I should hurry to do whatever I was planning. She accepted a regular check from me, so I paid for the property for you. It amused Betty how it unfolded because you two had made quite a favorable impression on her. I stayed out of sight while she played her little game with you, and although undercover, I was so happy to have her contact you. Unfortunately, the hurricane dragged this little prank out longer than I'd intended."

"I'd decided to thank the person who so generously paid for our farm, then I would beat his sorry ass for putting us through that insane game," said Carly, laughing.

The three laughed together. Then, more seriously, Carly told Uncle Matt how important he had been to Josie's life and his and would always be. He said softly, "Josie cherished the moments she shared with you. You've always been a beacon in our lives."

Soon they were wrapped up in stories, reliving old memories and creating new ones. Eva listened intently, fascinated by the tales of Carly's youth and the adventures he and Uncle Matt shared.

As a raconteur par excellence, Uncle Matt had a way of drawing one in with his stories. They were vivid, full of life, humor, and emotion. The kind of tales that made one laugh one moment and cry the next.

Uncle Matt seemed reluctant to change the subject, but he said he had come to deliver a message and a warning. "The tightly guarded scuttlebutt at the farm and about has it that Terry Baker is organizing a group to come to your farm to burn your house and barn and kill you and Eva. You are not to worry about this, because I will handle it. Do you understand? You must follow my directions without pushback, and I won't answer questions. When the time comes, I'll ask you two to come to my house for a night, maybe two, take a well-earned vacation, and that's all that will be required."

They were quiet, trying to absorb everything that Uncle Matt had said, and they asked no questions.

"I'm proud of the man, Carly, and the woman, Eva, that you two have become, with so much promise for the future." Uncle Matt said, "I'll be off now."

After they thanked him and said their goodbyes, Carly fell into deep thought. Uncle Matt's visit, unexpected as it was, brought a wave of healing and renewed hope to Carly's heart. The bond of family, once thought lost, was not yet strong, but developing.

Carly asked Eva, "How would you like to go to Marston? Do you fancy a dinner out?"

"Of course," Eva said. "I would love it, but do you want to risk it? It could be a re-run of the night at the ice cream parlor."

"To hell with it." Carly said. "We can handle ourselves in dangerous situations. That's why we enrolled in martial arts. We are entitled to be human and enjoy the fruits of life, just as much as the rednecks."

They got dressed in their nicest clothes. "What do you say we visit Evangeline's?" Carly asked. "It's a place that's always been out of my class, but I want to take you there."

Eva was delighted. She'd heard of the restaurant, but she was sure no Blacks had ever been there, and the idea that she would be the first to visit set her imagination afire. But why would she be the first Black to dine there? She thought the answer was twofold. The local Blacks were kept out by Jim Crow since long ago. They likely would have been turned away at the door. But the reputation of The Hanford was such that, surely there were Blacks from up north who stayed there. Would they be turned away? The second reason, she thought, was economics. Most local Blacks couldn't afford to dine at Evangeline's.

Taking Eva to the hotel for the first time reminded him of his first visit to the Hanford Hotel. As they walked through the lobby, Eva was beautiful, dressed in a pastel blue dress, high heels, and her hair was so lovely. As they walked down the short hallway to Evangeline's, Eva was in awe of such ostentatious wealth. They were seated at once near a window overlooking Marston's Main Street. A small loaf of fresh-baked bread with soft salted butter was delivered to their table, and they thought they didn't need to order anything else. It would satisfy them to dine on the delicious, buttered bread.

A well-dressed gentleman approached their table and introduced himself. I'm Harman, your waiter, and he handed an extensive menu to each, more striking than they had ever seen.

They tried to appear experienced when they opened them, but that façade dissipated when the descriptions of the Cajun dishes were foreign to them. Wrestling with the names of the Acadian dishes, Harman suspected they were unfamiliar with the terminology and offered his help.

"Most people are unfamiliar with Acadian or Cajun words, so let me help." He patiently explained each dish as they soaked in each word. He suggested they each get a bowl of turtle soup. "Out of this world," he added, "For a salad, "Perhaps something simple like a wedge salad with balsamic vinegar dressing. Balsamic vinegar is a special order from Modena, Italy." They asked for a suggestion of something with the essence of New Orleans. He explained the muffuletta, a New Orleans dish that was quite large. They ordered two, but Harman suggested, 'Why don't you get one to share, one side dish of red beans and rice, and a second of roasted sweet potatoes, to share?"

While waiting for their meal, a gentleman approached their table, and Carly thought Oh hell, here's trouble. The gentleman was well dressed, had bright red hair, and Carly recognized him, he was Hollister "Red" Adair, the manager of Evangeline's. Carly was at once defensive and flooded with apprehension. The man came tableside, held out his hand to Carly, and Carly stood and took his hand.

"Carly, I want to express my deep sorrow over the death of your sister, Josie. I was so surprised, and I literally wept when I read of her death in the newspaper. She was the smartest and loveliest little girl I have ever met. She, and you, made such an impression when you sold squabs, chickens, and yourselves to me."

"Your thoughts mean so much, I thank you from the bottom of my heart," said Carly.

"I would like to welcome you and your lady friend to Evangeline's."

Carly introduced Eva as his dearest friend. "We have been close friends since my earliest memories. I sincerely thank you for allowing us to dine."

"But of course, Carly. We are hopeful the people of this state will eventually come peacefully into the twentieth century."

"We would like very much to get to know you better. Perhaps I could call, and we could get together," said Carly.

"Call anytime, I'll be waiting," They shook hands again. "Enjoy your evening with us."

The two enjoyed the feast and the magnificent and sophisticated service to the Nth degree. Neither had ever tasted food as flavorful as those dishes. Then came the dessert. Harman suggested Bananas Foster. Neither had heard of it. When it arrived, they were excited to see the spectacle of the flaming dish performed at their table-side. Tasting it, they thought they'd died and gone to heaven!

"I've never had sex, but if I were given a choice of sex or this dessert, I would choose Bananas Foster," Eva said amid laughter. Carly blushed and kept eating.

After they paid and left a tip for Harman, they happily waddled out to Mary and their buggy, climbed aboard, sated and happy beyond words. Mary navigated, and they made out. As soon as they crossed out of the city limits, a car full of men or youths started harassing them, yelling obscene racial epithets. The car sped by, stopped quickly, and turned crossways in the road, blocking their progress. Five males, appearing between late teens and mid-twenties, piled out of the car, eager to "Beat some motherfucking ass!" They were in a hurry to get on with it. When they saw only a young white man and a young Black woman unload from the buggy, the racist hotheads started yelling and cheering, gaining support from group psychology and strutting up to Eva and Carly, trying to grab Eva's breasts and taunting Carly. "Fresh meat," two of the men heckled Carly, knowing he would take the bait and they would beat his ass.

Both Carly and Eva tried to reason with the men. Carly said, "You won't like what is about to happen to you." The men howled with laughter.

"An just what chu gonna do, honky?" Finally, one of the men grabbed Eva's breast, she slapped away his hand, and he slapped Eva. The Martial Arts training of Carly and Eva kicked in, and in less than two minutes, strewn about in the road, all the boys were lying, groaning but not moving. Eva went to the side of the road, found a used brick, and broke both elbows of the man who slapped her. She propped each elbow on the brick and stomped it, listening for the crack of the broken bones.

Carly didn't stop her, but they had only one brick, so he couldn't help. He had calmed enough to be thankful she wasn't doing what she was capable of. When finished, she walked to the buggy, climbed aboard and said to Carly, "Those racist pricks need to learn who their friends are because tomorrow with both arms in a cast, he will be begging someone to wipe his ass. They need to learn to respect women. Their mamas should have taught them better. They will be less sure of how tough they are when they put all this together. I'm sure I'll regret this tomorrow, but right now, I'm happy. I dislike rude, crude, uncultured, and racist sons of bitches, white or Black."

In the morning, the sun was preparing to peek above the horizon, painting the sky in hues of red and blue. And as the new day dawned, it was a day filled with promises and memories yet to be made.

42

....

CARLY'S SILHOUETTE AGAINST THE dawning twilight was a lonely figure, one that seemed to foreshadow danger as he strolled into Marston's aging police station. Whispers had crept through the countryside that had made him aware of what the local rumor mill was grinding out about Terry Baker and his KKK and their macabre intentions to murder Eva and him and burn down their house and barn. What made it worse? He knew they would stonewall him because the chief of police and sheriff were liars and would be uncooperative. The law was complicit, their allegiance bought or threatened into submission.

Police Chief Deek Potter saw Carly as he entered the police station and called him into his office. Greetings were short. Carly knew Police Chief Potter had a facade of a good-natured, friendly fellow, but wasn't too bright. "Carly, your face looks like a storm's brewing. What's that about?"

Carly nodded and got to the point. "The word on the street says Baker's gathering men to kill my friend and me and burn me out. I know you already have the full story, but you won't tell me. And I can't depend on you or the sheriff for help, nor will you call the FBI or the State Police. Potter smirked, dismissing those stories. "Carly, there's nothing to those rumors. You've made your bed, and you can now sleep in it. You've made enemies in this police station and the sheriff's office."

But Carly's parting words left an icy chill in the room. "When you call Baker after I leave, give him this message from me: If he wants another humiliation, he knows where to find me. But I'm thinking it will be more than a humiliation."

Carly left the police station with steam blowing from his ears. But he wasn't done. He walked directly to the sheriff's office a few blocks away and had an almost identical conversation with the sheriff. However, the sheriff didn't suffer Carly's insults happily, and his two deputies manhandled him and threw him from his office.

He had expected that treatment, but every push, every mocking sneer was data for Carly. He was collecting markers for a future reckoning when the shit hit the fan.

Carly didn't tell Eva about the contretemps at the police station and sheriff's office. When Eva asked questions about his visits, Carly explained that he'd learned nothing new. Carly and Eva were talking when Uncle Matt drove up. They were happy to see him, but he seemed focused, not amenable to small talk. He told them, "Baker has given the word, he's moving tomorrow night." Carly then outlined his preliminary plan for Uncle Matt's consideration. Eva gave him her rapt attention because Carly would ask her to help implement it. They needed four rolls of barbed wire. A roll measured 1,320 feet, a quarter of a mile, and would be unrolled to encircle about 150 feet from the house, over three times around the house, leaving a single space on the west side of the house, opposite from the parking area, wide enough for a vehicle to pass. The multiple spirals of barbed wire would be about three to four feet high, designed to damage and stop unsuspecting intruders. They could go to the garbage landfill to collect as many metal cans and lids as they could haul in the pickup. Tying metal cans and tops throughout the coils should create an early warning system and a signal to the intruders when they wandered unsuspectingly into the coils that they were now in deep shit.

Carly said he knew Terry Baker wouldn't show up in the daylight hours. Bottom feeders of his ilk preferred to do their dirty work in the dark of night. He expected Baker to confront them with a party the size of their recent encounter. This time, Carly felt Baker would arm his troops with guns, knives, and torches to be lit after they were onsite. They would park away from their house, and walk in without lights. The illegitimate sons of whores would separate and attack from two or three directions. The law enforcers made the KKK aware that no law officers would be around to interfere.

Uncle Matt liked Carly's plan, and they headed to town to get the barbed wire from the Hardware store and cans from the dump site. Carly bought ammunition for the two 38 caliber double action revolvers that had come into his possession.

They returned to the farm in mid-afternoon and began developing the defense system as planned. It was rudimentary, but Carly hoped it would give the defenders a fighting chance against the shadowy thugs converging on them. They completed it as the sun sought the western horizon, turning the scattered clouds to lovely shades of red, orange, and yellow.

Uncle Matt settled down to rest before going home. Carly asked if he needed coffee.

"Not tonight, but tomorrow night, for sure. Leave the coffee and the percolator out, and I will be okay."

Carly sat across the table from Uncle Matt and listened closely. Eva sat beside him.

"I want you to come to my house early tomorrow in your buggy. Drive your buggy to The Landing and walk around as if sightseeing. Talk with as many people as possible. Introduce yourselves and get the names of everyone you talk with. Talk with people during the day and around sunset or after and do the same the next day. You should be ready to come home in midafternoon. I'm sure this needs to be clarified because you wonder how that will defeat Terry Baker. Don't worry about that aspect. I'm giving you plausible deniability, something I hope you won't need, but you will have it if you do. We will have plenty of time to discuss this after the fact. For the time being, you must trust me."

That night, before going to bed, Carly penned a chilling letter to the editor of *The Marston Herald* describing the talk passing through the community by Terry Baker, the KKK, and their associates. He documented his interactions with the chief of police and the sheriff, the reception he received from each, and their refusals to supply aid. He quoted the chief, saying, "Carly, you have made your bed and can now sleep in it. You have made enemies in the sheriff's department and this police department." He said he would leave his farm on the date of the letter to protect his family. He didn't include an address on the envelope, only: Editor, *The Marston Herald*, to be opened in the event of an attack on me and my farm by the KKK. It was an insurance policy of sorts, in case the night turned deadly. He dated the letter that day. Now to wait for the shit to hit the fan.

The dawn of the new day was clear, the eastern sky was ablaze with red and blue hues, and Carly, Eva, and Jenna arrived at Uncle Matt's house. Uncle Matt had made many changes reflecting his personality and passions. He invited them in, offered them coffee, iced tea, and lemonade and proudly showed them through his neatly organized house, so tidy it resembled a doll house.

As they sat, he reiterated his instructions from the prior evening, cautioning them to take the visitations seriously and work hard. He left later in the morning, and as he went, he said, "I want you two to relax, read, and walk around. Eva will probably already know several people, and that's good. I have a television you can watch. Make yourselves at home and don't worry. Don't wait up." As he smiled and turned to leave, Carly handed him his envelope and asked him to give it to the newspaper editor that day, and he should call the editor after they had settled the score. Uncle Matt carefully placed the letter in his coat pocket, said he would make the call.

After Uncle Matt left, Carly and Eva sat, chatted, drank coffee and lemonade, and pretended the scheduled events weren't a mental bother. They rode to The Landing knowing they would exercise their legs walking throughout the community, and it would relax their minds. Jenna was excited about exploring new houses and people.

In a twist reminiscent of a game of chess, Carly and Eva spent the day blending into the community of The Landing. Uncle Matt had arranged it, a cover, a way for them to be safe and build an alibi. The goal? Plausible deniability.

They rode into the quaint, historic village of The Landing. Carly had no memory of visiting The Landing, but Eva had visited several times with Dottie Mae. He took copious notes in his little notebook as they wandered around the village.

The houses were attractive, and their well-maintained condition suggested pride in the community. Some places were owned by the farm and rented to farm workers, but most people who lived there owned their homes. They had worked on the farm for years and wanted to own their homes, and the farm made purchases available with unusually accommodating terms.

The two days were an eerie distance from their daily routines at home. The village was serene. Eva met many acquaintances of Dottie Mae and introduced them to Carly, and they had conversations about kids, schools, and jobs, though most were working or had worked on the farm. Carly was interested in how they enjoyed working on the farm, but he asked Eva to pose the questions, thinking the answers might be more truthful. It surprised him when Eva told him all but one said they enjoyed working on the farm; however, they described the work as hard.

Eva met an older lady acquaintance, Annabelle Johnson, who was so happy to see Eva and to meet Carly. After talking for half an hour, she invited the two to supper that evening. Eva said she was the best cook in the county. They eagerly accepted.

As the sun dipped in the west, they made their way around a vast cornfield and met a man who was Eva's relative, the brother of her Uncle Rodney and Dottie Mae. He and Eva talked at length, but he ignored Carly. Afterward, Carly asked why they had excluded him from their conversation. Eva said she was uncomfortable with him, and he seemed to have something on his mind. It puzzled her, she wanted to know more, but he suddenly had no more time and walked away.

They took the buggy back to Uncle Matt's home. They relaxed after taking their showers, and Mary took them to Annabelle's house. Annabelle was charming, making them feel welcome and comfortable in her home. The kitchen aromas tortured their empty stomachs after eating a light breakfast, but no lunch.

Annabelle served them a soul-food supper to die for. Crispy fried chicken, collard greens with ham hock, cheese grits, black-eyed peas, and cornbread covered the table. The beverage was a choice of iced tea or buttermilk. The dessert was the most delicious banana pudding Carly had ever tasted. He had not eaten so well since long before leaving the farm, except the night at Evangeline's.

After chatting well beyond a polite hour, they said their good-nights and waddled with full bellies to the buggy, and with a slow walk, Mary took them back to Uncle Matt's house. Neither he nor Eva was remotely familiar with a TV set. Curious, Carly turned it on, and turned to a show called The Honeymooners that was starting. There was a lot of laughter, so they watched. Jackie Gleason and Art Carney soon had them both laughing so hard tears were streaming down their faces. It ended, but they were tired and sated, so they were off to bed. But the tension, always in the background, was pal-pable.

In the morning, they ate breakfast and planned their day. Eva said her understanding of plausible deniability meant they should meet the so-called mayor of The Landing, and she knew him well from her many visits. His name was Joseph Ross, but everyone called him Preacher Joe. Eva said he was a good man, intelligent, and was the preacher for The Landing.

After hitching Mary, they rode to The Landing and walked into an area new to Carly. Eva took him to Preacher Joe's house. A pleasant man, Preacher Joe was about 40, handsome, educated, and enjoyed talking, especially about himself, but his charisma, intelligence, and confidence pleased Carly. They spoke for almost forty-five minutes and would have talked longer, but Preacher Joe had a group at the church that needed his attention. Carly and Eva continued through the community, meeting dozens before they finally took their leave in the late afternoon, heading back to their farm.

Late afternoon was approaching when they arrived home. Their protective traps, the barbed wire was gone, there was no trash, and everything was normal. Nothing was amiss. If something had happened in their absence, there was no evidence, and they assumed nothing had. But it was too clean, too deliberate, and Carly noticed something he wouldn't show Eva. He had noticed multiple spots of freshly removed grass and topsoil and an irregular patch almost twelve inches in the most significant dimension, dull red, typical of a patch of drying blood, next to a Redbud bush. The clean-up had missed it. He hid it by covering it with straw and grass and would remove the topsoil after dusk. The two relaxed around the spring and the Weeping Willow and nearby magnolia. Jenna was happy to be home, relaxing with them at the spring.

When the clouds of the western sky were turning golden red, as the sun bled into the horizon, they heard a vehicle in front of their house. They waited, concerned that it was someone who might have come to harm them. When Uncle Matt walked around the corner of the house toward them, they jumped to their feet and met him when he was halfway up the slope. Carrying an old cotton picker's sack, a large cloth bag with a strap to fit over his shoulder, he came to the spring and removed the pack from his shoulder. "I brought hamburgers, sandwiches, and various drinks. So, we shall eat, drink, and try to be merry," said Uncle Matt.

Carly thought Uncle Matt was tense, as he had been when they last met. They were dying to know what happened in their absence but remembered their admonishment to ask no questions.

"Uncle Matt only said he wouldn't answer questions. He didn't say they weren't to ask them," Carly whispered.

"But his intention was for us not to ask questions," Eva said in a whisper.

"Oh dammit, I need answers," Carly whispered irritably. After eating and chatting, Uncle Matt became more relaxed, looked tired, and could have easily drifted off to sleep. Carly mustered his courage and asked, "Uncle Matt, will we go to sleep tonight and be unafraid, or will Terry Baker and the KKK murder us and burn our house?"

"I heard you whispering, and I wondered if you would scrounge up the courage to ask that critical question. You're right; I didn't say you couldn't ask questions. I said I wouldn't answer them. But I will tell you what is pertinent to your future. Baker and two KKK henchmen escaped, and we don't know where to look. Baker is such a slimy creature he can escape almost anywhere. I wish I had better news," Uncle Matt said.

Although somber, they ate, drank, and pretended to be merry. The elephant in their midst, Baker's escape, wouldn't allow it. Uncle Matt said his goodbyes and said he would be back soon.

After he left, Carly and Eva planned their next move. "This is going to be over tonight," said Carly, emphatically.

"But how can you say that when you don't know where Baker is hiding?"

"But I do. Think, where would you go if you were Baker?" Carly said.

"Not home, I'm sure."

"That's correct," Carly's eyes sharpened. "I would bet dollars to donuts Baker has gone to his boarded-up drugstore, and I'm going after him," Carly said firmly.

Eva spoke with trebled anxiety. "Carly, why don't you just let the sheriff handle this. This is too dangerous. They will arrest Baker."

"Eva, can you honestly say that, knowing the history of the police and the KKK? Do you remember the slap on Baker's wrist the last time he was arrested?"

"I know, you're right. But Carly, don't even think about going by yourself," the anxiety now gone from her voice, and her martial arts persona kicking in. "I'll be there, holding your hand if I must, but I have a vested interest in killing the son of a bitch, as much or more so than you. Don't deprive me of this immense pleasure."

"Oh, hell! I'm smart enough to know when you've beaten me, so let's launch this operation. I would like to head for the drugstore. But I'd like to get home at a reasonable time."

"Let's do it!"

He gathered the two revolvers and ammunition, and they were

on their way. He handed the revolvers to Eva and asked her to load both.

He parked a few blocks from the drugstore, and they walked quickly and quietly along the pavement, trying to stay in the shadows. It was raining lightly, and the air was foul with the stench of wet garbage. Eva waded through puddles of standing water, and Carly followed. They slowed their pace as they approached the drugstore, moving into a stealthier mode. A feral cat hauled ass out of a dark alley and ran between two overflowing, foul-smelling garbage bins, crossing the sidewalk and street before them, hissing, snarling, and screaming, scaring the bejesus out of them! Eva was on the verge of screaming but caught it in time. Carly's heart was racing and skipping beats simultaneously as his brain and cardiovascular system tried to process the adrenaline dump infusion. "I think I peed my pants," Eva whispered.

Approaching the vacant, boarded-up drugstore, they continued to sneak through an alley alongside, and headed to the back of the building. They were looking for an entrance, but there were no windows or doors along the side of the building. Sneaking forward, they reached the back of the building. Visibility was worse than poor, but as they slowly crept along the backside of the building, they saw a door five or six feet away.

Carly silently slipped up to the door, expecting it to be locked, but, surprise, someone had entered and left it unlocked. Opening the door slowly, praying it wouldn't squeak, it protested with a mild squeak. Inside, with no lights or windows, Carly was sure they had found the darkest room in Marston. He was sorry he had forgotten a flashlight. Dawn was still hours away, and Carly hoped they would be on their way home in another half-hour. Sweat from his forehead covered his face and neck.

Eva handed him one revolver and kept the other. As they crept along the interior wall of the dark building, they bumped into an enormous maze of old newspapers, magazines, broken furniture, and unidentifiable trash. Stumbling through and around the mountain of trash, Carly saw a thin line of dim light escaping from under a closed door, and he heard men's voices. One voice belonged to Terry Baker, and he whispered it to Eva. They quietly moved the enormous pile of newspapers, magazines, and pieces of broken furniture and placed the junk against the door to Baker's room. After the trash pile was higher than his head, he opened the outside door for ventilation, lit a book of matches, and started one hell of a bonfire unlike anything he had ever seen.

The men's voices sounded muffled. Although the flames were blazing hot within minutes, he added more fuel. The door caught fire. The voices behind the door were becoming louder and more excited. Smoke filled Eva and Carly's room, and they guessed the men's room was as well. He could hear them coughing like crazy.

Baker yelled for one henchman to open the door, and a scream erupted when the man tried to turn the red-hot doorknob. Suddenly, the room erupted in panicked chaos. One man yelled he would use his robe as padding on the hot doorknob to open the door, and when he did, fiery flames from the floor to the ceiling met him.

He let loose a shrill, panicked shriek. "The damned place is afar!"

"Damn. How the hell did this happen? Damn, I'm having all kinds of bad luck. Whose side is God on?" cried Baker.

Another voice chimed in. "Whatever, we have to get the hell out of this blazing inferno, quick like, or we're bound to be barbecued."

Carly wanted to stand near the door, but the heat forced him to retreat. He hoped the men would come out one by one, and when the first man sprang headlong through the fire, Carly met him head-on, flipping him hard, landing him on the concrete floor in the fire. He wasn't unconscious and returned to his feet, heading toward Carly, who smashed the man's face with his revolver. He fell, unmoving. Carly fired a single gunshot into the man's right temple and dropped the revolver beside the body. He was dead without calling out to his companions inside. Another white-robed cretin was leaping through the fire. Before the cutthroat got his bearings, Eva was close enough to prove her training in Martial Arts, and gave him a flying kick to his face, and when he was back on his feet, she placed a solid kick to his groin. He grabbed his crotch with both hands, and while leaning forward, Eva walked to him and shot him in the forehead with the second revolver. Dead before he hit the floor, he tumbled backward into the blaze.

Carly was waiting for Baker to make his appearance. It seemed unlikely he would be brave enough to face the blaze, and his idea to remain inside the room and suffocate and roast didn't sit well with Carly. Since Baker had the spine of a nightcrawler, he might wimp out, and he might prefer to stay in the room as his preferred way to die. Carly jumped through the blaze and at once faced an existentially panicked Terry Baker aiming a pistol at him. If Baker believed he was in control, he would be more courageous.

Carly made a head-on fools rush, surprising and confusing Baker. A blast from his pistol sent a bullet through Carly's left shoulder, which hurt like hell, but Carly's momentum slammed his body into Baker, causing the second shot to splat closer to the ceiling than Carly's body. Baker still held onto the gun. Carly was now fighting with only one good arm and fist. Moving closer, Carly led with his knee into Baker's solar plexus with all 215 pounds of his body mass. Baker's eyes bugged out, and he wasn't breathing. After long minutes, air rushed back into his lungs, followed by an uncontrollable fit of deep coughing, so deep and excruciating it sounded like he might cough up his spleen or a kidney. The gun had spiraled across the room.

Baker had the ferocity of a rabid animal. Even though he no longer had the gun, he continued to fight more viciously than before. When a man senses his mortality, he becomes as fierce as a wild animal, and animal fury became Baker's first line of defense and offense. Carly stomped on the top of Baker's foot with all his weight and force, prompting the familiar crack of broken bones, which elicited a piercing scream like a wounded animal. Carly aimed a solid, massively hard blow towards Baker's midsection, but he ducked low, and the impact smashed hard into his mouth and nose and produced more sweet sounds of bones breaking. A geyser of blood reminiscent of Old Faithful spurted into the air. The volume of blood was astounding. Baker was conscious, lying on his back, and had a wild, scared look in his eyes. Carly turned to retrieve Baker's revolver and almost collided with Eva, who was holding it in her hand, going for Baker. Baker was beyond panicked when he recognized Eva standing over him, smiling, with a revolver in her hand, aimed at his head. He was crying, apologizing, and begging. He didn't remain panicked for long. Eva smiled and fired two bullets into Baker's head, killing him instantly. They arranged the bodies as if facing each other, strategically placing the three revolvers close to them, making it appear that a loud and fatal disagreement had resulted in a murder-suicide confrontation. They were assured the bodies would burn.

Eva told Carly she'd never driven a car but would drive him to the hospital. At the hospital, she called Dr. Fischer, who arrived about fifteen minutes later. He took Carly's history as he examined him. But before he discussed treatment, he looked at Carly and shook his head.

"The first thing I will do is to prescribe a padded room to keep you." He chuckled.

"We'll need an x-ray of your shoulder after we splint it. There are no definite findings of a fracture, but we'll be cautious until we know. Then we'll get some lab work cooking and clean you up."

After about a half hour, the x-ray of his shoulder showed multiple small metallic fragments that followed a straight path through the shoulder, with concomitant soft tissue swelling, typical of a gunshot wound. The bullet fractured the cortex of the upper humerus, but with no resulting displaced fracture. Doctor Fischer debrided the wound and placed Carly's arm in a sling. He told Carly that, since the cortex of the bone was fractured, he would admit him for IV antibiotics. Nurses started the intravenous antibiotics, and he was admitted. Carly received a promise from Dr. Fischer to discharge him as soon as possible with the required prescriptions for oral antibiotics.

He remained hospitalized for two days and Dr. Fischer released him with prescriptions for antibiotics and pain relief. Carly wanted to return to his academic program without more absences.

＊

Uncle Matt came to their house the afternoon of Carly's discharge to deliver news, and he was surprised to find him in a sling. Carly said, "Oh, it's nothing. After you visited, I walked to the barn to feed Mary without a light. I tripped and banged my shoulder hard on the ground. A small dry limb penetrated the muscle, requiring a surgical clean-up. I was in the hospital for a couple of days for antibiotics. I may have torn a ligament, but I'll wear a sling for a few days, and it should be okay."

Uncle Matt said, "I came over several times, and no one was home. Your accident explains why. I'm here to fill you in with some good news. Terry Baker and his two KKK compadres are dead, apparently from a three-way murder-suicide confrontation. The on-going investigation may bring out the details. An arsonist, perhaps Baker himself, set the Baker Drug Store and Soda Fountain building ablaze. When someone called the fire department, the blaze had already destroyed the building, literally burned it to the ground. The fire chief said they found no accelerants. When the firefighters combed through the rubble, they found three charred bodies in the area of a room in the back. The medical examiner named one body as Baker, and the other two were his cohorts, second and third in the line of command of the KKK. All had gunshot wounds, but the medical examiner did autopsies to decide if they were the causes of death. The results are not yet available. Three double-action revolvers traced back to the KKK were lying close to the bodies. Those deaths leave the KKK without leadership, and that is good. They have blown the brains out of that damnable organization, and I hope it will never recover from that loss. When no one showed up to burn down your house and barn and murder you three, we collected all the defensive materials and delivered them to the farm." Carly kept a straight face, but a knowing look might have escaped.

Uncle Matt stood to leave and asked Carly if he had any guns. Carly answered, "No, not anymore."

Uncle Matt's eyes met Carly's, and a coded, unspoken message passed between them, along with perfunctory nods. Uncle Matt shook Carly's hand, holding it longer than needed, and the two parted with a friendly smile, acknowledging the message was transmitted and received.

Uncle Matt gave Carly a friendly request and said, "Carly, consider going to the farm to make peace with your Mama. If for no other reason, do it for me. You might find things a little different now than when you left. Take Eva with you. I think she would enjoy seeing the place, and I'll bet your Mama would enjoy seeing you both." Carly remained silent, but Uncle Matt hugged him, and whispered, "I'm proud of you, my boy." He descended the steps and left.

The next regular edition of *The Marston Herald* had a front-page article about the recent murder-suicide confrontation of Terry Baker and his henchmen. Firefighters found three revolvers at the scene and traced them back to the KKK, and all three guns were involved in the killings. There was a second-page story of a mysterious incident of nine men showing up at the hospital in the middle of the night with gunshot wounds on their feet, ankles, and legs. No one would say who shot them, nor did they know who took them to the hospital. The police showed little interest in questioning the men, and they claimed the men refused to talk to them. As far as the police were concerned, the case was closed.

Carly and Eva read the newspaper article, didn't comment, but their knowing looks spoke volumes. Someday they will return to their academic pursuits, always looking forward, trying to stop looking back.

43

1960
· · · · · · ·

AS HE DID EACH MORNING, Carly dropped Eva off early at the store and drove to pick up Mr. Mallory at his house. Last evening, he and Mr. Mallory had an excellent discussion of Britain's complex yet well-documented history. They'd been discussing this subject over the past two weeks, and Carly's understanding of the United Kingdom had expanded exponentially because of Mr. Mallory's depth of knowledge.

Entering the driveway, Carly noticed a patch of colorful, multi-toned crocuses blooming their little hearts out beneath a pecan tree. How could he have missed that patch of beauty? They must have blossomed overnight. Mr. Mallory had not retrieved his newspaper. As usual, Carly picked it up, petted the community cat, and went inside without announcing himself. Because Mr. Mallory hadn't turned on the lights, Carly flipped the switch, but his pulse rate increased as he felt a mild adrenaline rush. After leaving the living room, he walked to the kitchen and became more anxious as he called for Mr. Mallory, but there was no answer.

He hurried to Mr. Mallory's bedroom to find him sitting in bed, propped on pillows and a book on his lap. The covers were neat across his legs to his waist. Carly rushed to his side, but he was un-responsive. His eyes were open, staring ahead but unblinking and vacant. His skin had the wan, pale, bloodless pallor of a corpse. Carly felt his neck for a pulse, his skin was as cold as the room, and he felt no pulse. His body was stiff from rigor mortis. Mr. Mallory was dead.

Carly tenderly closed Mr. Mallory's eyes, but he wasn't sure why. Death cannot be faked. Life's absence leaves a void like no other in the now-useless body. Carly's pain was sudden and immense, and the mental anguish was horrendous as he felt a pang in the depths of his soul. Twice before, at Winnie's horrible death and Josie's sudden, heart-breaking death, he had experienced that terrible hurt. Now he would suffer another excruciatingly painful loss with the death of his best friend. His tears flowed as he sat on the edge of the bed, unsure of what to do. A hint of a smile appeared on his lips when he saw the title of the book Mr. Mallory was reading, *A History of the British Empire*. Carly smiled slightly as he thought why that sneaky son of a gun. That's why he was so knowledgeable about British history. Carly left the house to tell Eva that Mr. Mallory had passed away. Her sadness was intense, and she returned with Carly to Mr. Mallory. Unsure of what to do next, they called Dr. Fischer.

Dr. Fischer's arrival was a considerable relief for the two because they were out of their element, having no experience of handling the processes and decisions that were needed. He promptly got the details and took charge. He called the coroner. When he arrived, the two conferred, and the coroner left. Then the funeral home attendants arrived, they asked Carly and Eva to step into the living room and gently removed Mr. Mallory's body.

Dr. Fischer told Carly and Eva that Mr. Mallory had lived longer than he had expected. The vast cardiac destruction by the massive myocardial infarction had prompted Dr. Fischer to recommend that he bring his affairs current because death was imminent and would be unannounced.

After Dr. Fischer left, they visited Mrs. Brownlie at her home, feeling a phone call would be tacky and disrespectful. Her pain was obvious, but she accepted the news more stoically than they had expected. She said his death was not unexpected because he had told her he had only an abbreviated time to live. They had talked at length about his imminent death. It saddened her, but it had honored her to assist when he asked her to help arrange his affairs, bring them current, and keep them so. They worked together, and she felt confident that handling his matters would happen like the workings of a fine watch. She said, "Expecting his death doesn't make it less painful because in my eyes, he was a great person."

A week later a memorial service was held for close friends. A large crowd filled the local church. Among those attending was Chester Pilkington, Esq., Mr. Mallory's attorney. He was introduced to Carly and Eva by Mrs. Brownlie. He said he needed to meet with them as soon as it was convenient to discuss the store and other matters. They arranged an appointment two days away.Carly and Eva agreed to keep the store open for two more days, and then they would begin looking for jobs. He would give the new owners the three-ring binder with crucial information about the store's operation. Carly thought poor Mr. Mallory had not gone on his vacation. Then it came to him. Mr. Mallory knew his death was imminent, and that would be his vacation. What would be the point of him asking Carly to cover while he was on "vacation?"

*

Mr. Pilkington arrived at the appointed time. A natty dresser, he wore a dark gray pin-striped suit, a colorful tie, and a tab collar. His graying temples and immaculate Van Dyke completed the picture of the consummate English gentleman. Carly welcomed him, posted the CLOSED sign, and he and Eva went with him to the office. He placed his briefcase and files on the large table in the center of the room, the work site of Mr. Mallory. After offering his condolences for the deaths of Josie and Mr. Mallory, Mr. Pilkington got down to work. Taking out a file folder from his briefcase, he removed papers clipped together.

Carly and Eva exchanged questioning glances as they wrinkled their brows and shrugged their shoulders. Mr. Pilkington cleared his throat and smiled. "I will read Mr. Truman Mallory's last will."

Their questioning glances developed into disbelieving frowns, wondering if there was a mistake. Mr. Pilkington said he would dispense with the boilerplate legalese and get to the reason for their meeting with plain talk.

"Mr. Mallory leaves the Mercantile Store, its contents, and bank accounts to Carlton Turner and Eva Lou Swain." A gentle breeze could have blown them away. He continued. "As you will see before we finish, the bank accounts are substantial." Carly asked him to repeat the statements, since he was sure he had misunderstood. Mr. Pilkington assured him he had not, and he continued. "Mr. Mallory leaves his home in Marston, the household goods, and the automobile to Carlton Turner and Eva Lou Swain." At this point, they were hyperventilating and sweating.

Mr. Pilkington continued. "Mr. Mallory leaves his entire portfolio of stocks and bonds and all the monies in his bank accounts to Carlton Turner and Eva Lou Swain. This portfolio is beyond immense."

They were quiet for a long moment trying to assimilate the earth-jolting information. No one spoke.

Finally, Carly cleared his throat and asked, "Why us?"

Mr. Pilkington turned in his chair and said, "You and Josie made an impeccable and indelible impression on him early on. Then Eva came on site, and you three impressed Mr. Mallory with your intelligence, how well you work together, your ethics, and your interpersonal attitudes. He watched as you met problems head-on and mastered trials that would have defeated most mature adults. When he shared your history with me, I wondered if it was a fabrication. You deserve all that he has left you. To have been a part of Truman's life was an honor. It is so extremely sad Josie passed away recently. I would have loved to have met her. It is a genuine pleasure to have met each of you."

The new owners of Mallory's Mercantile Store, Eva and Carly, discussed their immediate problem: who would run the store? Carly suggested calling Mr. Mallory's CPA. In the three-ring binder, they found Smith and Hudson, Certified Public Accountants, and Mr. Henry Hudson, Mr. Mallory's CPA.

Mr. Hudson offered his condolences and spoke highly of Mr. Mallory. Carly explained their problem, and Mr. Hudson eased his anxiety.

"Don't worry about this. I know a person who can manage the store."

*

The FBI sweep of the KKK resulted in the convictions of eight local members of the KKK, local lawyers, police officers, and a local judge. Special Agent Salter said lawyers had gotten delays, but they would eventually pay the piper. They would have to do prison time. After serving their prison time, their illegal operations will have destroyed their professional lives, so they'll have nothing left at home. The results of the KKK trials, the first in Eva's memory that a jury had convicted KKK members, gave her optimism she had never experienced. Carly suggested these trials were in a Federal Court, not the more capricious state courts, accounting for the convictions.

*

Mrs. Brownlie had recuperated, and the extended relaxation in the months since her brutal abduction had reinvigorated her. She regained her psychological composure and was ready to re-stake her claim to the Stars of Infinity Program. The Ben Griffin Foundation assured her they would return the program to its original stature with complete funding. Mrs. Brownlie received a call from Special Agent Salter, who gave her an update on an essential aspect of the investigation that interested her. The FBI had arrested the dean of students, Theron Johnson, and his secretary, Carolyn Crawford. She and the dean provided the Grand Wizard with information about the Stars of Infinity Program and gave information about the students to the KKK.

Miss Crawford said she and Dean Johnson collaborated on the notifications to the Grand Wizard, but the dean always insisted on personally contacting Baker. City University's president fired the dean of students, Theron Johnson. The Federal Grand Jury indicted the dean and Miss Crawford on seven counts of manslaughter and many more charges, and both were awaiting trial. Since receiving that news, Mrs. Brownlie had made spectacular recuperative progress.

These bits of information encouraged her to set a tentative date for re-opening the Stars of Infinity Program. It would resume the following July, four months away. When she gave the news to the twelve student members of the program, everyone groaned and grunted, but they accepted it without further protest. She gave them ponderous assignments that should keep them busy until their classes began, and they groaned and moaned even more.

44

1963
·······

THE STARS OF INFINITY PROGRAM had been efficacious in furthering the integration process of the university when classes began in the fall of 1963. There were now twenty-seven Black students enrolled in the university. Carly had the radio tuned to the City University station, listening to classical music while he completed the paperwork for an extensive Physical Chemistry lab project. Eva had been up much earlier to do last-minute polishing of a speech she would present to the Mathematics Club the following day. She had worked diligently to prepare the paper, *Large Subsets of Fqn With No Three-Term Arithmetic Progression*. Eva laughed when Carly told her his eyes were glazing over listening to the title.

The national and state news came on, grabbing his attention. Birmingham, Alabama's ultra-segregationist Commissioner of Public Safety, Theophilus Eugene "Bull" Conner was the architect of a disastrous heavy-handed put-down of peaceful protests by Black high school students. The Black students peacefully protested school segregation, and Bull Connor unleashed water cannons and police dogs on them. Martin Luther King said, "Bull Connor wants to ensure that Birmingham remains the most segregated city in America."

Eva and Carly were midway their eighth and final year of the Stars of Infinity Program, and thoughts of graduation and postdoctoral programs were heavy on their minds. They spent long hours in chemistry and physics labs, philosophy, and Russian literature and the volume of reading was astounding. They adapted, and a bright light at the end of a long tunnel beckoned them forward.

Eva began displaying troubling signs in her relationship with

Carly more than midway through their final year. Eva used several excuses but usually said she was too tired to walk with Carly and preferred to be alone in her free time. At first, Carly suspected nothing, but weeks passed, and things worsened. She spent no time with Carly and avoided him completely. What the hell was happening? He gave her space, no crowding, and no pushing to talk. But she offered neither indisputable nor disputable reasons for her behavior. He must assume something terrible was happening, but he didn't know what it could be. Was she having an affair? He couldn't imagine with whom, and because of severe time constraints, when it could even take place. She was so deathly afraid of pregnancy; he had serious doubts she would take that risk. Something was afoot, but he wasn't sure what, and so far, she refused to talk with him, and he lacked the courage to confront her.

Enroute home, he thought I don't know what is going on with Eva. She is avoiding any contact with me, and she has shut me out of her life. Sometimes I watch her as she sits alone, appearing dreadfully sad and often weeping. But when I approached her in those moments, she asked to be alone and walked away.

He had exhausted his limited repertoire of ideas on how best to approach her. None was successful. Carly understood that love may sometimes result in lies, and we imploringly present them with the best intentions when they occur. But Carly remained unconvinced that was happening with Eva, although he had nothing to support that supposition. Her actions were suspicious and suggestive that someone else was in the picture, but he wouldn't believe that. Their relationship had been too honest and open for him to acknowledge that it could be possible, but it was a painful predicament.

At Mrs. Brownlie's house, he walked to the door unannounced, and the door opened just as he was about to knock. Mrs. Brownlie invited him in and asked him to sit. After exchanging brief small talk, she went straight to the point.

"My boy, something is seriously wrong with you today. Do you want to talk about it?"

Broaching the uncomfortable subject, Carly shifted in his chair and began. "Mrs. Brownlie, Eva's recent actions have baffled me. She has shut me out of her life, and I can't imagine what caused her to discard her best friend. She grows more distant daily. I've seen her sitting alone, sobbing, but she turns away when I approach her, so we haven't discussed the problem. I know she's in enormous emotional pain, but I'm not privy to the source. She's not eating or sleeping. I'm afraid she'll become ill if this continues. I'm disturbed, hurt, and in total darkness because she won't talk to me. Do you have any ideas?"

"No, my boy, I'm sorry, I do not. The two of you were so in love. I also have seen that something is bothering that poor girl. I think she has received incorrect or incomplete information from someone. She's shut me out as well, and it breaks my heart. She is an exemplary young adult and student. Nothing can detract from that record. I'm fearful she may never resume talking to us. Sadly, I don't know why."

Carly had no labels to catalog Eva's actions, or non-actions. He was ready to listen to anyone and try anything, but nothing had appeared on his horizon, and nothing helpful was readily apparent from his meeting with Mrs. Brownlie. Carly had become terminally desperate. He would have employed the services of a crystal gazer, but he didn't know one.

Carly was up early, ready to go to his lab. Eva remained in bed. He assumed she wanted to be alone, so he didn't disturb her and made his way to the campus. But a productive day was not to be, for research was the furthest point from his mind, and he couldn't focus or stay on track. In joyless desperation, Carly wondered why the hunger for connection increases exponentially when a relationship becomes questionable. It isn't jealousy. Jealousy is an immature and adolescent emotion, and he knew they were beyond that stage, leading him to his next thought. What the hell was going on?

He notified his mentor he was taking the rest of the day off. He had no desire to go home but had no alternative ideas about where to hang. Carly had the facetious thought too bad the soda fountain wasn't around anymore. He had become persona non grata long before it closed, and he need not remind himself why. Why don't I walk around the park? It's a beautiful day, the flowers are blooming, and it should help dispel this vicious anxiety. This degree of mental disturbance is something he would not like as a long-term friend.

As Carly entered the park, he saw an older man with one leg. Someone said the man was a veteran of the First World War, and a grenade had blown away his leg. Carly continued to his favorite place, a beautiful lake at the back side of the park. The air was still, and the calm water had a glassy surface. He walked a quick path along the water's edge and watched a large fish make a jump, making a loud splash and sending concentric wave ripples across the water. Dr. Fischer was sitting alongside the central fountain, relaxing. Carly walked over to him, and when Dr. Fischer saw him, he invited him to sit. Carly preferred to stand and said, "With the lovely, addicting aroma of these beautiful flowers, I can see why you chose to come here."

"Yes, I come here often when I have a day off, like today. Few people are out today, but sometimes there are more. I enjoy people-watching, and when one studies them, people can be seen as amazing creatures." Dr. Fischer updated him on the events in his life, or non-events, as he described. He was still single, with no one on the horizon, and he said the pickings for educated girlfriends were slim in this town.

"So, am I to assume your girlfriends are uneducated?" Carly asked.

Dr. Fischer laughed, saying, "That's a dead ringer for something Josie would have said." He laughed again and commented that he had missed her refreshing wit.

"I too have missed her something terrible, daily and every night," said Carly.

Carly brought him up to date on the activities of his own stodgy life, and Dr. Fischer was more than a little impressed. He said Carly's achievements were categoric and asked about Eva. Carly described her activities, painting an exact picture of her superb achievements but leaving out their recent tragic lows.

Dr. Fischer listened courteously, then replied, "Carly, what are you not telling me?"

Dr. Fischer's people-watching skills were impressive, and now they appeared preeminent. Carly then vividly described how Eva's behavior had gone from ordinary to bizarre to Kafkaesque, with no idea why. Still, he hoped by telling him the truth, Dr. Fischer might have valuable suggestions.

Dr. Fischer listened quietly, and, almost reluctantly, suggested he could explain the origin and continuation of Eva's peculiar behavior.

"Carly, this will be painful for you to hear, and difficult for me to say to you. I met with Eva weeks back because I worried about a problem that I felt obligated to address and try to prevent, if possible, a potential disaster. Neither Eva nor anyone else had asked me to intervene."

The subject was complex and challenging; it was close to Dr. Fischer personally, and caused him to squirm.

"I admit to ignorantly blundering into an abyss that I still worry about, and it promises to become much more of a trouble spot than I initially conceived. But if it prevents the catastrophic problem that I envision, I will have succeeded and we will survive the onslaught. To paraphrase William Ernest Henley in his poem "Invictus," 'My head will be bloody but unbowed.'"

Dr. Fischer continued, "I will present my concerns to you, and you can either provide me with more information, ask me questions, or tell me to go to Hell. Carly, I realize you and Eva are a loving item. Your relationship may or may not be sexual. If not, and your close physical contact continues, it will become sexual. I envied you, experiencing a beautiful romance with the love of your life. And I understand your relationship with Eva began early in childhood. But I have concerns. She shares an excellent IQ with you and Josie, but there is no evidence of exceptional intelligence from her Black parents. You three, I will include Josie for this comparison, have identical blue eyes. Her skin is light colored, and she has beautiful blue eyes, and

Caucasian or European light brown hair consistent with a Caucasian parent. She had a parent with dark skin, I won't put a label on his ethnicity, but she has been raised as a Black person. I approached Eva about my concerns; again, none of my business, I admit. As I expected, she became quite upset and despondent. If my observations are correct, and if she were to get pregnant by you, that could be a disastrous event of a magnitude that you two cannot imagine. I asked her to allow me to explore how you three might have the same father. She became angry, then severely depressed, and because of this question has not allowed me to pursue the question of paternity. Still, it needs answering before a potential disaster becomes a reality."

Carly was no longer standing. He had sat down clumsily with his ass angled half on and half off the bench. His feet and knees were nervously bouncing up and down. His mind was too foggy to think clearly. Hyperventilation was imminent and he felt a sudden rush of recurrent anxiety and the onset of an acute panic attack. His life was disintegrating like a seashore sandcastle in a rising tide. Carly listened as Dr. Fischer talked, but as the blood rushed to his head, a loud, high-pitched roaring sound had overtaken his inner ears, a panic-driven white noise. It was blocking whatever the doctor was saying, but he was aware enough to realize he was alone in hearing the roaring noise. Dr. Fischer had made his point.

"Proceed as you see fit. Please discuss our conversation with Eva. She is a model student and an exemplary person, and I want to see her continue her outstanding work when she leaves to begin the next chapter of her life. I want her to continue to be just as great and the same for you. Your and Eva's potential is too great to allow the disruption that a disaster of this magnitude could invoke. This potential catastrophe is preventable. But if true, it will require you, Carly, and Eva, to make difficult life-altering choices. But we need more information before we can address those hard choices."

Carly looked blank; obviously, he had no clear vision of how to proceed. He was stunned, and it would not be beyond reason that he would need help to get home.

"I will bid you a good day, and I am so sorry to be the bearer of this potential shipwreck and tsunami news. You can tell me how you prefer to continue or if you don't want me to continue. Please understand that this discussion falls within doctor-patient confidentiality, and no one else is privy to this conversation. You should not confide in anyone who is not a physician."

He rose, gave a slight nod, shook Carly's hand and walked away with slow, uneasy steps as if he had aged fifty years. Carly had never seen him appear so weary.

This information had blindsided Carly, leaving him in disbelief, and his mind paralyzed. His world had spun out of its orbit. Carly mumbled incomprehensible monosyllabic words to no one, bombinating, sitting on the park bench, numb. What the hell could happen next? What could be next on God's vengeful agenda?

Standing briefly, he muttered, sotto voce, "I'm praying this ground will open up at once into a pit of alligators."

As if in a possessed state, he sat again and had no thoughts for comfort for the first time in his memory. None existed.

On the way home, he was in such a dazed state that he couldn't even cry. Fortunately, Mary was in control and saw him safely home. When he arrived at the farm, Eva was out of bed, but not in a peaceful state of mind.

"Good night," she said abruptly and turned away.

Before Eva could walk away, Carly started to explain in staccato fashion that he had just returned from an accidental meeting with Dr. Fischer. "He told me about his conversation with you. The conversation left me completely blindsided, leaving me devastated and speechless. While hurrying home, I realized how terrified and lonely you must also feel."

"Eva, you must feel so frightened and alone."

They hugged. As she loosened her embrace, Eva had the frightened look of a child, praying, pleading, as she looked beseechingly into his eyes. "It's been a living hell. I cry all day and all hours of the night, and with no appetite, losing weight is a guarantee, but I have nothing to lose. But, Carly, what if it's true?"

He held her in his arms to console her, and tears flowed down his cheeks. They clasped each other in a tight embrace, and Eva cried.

"Let's find out the truth as fast as possible and stop this train wreck before it destroys us. Working on assumptions, not facts, is the poorest basis for a scientific hypothesis. Eva, do you know your blood type?"

Eva turned to sit. "No, I haven't any idea. Dr. Fischer wanted to take my blood sample for typing, but I haven't given my permission yet. Carly, I don't know what to do."

They sat and tried to plan a way forward. They agreed they were in this psychological paroxysm together, and neither should feel it was a lonely journey. The two stared at each other in consternation, and neither knew what to do.

*

Dr. Hiram Baldwin, chair of the English Department at City University, had studied and earned his DPhil in Literature and Arts at The University of Oxford. He had remained in contact with the revered university's Department of English Literature chair. Dr. Baldwin contacted the chairperson in the interest of Miss Eva Lou Swain, giving her his highest recommendation for admission to study the works of Wordsworth. Dr. Baldwin and Eva completed the paperwork, and the prospect of attending the hallowed halls of that honorable institution was a reason for celebration. Eva had never dreamed of admission to such a prestigious university of higher learning. Alert and conscious of the challenges, she knew she could meet them. The Department of Literature and Arts at The University of Oxford accepted Miss Swain.

When she gave Carly the great news, he was serious.

"Eva, I'm bursting with pride for you, but I hope you understand when I say it is with mixed emotions that I offer my sincerest congratulations. I wish you every success in your incredible endeavor. You have earned this excellent academic achievement and the great honor going with it. But I will miss you."

"Carly, what are your postdoctoral plans?"

"I'm spending a year at The Princeton Center for Theoretical Science. I'm anxious to continue studying quantum physics. I'll try to figure out if this life is for me, or will it be a career in medicine."

"Good luck, Carly. I know you will be that shining star that you talked about when we started Stars of Infinity. You should know you'll be in my thoughts daily."

✳

Grand Master Ronen Hanegdi called Carly and Eva into his office to congratulate them on finishing their eighth year of extreme martial arts with perfect attendance. He awarded them the 2nd DAN (2nd degree) Black Belt. He also gave them a confidential award, "To be placed in the back of your safe deposit box, never to see the light of day or spoken of, even to your closest friends," and he awarded them the First Level, Yellow Belt in Krav Maga.

Grand Master Hanegdi explained Krav Maga as an Israeli Martial Art, developed for the Israel Defense Forces. It is practical and intuitive and leaves out the spiritual and ethical aspects of other martial arts, leaving only the lethality of defense and aggression.

They were confused, and Eva asked, "When did we compete in Krav Maga?"

GM Hanegdi said, "Without your explicit knowledge, I have taught Krav Maga to you for the past four years. When I started it, you both began pissing and moaning about how difficult it had become. It got tougher, and you got tougher and stopped complaining. I guess you thought I was punishing you for complaining."

They looked at each other and chuckled.

"You both have excelled, although you were more accomplished than your opponents who didn't fare as well. I trained you to protect yourselves in any hand-to-hand combat situation, and to incapacitate any opponent. It has been a distinct pleasure to have been your instructor. Certain alphabet federal agencies will contact you, I'm positive. Do with them what you will. When you reach your next destination, contact me, and I will set you up for your future martial arts experiences. Please stay in touch. I don't want to lose contact with you." He gave each of them his card, which was unusual. When they were outside, Carly noted his address was in Israel.

They were preparing for their upcoming separation and were subdued, a little sad. He and Eva reminisced, and she wanted to hear more about Josie's and his almost preordained landing at the abandoned house and farm, which became their permanent home. Long-ago experiences came to mind; they laughed at some, others not so much. They talked and laughed, taking the time they had not allotted for themselves during their years of intense, complex study. Separation would be difficult, but theirs was an infrangible bond.

45

1965
·······

AT PRINCETON, CARLY DEVELOPED a strong passion for teaching and research that galvanized his desire to become a physician. His postdoctoral had been an excellent move. Eva was still on his mind, and often he daydreamed of sitting with her beside the Weeping Willow and enjoying a pleasant conversation. Her contagious laugh still echoed in his memory, one of the most captivating sounds he had encountered. The beautiful halo of her smile and the addictive redolence of her body remained imprinted on his dreams and thoughts. He enjoyed talking with her weekly. Since the unproven question of consanguinity had reared its malignant head, would Eva in the flesh be as enchanting as in his memory? He lived on campus in graduate housing and made friends but didn't date. He wasn't ready yet.

His postdoctoral program ended, and Carly planned to drive to Marston. While away, he had found someone who was perfect to take care of their house and farm. David Maxwell was a handy young man raised on a farm, now in his mid-twenties, and Carly felt their farm would be in reliable hands. The electric co-op utility had connected electricity to their house. David wired the house and informed Carly that Southern Bell had installed a phone line and telephone.

On a beautiful, sunny morning in mid-June, he left Princeton. Cirrus clouds and a mare's tail streaked across the sky, predicting rain.

He arrived home mid-afternoon and found that David had groomed the acreage between the house and the road, and a vast expanse around the house, using their new tractor and bush hog. The entire area had a park-like atmosphere, much like a golf course.

As he approached the house, old Jenna greeted him with a tumultuous, emotional welcome. She bathed him with kisses, always by his side, like his shadow.

As he walked through the spotless house, it delighted him when he flipped a wall switch and turned on a bright, beautiful electric light. There was brighter light than he thought possible. A pleasant, exciting, and unexpected greeting welcomed him when Eva stepped out of her bedroom, wearing her trademark smile as her "Hello." She was dressed in a stylish, pastel yellow-green dress with a low neckline, and a lovely string of pearls adorned her neck. He wasn't aware she was returning home from Oxford, and they hugged and talked non-stop, catching up.

Mary neighed as Eva and Carly approached the barn and trotted over to greet them. David had planted a garden, which was now producing vegetables, and Mary ate two carrots from Eva's hand in one bite. The air was fresh, the discordant, loud buzzing of cicadas came from every direction, June Bugs were out in large numbers, oppressive heat and humidity were palpable, and it felt like home.

As they retreated to relax in the shade of the beautiful, sprawling Weeping Willow they breathed the addictive fragrance of the magnolia and discussed how they had missed it. They talked of their post-doctoral programs and personal lives. The Department of Literature and Art at The University of Oxford had accepted Eva to pursue her DPhil degree. It bowled Carly over with joy and he congratulated her. They discussed their martial arts programs. Each had continued in Krav Maga and was pursuing their 3rd DAN Black Belt. Personnel of alphabet agencies of the federal government had approached both, but neither held any interest, so nothing came of it.

They sat, thoroughly enjoying the unfamiliar sensation of being unrushed with an empty to-do list. Eva was sitting close to Carly and placed her head on his shoulder. He put his arm around her, and his pulse rate doubled.

Carly smiled as he welcomed Eva, aware she was even more beautiful than when they left for their postdoctoral. "What a lovely surprise that you came home. It's so nice to have you here."

"I wouldn't have missed this opportunity to be with you," Eva said.

"I toyed with visiting you at Oxford, but I decided it would be an intrusion into your private life, and I don't have that right anymore," Carly said, somewhat subdued.

"Carly, sweet Carly, why do you say that? I'm your sister, aren't I? I would love for you to visit me. We could see London together." she said.

"That you are, big sister. Do you like London?" They chuckled.

"I don't know, I have no desire to explore it without you. Are you seeing anyone? I know I shouldn't ask that, and if you don't want to answer, I'll understand, and I realize I may not like your answer," Eva said, in a serious tone.

Carly said, "Oh, Eva, I don't mind. I have no secrets from you. No, I haven't dated anyone. I'm not ready; honestly, I don't know if I will ever be ready. I have no interest in girls, or boys either for that matter." Both laughed.

She asked, "Aren't you going to ask me if I'm seeing someone?"

He thought, no, because I'm a coward and may not like the answer. But he said, "If you are, that's your business Eva, and I have no right to ask that of you."

"Carly don't be that way. I've dated no one. Like you, I don't have the slightest interest in any relationship. You are still the love of my life. Having put that to rest, could we just cuddle? I want us to hold each other. I'm so starved for it."

They sat quietly, snuggling, and Eva asked, "Carly, what will we do with our lives?"

Carly was silent for a spell and finally said, "How would you like to live in Appalachia?"

She asked, "Why in heaven's name would I want to live in Appalachia?"

He said, "I hear there are places where it's okay for brothers and sisters to marry."

She sat bolt upright, hit his shoulder, and said, "Carly, you damned idiot! I thought you were serious."

They cracked up with laughter, and she struck him on his shoulder again, causing him to feign a crippled arm. Then they returned to snuggling.

Eva said to Carly, "I want to learn to drive. Will you teach me?"

"Of course. What a great idea! Let's go into town tomorrow and get the driver's manual. If my memory serves, you drove me to the hospital in an exemplary fashion. Oh, I almost forgot. We now have a telephone."

Eva sat upright again, as if startled. "The hell, you say."

They cracked up with laughter again.

A gray rat snake slithered past with a field rat in its jaws. Aside from admiring its beauty and stealth, they appreciated its contribution to reducing the local rodent varmints.

A gentle breeze blew, swaying the tops of the nearby longleaf pines, and the soughing was their hum of approval. There was a raucous dispute among a nearby murder of crows in their nesting area. As dusk approached, the sun moved westward to the crest. The sweet aroma of Arabian Jasmine wafted through the air as the willow shivered placidly in the breeze. Crickets were chirping discordantly, and frogs were croaking and answering in unison. Jenna sat between Eva and Carly as they quietly tossed broken twigs into the water and watched them float away.

Carly thought her warm smile was like a ray of sunshine on a stormy day, and it was impossible not to feel uplifted by her presence. Eva was angelic, as beautiful as ever and this brought back lovely memories. Her eyes sparkled in the shaded sunlight. Her gentle demeanor always made him and everyone in her zone feel comfortable and loved. She sat with her feet dangling in the cool water, enjoying the moment's serenity. To make conversation, Carly asked if she had seen her Mama, and, suddenly unsmiling, she tersely dismissed the idea. "I have no reason to see her."

They continued to sit silently beside the spring after dark had settled. The vast black sky twinkled with untold numbers of stars, and no clouds were present to obscure the brilliant quarter-moon. Carly recalled a quote from Dostoevsky's *Crime and Punishment*, "The darker the night, the brighter the stars, the deeper the grief, the closer is God." The flickering luminescence of thousands of lightning bugs brought calm, happy memories.

Carly discussed a subject that had played in his mind since he last saw Uncle Matt. "I would like to bring up an issue to get your reaction. When I last saw Uncle Matt, he gave me a gentle nudge and asked me to consider seeing Mama because things may differ from when we left. He said I should bring you when I decide to see her. That has been like gravel in my shoe, and it continues to occupy my thoughts. Give me your take on this."

Eva turned to look into Carly's eyes. "I know I don't have the history with your Mama that you have, but I want to meet her to sit and talk with her to gain insight into her identity. Is she the boil on the ass of evil that you have described in the past? Is she the same person who was so wicked and hurtful to you that you avoided her at every turn? Your thoughts after seeing her could be interesting, but independent of your thoughts, I want the opportunity to form my opinion of her. What are your thoughts?"

"I'm leaning toward going to see her. I agree with you. I should have questioned Uncle Matt about the meaning of 'things may be different,' but that opportunity has passed. The only way to answer these points of curiosity is to meet with her. But I will neither now, nor will I ever meet with the son of a bitch who murdered Winnie. Someday, I hope to piss on his grave if he has one. If you agree, we can visit Mama at the farm someday soon."

Carly chuckled as he told Eva about a paranormal conversation that he was having with himself. When he came through town on his way home, he stopped for gas and saw a brochure announcing a homecoming event at the Old Antioch Presbyterian Church, close to the farm where he was born.

"I know where The Old Antioch Church sits. It has a large cemetery, and I used to get scared when I walked past it, especially at night," said Eva. "There are gravestones going back to pre-Civil War Wars days."

"There's an ensuing powerful urge for me to attend the event, and it's annoying me. I have never attended the church, have never known anyone at the church, have never taken part in past home-coming events, and I can't understand who or what is hounding the hell out of me to attend the homecoming event. According to the scant brochure, the church's history dates to the antebellum era. The event attracts families from most of the southern states. The event is next Sunday, so if my prayers for a cyclone are unfulfilled, I probably will go. Are you interested in attending an event with a bunch of boring old white people?"

"I don't even attend events with a bunch of boring old Black peo-ple," Eva said as she chuckled. "Besides, you might find an old crone that thinks you're the apple of her eye. If you don't come home Sun-day evening, I'll know you got lucky." They both laughed.

46

. . . .

SUNDAY MORNING CAME, there was no cyclone, so Carly was yielding to his so-called paranormal urge. He picked out pants and a shirt he bought in Princeton. Eve gave him a complimentary smile and kiss. He wanted to be a bit late and left for the Old Antioch Presbyterian Church.

He was astonished at the many cars in the parking lot as he drove onto the long driveway leading to the churchyard. Where did all these people come from? His plan was an early exit, and he found a parking spot that looked promising. He walked toward the crowds, trying not to trip on the gravel surface. To fall in front of all those people would be extraordinarily bad form. A large group of people stood beside the food tables. Looking over the crowd, he saw no familiar faces. He walked slowly toward the tables and passed the most delicious spread of food imaginable, which promised to be more than enough for everyone.

While he had an excellent view of the table, which had become the focal point of most everyone's attention, he was distracted by a lady standing by the picnic plates and flatware before reaching the punch bowl. She wore a beautiful pastel green dress that stood out among the drabber colors of the crowd. She was thin, had grayish-blond hair, and appeared in her 50s. In the nanosecond glimpse of her face, he didn't recognize her. Perhaps she was someone he had once seen, but he couldn't place her. A glance around didn't reveal anyone he recognized.

Continuing toward the punch bowl, he caught another glimpse of the green-dressed lady, a brief second before she turned away.

While her facial features appeared old, she was slender and moved with a youthful gracefulness. Had he seen her before? He stood next to the punchbowl and ladled a paper cupful of clear red liquid, which tasted like typical large gathering punch, and he edged close to a garbage can and sneakily dropped it in.

Trying for a change of scenery, Carly moved to the long end of the L shaped table, nearer the church building where a larger group had gathered. Again, the lady dressed in pastel green caught his attention, about three yards to his right, but she wasn't on his path to the church. She was standing with her back to him. He wondered why he had become so absorbed in this little game of cat and mouse. Was it because he was bored and had nothing better to do? Was it because of the lovely pastel green dress, more blue-green than yellow-green, which made her stand out in a drab crowd? She was looking around. Was she waiting for someone or trying to find someone? She had exchanged greetings with other ladies she knew, so she lived locally or had in the past. This game of hide and seek had stirred his curiosity. Keeping her in his peripheral vision, he edged closer and looked over his shoulder away from her. Despite his best efforts, he hadn't seen her face even as he walked toward her. While walking away from him, she turned around as if looking for someone. As he approached within two yards, he cast a furtive glance in her direction as she turned her head, and he saw her complete profile. Carly's heart was racing, and, standing paralyzed, he knew at once. But she still had not seen him.

"Hello, Mama."

She whirled in search of his voice, then unmoving, she appeared dizzy and likely to fall and with partway extended arms, she steadied herself against the table. Mama stared deep into Carly's eyes trying to discern his intention. Her mouth was agape, both arms partially extended; still uncertain of his response, she seemed reticent to reach out to him for fear of rejection. She still had not spoken. Carly fought an involuntary, almost overwhelming urge to vomit, and his instinct was to run away as fast as his legs could carry him. He turned a full circle surveying the crowd with a desperate Pavlovian search for Papa because he knew the SOB would be close, but he wasn't in view yet. He remembered the terrific fights Papa and Mama had and wondered if they were still living in the same house.

Seeing Mama's frightened, begging countenance, her beseeching blue eyes, Carly walked toward her and clasped her in his arms. He and Mama embraced for the first time in his memory. Both seemed reluctant to let the moment end. After all those years, it felt right. She was crying. Carly cried, too.

Her appearance was a surprise to Carly. She was wearing makeup, had beautifully brushed graying blond hair, and a lovely perfectly placed barrette neatly held a lock of hair in place. Her face appeared older than Carly expected, showing wrinkles, but time had that effect. She displayed a profound surprise. A blanket of sereness had enveloped her, an indescribable peacefulness had suffused her essence, filling her with an appearance of liberation and purpose.

They edged away from the crowd and discussed safe superficial history. How are you, Mama? I'm fine, how are you, Carly? That type of stuff. Carly wanted to get away and go home. He didn't want to tell her about Josie's death until they were in a more private setting because he wasn't sure what her reaction would be. Carly asked if he could visit her the following day, and she was overjoyed. He fast-tracked their conversation, he said he would leave, and he would see her early the next day.

"Carly, you've made this day the happiest in my memory," Mama said.

47

1966
·······

AFTER SUNRISE, CARLY AND EVA arose early to drive to the farm on a beautiful day with fat, fluffy white clouds floating lazily. The sun was struggling to dominate the immeasurably deep blue sky, causing them to squint. The deciduous trees were bare of leaves. Stately live oaks had green leaves and gave a sense of life among the dormant colors. The farmers had picked the cotton, and the fields were blending with the colors of the countryside with their brown stalks. They had gathered the corn, and the fields were now shades of taupe, wheat, and mustard—all well suited to the monochromatic look of earth-tone brown stalks, barren of corn. Jenna joined them for what promised to be a fantastic experience. Palpable anxiety with subdued conversation permeated the car. Carly had not decided his best approach if Papa tried to accost him. He knew from his martial arts training that he would tolerate no shit from him.

They entered the long driveway, and the expansiveness of the farm was almost overwhelming, monolithic in proportion, and it extended for miles in all directions. He had escaped from the farm years ago and didn't remember the house and farmland being so immense. Few of Carly's memories of life on the farm were wholesome, sound, or worthy of recalling. His most vivid memory was Winnie's murder, and his escape with Josie to freedom wasn't far behind. Though Carly had tried unsuccessfully to banish the awful memory of Winnie's bloody execution from his mind, it lingered, and it visited him daily. Winnie's swollen, bloody, unrecognizable face remained as clearly imprinted in his mind as the night Papa murdered him.

Eva and Carly parked in front of the enormous Georgian house, guarded by a massive portico and an impressive colonnade of six large Ionic columns supporting a towering roof. The giant column's miniaturization effect on the entryway and adjacent windows was striking as they stepped onto the porch. The grand old lady's inherent beauty awed Eva; however, Carly harbored deep feelings that it had stood for a legion of humanitarian, societal, and personal transgressions, and its beauty did not stir reverence in him that seemed to abound in Eva.

They walked slower than usual as they climbed the steps onto the porch because Carly had not predicted the apprehension pervading his mind and soul. Finally, reaching the door, deciding whether to knock or ring the doorbell, seemed insurmountable. They quietly discussed the problem, but Carly finally stepped up and knocked on the massive oak door. Nervously waiting, they heard footsteps coming. Carly was anxious. Mama opened the door. Carly said, "Good morning, Mama."

They embraced, and Carly checked the doorway in case Papa showed up. He remained unsure how he would react if the murderous cretin showed up.

She looked at Eva standing with a beautiful smile on her angelic face and seemed startled. Before Carly could introduce her, Mama stepped outside the door and wrapped her arms around her.

"Eva, I'm so delighted to see you. I understand you are studying at the University of Oxford, which is so impressive. It's a pleasant surprise that you have done me the honor of visiting. My, you have grown into such a lovely young lady."

They had questioning looks on their faces. How could she remember Eva? How had she known that Eva was studying at Oxford?

Facing Carly, Mama asked, somewhat timidly or scared, "Where is Josie?"

Carly answered ever so softly. "Mama, I'm so sorry to be the bearer of this news. Josie had severe pneumonia, requiring time to get a special antibiotic, and it resulted in delayed treatment. The delay caused prolonged bed rest. Josie died. She developed a massive blood clot in her lungs and died instantly."

Mama screamed, cried out as if she was in excruciating pain, not physical pain, but a pain that doesn't respond to medications, a shaman's remedies, or Papal prayers, emanating from the depths of the essence of her being. Unable to remain standing, she sat abruptly on the door sill, rocking back and forth and sobbing, trying to alleviate the extreme, gut-wrenching pain. Continuing to weep uncontrollably, Carly sat beside her and held her close. After many long minutes, her weeping slowed and, with help, she stood, but her first cheerfulness had gone. Still crying intermittently, she embraced them again and invited them inside.

Critical structures in the house triggered marked anxiety in Carly. As they stood, Eva placed a tight grip on his hand, and it was comforting that she was there for him. He put an arm around her to reassure himself that no harm would come. She put her arm around him and held him close. Although the interior structures of the house didn't precipitate a full-blown panic attack, he stopped, closed his eyes, and tried to avoid hyperventilating. It required time to decide whether to enter the living room. The wall outside the room where Papa had murdered Winnie was where he and Josie had stayed hidden and endured the horrible sounds of Winnie's bloody slaughter. Was it too forbidding to view the scene of the bloody execution? The massive fireplace drew Carly's attention as he glanced into the room, appearing spotless, as if new. Eva felt his arm tightening around her. She gazed into his face and followed his fixed stare to the fireplace. He was where the horrific tragedy occurred.

The images of that tragedy, which were permanently imprinted in his mind, had remained unchanged. He relived the horrific scene with the awful sounds. His eyes remained closed, and he could barely move. He slowly opened his eyes. Eva took his hand and they walked into the living room. Eva's hand stiffened, and Carly trembled as he put his arm around her again. Carly tried to imagine what she was experiencing. His eyes scanned every inch of the newly painted walls, scrubbed floor, spotless windows, new curtains, and the replaced paintings. The entire area was immaculate. Someone had replaced

Papa's chair with a different one. But slowly, his eyes drifted to the ceiling, and dark stains were visible above where Papa murdered Winnie. It was Winnie's blood, now brown from years of aging!

"I can't be here any longer!" Carly gasped and cried.

Mama recognized what was happening, took Carly and Eva's hands, and promptly ushered them onto the patio. Along with coffee and lemonade, she offered freshly baked cookies.

Mama spoke, barely loud enough to hear, "Carly, I never gave up hope. Everybody kept telling me you both were dead. The sheriff declared you dead, and he and everyone stopped searching for you, got on with their lives, and forgot. But I never forgot and couldn't accept that you were dead. They kept me at the institution six months longer because I refused to accept the edict of the psychiatrists that you and Josie were dead. They said I wasn't ready to face the realities of life."

With a surprised and questioning look, Carly asked, "What institution, Mama?"

"I suffer from Substance Abuse Disorder. I'm an alcoholic, and I have Schizoaffective Disorder and Bipolar Disorder. The Court declared me mentally incompetent, and they institutionalized me at Bryce Hospital in Tuscaloosa for almost four years. I've been sober since Winston's murder and Aldrich's suicide."

It was that last, somewhat incidental statement, that sent Carly's mind spinning out of control, about to leave its orbit! Speechlessness had become his new norm. Finally, Carly could mutter a few words, "What the hell, Mama, are you telling me Papa is dead? Can you understand that Josie and I have lived in absolute fear every day and night since we left, afraid the murderous cretin would find us and murder us the way he did Winnie? What happened when you discovered Winnie's body on that horrible day."

"The day after he murdered Winston, Aldrich and I sobered up enough to realize the unspeakable tragedy we had caused. I lost my entire family on that day. My two sons and my daughter were gone. When he finally regained his senses, Aldrich realized he had murdered Winnie. He sat, calmly put on his shoes, went into the library, removed the English double-barreled shotgun from its rack over the mantlepiece, loaded it, and walked out back. I didn't stop him; I didn't even try. When I heard the blast, I knew it was over. I slowly went to check, and he had shot himself straight in the face with both barrels and blew off his face and most of his skull and brain."

Almost as an afterthought, Mama added, "Carly, you now own the farm."

"Mama, how do I own the farm? What the hell?"

"When Aldrich's Papa disinherited him, the farm would go to his firstborn, Winnie. With the death of Winnie, you are now the farm's owner. But the Court will declare you dead in about six months, so we must deal with that."

He thought that was what Papa was referring to when he murdered Winnie. "You're stealing my farm!" He was staggered by the memory. "Mama, I need to find a place to sit. My head is spinning from too much sensory input, and I'm sure I'll fall flat on my face."

She had him sit beside her and Eva in a comfortable patio chair at a gigantic wood table that had endured many seasons, good and bad. An enormous, sprawling Live Oak with pale gray Spanish moss hanging from its radiating, downward-sloping branches shaded the three. While he and Eva were drinking lemonade and relaxing, Carly looked closely at Mama's face, especially her eyes. He remembered them bright blue, but now they seemed faded to a paler blue. Could that be the result of time or the toll of her mental challenges and alcoholism?

"I'd like permission to visit Papa's office to browse."

"Of course, dear, go ahead. You own this place now, remember? But it'll be dusty because I haven't been inside it since before his death. Eva and I will continue to carry on our conversation."

He steeled his resolve and went upstairs to the office. Mama was right. No one had cleaned the office since before Papa's suicide, and dust covered everything. Grandpa Turner's contract with the legal firm managing the farm was in a desk drawer, but he could find neither a contract for an accounting firm to perform the audits, nor did he find a ledger. He placed the agreement into an empty file folder and Grandpa Turner's Last Will from many years ago. He found a ring of keys on a lower bookshelf and tossed them on the desk. A true artisan had built the bookshelf, but the upper section lacked the meticulous joinery of the lower shelves. Pushing on it and cranking on it to correct its fit was useless. He finally struck it with his fist, and the bookshelf slid to one side, revealing a door.

The door wouldn't open because Papa had locked it long ago. He took the keyring from the desk and randomly checked the keys. After five or six attempts, he unlocked the door. Inside was a vault with reams of old paperwork related to the farm. A built-in tray near the vault's front, beside the door, held two weird-shaped keys unlike any Carly had seen. The keys were oddly fascinating, but he wondered if they would ever be useful. A cute, small tape measure was also on the tray. He pocketed the keys and tape measure.

Despite scouring the vault, he found no accounting contract or ledger. Carly locked the vault door, hit the bookshelf, and it slid back in place. He returned the keyring to the lower bookshelf, tucked the folder under his arm, and left the office.

Shuffling along the hallway toward Winnie's bedroom, Carly took slow, deep breaths to ease his increasing anxiety. When he opened the door, it was plain that Mama had not moved a single item since Winnie's death, but the room was spotless. He couldn't see even the tiniest dust mote. Carly looked around and experienced sharp anguish, so anxious he had difficulty breathing. An envelope lay on the chest of drawers. He picked it up, carefully examining it. Mama had left the envelope unsealed. He opened it slowly and discovered there was money inside. Carefully removing the bills, he counted them and found seventy-eight dollars. He stood motionless. This was the money he and Winnie had saved for their survival when they escaped from the farm. It was to see them through until they could sell their horse. Carly's discovery of the untouched room and the money was a poignant moment that triggered memories of his past. Before Winnie could put the money in its pouch on the buggy, Papa murdered him. Instead, Carly and Josie arrived at their destination with thirty-eight cents, which they had never spent. Tears blurred his vision as his thoughts traveled to that event so many years ago. Now it seemed like they had made those plans only yesterday. Carly replaced the money in the envelope and returned it to the chest, so it appeared untouched.

With a heavy heart, Carly left the room, closing the door behind him for the last time. As he walked away, he took a deep breath and wiped his tears. He felt a faint sense of closure, always remembering his love for Winnie.

He walked down the hallway to the library, his favorite room in the vast house. The beautiful fireplace drew his attention. Its ornamental andirons rested above a half-burned log and ashes untouched from the ages. The sprawling mahogany desk sat off center toward the windows, covered in dust and spider webs, unaltered since his earliest memories of the room. Bookshelves were on three walls of the room, and hundreds of old, musty-smelling books occupied permanent spaces on the shelves. Portraits of men from past generations adorned the walls. Lighting was inadequate and entered through two large windows with dusty panes that should have been cleaned years before, dimly lighting the desk, fireplace, and bookshelves. A beautiful shotgun rested on its rack above the mantlepiece.

Mama said Papa had used the gun to commit suicide, and he removed it from the gun rack and carefully examined it. The weapon was a marvelous gem manufactured in London in 1900 by Russell Hillsdon, as seen on an engraving on the steel receiver. Carly noted the gun barrels were extra-long, and with the tape measure he found in Papa's office, they measured 36 inches. Add the length of the lock, chamber, and stock, and it was a very long gun. How could Papa possibly hold such a long gun to shoot himself in the face?

Carly had no desire to visit his old bedroom; he had seen enough. Walking down to the tool shed to look around should help regain his composure. Soon, he rejoined Eva and Mama on the patio.

Catching up continued to last for hours; although painful at times, she coped with all the questions.

Mama readily admitted to being a recovering alcoholic with mental challenges. She had few actual memories from before her treatment. The psychiatrists had interviewed Dottie Mae, who supplied, in large part, or likely most, of Mama's history which helped form her memories during the regimen in the state institution. There were some terrible memories. She remembered how evil she had been toward her children and how that had led to Winnie's murder, directly or indirectly. When Papa should have been there to receive his rightful share of the blame, Mama discussed every question and accepted responsibility.

Carly wondered and asked, "Do you have a photographic memory?"

"Yes, I do. I should qualify that. I did in my earlier years. It has dimmed with my increasing number of birthdays. Do you?"

"Yes. I have it, and so did Josie."

Eva became anxious, appeared troubled and ill at ease, stood and asked to be excused. She went inside.

Carly continued with the questions. During Mama's late teens and early twenties, she experienced weird symptoms of depression and hallucinations, specifically hearing voices and seeing things that weren't there. A physician told her no medication was available to treat the disorder. Vicious depression often pushed her to suicidal ideation.

That night at the farm, Eva and Carly discussed the visit and agreed it was a fantastic event. Carly said he would have never predicted the Mama he remembered could make such a seismic change. They gave thanks to modern medicine. Eva tried to reconcile how Mama knew so much information about her. She couldn't figure out how it was possible.

Morning dawned, and they were still riding high from the psychological boost from the day before, and they could think of nothing that had gone sideways. Still, Eva said, I wonder how your Mama knew so much about me.

A little more than a year earlier, Dr. Fischer had raised a serious question of potential consanguinity that still needed to be resolved. The question often plagued Carly, causing anxiety, putting him in a blue funk, and making some days almost unbearable. Occasionally, he felt cursed by the possibility that Eva could be his sister. Listening to Dr. Fischer convinced him that a significant probability existed that Eva could be his blood relative. The dreadful pain could endure forever if it didn't end well. However, he and Eva would dance with glee if the answers were favorable, and that prospect had lured him on. He and Eva had silently chosen to procrastinate trying to untie the damnable Gordian knot, unconsciously hoping that time alone would solve the problem. Carly felt alone and knew he must persevere in resolving the etiology of that mental anguish. Neither he nor Eva knew their blood types. Carly asked if Eva would join him in having their blood types done before she returned to Oxford, and she agreed. They had their blood drawn in the hospital laboratory.

Carly asked Dr. Fischer if he could have the hospital search for old records that might have blood types for Papa, Eva's dad, and her Mama, Dottie Mae.

Dr. Fischer contacted him after a week to report finding an old hospital record for Eva's father that showed His blood type was OO. They could not find old records for Papa and Dottie Mae. Because of this development, Carly had no choice but to talk to Eva or Dottie Mae.

Carly would talk to Dottie Mae, risking life and limb, hoping and praying Eva had already spoken to her. Eva sat, sipping her coffee the following day, and he asked her about Dottie Mae's blood type. She was evasive at first, but she knew Carly would persevere.

"Type OO, I'm sure."

After hearing this information, Carly was relieved because he was sure he would have suffered broken bones and concussions from Dottie Mae's cast-iron skillet if he had faced her. Eva asked that this topic remain between them, and he agreed. Carly assumed, was sure, Eva's blood type was OO. But neither revealed their blood type.

Carly went to the back bedroom where the chest sat, removed the two weird keys from his pocket, and tried the first to see if it fit the lock. It didn't, but the second key passed through the aperture and unlocked the chest. The chest builder had cleverly, skillfully created the illusion of drawers, but they were fake. There was a single door that swung open.

Inside the chest was a metal safe with a lock. The remaining weird key opened the safe. Many papers were inside, some dating to the 1830s, including the farm's original deed.

He found Papa's military dog tags, which he stared at in silence, examining them carefully. He didn't know Papa had been in the military. Papa had stashed many old coins in mint condition inside the safe and a considerable amount of US currency.

He took the currency and old coins, locked the safe and the chest, and replaced the keys. Before talking with Eva, he sat in the living room for long, contemplative, dreadful moments. When he asked her blood type, Eva answered without hesitation, "OA." Carly told her he had just seen Papa's military dog tags, and his blood type was OO. After long minutes of silence, in a whisper, they said goodbye, and Eva slowly walked away.

Eva slowly returned after a half-hour, and she was crying, intensely, desperately. She looked beseechingly into Carly's eyes, hoping for a last-minute miracle.

Finally, she said, "I am your sister, but you know that, don't you? We don't have the same father. We have the same mother. I had almost figured it out before I left Oxford to come home, but I needed more information. When we visited your Mama, our Mama, she clinched the deciding factor when she admitted she had a photographic memory. I also have a photographic memory, and so do you, as did Josie. It's a genetic trait, so it answered the question. But when you said your Papa's blood type was OO, that made it 100 percent. I assume you will soon visit your Mama, our Mama. Do you mind if I'm present for the meeting?"

He replied with encouragement for her to be beside him. "I insist you go with me to meet with her because this matter involves both of us. We are brother and sister. I'm trying to remain non-judgmental, but it isn't easy. She owes us an explanation," said Carly.

The next morning, they set out to meet with Mama. When they arrived, Mama answered the door in a silent, praying, eyes-wide-open stare fearfully and pleadingly into Carly's and Eva's eyes.

Carly was uncomfortable as he sat in this situation, and he shifted onto his left butt, then his right as they sat on the patio. He spoke first, with difficulty, directed to Mama. "Dottie Mae isn't Eva's Mama."

Mama began to weep. Mama shook her head, and in a voice barely above a whisper, said, "No, she isn't. I have blood type AA. When you began your detective work, I knew you would realize that Dottie Mae could not be Eva's mother, and you would circle back to me."

Soon, she regained sufficient composure to supply her story of events as much as she could recall. Carly and Eva told her it was unnecessary, what's done is done, and nothing could make it otherwise, and she shouldn't feel she must explain.

Mama stopped crying but continued, "No, I want to finally tell my side of the story, and I wany you two to hear this. I allegedly had a onetime fling with a farmhand, or so I'm told, when I was in the depths of the schizoaffective disorder, severe depression, and alcoholism. I have no memory of the incident or the individual. A psychiatrist at the institution told me he got that information from Dottie Mae, and he told me, over and over, ad infinitum, that was how it happened. That's all I recall, what they told me. I have often wondered if someone raped me. Artentious Jackson, the midwife who delivered all my children, delivered Eva, and Dottie Mae helped her. When they realized Eva was Black, Dottie Mae took my baby out of my arms, abducted her, and raised her as her child. Dottie Mae and Artentious spread the word that I had a stillbirth. They even gave that story to the Psychiatrist at the institution. Dottie Mae delayed filing for a birth certificate more than a year after Eva's birth to further cover the abduction.

She paused. "Eva, I believe you had a good upbringing, although Dottie Mae was a kidnapper. I guess I must give the devil his dues. Since I have been sober, I have gathered this information from my memory, not the memory they brainwashed me to repeat. It has been my special quest to keep track of everything you've done in and out of school. Your personal growth and life have been impressive, and with all you've carried out, I'm not surprised you are studying at Oxford. When you entered the Stars of Infinity Program and stood against the KKK, I was exultant. I was ecstatic when I learned that you were attending Oxford. I'm so proud of you. One of my greatest regrets is not being a part of your life when you were growing up.

Eva nodded.

"But they abducted my baby, my daughter, and stole her away from me, and that was one of the two most horrible days of my life, and that dreadful scene has remained with me every day since. That is still one of my most distinct and disturbed memories. As she stole my baby from my arms, Dottie Mae told me Eva deserved better than I would ever be. But I had neither the emotional nor physical or mental strength to refute that. They made me feel like dirty, shameful trash, and I didn't know what I could say to the police for them to believe me. So, I withdrew from everything and everyone, as if in a shell. My heart has ached every day for what happened to my daughter. I believe the act of abducting my child was based on race, not on my circumstances. I admit to alcoholism and severe mental challenges, but that was an act of blatant racism."

Eva was in tears as she walked to Mama, and the two, in a tight embrace, wept quietly for long minutes. Carly sat quietly while mother and daughter bonded in a secure, permanent connection. Carly said, "Let's never discuss the subject again, and there should never be a need for anyone but Eva to discuss the matter with Dottie Mae." But Eva said at once, "No, Carly, I want you with me when I talk with her because she owes us an explanation."

The bombshell revelation had created an abyss of change of such size that it would forever affect all their lives. Eva was now Carly's sister. But he and Eva would have their memories.

Eva needed to talk, and that night she sat with Carly on the side of his bed. She said, "Assuredly, it's now a strange, new beginning for all of us. I don't have my head around it yet, but I will tell you this for certain, Carly, sweet Carly; no one will ever love you as much as I love you, and I use the present tense because I still do. You have been my hero, lover, life, my everything; those memories will never fade. I will never stop loving you."

Carly's tears streamed down his cheeks, "And I will never stop loving you, Eva. Like you, I am confronted by impalpable and intangible intimidation, directing me against every atom of my will to place my love for you on an inaccessible and unfamiliar plane."

"How do I turn off my love for the love of my life? I can't," Eva said. "But now I'm told to place all my love for you on this strange, new, unfamiliar plane against all my will. And I ask you, Carly, who or what is this invisible force telling me to do this, and what is its authority?"

"Eva, I can't stop loving you. Even if miles, states, oceans, and continents separate us, my love for you cannot be diminished. You were my first love, my only love, and the love of my life."

"Carly, my feelings will remain on that bewildering plane, so remind me if it takes time. I must ask you, Carly, do you still love me, and will you still love me, not only as your sister, or do you need time?"

"Eva, I will need time to make formidable mental adaptations. I cannot, will not, stop loving you. Please don't ask me to do so. I will try to abide by the rules of our culture and society, but don't be angry if I slip up."

He put his arms around her, and their embrace was long. They kissed without passion, but as their kiss lingered, they continued to clasp each other in a tight embrace, never wanting the moment to end, and as their tears blended, he placed his head on her shoulder and inhaled the evocative redolence of her neck, hair, and body. At that moment, he knew he would miss her forever and would never stop loving her. He couldn't imagine loving another person; she would be the only woman he could ever love; the love of his life. Confused, heartbroken, defenseless, and shattered, he knew, from that moment forward, these events had changed their lives forever. Carly knew the gods had assigned him to a life in Hell.

Carly went outside.

Dark cumulonimbus clouds stood tall in the sky, bringing a darkening, rainy overcast and a forecast of severe thunderstorms in the afternoon. Carly sat alone on the enormous rock under the Weeping Willow, with nothing to console him, only his troubled thoughts and memories. The fragrance of the nearby magnolia blossoms hung low around him, but he now hated that redolence because it brought back joyous and hopeful memories, now they were dismal. He knew everyone lives with their demons and deals with them in the privacy of their minds. Despite friends, family, and faith, their strength comes from within, and we are ultimately alone. We can't share our last breath. Death is private, to be shared with no one. Afternoon rain dripped from the Weeping Willow's slumbering branches and leaves falling like tears to the ground, and in the spring water making tiny ephemeral circular waves. It began as a drizzle and soon became a steady downpour. His painful, lonely thoughts kept Carly sitting for hours, dismissing the rain, sounds, and scents around him without moving. A bolt of lightning and a sharp, loud clap of thunder, typical of a close-by earth strike, barely caused him to blink.

The rain, thunder, and lightning were intensifying, but he sat and looked upward. "What the damned Hell, Strike me! If you want to take my life, so be it. I don't really give a good God Damn!"

The storm brought back Carly's memories from so long ago when he huddled with Winnie beneath his bed in the cloak of darkness, a severe thunderstorm raging outside while they listened to their parents fighting ferociously in the next room. Life was not like he pictured when he left the farm. He had labored under the misapprehension that if only he could leave the farm, he would be in control of his life. Now, he felt he could control nothing. He had gone full circle since he had left, and what had he done with his life? Exhaustion consumed him, and he felt defeated and a profound failure. He was tired, and life had exhausted him for a long time. He needed rest, an escape from this hell on Earth, and maybe life itself. It was a dark night of the soul.

But in the immeasurable depths of the deepest chasm of his soul, he knew he must hold onto his dream, even if only by its fringe, and never give up or yield. Life confronts us daily, threatening us with failure. Our life's responsibility is to never give up, never surrender, always face up to our failures. He knew sometimes those failures involve people we love.

As he thought of Eva, he knew he didn't want her now. He wanted the person he once thought she was, now she was as unattainable as if she were dead.

He felt an acute desperation to return to his research bench at City University. That was the only entity left in his life that made him alive. And in his brokenhearted, dejected depression, he needed to feel alive.

48

1966
·······

CARLY SAT WITH EVA on the limestone rock beside the Weeping Willow. Dark, towering cumulonimbus clouds had gathered, and light mist was falling, but forecasters predicted harder rain. They were making Eva his sister, not only in name but also in fact. They were adding her name to the Live Oaks Meadow deed, and to the deed and title for the section of farmland and buildings that had been owned by Josie and him. Now Eva owned it with him. Her name was already on the inheritance from Mr. Mallory. After that, nothing else of significance came to mind. Eva was now in a lovely, light-hearted mood for a change, and she and Carly laughed at memories from their early childhood. He said, offhand, "I still love hearing you laugh, it's my favorite mood lifter."

The afternoon downpour began. A bright flash of lightning preceded an earsplitting clap of thunder by a mere nanosecond. The rain poured, and Eva dashed inside to safety. Carly was slow to follow inside, still taunting the gods to take him on.

✳

Eva announced to Carly that she was ready to meet with Dottie Mae to discuss the newly gained knowledge of her parentage. Eva had not visited Dottie Mae since she was banished from home. She felt an obligation to Carly, Mama Turner, and herself to hear Dottie Mae explain why she abducted Eva from Mama Turner.

Carly asked if they should call to announce their planned visit. Eva said, "No, because if we let her know, she would sneak over to somebody's house, and we wouldn't find her. I want this over and done with today."

They rode to Dottie Mae's house and received an unfriendly

welcome. She looked into Eva's eyes. "I told you when I saw you last time, I was through with you," she said. "Why are you showing up here with that person?"

"That person is Carlton Turner, my best friend and my brother. When I agreed not to come around anymore, it was before I learned you aren't my Mama, never have been, and, I will add, never will be," Eva said, with a mindset to do battle.

Dottie Mae's fierce countenance melted instantly, and she sat in the nearest chair. Her panicked eyes were fixed on the linoleum floor, no longer staring at Eva, trying to avoid even looking in her direction. She offered no acknowledgment of Carlie's presence beyond her first snotty comment.

Without dancing around the subject, Eva asked, "Why did you abduct me, steal me from my birth Mama and my family? And don't insult my intelligence with bullshit denial. I know what happened. I want to hear your explanation of why."

Dottie Mae looked frightened, and Carly was worried Eva would see her fear and give her a pass, but it wasn't happening that day. Dottie Mae sat, staring at the floor, unable or unwilling to answer.

Eva came back in a much louder, fiercer tone. "You may think you can sit like a damned knot on a log, not say anything, and hope I will go away. But you can either talk with me and answer my questions or talk with the detectives. You decide but make it damned quick because the clock is ticking."

Dottie May was terrified. "Eva Lou, when you were born, I saw you had Black blood, and I wanted to do what I thought would be best for you." She continued, "I knew mixed-blood children have a tough life in the South, so I took you home and raised you like you were mine. I thought Mrs. Turner was unfit to be your mama. I talked to Mr. Aldrich Turner and explained the situation to him, and he told me that he didn't want you, and if I took you, he would pay me two thousand dollars. That was more money than I had made from all my years of domestic work. That's when I decided to tell everybody to claim there was no baby. I did it for the money and to hurt Mrs.

Turner. Now, you know the rest." But she continued, now becoming angry. "With time, I grew closer to you, but I never loved you because you were mixed blood, and every day you grew more and more like the Turners."

Eva was becoming heated. "You took money to abduct me from my mama and family! You knew what you were doing was wrong, and you lived with that vile, wicked deed all these years, robbing me of knowing my actual family." Eva said, and turned to Carly, "Do you want to say anything?"

Carly said, "Mrs. Swain, I understand your reasoning, but it was illegal and wrong to rob Eva, Josie, and me of growing up together. Eva has been especially outspoken in paving a path for Blacks to have better lives through education. She is a credit to the Black and white races, and she excelled in an all-white university and helped break the racial barrier. Since Eva has been living at my house, she has become my best friend, and I will never forgive you for robbing us of so many years of the happiness that has come with that relationship."

Eva said, "Now, I have more to say. It was hurtful when you told me never to come back home. Carly could see how badly it hurt, and he welcomed me into his home, and his friendship made the pain bearable. Since I have learned the truth about what you did, I don't hurt, but I'm damned mad as all hell. I have believed a lie all my life, a lie that began 27 years ago and hasn't stopped. I don't object to having been raised a Black girl, but I strenuously object to your damned dishonesty, one damned lie stacked upon another, again and again, year after year. I should report you to the police, but I will let you work out your sins with your maker, and I hope guilt consumes you. Abducting me from my mama was blatant evil racism. May you rot in Hell. I'm sorry I ever thought of you as my mama. Damn you."

*

Eva was in a talkative mood at home and wanted to get everything said. "Mama became rabid when I told her I was coming to spend time with you. I had never seen her so upset and angry. It was such an uncharacteristic emotional explosion. I couldn't understand why she had become so unhinged about me living with you and Josie. But she was specific. It was you she objected to. She threw me out and told me she was through with me. We haven't spoken in the years since. But after we solved the mystery of my parentage, I needed to communicate with her to let her know I understood why she was so upset. As we talked, I almost felt sorry for her because her face expressed more intense fear and guilt than I had ever seen. I have much work ahead to resolve my psychological challenges. Many problems may remain unresolved because the more I search for answers, the more complex the issues become.

Carly nodded.

"Laboring under the misapprehension that Mama Turner gave me away because I was Black proved a fool's errand. While talking with my birth mama, our birth mama, Mama Turner, I found she didn't throw me away or give me away because I am Black. It doesn't matter to her I am Black because she loves me. Dottie Mae abducted me, kidnapped me, stole me from her, against Mama Turner's will, because of my immutable characteristics of being Black and female. Mama Turner lost her heart and soul because of my abduction, and I don't find a scintilla of racism in her. It bothers me to say this, but I know racism dictated Dottie Mae's actions. She was worried about what other people would think. My abduction, her baby stolen from her, sent Mama Turner deeper into the dark abyss of mental disease and alcohol abuse.

Carly could easily see the cathartic effect this talk was having on Eva, and he didn't interrupt.

"She described her great excitement when she was pregnant with me because her four-year-old daughter, my sister, Tillie, had died, and she knew I would be the joy of her life, which would help her deal with her severe depression. She said her pregnancy with me gave her a precious reprieve from the ravages of her mental challenges. Still, Dottie Mae abducted me from Mama Turner, my rightful mother, who had neither the physical nor psychological means to fight, thus ensuring a lifetime of Hell on Earth for her already netherworld existence. Dottie Mae made Mama Turner feel so dirty and trashy because she had a mixed-race child. Mama Turner was ashamed to go to the police because she knew they would only make matters worse with their ridiculing, sexual innuendos, slander, and laughter. Knowing she suffered from mental challenges and an addictive substance disorder, the shaming would have been unbearable for her, and to what end?" Eva continued, "I'm also trying to deal with the factors leading up to Winnie's death and what part my abduction may have played in that eventual tragedy. Did my birth so embitter your Papa that he became mentally challenged to the extent he murdered Winnie?

"Mama Turner has kept an almost daily diary of all my endeavors and accomplishments. In Harper Lee's *To Kill a Mockingbird*, Atticus Finch said, 'You never really understand a man until you consider things from his point of view… until you climb into his skin and walk around in it.' I'm trying to walk in Mama Turner's skin for a while. She has a great love for me. I'm trying to reconcile Dottie Mae's action of abducting me from Mama Turner, and it isn't straightforward. Dottie Mae was my mama for so many years, and she was the only mama I knew. But that has changed forever. That she so readily rebuffed me and kicked me out when she knew I was close to learning the truth speaks volumes about her character. Things won't ever be the same with Dottie Mae and me because she deceived me, and that deception makes it impossible for me to trust her. Maybe it's easier to give up in despair and move on with my life.

"I will join a counseling group when I return to Oxford, and, working with them, maybe someday, I'll understand all the facets of this atrocious psychological nightmare. My goal is eventually to be less confused, less bitter, and more accepting of these colossal changes. But I'm too old to believe in miracles and unicorns.

"This catastrophic circumstance has been more than one person should have thrust upon them in a lifetime. I'll survive, but now, more than ever, I'll need you to remain close to me. I'm going through phases of feeling alone and vulnerable, and I need to feel your closeness, a shoulder to lean on and cry. Please, don't bail on me. I plan to remain close to Mama Turner, and as I learn more about her, I hope to understand more about me."

Carly reassured Eva he would always be as close as her telephone. She looked at him sweetly, with an understanding smile, and his heart skipped a beat.

*

Eva and Carly sat beneath one of their live oaks, relaxing, acknowledging time was growing short for them to be together but knowing they would be in constant contact. Mrs. Brownlie drove into their driveway, and they were beside the car before she opened the door. They embraced, invited her to join them in the shade, and offered her a lemonade. Mrs. Brownlie said she knew how precious time was, and it would become even more so before they had to leave, so her visit would be brief. The purpose of her visit was to say goodbye, not permanently. She reiterated how they were so dear to her, not only as students but as two of her most precious friends, and she considered it an honor to have had them as students and friends, and if Josie were here, it would be three most cherished friends. She embraced them again and drove away with tears streaming down her cheeks. Carly and Eva were quiet as the car drove down the driveway, and they waved as tears welled in their eyes.

*

Eva and Carly entered a tall building on Peachtree Street in downtown Atlanta with an appointment to meet Mr. Harry Berkshire of the law firm of Berkshire, Goldberg, and Newton. They stepped off the elevator into the office of Mr. Berkshire.

Carly said, "Are you acquainted with the firm of Brown, Clarke, and Goss?"

"Very much so. Why do you ask?"

Carly used photographic memory and went into detail explaining how Brown, Clarke, and Goss had signed a contract with Turner

Farms over fifteen years earlier. Even though it was their fiduciary duty to conduct an audit, they never hired a CPA firm to perform an audit. The firm had paid the employees' wages, but neither Mama nor the farm received any compensation in the interim.

When Carly finished, Mr. Berkshire spoke. "I have been waiting forty years to nail those sons of bitches, and I think we have it. They are the most crooked bastards of all law firms, and everybody hates them, but they've always been clever enough to beat the raps. We now have them by the short and curlies, and we'll bet the entire firm against them. We'll sit with you and get all the information you have, including the material you brought today, then we'll combine it with what we have, and I think we'll have more than enough data for you to have a nice payday."

✳

Carly received a call from Mr. Harry Berkshire of Berkshire in Atlanta. He said this was one of the most uncomplicated cases he had managed. Because of Carly's extensive material, the defending firm, Brown, Clarke, and Goss, had to admit defeat and settle out of Court. "They agreed to our demands, resulting in a full refund of all funds collected from the farm for fifteen years and seven months. If we had gone to court, they would have lost big-time, amounting to destruction of their firm. You have a pleasant bonus to reinvest in the farm."

49

1966
·······

ON A HAZY, STUFFY DAY in late summer, Carly drove with Jenna to the farm to chat with Mama, pursuing no agenda. Their looming departure date had created a precious commodity of the small amount of time before he and Eva left. Eva had procrastinated, and she now worked on a tight deadline to finish her literature paper. Mama was cheerful when greeting Carly and Jenna. Carly told her about the substantial payment the farm would receive from the legal settlement. She was surprised and extremely happy since she was unaware that he had begun legal proceedings. Her enthusiasm was remarkable but not contagious. Given the torrent of vicious headwinds in Carly's recent private life, a visit by the Virgin Mary to their environs wouldn't have made the difference of a tinker's dam. Carly hoped his gloomy mood wouldn't invite Mama to descend into the darkness of his depression.

Mama brought a pitcher of ice-cold lemonade to Carly, who felt most comfortable sitting on the patio in the shade of a sprawling Live Oak. He wanted to ask questions about Papa to augment blank spaces in his sparse store of information concerning him, and she agreed at once.

Carly squirmed in his seat, not comfortable asking the questions. "Papa was a viciously mean alcoholic every day that I knew him. Winnie said he thought he'd started drinking after the death of Tillie. Is that correct?"

"No, Carly, it isn't. I'll try to give you a glimpse of your paternal history from the beginning. Your Great, Great Grandfather Andrew Turner came to America from England as a young man in the 1830s.

His family was wealthy, and he bought this land and developed it into a plantation, Live Oaks Meadow. He finished building this big, spacious house in 1843.

"When he landed in America, he brought a shipload of belongings, including an interesting object, a unique chest, an artisan's work constructed in Morocco. Aldrich showed it to me more than once. It had front, top, and sides covered with beautiful inlay work and rare gemstones, but I don't know where it is today.

"Great, Great Grandfather Andrew Turner died in 1876, and his son, Great Grandfather Albert Turner, inherited the farm as a young man. The Civil War was over, and there was an end to slave ownership and the term 'plantation,' but farming was quite profitable despite the Reconstruction. From all indications, he was at the tiller through rather exciting times.

"When he died in 1923, his son, Grandfather Bernard Turner, your papa's dad, inherited the farm as a young man. When your papa turned twenty-one, Grandfather Bernard gave the chest to him, which thrilled him to no end, not because of the value of the chest, but because it was a gift from his papa. Aldrich and Grandpa Bernard were never close, and Aldrich tried many times to win his affection, but Grandfather Bernard rebuffed Aldrich's efforts. He longed for his papa to go fishing with him, swim in the creek or river, walk, work in the fields, or sit and chat. None of those things happened. So, the gift of the chest was unexpected and out of character because they had never bonded. Aldrich worshiped his papa when he was younger, but he became more aware of his papa's disdain for him as he grew older.

"Grandpa Bernard had a couple of field hands move the chest into an upstairs room Papa used as an office. Someone had taped an envelope to the chest holding two unique keys, unlike any Aldrich had ever seen. He sent no birthday wishes, description of what or why, or history of the chest. The gift elated Papa because it was the only communication he had with his Papa. The gifting mode was the coldness that his papa always showed. It symbolized his papa's disrespect, loathing, antipathy, and hostility toward him. He would have preferred a hug or a tousle of his hair to show genuine feelings of love."

"Aldrich had hired a carpenter, Francis Ellingson, to build an office upstairs. When it was complete, Ellingson's men moved the chest into the office. Aldrich had given Ellingson a key to the place for access while he constructed an office. He still needed to ask for the key from him when he completed the job, which he did not do. Aldrich and I left for a day; the chest was gone when we returned. It was clear Ellingson had stolen the chest, but the sheriff did a cursory investigation, did not find the chest, decided the evidence was circumstantial, and closed the investigation. But Papa still had the unique keys needed to open it so that Ellingson couldn't gain access to its contents. His papa's temper exploded when he learned of the theft, not at Ellingson but toward Papa. His papa screamed at him and accused him of being a careless and irresponsible idiot. He disinherited Papa, signifying the culmination of his disdain for Aldrich since his birth. That act was the nadir that brought Aldrich to his knees, and he was never to recover.

Carly interrupted her, "Mama, Francis Ellingson, the man who built Papa's office, also built our house, and, as you said, he stole the chest and hid it away, and I recently found it at our house, but it belongs here. I'll have it delivered before we leave. Did Papa show you the inside of the chest?"

Mama, happily surprised, replied, "That's great news. It will be so nice to have it here, where it was intended, and I'm eager to see it again. No, I haven't seen the inside. Is it something special?"

"It's interesting, but I won't spoil the surprise. I'll show you when we bring it out."

"Winnie was born and proved quite clever. Within months of Winston's birth, Papa hated him and refused to hold, talk to, or touch him. Grandfather Bernard left everything to Aldrich's firstborn child, Winston, as a final blow to Aldrich. He carried his hatred for Aldrich to his grave. By then, Aldrich had suffered from severe depression and alcoholism for years. He never had a sober day after they read the will. He was severely depressed and furious with anger, displayed no interest in life, had no hobbies, and never exercised. He withdrew from society and became a recluse, a misanthrope. The old bastard destroyed Aldrich.

"When Grandfather Turner died, as you know, a contract setting up responsibility for running the farm went to an outside firm, Brown, Clarke, and Goss, and it stayed until you changed it. I had suffered from Schizoaffective Psychosis and severe depression since I was 19. Psychiatrists renamed the psychosis, now a disorder, but it didn't mitigate my suffering. There were no medications for treatment, or so my doctors told me. I received several prescriptions, but not one was effective. There was a brief respite when I was pregnant with Tillie. I was so happy when she was born; such a beautiful, bright, and delightful child. When she became ill with the fatal Bright's disease, things became grave. Tillie suffered for more than a year and died when she turned four. Was that God's way of punishing me? Making me watch my little Tillie die a little more each day.

"When Tillie died, Aldrich brought home two brown paper bags, each holding a large Mason jar filled with moonshine whiskey. One was for me, and I drank every drop. I wasn't even sober when I attended Tillie's funeral. After that, we both got drunk practically every day and night.

"My pregnancy with Eva relieved me, and I remained sober. It was a brief enchanted respite in a dark, turbulent time. I looked forward to Eva's birth as if it were the second coming. But the tragedy of Dottie Mae abducting my baby from me sent me for a terrible mental tumble, one I could not recover from without help, and help wasn't available. With my impaired and limited mental ability, I turned back to alcohol because it was a familiar recourse."

Carly was pale when he said, "Josie and I were close enough to hear the bloody execution of Winnie, and when Papa started snoring, I went to Winnie's side, but he was dead. Papa sat up as if he would come for me, and I kicked him in the face with all the force I had, and he dropped into his chair and didn't move. When I turned to run for Josie, she was standing, watching everything. I went to your room and tried desperately to wake you, but you had passed out, drunk. What was it like to wake to such a horrific scene?"

Mama looked at him, "When Aldrich murdered my boy, as you said I was drunk and knew nothing about the tragedy until the next day. I found my murdered boy's horrific, bloody, unrecognizable body, and Aldrich had passed out in his chair. Blood covered him, his chair, the wall, the floor, the fireplace, and even the ceiling. I finally roused him, and in our hungover state, we tried to figure out what had happened. When we thought more clearly, I told him he had murdered Winston. He stood, stunned, trying not to believe it, but when he accepted the blame, he said he had to do it because Winston was stealing his farm. He went to the gun rack in the library, removed his double-barreled shotgun, and walked out the door without another word.

"I didn't stop him, but I was pleading with him to kill me first. The thunderous blast from the shotgun echoed all around, and I knew it was over. When I checked, Aldrich had shot himself straight in the face, had blown off his face, skull, and brain, and had fired both barrels of the shotgun at once. The shop supervisor heard the shotgun blast and came to see what had happened. The horrible scene shocked him, and he left to call the sheriff. I stopped drinking that day, but it was years too late. The judge eventually declared me mentally incompetent, and I spent the next three years, seven months, and seventeen days in the mental health facility. But I'm alive today because of that institutionalization."

Carly interrupted her, and she smiled as he said, "Mama, I want to say something. Papa didn't commit suicide. When examining and measuring the shotgun, I tried to re-enact Papa's suicide and concluded the gun length was too long for him to shoot himself straight in the face. You took the gun from its rack over the mantlepiece, loaded both barrels, followed him outback, called to him, and when he turned, you shot him in the face at point-blank range. I will be forever grateful that you did so, and Josie would also be thankful. There won't ever be repercussions for that act, and someone should give you a medal. This is the last time I will speak of it."

Mama was not upset that Carly had unveiled her secret. Instead, she held her head high, smiled, and said, "Carly, you are brilliant, and I'm proud of you because that's how I did it. I called to him, he turned, and I placed the shotgun barrels about a foot from his nose and fired both barrels at once. I'm happy to say I finally had done something I was proud of because he murdered my boy, and my other boy and my daughter were missing. I could not let him live in the same universe as me. I will deny ever making this admission."

Carly stood and put his arms around her in a confirming embrace.

Mama continued, "After a brief investigation, the sheriff told me you and Josie were dead. He closed the case, and they would do nothing further to find you. Everyone took the sheriff's declaration at face value that you two were dead. In the eyes of everyone, you were dead. Newspaper articles supported the sheriff's statement of your deaths, even without your bodies. But I would not, and could not, accept you were dead. Telling myself, over and over, you were alive allowed me to live.

"A few months later, the field supervisor, Sam Mattison, came to me the day before the Court sent me away, 'Mrs. Turner, two things are missing, the Amish Buggy and the black mare. Carlton and Josephine are not dead. They will come back someday. Just keep believing that.' Those words became my mantra. In a single day, my entire family disappeared. No act of expiation will ever relieve my guilt and shame, but I must keep trying."

Astonished, Carly tried to assimilate the abbreviated history of his paternal ancestry, but it would require introspection, study, and time. Mama's summary description of Papa's dead body described the remaining puzzle of the wraiths in his hallucinations. The adult male figure must have been Papa, without facial features, and the boy must have been Winnie. He wouldn't even try to analyze why or how they appeared as a figment of his imagination.

The generational connection of the chest seemed as consequential as the farm, despite being minute in comparison. Who was to say, if Grandfather Bernard Turner had taken a different tack with Papa when Ellingson stole the chest, Papa might not have suffered from severe depression. Grandpa disinherited Papa by cutting him out of his will, leaving the farm to Winnie. That explains why Papa was always angry at Winnie and eventually murdered him. But would alcoholism not have played such a destructive role, and their lives could have been much different on many levels?

There were many what-ifs. But if frogs had wings, they wouldn't bump their ass when they hop. Carly smiled at the silliness of that old expression, but it was no sillier than to "what-if" scenarios in his own life.

Winnie hadn't known Eva's birth was the pregnancy he talked about so often. There was no baby at birth, and no one discussed it because Dottie Mae abducted Eva at birth. Knowing Eva was his sister, would Mama have allowed him to marry her? Carly sensed a conflict he didn't need, and he looked forward to the mind-cleansing adventure medical school promised. Fate and destiny had led to that moment, and nothing could make it otherwise. So, let it go.

After an eternity of silent contemplation, Carly stood.

"Mama, I must go. I love you, and I will stay in close contact. Papa's office has a hidden vault, and I'll explain how to enter it when we deliver the chest."

As they embraced, Mama looked into his eyes and holding both his shoulders, she spoke softly but passionately. "This is the stone the builders rejected. The same has become the head of the corner-stone."

Carly recognized the verse from the *Book of Psalms* in the Bible. She kissed his cheek, gently touching it with her soft fingers to seal the kiss forever. He turned slowly and trudged away, feeling years older than only weeks earlier.

*

So, it had come to this. Miles, states, continents, and an ocean would separate them. Eva and Carly had closed these fulfilled chapters of their lives. With mixed emotions and altered fundamental cornerstones for their interpersonal relationship, they were excited to welcome the facets that would follow.

They drove north from Marston to Idlewild Airport in New York City, where Eva caught her flight to London's Heathrow and on to The University of Oxford. Carly returned to Baltimore, Maryland, to attend Johns Hopkins University School of Medicine.

Carly recalled old Farmer Jackson's words, "Y'all will go fer." They had made a decent start; now, life was waiting.